Burning Embers

Sam Silver

Countdown Minus Five:
Ignition

Chapter One

Those had been Maria Longsworth's words just hours earlier. They returned to Jenny Campbell with a vengeance as she trudged angrily through the valley in the dead of night. This party, in this remote location of nothing but forest, was meant to be the party to end all parties. Everyone from school was going, the self-proclaimed popularity queens of Carrington High had said over and over. This mother of an event was going to be massive, colossal, with a smorgasbord of guys to choose from, and it had shot Jenny's hopes through the roof.

It was the first real party she'd ever been invited to. She'd made out like she'd been to hundreds of them but in truth she was always trying to crack her way into one, just one.

So she'd rocked up and found out, in actuality, that the party was much smaller than she'd expected. Maria had said there'd be hundreds of people. Instead, there were about thirty kids from school at most, and aside from Maria Longsworth and her posse standing around acting like royalty, everyone else was playing with their phones and not talking. This was the party of the century? Please!

Even worse, Maria and the girls started having digs at Jenny. Little jibes here and there about Jenny being the nerd who'd recently scored big by coming top of the year in English Lit, but Jenny was anything but a nerd. An outsider? Yes. Persistent and hardworking? Definitely. A nerd? No way. She was too much of a fighter for that, and if she had something to say she'd sure as hell say it.

Which was what happened. When Maria started getting extra smoochy with Mike Adams and led him to a room, Jenny snapped and stormed from the party with Maria's shallow laughter echoing behind her, making quips about her being a precious *'Little Miss'* who couldn't take a simple joke. Jenny knew that the real reason Maria was riling her was because she was bitter about being trumped in school. Topping English Lit at such a high level meant that Jenny would receive a special award, and in a ceremony that recognised the state's greatest achievers. The official term, slightly tongue-in-cheek, was the Academia Awards. Unofficially around school, however, it was termed as the *'Macadamias'*, meaning that a bunch of try-hard nuts would be put on show to bare all. The fact that Jenny came from the East Side, and lived in a rental house with her father who worked his butt off to make ends meet, didn't raise her any higher in the popularity stakes.

Reality hit back hard when Jenny stepped out the door to see a long stretch of valley laid out before her. She'd totally forgotten that it was Maria who'd driven her and a few girls to this hell of a place. Now she had no idea of where she was or how to get home. Even worse, her phone had no signal.

When she'd heard the girls' laughter from inside the house again, she'd made up her mind to go somewhere, anywhere, just to get away from them, and furiously charged off into the night, determined to find a way back to the main road and hitch a lift.

"This party's about to heat up."

Yeah right.

"Party of the year my butt," she muttered, trudging on. She stumbled over a fallen branch. "Damn it!"

She tapped her phone for the umpteenth time. Still no signal. She tried again, hoping in vain that it would magically activate.

Nothing.

She swore under her breath and trudged on, doing her best to follow Mother Nature's path in the dark.

A glimmer ahead caught her attention. A car headlight? No. Too high for that. Much too high. A plane? Wrong again. The light was bright yellow, growing rapidly, and highlighting a mass of ants scuttling over a tree trunk. Jenny had never seen ants that large and green before. Some were as big as her hand, and they were going crazier by the second, as if sensing something.

She half-covered her eyes and stepped sideways to get a better view of the light above. It grew brighter, captivating her, then her leg hit another upturned branch, making her yelp and topple over. The ground rushed to greet her, along with a small pool of God knew what, then –

Splat!

She cringed, feeling some slime stick to her skin.

"Damn Longsworth!" she seethed, blaming her high school nemesis for everything that she hated about this place.

She pushed herself up.

The yellow light grew even brighter, accompanied by a piercing whine.

She started to scramble away.

Her hand caught hold of something soft and squishy.

Something that resembled a small body.

She looked down.

The face of a toy clown stared back up at her, grinning with blood-red lips from beneath the black circles around its eyes.

She tried to pull her hand away but couldn't. It was frozen. Rooted to the spot, like a magnetic force was keeping it there.

Psycho toy was freaking her out. This thing was wrong, totally wrong. It felt alive. Filled with dark energy that tingled in her touch. She grimaced as a sudden charge swept up her arm, sending a presence into her head.

Her eyes rolled back and she fell to the side. Her arm was released and, like a limp doll herself, she rolled down a small slope before coming to a splayed-out halt at the bottom, her right cheek covered by mud.

Then the party really started.

The night split open.

A massive explosion ripped through the valley, sending a cacophony of fire and debris billowing everywhere. Trees were uprooted, falling heavily as hysterical flocks of birds fled for the horizon, all whilst crackling flames reached high into the night like the smouldering fingers of hell.

Through it all, the face of the toy clown stared up insanely, its grinning red lips stained with ash and its frills dancing in the searing wind.

Nearby, some groans and raspy breaths rose, from someone who'd been caught up in the blaze. Painfully, they reached out for something, anything, to hold onto.

Their blackened hand fell upon the clown.

A sinister voice chuckled in their head as the newcomer's hand was suddenly magnetised to the toy, clutching it tightly.

The dark laughter grew.

"Whoa!"

"What the hell was that?"

"Did, like a plane just crash or somethin'?"

"I'm getting out of here!"

The partygoers stood on the edge of the burning valley, watching the scene from a small building. Some stood on the balcony. Others were too scared to even venture outside. Thick smoke clouds were sweeping in their direction. The flames were still some way off, but getting closer, crackling through the trees like they were matchsticks.

Murmurs rippled throughout the crowd. Cries followed and several people ran for their cars. Others stood in shock, not knowing what to do.

One girl, Johanna Seymour, hurried down the slope towards the valley.

"Jo, what are you doing?" a boy called from the balcony.

She turned to face him. "Sam and Sarah went for a walk. I'm gonna see if they're okay."

"Have you got a death wish? Get back here!"

"Not scared are you, Baz?"

He shrugged. "They could be in the middle of something. Or coming to the end of it."

His friends snickered.

Johanna shrugged back. "I don't know, but at least they're not standing around with a drink in their hand talking about it, hey Baz?"

A louder laugh went up.

"Come if you want," Johanna said, "or else you can stand there and prove that you really are all talk and no action, for the second time tonight, according to Beth Chalmers anyway."

She turned and ran.

Baz downed his drink, disgruntled. One of his friends cackled and got smacked in return.

"Shut up!" Baz snapped, and went inside.

Johanna ran on.

"Something's gone down, big time."

Sarah nodded, feeling Sam's hand clasp tightly over hers. They stood in shock, halfway down the valley slope. The fires of hell were heading in their direction at an all-consuming speed, with some smaller blasts igniting too, like tanks of petrol erupting.

Her night walk may have gone to hell, Sarah reasoned, but it was peanuts compared to what her friends were going through. No, she knew what she had to do, and it may well be the stupidest thing in her life, but right now she didn't have a choice.

She stepped ahead, pulling Sam with her. "Someone may need our help…"

He pulled her back. "No! Fire travels fast. Smoke even faster."

She whirled around to face him. "Sam, we can't –"

"We can't do anything!"

"Sam!"

Bang!

A powerful line of fire shot up high over the valley.

A cry went up from the partygoers.

When the pillar of fire reached its peak, it arched over, pummelling downwards.

Sarah cried out in horror. The fire was heading straight for them.

Sam pulled her away. "Move!"

Sarah had no choice but to run with him.

The flames came down and her screams went up, along with a large section of the valley.

Further up the hill, Johanna fell backwards. High above, several fiery pillars burst into the night, arching out in all directions, carrying bits of machinery and forest debris with them.

She hit the slope with a thump and groaned. Now painfully defeated in her search for Sam and Sarah, she pushed her dishevelled hair away from her eyes and rose. There was nothing more she could do, only retreat. Dismay welled inside her. She hated having to back off from her search, but at least she'd made more of an effort to find the others than big-talking Baz back at the party.

The smoke was suffocating. She covered her mouth with her shirt and stumbled up the hill the way she'd come from. She'd only gone a mere few meters when something slimy wrapped around her leg.

She looked down.

It was a plant. No, more like a tendril. A strong, thick tendril holding her tightly.

She tugged her leg sharply, trying to break free. She couldn't.

"What the hell...?"

A shape slithered over the ground behind her. She barely noticed it before another tendril grabbed her other leg with a slimy squelch. Another swept in, then another and another.

Two more covered her arms, crackling, while a third clasped her neck, pulling her to the ground.

"Oh god! Oh shi –!"

A crunch followed.

Silence.

Emergency personnel in a chopper saw the blaze first. Amidst the chaos, kids from the party were fleeing to their cars and tearing down the highway as fast as possible.

Several emergency services vehicles soon approached the small building. In the lead fire truck, sat a firefighter called Tank Jordan, so-called because he was built like a tank. He emerged grimly from his truck and observed the scene.

These kids hadn't started the fire. He sensed that much. Many had run. Others had stayed to help their friends who were suffering from smoke inhalation. The surroundings were already being scouted for survivors who may have ventured away from the building. Luckily, some had been found.

Tank approached a small group of ambulance workers carrying two stretchers between them.

"What have we got?" he asked.

A man spoke, "A couple of kids. Names are Sam and Sarah, going by their IDs."

"They alive?"

"Yeah. They'll make it. The girl got hit the worst."

"Get 'em out of here."

"Yes, sir."

They headed off, leaving Tank to stare out at the burning valley. He inhaled some smoky air with a sharp breath, seeing the sheer scale of the task ahead. This wasn't going to be easy. The flames were fierce. There were fires, and there were fires, and this one was turning into an all-out mother inferno from hell.

Someone walked past him, heading smoothly down the slope in the direction of the fire.

Tank frowned. This person, whoever they were, wasn't part of his team. They weren't wearing any kind of uniform either, just a leather jacket over jeans. Strangest of all was their ultra-dark sunglasses at this time of night. *This guy had to be on the crazy side,* he thought.

"Hey!" Tank called.

The man stopped.

Silence followed.

Tank tensed, ready for a fight.

Mechanically, the man turned, facing him.

Tank's head rose as he stared into those jet-black sunglasses. Despite the dim light, he saw shifting shades in the man's lenses. Was it a reflection? No. This was something else entirely – a presence drawing him in.

Tank shook it away and said, "You can't go down there."

The man paused, analysing him, then spoke in an infuriatingly calm tone. "Yes. I can."

His voice, along with his glasses swirling shadows, mesmerised Tank, and he found himself submitting to the stranger's suggestive undertones.

"Fine," Tank relented. "Go on. Get out of here."

The man's gaze bore deeper into Tank's.

"Forget," the man ordered.

Tank found himself complying. "Yes."

Tank turned away while the man headed down the slope for the blaze below. Tank had only taken a few steps when he stopped. There was a gap in his mind, like he'd forgotten something important. Try as he might, he couldn't recall the last few moments, no matter how hard he thought. It didn't matter. He had work to do.

He hurried to his truck.

The man who'd spoken to Tank strode through the valley. His face was blank and focused solely on the path ahead. He descended the slope, unaffected by the growing clouds of smoke and searing heat, neither coughing nor reacting as he moved past the sizzling trees.

A natural response, for an Agent.

Agents were above such conditions. They were trained to be. Mentally, physically, and emotionally. Objectivity was paramount over all else. Most of his emotions had been purged when joining the Agency, making it almost impossible for him to feel anything. Only the essential ones needed to complete his mission remained. The Authority on the Homeworld had made sure of that.

Since being assigned to this sector, he'd been patient for the last several months, watching, waiting, monitoring.

Preparing.

Tonight, things had kicked off. An enemy vessel had finally arrived. One which now lay as a burning wreck, savagely mutilating the valley's landscape. Despite this, the threat wasn't over.

The Agent moved on.

A crackle rose from nearby. Not fire, he determined. This noise was alive, filled with raw fury.

Something wrapped around his leg.

A thick, slimy tendril.

The Agent stopped.

The tendril's grip tightened.

The Agent lifted his foot, pulling hard. The long tendril ripped in half with a sharp snap.

Unmoved, the Agent continued walking to the source of the blaze.

Another tendril slithered in, wrapping around his other leg.

That too was ripped away.

Two more tendrils rose, binding his wrists.

He wrenched both tendrils from the ground, effortlessly, hurling them far over the treetops, into the night.

Getting the message, the tendrils retreated.

The Agent resumed walking. He hadn't gone far when he saw a girl slumped at the base of a slope. This needed to be investigated, he reasoned. Too many factors were present to leave anything to chance.

He approached the girl, knelt before her, and leaned in. Digital readouts flashed over the interior of his lenses, visible only to him.

Her breaths were faint but present. Although wounded, blackened with ash and covered with forest debris, she would survive, but only if he got her to safety.

An open purse lay by her side, revealing a name.

Jenny Campbell.

There was no choice, he concluded. Protection of all intelligent life, unless they were a direct threat, was the primary mission of every Agent assigned by the Authority.

He took her in his arms, stood up, and turned in the direction he'd come from.

Jenny's eyes half opened. The air was hot. Swelteringly so. She could just make out a blurry haze as she felt herself being lifted off the ground. The blur solidified, if only slightly, revealing a man's face. One wearing sunglasses.

The horror of the night faded away and Jenny would have swooned if she could. It was like being rescued by a muscular firefighter from one of those romance novels she indulged in at times.

"Holier than God…" she muttered.

Her head slumped sideways and she passed out.

"Hey man, look!"

The firefighter's head rose to his buddy's call. Together, they watched a man with sunglasses ascend the hill, carrying a limp girl towards them. Strangely, the newcomer wasn't staggering, stumbling, or coughing, and seemed unaffected by the surroundings. His glasses mesmerised them too, and they stood in awe as he glanced at each of them in turn, before staring directly at the taller one.

"Take her," he ordered.

The firefighter nodded and did so.

The newcomer spoke firmly. "You both found her on your own."

They spoke in unison. "Understood."

"Go."

They moved away.

They didn't see the man watch them go, nor did they see him turn and head back down the slope for the fiery valley.

Jenny's eyes half opened again and she peered groggily at the man above her.

"Where'd your sunglasses go?" she muttered, before her head slumped down and she passed out once more.

The firefighter quickened his pace.

Poor kid, he thought. *She's delirious.*

A paperbark tree flared up.

The flames flickered high into the night, charring the tree's flaky exterior into black, crumbling wisps of ash that danced on the wind, sweeping over the Agent, who calmly walked through it all. His glasses whirred, scanning for specific signs of life, as he descended to the explosion's source.

Several large ants scuttled over a tree trunk. He observed them. The ones at the tree's base were crawling over a hideous find.

He stared at it curiously, then swiped some away, revealing an object below.

The blackened face of a toy clown grinned up at him with maniacal glee. He picked it up, unaffected by its searing heat, and examined it. Its back was ripped open, exposing an empty cavity, like something was missing.

A screech erupted behind him.

He whirled around as a heavy shape thudded into him, taking him by surprise. The body he felt resembled a giant insect. More of its kind swept in, burying him under a fierce mound of guzzles and high-pitched squeals. It was impossible to fight back against so many.

His sunglasses fell from his face, landing beside him. They flickered rapidly, making a silent distress call. A call that was only active for a few moments, then silenced as his glasses were trampled on. They bent a little but didn't break. Like him, their alloy was much too tough for that.

His hand landed limply beside them, his fingers twitched, then were still.

The toy clown lay nearby, having dropped from his hand. A rippling sound rose from its back as it sealed up smoothly, of its own accord.

Making the toy seem as good as new.

Tank looked up to the sound of approaching engines. They weren't reinforcements. Not from his base anyway. They were louder and fiercer than the usual emergency vehicles.

Military.

A convoy of jeeps and trucks appeared before him, coming to a grinding halt. The doors clicked open, their personnel disembarked, and began removing equipment.

Tank headed over.

"Something I should know about?" he called.

A man turned to him.

Tank was unmoved. "Name's Tank Jordan. I'm in charge here."

The man stepped in. "Yeah, well, you can just go on home and have yourself a break now, okay?"

"Oh really?" Tank retorted.

"That's right, son," the man replied. "Captain Jack Tucker, ECG, but you can call me JT. We'll take over."

"ECG?" Tank scoffed. "What the hell's that?"

"Elite Control Garrison. We're the ones who put things right."

"Pfff! Means nothing!"

"Shouldn't either. It's classified."

"Is it now?"

"Sure is. Why don't you just leave this to the experts, huh?" He gave a small smile and walked past.

"Not gonna happen," Tank called after him. "We're staying put."

JT turned to Tank. "I'm not asking you, boy. That was an order. Everyone has to follow orders, and my men's are to use a little force on you, if necessary."

"Bit extreme, isn't it?"

"We don't take the safety of your workers lightly."

"Something tells me this isn't about *my* workers."

JT shrugged. "Maybe. Maybe not. Whatever the case, go. Get some rest. Have a night off. Let us take care of the dirty work."

Tank moved in.

JT stayed put.

Two military men stepped in on either side of JT, looming over Tank. Seriously outnumbered, Tank relented.

"You're the boss," Tank said, "but we're not done."

JT was infuriatingly smug. "Let it go. Your night's finished."

"Yeah, but we're not," Tank warned.

"Oh, I think we are," came the smooth response.

Tank felt the urge to hit JT. It took herculean strength to hold his anger. Somehow, he managed to walk away with a burning seethe, heading up the slope for his truck.

"Let's go, people!" he called. "Make sure everything's accounted for."

A few groans went up as the firefighters stopped their work. Engines soon started as the emergency vehicles pulled out.

JT watched the fire trucks leave. Once they'd gone, he called, "Okay, people, time's short and there's plenty of stuff up for grabs! Let's have some fun!"

The Elite Control Garrison moved past him, heading down into the valley and the burning landscape beyond.

If it's one thing they were good at, JT thought, *it was living up to their name.*

The next morning, long wisps of smoke rose over the devastated valley as the clean-up operation continued.

The media wasted no time in arriving, its many reporters broadcasting live.

"… and reports just in show that the valley fire has been extinguished. The cause of the blaze is still unknown, but it's believed to have been a light helicopter that went down during the night and exploded upon impact. At least four people were caught in the blaze, and search parties are scouring the area for other survivors. Whether these four people are alive or dead is unclear, and their identities are yet to be released, but one thing is for certain. This is a devastating catastrophe which will affect this community for years to come. This is Jodhi Summers, reporting."

Chapter Two

Three Months Later

Jenny Campbell stormed down the school hallway, fuming as she passed the long locker rows on either side of her. This couldn't be happening. Detention! After-school detention! Her of all people! It wasn't even her fault!

Okay, so she hadn't exactly kept up with her homework lately, and had been a little distracted too. Migraines, headaches, dizzy spells, all of which were getting worse. She'd never had them before. They'd been flaring up ever since that valley explosion, that everyone in school had dubbed, the Hurriflame. The media had picked up on this term too, and it was now its official title, thanks to one Carrington High.

As a result, she called the occasionally flaring storms in her head the Hurripain. It raged every so often, of its own accord, blowing up in times of stress. Luckily, it went down just as fast. Her doctor said it was a traumatic injury that would eventually pass, but he had no idea when.

In the meantime, that damn Hurripain had made her fall behind on her homework. Maria Longsworth hadn't exactly helped either. Maria had gone missing for ages during the Hurriflame, and when she'd finally turned up again, she looked like a ghost. Her personality hadn't improved either. She'd grown more paranoid than ever and wanted to take her anger out on Jenny. All it took was a little gaze from Jenny, or something said in the wrong way, and Maria would lash out. Trouble was, Maria was the most popular girl in school, with all the power and influence over a group of mindless sheep with matching accessories to follow. Now they were all turning against Jenny, who incidentally couldn't believe their level of stupidity.

A couple of snaps with Maria in class that afternoon had been the final straw for Miss Ford who'd sent Jenny off to detention, whilst recommending she see the school psychologist.

Swearing under her breath, Jenny headed for the *prison door* at the end of the hallway.

"Jenny Campbell!" Miss Ford called from the room ahead. "In here, please!"

Jenny sighed, walking up to the door.

"Phone," Miss Ford ordered, holding her hand out.

Jenny pulled out her phone, slapped it into Miss Ford's hand, entered the empty room, and sat at a desk wearily.

"You've got work to do," Miss Ford said icily. "Get started. I'll be back in a second."

She walked out, closing the door.

Jenny made a face and looked out the window. Silence followed. Peaceful, quiet silence. She stared into the distance, doing her best to relax then —

"Arrrgh!"

The damn Hurripain.

She pinched the bridge of her nose and clenched her eyes tightly, waiting for the pain to subside. Finally, it did.

Footsteps sounded from outside. She blinked a couple of times, shook the pain off, and heard the door open. She fully expected to hear Miss Ford laying into her about why her schoolwork wasn't out. Instead, she heard the door close, and another voice say, "Jenny Campbell?"

It was hard to tell if it was an order or a question.

A girl her age stood before her. The newcomer's blonde hair was tied back and her clothes were almost masculine. Dark jeans, a white shirt, a leather jacket, and all without any trace of softness. The girl was expressionless, but what stood out most strikingly was the jet-black sunglasses on the newcomer's face.

Jenny stood up, sensing the worst.

"What if I am?" she asked.

"We need to talk," the girl said.

The door opened and Miss Ford entered, stopping in her tracks.

"Why are you out of your seat, Jenny?" she asked, then saw the new girl. "Who are you?"

New girl's head turned to the teacher.

"Get out," the girl ordered.

"Right," Miss Ford replied, and left the room, closing the door behind her.

Jenny was impressed. "Okay. That's cool."

New girl's head turned to her mechanically. It was bizarre, Jenny thought. She couldn't see the girl's eyes behind her glasses. There were only dark patches, swirling rhythmically. It was mesmerising. Entrancing. So -

A searing stab from the Hurripain made her wince and look away.

New girl tilted her head to the side, observing her curiously.

"You're resistant," she noted.

"Duh!" Jenny scoffed, indicating the room around them. "That's why I'm here. Detention, remember? What's with the glasses anyway? They're freaky."

"You shouldn't be this way," the girl replied, unemotionally.

Jenny's jaw dropped in realisation. "You got me out of the Hurriflame! I recognise the sunnies."

The girl was unmoved. "Your delirium at the time betrays your memory."

"So who saved me? One of your friends?"

"Friend, no. Associate, yes."

"Who are you, then?"

Silence.

Jenny made for the door. "This is too weird; I'm getting out."

"Try," the girl responded, standing in her path.

Jenny stopped. "Yeah, well, can you like, move?"

"No," came the firm response. "As I said, we need to talk."

Jenny stood firm. "You're scaring me."

"There is no need to be afraid. My associate saved your life, if you recall."

"You talk like a robot."

"My name is…" The girl paused. "Susan Chambers."

"Fine," Jenny said. "What do you want, *Suzi*? Who do you work for?" A thought struck her. "Hang on, how can you work for anyone? You're my age."

"To answer your questions in order, Jenny Campbell," the girl began, "I require information from you, I work for a collective known as the Authority, and I am not your age."

Jenny raised her hands defensively. "Authority? What authority? Whoa wait! What are you? A secret agent?"

"Agent, yes. Secret, no. Discreet, very."

"What about your associate?" Jenny pressed. "Where's he?"

"Missing," the girl answered. "Like Johanna Seymour." She paused. "Things have changed in the three months since the Hurriflame. You've been getting migraines since that night. I heard that another girl, Sarah Eastman, has also changed significantly in her behaviour patterns. I need answers."

"So go ask her."

"I'm asking you." Her head lowered a little.

Jenny felt a force trying to penetrate her mind. That only flared the Hurripain up even further. She winced yet again.

"Stop doing that!" she snapped. "It's annoying!"

The girl seemed to be analysing her. "Your mind is overriding my sub-liminal commands. Your ability to do that is not natural. Something happened to you in the valley before you were rescued. You're in continuous pain. Why?"

"Get stuffed!"

"Did you see or touch anything?"

Jenny paused, recalling a memory. She'd touched something, yes, but couldn't think what. It hurt like hell when she tried to recall it. The only image she did remember was a clown's sick grinning face. Why that remained when everything else had vanished was beyond her.

"You know everything, you tell me," Jenny retorted. "I'm not scared of you."

"Your rapid blood pressure tells me otherwise."

"Shut up."

"So do your defensive speech patterns. They make no sense."

"What makes you think you're so damn superior?"

"I am superior."

"Get lost. I don't have to tell you anything."

The girl stood firm. "We cannot afford to waste time. Events are in motion."

"For what?"

"War."

Jenny was taken aback. The response was harsh, yet this girl had said it matter-of-factly, like she was used to it. A little too used to it.

Jenny shivered, doing her best to hide her growing fear. "A terrorist attack? Another world war? What?"

The girl's tone lowered. "Things are getting big. Even for my people."

"Wait a sec, what do you mean, your people?"

No response.

"So, you're here to fix everything?" Jenny pressed, holding her ground.

"No," the girl said. "I'm part of a strategic foundation to minimise casualties."

"Minimise? Seriously?"

"Deaths will occur, Jenny Campbell. Many of them. It is imperative you tell me what you know."

Jenny threw an arm up. "I don't *know* anything!"

"Your vocal tones indicate you're lying. There is fear in your voice. Talk."

"I *can't*"

Jenny saw the shades in the girl's glasses enflame yet again, making her feel like a bug under a microscope. She'd always hated being intimidated, even as a child. Damn Longsworth, damn teachers, damn detention and damn this girl!

Jenny Campbell had finally had enough.

She glared right back at the girl, pushing deep into her optical shadows with sheer attitude. The girl wasn't taken by surprise, but it was hard to read her face, for she wasn't affected in the slightest, and seemed like a freaking robot. Worse, the Hurripain was welling in her brain again, and just when she felt it about to erupt through her head, the girl stepped back and said, "Impressive. I see that nothing more can be gained from this meeting, Jenny Campbell. You may go."

Jenny blinked as the pain in her head subsided. "What? Just like that?"

"Yes."

"What about all that stuff about war?"

"It will still happen."

"So, what? You're backing down from me, now?"

"I never back down. From anyone." The girl stepped to the side, indicating the door with a glance. "Time is being wasted and I have other avenues to investigate. I came to you first because you are at the centre of events. Now I must examine other elements on the periphery. You may leave when you are ready."

Jenny could hardly believe it.

"What about detention?" she found herself blurting out.

The reply was formal. "I will make sure that your education facilitator doesn't pursue you for further reprimands."

Jenny's head swirled with a mixture of physical pain and confusion. Not wanting to argue, she hurried past the girl to the door, unwilling to spend another second in this God-forsaken place. She just reached it when she heard the girl say,

"The Hurriflame was the match. The rest of the explosion is soon to follow. Things are far from over."

Jenny stopped, looking back. The girl stood motionless by the window, staring out at the darkening day.

"Screw you!" Jenny snapped. She pulled the door open and stormed down the hall. The girl had rattled her, and she wanted to leave as fast as possible before Miss Ugly, aka Miss Ford, returned and threw her straight back into detention with Miss Freakshow.

Enough was enough.

Swearing in disbelief, with several phrases of the inhumanely impossible, she headed off.

Back in detention, the statuesque Agent reviewed the situation from all angles. Jenny Campbell was resistant to subliminal manipulation, and was also lying to keep secrets, meaning she'd have to be monitored closely.

Forcing her to talk would only lead to further resistance. It was improbable that the girl would say anything about their meeting to anyone. As far as alliances went, Jenny Campbell didn't have many friends in school, and few people would believe her.

However, their meeting held one benefit, trivial as it was. Jenny Campbell had called her Suzi. This term was more fitting than Susan Chambers, the name she'd spotted from a magazine on the teacher's desk when entering the room. Suzi. A shortened abbreviation of her chosen identity, but one the inhabitants of this world used frequently. It would help her blend in effectively. Yes. That was fitting. Suzi it was.

Satisfied with her new name, Suzi moved into the corridor. The only person present after these school hours was a woman pushing a pram holding a baby.

"Oh, thank God!" the woman said at the sight of Suzi. "Look, I've got to duck into the ladies and fix my face. My other daughter's coming out of her recital soon and I'll only be a minute. Could you watch this one for, like, two seconds?"

"No," Suzi replied automatically.

"Thanks," the woman said. "I'll be right back."

She hurried through a door.

Suzi looked down.

The baby's lips quivered, before letting loose with a full-blown wail.

Suzi glared into its eyes, remembering a human term she'd observed others use. "Shut up."

The baby quietened and went to sleep.

Suzi started to walk away, then halted, hesitant to leave this tiny creature by itself. It was Agency protocol to protect all human beings, a notion that was drilled into her before coming here.

Her face hardened. The sheer magnitude of this mission was immense and here she was, wasting time with this *thing* in the pram.

She turned back and stood in silence, fuming, while the baby snored peacefully in front of her.

Chapter Three

What the hell was that? Jenny thought, shaking her head in disbelief as she walked across the school's freshly cut lawn. *Am I actually walking away from the Big D?*

'The Big D' was her term for detention. She couldn't believe she'd just left it, and with no consequences. Not so far anyway. She thought about turning around and going back inside to settle things with Miss Ford, but that might lead to more trouble, especially if that freaky girl with dark glasses from some weird kind of "Authority" interfered.

Baffled, she strode on, figuring that everything about today was a massive Hurripain delusion. Even the mere thought of the Hurripain made her temples flare with a vengeance. She stopped, closing her eyes. It took a few moments for the pain to subside.

A plant-like rustle came from the ground, along with a soft crackle. She opened her eyes, looking down. "Whoa!"

A freaky, slimy plant lay in the garden bed, with thick green tendrils protruding from a long stalk. Similar plants were growing behind it, and growing meant growing. They were shooting up way too fast for her liking, as if responding to her presence.

Convinced she was going crazy, she hurried away.

The plants grew rapidly, their crackles growing into long drawn-out creaks. In the space of a few minutes, they'd almost doubled in size when —

Squelch!

A plant squealed as it was savagely stepped on. A spray of green liquid squirted out, sizzling into the grass. One by one, the plants were ripped from the ground and hurled over a fence into a dumpster beyond. Soon all were contained. A gardener's shovel was picked up and thrown into the dumpster's lid, making it go up a little before slamming down, sealing the plant debris inside.

Her task complete, Suzi's head clicked to one side, activating a small chip, known as the Earwig, behind her ear. "Echo, the mutations are escalating…"

Jenny hurried down the street, hoping to get home as fast as she could. All she wanted was to go to bed, wake up a few days later, and find out that everything from today was a Hurripain nightmare. Another visit to the doctor would fix the rest of her symptoms.

Or not.

A rustle came from the roadside. Another plant. This one seemed to be peering out of the bushes, observing her.

She gulped, took a few steps back and thumped into a tall figure. She whirled around and recoiled.

The school cleaner stood before her, doing little to ease her tension. He was new, and everyone knew he was creepy. Now, he seemed like a stalker too.

She swallowed hard. "Okay, awkward, awkward, awkward." She backed away. "Sorry, I really gotta run, and I mean run."

He stepped in, indicating the plants. "Best not to bury your head in the sand. With these things around, it could get bitten off."

"Okay, *really* awkward, bye."

She started to leave.

He stepped in, blocking her path.

"You're open and vulnerable —" he began.

"Yeah, so are your legs…"

He grabbed her shoulders, making her jump.

"Don't touch me!" she warned.

"Look!" he snapped, roughly turning her to face the plants. "They're not native. They're new."

Jenny shuddered. This nutcase was right. The plants were all leaning in her direction, like they were stretching out just for her, crackling eerily.

"It's you they want," he said softly. "Things haven't been right since the Hurriflame, have they?"

"Get stuffed!"

She struggled to break free. He held her tightly, moving his head close to hers and making her freak out even more. Everything about him made her feel sick, and the rising Hurripain in her temples didn't help either.

"Listen!" he ordered. "I've seen the changes around your school. Things are sprouting that shouldn't be."

"And I hope to God you're not one of them. Get off me!"

She wrenched herself free.

He pulled his phone out and threw it at her. She caught it, seeing an image of a freaky plant.

"Take it to the local nursery," he pressed. "Or anyone who's a botany expert. They'll tell you they're not natural."

"Why don't you?"

"I'm a target too."

"Only for orderlies!"

She hurried away.

"What happened to you during the Hurriflame!" he called.

She threw the phone in a bin and rounded a corner. Moments later, her fury overtook her fear, and she stormed back, letting loose with, "Oh, and one more thing numb nuts…"

There was no sign of him. Only a black car speeding away.

She drew a shuddering breath and looked at the plants. They seemed to have grown another inch and were reaching out for her with their tendrils.

She bit her lip. Maybe it wouldn't hurt for someone to check the phone's photo out, just to be on the safe side. She pulled the phone out of the bin and headed down the street.

The nursery was nearby.

No doubt they'd confirm everything.

Suzi's shoes made no sound as she strode through the Carrington Hospital Burns Unit. Her pace may have been controlled, but her mind was working in overdrive with rapid calculations and possibilities. Her progress on this mission wasn't satisfactory. The consequences from the Hurriflame needed to be dealt with, and fast.

An admin officer approached her, pointing at the desk. "Miss, if you're going that way you have to sign in…"

Suzi glanced at her. "No. Go away."

"Right."

The woman went to her desk and sat down.

Suzi headed to a room.

A nurse was exiting. "Oh, you can't go in there —"

"Stop wasting my time," Suzi replied, giving another glance.

"Sure," the nurse replied, and strode down the hallway.

Suzi entered the room, closed the door behind her, and approached the heavily bandaged figure on the bed. Their head was covered completely, save for one eye that squinted, indicating a concealed grin below.

Suzi did a preliminary scan. Several numbers flashed inside her glasses, along with a readout. There'd been a significant brain change, she discovered. This was logical. A flood of ion particles from the ship's reactor during the Hurriflame would allow Sarah's mind to expand, allowing access to the vessel's data that should have remained confidential.

Yet there was another substance in Sarah's bloodstream that Suzi couldn't identify. It wasn't from the Homeworld. It was created on this planet. She'd sensed its traces in the air earlier. Somehow, it was interacting with the ion particles in Sarah's brain, further expanding her mental abilities.

Suzi spoke. "Sarah Eastman. We need to talk."

A snicker came from beneath the bandages, accompanied by a soft song. "You know I go from rags to rages…"

Suzi's head twitched. It was brief and barely noticeable, but the song had triggered an emotional response.

"Struck a nerve, have I?" Sarah asked cockily. "Agents are supposed to remain unemotional and detached. How very unprofessional."

Suzi composed herself, speaking cool as ever.

"How much?" she asked firmly, referring to what Sarah knew.

"Careful," Sarah warned. "If knowledge is power then the factions 'round here are about to go on a binge."

"Who are they?" Suzi demanded.

Sarah snickered again. "Things are delicate right now. They're all watching and waiting to gain an upper hand in this game. One wrong move'll spoil everything. The stakes are high." She chuckled. "So much simmering goes on beneath the surface, as *you* would know."

"The factions," Suzi pressed. "State them."

"Why?" Sarah asked. "Do you want to be the spark that starts a war? You've already done that back home. Your errors cost others their lives. Your recklessness has made you expendable to your superiors. That's why you were sent here as a replacement Agent. You're not as experienced as your predecessor." Her tone darkened. "Yet you also pushed to come to this world, didn't you? To find some leftover rags from the ravages of a war which *you* started."

"Enough!" Suzi ordered. The girl knew too much. She'd have to rectify this, and soon, but first needed to change tactics to get the information required. "What do you want from me?"

Sarah stared at her. "The game's out of my hands. You set off a war by infuriating a resistance group on your Homeworld. Your whole family's dead, save for one hybrid cousin. She came to this planet and hid. A *fugitive*' from the Homeworld followed her trail here before deciding to settle. Your predecessor Agent gave chase but couldn't find him or your cousin. What a mess."

Sarah's eye bore into Suzi's dark glasses, and she continued.

"The Fugitive built weapons to defend himself. Supplies got low. He called for help from his Resistance allies. They came to this world but were pursued by an Authority ship. There was a battle. The Authority ship was destroyed. The Resistance ship crashed here, killing its crew, igniting the Hurriflame *and* creating moi!" She cackled softly. "The Agent vanished, leaving you and I. So, what do I want from you?" Her voice lowered to a snarl. "I want you to stop interfering and to let me, and this world, die in peace."

Suzi showed no emotion, not liking that Sarah knew so much. The girl was taunting her. It was painful to be reminded of her past. Still, Suzi remained as formal as ever and said, "I cannot do that."

Sarah sneered. "Why? Do you think you can fix your mistakes, find your little cousin and tell her that everything's all right. Seriously?"

"We're both in circumstances beyond our control," Suzi stated. "We must assist each other. You, Sarah Eastman, have been granted greater insight than you could have ever imagined. Can you not see all the victims who have suffered so far? Jenny Campbell –"

"Ah yes," Sarah cut in. "The numero uno among us. What little secret does she hide in her head? Then there's Gastoff. The invisible fury…"

"Explain!"

"If only I could. I see patches of light and dark, not the whole picture. Like you, my vision is clouded."

Suzi tried another angle. "What do you know of the mutations?" she asked, referring to the plants she'd seen outside the school.

"A little," Sarah answered. "One hundred and twenty flora specimens were on the Resistance ship that set off the Hurriflame. They evolved after encountering the ship's ion particles, mixed with another little surprise from this world that's floating around. Together they've sprouted some very nasty growths. Our plants are growing larger by the moment, and pollinating as we speak."

Suzi kept her nerve. "Are they one of the factions you referred to?"

Sarah submitted. "Yes. They're aware of the other factions and seek to eliminate them."

"Logically speaking," Suzi began, "another enemy is the Fugitive."

"Wrong," Sarah said flatly. "He's dead."

"How?" Suzi demanded.

"Betrayed by his own creation during the Hurriflame," came the answer. "It was to be expected. That monstrosity's now in charge."

"Define it."

Sarah tensed. "Can't see. Don't want to either. It's too powerful. All I know is that the Fugitive's arsenal is being improved upon. Rapidly."

"Meaning that the plant mutations and the Fugitive's replacement know about each other."

"Naturally," Sarah replied. "Plants can grow anywhere. These ones, strong as they are, fear this new player. They're creeping around them to find out what they can, but it's not easy."

"Is that all we're up against?" Suzi pushed.

"It doesn't matter," Sarah answered sombrely. "Nothing does now."

Suzi knew that the strain of the conversation, and the ion particles, were affecting Sarah.

"It matters to me," Suzi stated. "Surely with your extra sensory abilities, you can see further options for us?"

Sarah frowned. "There is… something. Only a glimpse."

"Speak," Suzi pressed.

Sarah spoke softly. "Humans."

"Elaborate."

Sarah winced, trying her best to penetrate her mental clouds. "They were on the scene right after the Hurriflame hit, sweeping in and taking what they could. They've salvaged your Homeworld's tech, planning to use it for themselves."

"If you know so much, Sarah Eastman, why has no one come for you?"

"You don't think we're being monitored right now?" came the bitter response. "I know *you've* taken precautions. You use your tech to scramble human digital signals wherever you go. Clever, but it only blocks a little enemy surveillance. Just by being on this world, you've hastened the countdown to this war."

"I have done nothing."

"Your presence here indicates otherwise. Clashes will soon erupt between the rival factions. There are the rogue humans of this world, along with the mutated plants who've evolved into Trans-plants, and finally, the greatest monster of all from your Homeworld who killed the Fugitive. All are massing in strength to fight one another, and all have been monitoring you since your arrival. Each seeks to assimilate you as a soldier for themselves. Who will you side with?"

"I work alone," Suzi said. "I always have."

"That's soon to change too," Sarah said simply.

Suzi didn't pursue this. She'd only get emotional if she did, and the last thing she wanted was to give Sarah the upper hand. She changed tack.

"This monster from the Homeworld is clearly the greatest threat. Where is he?"

Sarah paused, not liking to reveal the answer. "The Black Crossroads. Don't try scanning for him —"

"I already have."

"You of all people should know that he's familiar with your technology. He's a lot smarter than you too. He knows how to block your digital feelers."

"His location?"

Sarah paused again. "Unclear. Close, but hard to see. It's growing with his allies, but that's irrelevant now. I can tell you no more. Our conversation's at an end."

"I strongly differ."

"Then differ with them."

An eerie crackle came from the window.

Suzi looked. An enormous green tendril loomed outside.

Sarah spoke grimly. "It was only a question of who'd get to you first. The Trans-plants are the most reactive of the three factions, especially with the Germinator in charge."

"The Germinator?" Suzi asked.

"The most highly evolved Trans-plant," Sarah explained. "He's free from the geranium now. He's hardly the root of all your problems, nor the strongest of our factions, but he's enough to do a hell of a lot of damage."

"Good," Suzi said. "I'd like a word with him."

"Be careful what you wish for," Sarah warned. "He wants both of us converted to his cause."

Suzi wasn't fazed. "Is he outside, or has he planted his expendables to do his dirty groundwork for him?"

Sarah didn't answer.

"Where can I find him?" pressed Suzi. "He may be a link to the Black Crossroads."

Silence.

Suzi leaned in, her gaze boring into Sarah's remaining eye. "Talk!"

Sarah submitted wearily. "Carrington Nursery."

The tendril's shadow grew over them.

"What of the rogue humans you spoke of?" Suzi pushed.

"They're known as the ECG," Sarah answered.

"Location?"

"The Heartbeat."

"Be precise," Suzi ordered.

Sarah stared at Suzi curiously, sensing something.

Suzi returned the stare, twice as fierce.

The bandaged girl leaned her head to the side, speaking softly. "Your future is linked with Little Miss. You and she are the elements our enemies need to win this war. The Trans-Plants hunger growls the loudest. That's why they're here." Her voice lowered to a whisper. "End-Time… begins!"

Crash!

The hospital window shattered inwards.

The door opened and a nurse entered, stopping dead at the sight.

"I'm calling security!" she said shakily, and ran out.

Suzi remained motionless as the giant shape at the window towered over her. She didn't flinch, nor show any physical reaction. She simply watched as the massive humanoid with a green head crawled through the window on two of its four arms, sliding on its stomach.

Clearly this thing, whatever it was, had absorbed some humans into its form, then mutated further. Any human essence was gone, having been trans-planted.

Suzi analysed the readouts inside her lens. Much of this creature was composed of natural forest debris.

"Class 4, plant parasites," she stated. "You've absorbed your hosts faster than anticipated. Under my radar too." She stepped in. "I hate that."

The monstrous head loomed over her.

Suzi glared right back. The tension grew, then –

Smack!

A thick tendril lashed out, sending her sailing into the corridor. She smacked into a tea trolley, tumbling over in a terrific crash.

The tea lady screamed and recoiled. Suzi rose to her feet and headed back for the room, seriously annoyed. She wrenched a fire extinguisher off the wall, fully prepared to knock the creature's head off, but when she stepped inside she wanted to smash it through the floor.

The Trans-plant now had a second head.

Sarah's.

The mutant had worked fast, absorbing Sarah into itself. Suzi glared at the bandaged head protruding from the Trans-plant. Any humanity in the remaining eye was gone.

Suzi raised the fire extinguisher, ready to ram it on the head that wasn't Sarah's. The Trans-plant was faster, smacking it from her hands and sending it flying out the open window into a dumpster below.

Suzi had no concern about suffering the same fate as Sarah, since much of her own form was metal. She couldn't be digested, at least not easily.

Two more tendrils swept for her, one from either side.

Her arms were a blur as she grabbed the tendrils with both hands, pulled the Trans-plant in, kicked out hard, and ripped its green limbs off with a squelch. Her kick sent the rest of the monster flying across the room, smashing into the far wall. It bounced off and surged in again.

Two more tendrils clasped her metal throat, which sizzled in their touch, then slammed her into the wall, holding on tight. She retaliated by swinging herself around and whirling the Trans-plant into the side wall. The beast held fast, thrusting her back into the room's corner near the window.

The head that had once been Sarah's snapped for Suzi's chest. Suzi evaded the bite, feeling the tendrils tighten over her neck as she was pulled in. Unfazed, she savagely headbutted the Trans-plant's original head, making it squeal, before she was hurled out the window. She spiralled outside, rolled through the air, fell three stories, hit the ground heavily and sent several cracks rippling along the pavement.

The Trans-plant leapt down after her, landing smoothly and sending dollops of ooze and slime flying over her head.

Unharmed from the fall, Suzi stood up, facing it.

A shadow fell over her. One which steadily grew.

She looked back.

Several more Trans-plants were moving in for her, lumbering in with various heads and limbs.

She reached into the dumpster, pulled out the fallen fire extinguisher from the room above, and hurled it at the closest Trans-plant, severing one of its heads in a clean sweep. The creature recoiled, wailing.

Another Trans-plant's tendril swept in.

She grabbed the dumpster's handle and swung the whole thing around with monumental strength. It flew in a blur, hitting the Trans-plant and splattering it into the wall in a mass of green liquid. Wasting no time, she ran in, grabbed the dumpster's handle again and swung it hard, slamming another Trans-plant into the opposite wall. Two more Trans-plants were condensed next, leaving only three standing, one of them being Sarah's.

All got the message and backed away.

They couldn't be allowed to live, Suzi reasoned. It was an unpleasant notion. She'd seen more than enough death and hated killing anything, but they'd be a threat to all human life.

With no other choice, she flung the dumpster at two of them, ending their existence.

Only the one with Sarah's head remained.

Suzi stopped. The girl's eye had made her hesitate. A faint, emotional trace of the old Sarah trying to surface.

The eye looked at her sadly.

Suzi knew the eye's intention. She'd seen that gaze before, many times. She wanted to say something, do something, to plead with it, but Agents could never show emotions. Feelings hindered their missions and were against regulations, so she stayed silent.

The eye closed.

The Trans-plant rumbled, retreated a few steps, then exploded into a mix of tendrils, human body parts and forest debris, some of which flew past her, hitting the wall with a sizzle. The rest dropped to the ground in a slimy dollop.

Suzi was far from satisfied with the outcome. These Trans-plants were cowards. This one had self-destructed, destroying any humanity inside it, rather than evolve or risk interrogation.

Her anger grew. Things were not going as planned. She should have been able to save Sarah. Her inability to do that meant she'd failed. She wouldn't allow it to happen again.

Seriously riled, she strode towards an alleyway.

Chapter Four

Jenny's stomach churned as she hurried down the street. Her house wasn't far. All she wanted to do was flop on her bed and hide her head under her pillow, then all would be well.

The stress from the last hour had ignited the Hurripain, which flared greater than ever. Somehow, through its intensity, she'd seen a black car tailing her. The Hurripain then vanished the same time as the car. Paranoia struck next. Was she being followed? What if this was a big conspiracy? Were people really after her? Or was she going mental?

Only one place would give her the answers she needed.

Carrington Nursery.

It was just across the road. The place that creepy school gardener had told her about. She still held his phone. If she could get confirmation that those ugly plants were just rare, exotic freaks of nature, she'd feel a hell of a lot better.

She hesitated, staring at the ominous building ahead.

"Here goes my whole day…" she muttered, walking towards it.

The digital readouts in Suzi's glasses deactivated. They'd reported that Carrington Nursery was on the other side of town, meaning she'd need transport to get to this Germinator.

A loud motorbike pulled up next to her. A big man with several tattoos dismounted.

Suzi caught his gaze.

"I'm taking your bike," she told him.

He complied willingly.

"Yep," he said, walking away.

She mounted the bike, revved it with a sharp kick, and roared off down the street.

"Hello?"

Jenny stepped into the nursery, peering around. Save for the usual garden centre plants, it was empty. Weird, she thought. There were usually stacks of people here this time of day.

She observed the different plant species, comparing a few to her phone image. There were colourful flowering plants, along with tall green ones for indoors, as well as cacti and bonsai, but nothing matched her phone image, and this place was huge. The last thing she wanted was to waste her time.

A man in a black t-shirt and jeans emerged from an office. Crappy dress sense, Jenny thought. He wasn't that good-looking either. A little too skinny for her liking, with an elfin face and hair so black that it had to be dyed.

Jenny approached him, holding the phone out. "I'm looking for a plant. This one. Have you got it?"

The man didn't move.

"I need to know kind of fast," Jenny pressed. "Today would be good."

His gaze didn't waver.

"You gonna look at it or what?" she asked.

He kept staring.

"You're off the planet," she said. "See ya."

She turned to leave.

Smack!

A sharp weight thudded on the back of her head. The world swirled and as darkness closed in, she realised she'd been struck.

Make my friggin' day why don't ya? were the last words she thought of before a blanket of black descended and she slumped to the ground.

The shovel clanged to the floor, dropping beside Jenny. The man stepped over her. His lips curled up to reveal a pair of fangs.

A long green tongue emerged. A pointed tongue that resembled a leaf. Or that of a perfect Trans-plant. The most highly evolved of all.

Her words echoed in his mind.

"You're off the planet."

He leaned in, reaching for her.

Suzi weaved her bike through the traffic, ignoring the blaring horns from the surrounding vehicles. She shot between two cars with precision and control, raced through another set of red traffic lights, skidded under a semi-trailer in a shower of sparks, righted herself on the other side, and rode on.

An observing cyclist was blown away by the spectacle.

"Holy crap…!" he whispered.

Jenny opened her eyes. Things were hazy. The exotic plant aromas reminded her of where she was. Her vision returned, along with her memories.

Her head, however, hurt like hell. She sat up, wincing. Her temples still flared from the Hurripain, but that was minuscule compared to the back of her head which throbbed like crazy. Even worse, the freaky suckhole who'd hit her with the shovel stood over her. They were no longer in the garden center's foyer, but a greenhouse.

The bridge of her nose tingled, making her wince again. The Hurripain was stronger in here, like something was irritating it.

A rustling noise rose, like a breeze rippling by. Strange, she thought. The door was shut and there were no open windows.

The greenery crackled, before most of the surrounding flora morphed into green-skinned leafy beings, with multiple heads and limbs. Distorted ears, noses, twisted mouths and other warped features, were littered throughout their perverse bodies.

She nearly gagged.

"Sanity officially departing," she whispered.

Instinct kicked in and she rose to her knees, trying the door behind her.

Locked.

She looked back as the man stepped in. His voice was thin and raspy. "Cus-to-dian!"

"Freak," Jenny retorted.

His green tongue flickered out and retracted.

She gasped in shock. "O-kay!" She composed herself. "What do you want?"

He loomed over her. "Your mind."

"Last sleaze who tried to pick me up said the same thing."

His hands rose, pointing his fingers at her, then curled them towards himself.

Jenny trembled. It was like he was trying to exorcise her. She knew she was right when the Hurripain suddenly grew tenfold, like part of her mind had dislodged and snagged on something, refusing to budge. She could almost see a black sphere between her eyes that was a hundred percent toxic.

With it came memories.

The toy clown sneers at her, filled with dark energy. Her arm's pulled down magnetically and her hand's forced upon it.

A hideous wave sweeps into her head.

More recent memories returned. They're of that new girl, Suzi, or whatever her name is.

"Your mind is overriding my subliminal commands. Your ability to do that is not natural. Something happened to you in the valley before you were rescued."

"Did you see or touch anything?"

"The Hurriflame was the match. The rest of the explosion is soon to follow. Things are far from over."

The cleaner's ghostly voice came next.

"Things are sprouting that shouldn't be."

Jenny returned to the present, struggling to gather her thoughts. "Let me guess, when I touched the clown from the Hurriflame, something sick passed into my head. You want it, right?"

The soft response made her shiver. "Not just me."

"What do you mean?"

He reached for her.

She grabbed an upright shovel, smacked his hand away, and rose to her feet.

He snarled. The surrounding freaks stepped in, towering over her.

She pointed the shovel at him. "I can't fight everyone, but I can make things real painful for you! Start talking before I sever your honkey nuts! Who are you?"

His tone was sinister. "The Germinator…"

She grimaced. "Gross."

"… And you're wanted," he added.

"Disgustingly gross."

He continued, unfazed. "You are the key. There are those who will stop at nothing to find you. Our enemies grow in power."

"So what are you? A toxic weed that's high on itself?"

The Germinator ignored her. "There are also these so-called human protectors of this world who strive for supremacy. We can shield you from them too. Submit to us."

Jenny ignored him. "Where do you freaks fit into all of this?"

He paused. "We were created as a weapon by a Resistance faction on the Homeworld. They made a grasp for power against a collective of leaders known as the Authority. One key Resistance leader fled to this world. He requested assistance from his allies. A Resistance vessel responded to his call, with us on board. Shortly before arriving, our ship engaged in battle with a pursuing Authority vessel and was shot down."

"So freaky robo-girl from school was on the Authority ship?" Jenny concluded.

"Wrong," the Germinator replied. "The Authority vessel was destroyed. Our ship was damaged and crashed. We were the only survivors."

"What about the guy who carried me from the flames?"

"He was already seconded to this world to track the Fugitive from the Resistance. The Fugitive had created many weapons and mutations. One such weapon, combined with one such mutation, brought about the evolution of the abomination. On the night you call the Hurriflame, the Fugitive came to meet us, but was betrayed by his abomination, which resided in a toy clown." His tone lowered. "The clown stole the secrets to the Fugitive's greatest weapon of all. It released itself from its master's hand moments before our ship crashed, then placed those secrets into your head. The Fugitive was killed later that night, upon the orders of his toy. Now this one-time puppet pulls its own strings."

"Yeah, sounds like a big puller," Jenny said. "Boy did I hit the wrong-place-wrong-time bullseye. Yet another reason to kill maggot Longsworth."

The Germinator ignored this. "Since then, we have *planted* our spies everywhere. We have seen you converse with the latest Agent sent from the Authority. She is loyal to them, except when her reckless attitude takes over."

Jenny drew in a sharp breath. "What's causing the Hurripain?"

The Germinator paused. "Our bargaining chip."

"What the hell does that mean?" Jenny retorted. "That you guys are gambling with my life in the hope that you'll come out on top?"

"We have evolved from what we once were," the Germinator stated. "So have others. The abomination is powerful and has expanded his arsenal. He seeks to assimilate my kind into his collective. We cannot return to our world. We must ensure our survival."

"Yeah, but what about mine?"

"That is insignificant. Time is short."

His hand rose again.

"No, wait —" Jenny began, then dropped the shovel and pinched the bridge of her nose. "Arrrgh!"

The Germinator reached out once more, trying to free the black presence from her mind. The tug worsened. Tears welled in her eyes. Nausea followed as dizziness rose. Her temples rippled with searing daggers of sheer agony. Somehow, as the world blurred, she heard a whizzing sound. It seemed like a side effect of whatever this freak was doing, until she realised the noise was external. It grew louder. A shadow loomed from outside, then...

Smash!

The greenhouse's side wall shattered as a motorbike sailed through the air, ridden by Suzi. She leapt off, leaving the bike to slam into a Trans-plant, smashing it through the opposite wall and into the fence outside, where all exploded in a mass of flames.

"Wicked as hell…"" Jenny murmured, then slumped to the ground and passed out.

Suzi observed the scene. Several greenhouse plants were already ablaze, and the place would soon ignite like a tinder box. She had to act fast. Jenny Campbell was the crucial element here, or else the girl would be dead by now.

Sarah's words returned. *What little secret does she hide in her head?'*

Suzi considered the possibilities. She'd scanned Jenny upon meeting her and found nothing, so why was she so valuable to her enemies? Jenny had been resistant to Suzi's dark optics and suffered severe migraines too. Something was going on and nobody was talking. Not good.

She noted the elfin-faced man. He was different to the rest of them and must be the one who Sarah had referred to as the Germinator.

"The girl's mine," she stated.

Two Trans-plants moved in, blocking her path.

The Germinator sneered. "For how long? Without our aid you won't stand a chance against those who seek her, nor will you free your cousin from the abomination."

Suzi had to restrain herself from hitting him. Her cousin? Imprisoned by the enemy? Impossible. He must be toying with her.

He continued. "I know what the girl, Sarah, has told you. Her memories were assimilated into our consciousness once we absorbed her. I have her knowledge, and I know where your cousin is too. We can be of use to each other."

Suzi was riled but didn't show it. "I disagree."

"You have no choice." He indicated Jenny on the ground. "You may be able to take this girl from us, but not the abomination. He won't let you."

Suzi paused. This information was new to her.

"Explain!" she ordered.

The Germinator ignored her. "He once belonged to the one you call the Fugitive. Since then, he's taken matters, and your cousin, into his own hands. Will you really let the last of your line perish?"

Suzi held her ground. Jenny Campbell's safety was her priority. There was too much at stake to reject logical thought now.

"I'm taking Jenny Campbell," she said flatly.

"It won't make a difference to the abomination," the Germinator warned. "He's evolved from hiding inside a toy clown and calls himself the Toymaster now. He's very creative. He likes to *play*." His head rose. "It matters not. We can play him at his own game."

"I don't play games," Suzi replied. "I work alone, and I get results."

"With consequences," the Germinator pointed out. "Homeworld records state that you've defied the Authority in the past. You can do so again for your cousin's sake. The Toymaster dwells in the Black Crossroads. I have plants there. *Bugs* too. I can tell you exactly where he is, as well as the secrets hidden in *Jenny's* head. I can take you to your cousin. I can fix *everything*."

Suzi considered his words. They were valuable, but these creatures were unstable reactionaries. It was too dangerous to ally with them. No, her resolve was final.

"No deal," she said flatly. "I'm taking Jenny Campbell to the Homeworld. They can extract whatever she's hiding. You and all the other factions can destroy yourselves. I'll return and finish off who's left."

The Germinator's face hardened, annoyed by her stubbornness.

"So be it!" he snapped. He motioned to the largest Trans-plant with a sweeping gesture. "Weed Killer! Shred her!"

The giant weed swept in, screeching, and struck out, sending Suzi flying through the greenhouse's glass wall and dropping heavily outside.

The Germinator indicated for his Trans-plants to grab Jenny. Two of them lumbered in, reaching for her.

Rooooooooooooowwwwww!

Suzi rose to her feet, holding a whipper-snipper.

The Weed Killer raised a tendril, releasing a spray of poison. Suzi ducked the black wave and lunged at him with the whipper-snipper, running him through and silencing him in a mass of splattering slime and ooze. She did the same to a second Trans-plant, then a third, then swiped for the Germinator who retreated.

Snap!

A Trans-plant's long tendril wrapped around her neck, sizzling into her with its toxic touch. Another wrenched the whipper-snipper from her hands.

She pulled on the tendril, whirled around, and sent the Trans-plant spinning into the fiery blaze from her bike that grew ever closer. The Trans-plant caught alight and rose to its feet as a screaming, flailing mass that ignited everything it touched.

The smoke thickened but didn't affect Suzi in the slightest.

Another tendril struck out. She dodged it, picked up an axe and hurled it hard, severing the Trans-plant's head. As both hit the ground, she grabbed the shovel that Jenny had dropped, slung it powerfully, and sliced one of the multiple heads off another mutant.

The flames flickered in.

She seized a plank of wood, ignited it, and threw it into the leafy chest of another Trans-plant who went up like a bonfire. He recoiled, igniting several of his kind. All screeched wildly as she grabbed a pitchfork and stabbed fiercely. Three Trans-plants were rammed through simultaneously and thrown onto the compost heap outside where they twitched and smouldered.

Leaving only the Germinator.

His long, green tongue lashed out, ripping her glasses off her face in a shower of sparks. Uncharacteristically, she wailed and fell to the floor, her glasses clattering out of reach. Painfully, she covered her eyes with one hand, whilst desperately reaching around with the other.

Jenny awoke groggily. "Whaaaaa…?" She looked up to see the Germinator standing maniacally amidst the roaring flames. "Whoaaaaaaa!"

She recoiled and saw Suzi blindly searching for her sunglasses. They lay on the ground a short distance away. The blonde robochick who was usually so calm, was shaking uncontrollably.

"Suze!" Jenny called. "Snap out of it!"

Suzi trembled. "Iyes! Where are they? I need them!"

Jenny was baffled. "Your eyes?"

"My… glasses!"

"Now's not the time for a damn fashion accessory!"

Jenny scrambled over, grabbed the glasses, and slid them across the floor to Suzi. They tapped against her hand.

Suzi wasted no time in putting them on. They clicked into place, there was a soft hum and her demeanour changed. Her face returned to its expressionless mask as her pain seemed to dissipate. Smoothly, she stood up, in complete control again.

The Germinator hissed, ready to strike with his tongue. Suzi picked up the shovel from the ground and threw another to Jenny who snatched it out of the air.

"I could hit something really hard today," Suzi said fiercely.

"Me too," Jenny replied.

They both lashed out, striking him in the head and sending him flying onto the flames which he hit square on. His flammable form ignited like a bonfire, and he dropped to the ground with a piercing cry before gazing up at them pleadingly.

Jenny quivered, not wanting to see anything in pain.

Suzi watched unmoved.

It was like robochick was used to it, Jenny thought. Perhaps a little too much.

Bit by bit, the Germinator crumbled, letting loose with a final wail from his charred lips which then imploded into his face, dissolving as a mass of black debris.

Silence followed, save for the crackling flames.

"There we go," Jenny said, slapping Suzi's shoulder. "Teamwork!"

Suzi glared at her. "I never do teamwork."

Jenny coughed heavily.

"Let's get you away from here," Suzi said. "Your lungs won't take much more of this."

"Yours will?"

"Yes."

"Duh, of course. You're so full of hot air anyway."

"I do not understand."

"Didn't think you would."

Jenny coughed harder. The smoke was suffocating and she could barely breathe.

Suzi pulled her out of the greenhouse, towards the main building.

"What's the deal with your glasses?" Jenny asked, with tears forming in her eyes. "Why'd you go to pieces without 'em?"

"They're not glasses," Suzi replied. "The correct term is *Iyes*. They're tuned to my biochemistry to enhance my overall efficiency. They also allow me to send digital messages into people's brains to ensure their obedience to my commands."

"Like hypnosis?"

"Yes."

"What freaky spy school did you go to?"

"One where we sacrifice our eyes in exchange for these."

"Oh god, yuck!"

"My Iyes aren't meant to come off so easily. Our enemy got me by surprise. He won't do that again. It is unfortunate that you saw me without them, Jenny Campbell."

"No, no I…" Jenny started to choke. "I… I…"

Suzi saw Jenny's eyes roll back. She caught her in mid-fall, picked up the unconscious girl and carried her to the door. Jenny Campbell was still breathing, she observed, if at a reduced rate. She needed medical attention and fast.

A wail came from outside.

Emergency services, Suzi determined.

She turned, approached the neighbouring fence, kicked it down and carried Jenny through.

Several firefighters entered the greenhouse soon after. Extinguisher spray followed as survivors were searched for. None were found.

Other discoveries were made instead.

A fireman stopped at the sight of the fallen Trans-plants. Not all had been incinerated. A few lay there, dead, with macabre expressions on their multiple faces.

"What the…?"

"I'll take it from here."

He turned to see a tall man in a long black coat standing behind him.

"You will, huh?" the fireman asked.

The man flicked open a badge. "Captain Jack Tucker, ECG Taskforce. Just call me JT."

"Really?"

JT ignored this. "You guys can do the basic clean-up. Leave the rest with us. Understood?"

"No," the fireman retorted.

"I don't have time for this." JT opened his coat, revealing a sleek gun in a holster. "*Now* do we have an understanding?"

The fireman backed off. "Yeah, sure man, whatever."

He left hurriedly.

JT scanned the debris through his dark glasses.

"Not the outcome I was hoping for," he mused.

Another voice spoke from behind him. "It aint all bad, Chief. There are still bodies here. We could open 'em up. See what makes 'em tick."

JT didn't turn to see who'd spoken. He knew the voice. "Good job today, Leonard."

The cleaner from Carrington High nodded. "Thank you, sir."

"You just make sure we've got a tail on those girls."

"Happening now."

"Good. How are my contact lenses comin' along?"

"Nearly ready. We've almost got the alloy right. We'll get the mould from your eyes when we're back at base."

"What about our latest recruit from the Hurriflame?"

"He'll be online in a day or so."

"I like the sound of that. Dismissed."

The cleaner walked away.

JT observed the area, satisfied. Things had worked out well, if not the way he'd intended. His taskforce had known about the Trans-plants here, along with their growing presence at Carrington High. He'd made sure that the nursery was empty for Suzi and Jenny to enter. He could have stormed the place with his people ages ago, but knew the Trans-plants held their own agenda, and he could learn more through surveillance. Suzi had taken care of the dirty groundwork, leaving him to reap the benefits. Now he knew about her weakness too, thanks to her glasses having been ripped from her face. Another bonus.

Despite this, he wasn't quite ready to meet Suzi yet. He needed to be wearing his new contact lenses when he did. The other alien secrets he'd salvaged from the night of the Hurriflame were still being readied for battle and would be operational soon enough. Even better, these Trans-plant corpses on the ground contained seeds. He could use them. Maybe even grow a little nest egg too.

Things were working out nicely.

Jenny hung loosely in Suzi's arms. Her hair, and one of her arms, dangled as Suzi carried her through an alleyway between two shops. Jenny was breathing normally again, Suzi noted, but it would be some time before she came to.

Suzi strode on, staying out of sight of the security cameras and other forms of surveillance. She knew she was being followed. She'd spotted several cars already. The same ones kept turning up, like prowling beasts. She'd seen them from miles away and knew how to evade them, but it prolonged her journey, and she didn't have time for it. She was focused on one thing and one thing only. To get away from this planet as fast as possible and to take Jenny Campbell with her. The girl was too valuable to be left alone.

She zigzagged through several more alleyways, losing her pursuers. A few extra turns brought her, undetected, within sight of an old house. It was crumbling and looked condemned. The paint was peeling, the roof falling in, and various holes exposed its interior to the outside world. For the moment though, it was her base of operations.

She quickened her pace. A light flickered over her as she entered the front gate. The light was harmless to humans, and barely noticeable either, unless one knew what to look for. Its tingling effect might make them feel slightly elated, if only for a second. Once it passed, they'd forget about it. The presence in the house would ensure that. The light shield was there to protect her base from electronic detection and to alert her if there was a security breach.

She approached the door and opened it. It wasn't locked. There was nothing inside the actual building to steal. She entered, carrying Jenny over the creaking floorboards and across the tattered, dusty lounge room for the cupboard. Her hand rose, she opened the squeaking cupboard door, turned around, stepped in backwards, closed the door, and stood in the darkness, with Jenny dangling in her arms.

"Descend!" she ordered.

The floor lowered with a hum.

A few moments later, a metal door slid open, and she stepped onto her ship's dimly lit bridge. Hums and occasional beeps rose from the surrounding terminal banks of the circular area, overseen by an onscreen map of Carrington.

Hovering in the room's centre, was the giant transparent head of a young female. The holographic image resulted from several lights shooting up from three small points on the floor, all interconnecting. Suzi knew the image well. It was a digital assistant with Suzi's face but without the dark shades of her Iyes across it. On the Homeworld, it was known as a Holler-Gram, and it lived up to its name. Its wail was so loud that it could blow an intruder's head off, though being a security system was only one of its functions. Holler-Grams were a form of superior artificial intelligence. They were assigned to Agents, if requested, to act as mentors and advisors on assignments.

The Holler-Gram spoke. *"Welcome back Agent. I see you've broken regulations by allowing an outsider in here."*

"I've no time for regulations, Echo, you know that," Suzi replied bluntly.

"Only too well."

"You can also refer to me as Agent Chambers now. I'm not just another unit working for the Agency. I'm me."

"Protocol states that names are forbidden upon joining the Agency…"

"I know, and I don't care. The Laybel please, Echo."

This was the term for her examination table, where specimens were laid out and examined. Once complete, their details were labelled in the ship's data core.

A whine followed as a smooth metal bench emerged from the wall.

Suzi laid Jenny on it. "We need to leave for the Homeworld immediately."

"You're prepared to break regulations even further I see," Echo noted. *"Outsiders are forbidden there."*

"Now, Echo."

"Yes…" Echo paused, considering Suzi's new name, then submitted.

"Yes, Agent Chambers. What is our current threat level?"

"Trans-plants taken care of," Suzi replied. "You'll need to do a sensor sweep for any we may have missed. We've no time for anything else. Not with this Toymaster hiding in the Black Crossroads, wherever that is, and a human taskforce active in the area. Both seek to use us to benefit themselves. Jenny Campbell also has a force hidden in her head that the Toymaster wants. We must get out of here."

"I agree," Echo responded, *"although I don't see how this child can be so crucial to everything. I detect no unusual brain activity from her."*

"Look deeper, Echo."

A light descended from above, scanning Jenny with a gentle hum. That hum turned into a piercing shrill, becoming deafening.

"Echo!"

A terminal burst into a shower of sparks. Several smaller explosions followed over the bridge as Echo wailed, *"Intruder alert! Intruder alert!"*

The engines died and Echo vanished, replaced by a giant holographic image of two blood-red lips over a painted white face. The lips sniggered, making Jenny groan, before erupting into shrieking laughter.

Suzi stood her ground. "Override protocol! Inoculate!"

The lips opened wide.

The control panel blipped and the lips disappeared, allowing Echo's familiar features to return once more.

Several sprays of gas extinguished the surrounding fires.

"Report!" Suzi ordered.

Echo spoke. *"My apologies, Agent Chambers. When I attempted to scan this subject's brain, a defence mechanism in her head released a digital virus that targeted our systems."*

"Jenny Campbell, does she live?"

"Yes."

"What's our status?"

Echo spoke sombrely. *"I've ensured that the virus is no longer in operation. Unfortunately, it activated a homing beacon to alert our enemies. Thankfully, the timeframe of the transmission makes it unlikely we were located. We can still maintain many of our basic functions whilst avoiding surveillance but..."* She paused. *"All our drive systems are disabled. We cannot take off unless significant repairs are completed."*

"Fine," Suzi stated. "Begin them."

"Your passion overrides your logic," Echo said. *"This world simply doesn't have the technology for our needs."*

"Build it."

"That takes time."

"How long?"

"Weeks. Maybe months."

Suzi's tone grew angrier. "So call for help."

"I've already tried," Echo replied. *"The signal's rebounded."*

"An obstruction?"

"Yes. When the virus disrupted our systems, our enemies were alerted. They may not have our location, but they've just activated an ionic shield over this continent. That prevents us from calling for help or locating its source. Given time, I might be able to break through the shield and request Homeworld assistance, though it will be difficult without giving our position away to the enemy."

"Meaning —"

"We're stranded," they said together.

The shades in Suzi's Iyes swirled, filling with rage. "I should have anticipated the trap in her head."

"As should I," Echo replied. *"We're not perfect."*

"We have to be, Echo. There's no other option."

"You needn't be so hard on yourself."

"You're right, I'll save it for our enemies. Whoever did this was good. The battle's begun. The only question now is, who can hit who the hardest first?"

"You wish to go on the offensive?" Echo asked.

"We have no choice. I go out fighting. Always."

"So your record tells me."

Suzi stayed silent.

"However," Echo said, *"I'm detecting residual ion particles originating from the south-west of this land mass. They've likely stemmed from a Homeworld vessel. Possibly the Fugitive's."*

"How long will it take you to zero in on its source?"

"I'm unable to say at this stage."

"Then keep searching. The Black Crossroads can't be too far away."

"A logical assumption. The odds, however, are against us."

"Damn the odds. Besides, there may be a quicker way into the Cross-roads."

"Really?"

"Yes. We have what everybody wants." She indicated Jenny. "The key to everything is right here. Jenny Campbell."

"You wish to use her as a negotiating point?"

"Forget negotiation. I'm putting her out there as bait."

Echo paused. *"Please remind me again why there are several reprimands on your records, Agent Chambers?"*

"I'll be monitoring her the whole time."

"You're taking an incredible risk. The stakes are high. We're up against insurmountable odds, with one bargaining chip and no allies."

"We're not going to surrender. If our enemies want us, they can come out of hiding. Any word on my cousin?"

"None."

Suzi went quiet. She'd expected as much. If her cousin was a prisoner in the Black Crossroads, and the odds of finding it were slim, the only logical thing to do was to track her last known movements. Aside from a few traces of residual energy from her cousin's vessel, there was no sign of her. Some time ago, Suzi had been annoyed that the little brat had stolen a Skimmer and fled the Homeworld once the conflict had started. Now she knew that the child was the only one who'd had any brains.

She looked down at Jenny. "Nothing must happen to Jenny Campbell, Echo."

Echo gave a little smile. *"I will abide by whatever decision you make, Agent Chambers. If you wish to use her as bait, I will ensure that we have the best possible contingencies for worst-case scenarios."*

"Thank you, Echo." She leaned over Jenny, gazing curiously at her. "So, Jenny Campbell, what lies inside your head? What's powerful enough to take out my drive systems but remains so small it can't be located?" She moved in, her shadow looming over her. "What secrets do you hold?"

The only response was a deep silence.

Chapter Five

The crunch of an apple, the flowing of its juices, the flavours on her taste-buds, these were the succulent sensations that Jenny had longed for, at least for the past hour anyway. History class had been long and boring. It came as a much-needed relief when it ended and lunch arrived. Now she could sit in peace with her apples under the schoolyard tree and watch the boys play soccer on the oval like the stupid apes they were.

She took another bite, gazing into the distance. She loved apples. They usually solved everything, but not this time.

Her head still hurt. Things were painful, and not just from the Hurripain. She was emotionally drained. Yes, she remembered the end of school yesterday and going to the nursery, but her memory grew hazy when it came to recalling just how she'd gotten out of there. The only thing she remembered after passing out was waking up in her own bed the next morning, convinced she'd gone completely nuts. What the hell, she'd thought. The best thing to do was to keep going, so she'd gone to school like normal. Now she wondered why.

She took another bite of her apple and looked out over the field. It was a beautiful day. So simple, so peaceful, so –

"Jenny Campbell?"

The voice came from that blonde robochick who stood nearby.

Jenny sighed, convinced that her precious few moments of peace had gone to hell. She finished the last bit of her apple, threw the core away and said, "Hey Suze."

Suzi paused, as if trying to figure out what to say. Finally, she came out with, "You're all by yourself."

"Duh," Jenny replied.

Silence.

Suzi spoke again. "Wouldn't you be more comfortable with your own kind? Like Maria Longsworth?"

Jenny glared at her. "Maria Longsworth is *not* my kind!"

"True," Suzi said. "She is driven by material wealth and the superficial approval of others. You have insight, intelligence and depth."

"What do you want?" Jenny asked.

Suzi went silent.

Jenny inhaled sharply. "You know, Suze, I can't figure you out. I…" She winced, putting a hand to her temple. "I can't figure out anything anymore. Arrrrgh! Damn this stupid Hurripain!"

"Yes," Suzi agreed. "Damn it."

Jenny blinked, shaking the pain away. "The Hurriflame, the plants, the school cleaner, you, what does it all mean? Why's the world suddenly going to hell?"

"It's not easy for me to make sense of either," Suzi answered, her tone softer now, "but we can't ignore it."

"I want answers, Suze."

"We have that in common, Jenny Campbell. When I carried you from the nursery, you were mumbling about your conversation with the Germinator."

"Oh yeah. The freak leader of the Vegetative State."

Suzi frowned. "Your words confuse me, Jenny Campbell. I must know the details of what he told you."

Jenny drew another sharp breath. "Always the mission with you, isn't it? You're not interested in me because of me. You don't care about what I'm feeling inside."

"That's not true."

"Oh really?"

Suzi paused, then spoke hesitantly. "I too know what it's like to be alone. I've been taught to work and fight, and nothing more. You are lonely. I see it in your eyes. I understand that. I have felt it many times. We are similar, Jenny Campbell. We have both striven to be part of groups that appear to offer so much yet deliver so little."

Jenny saw the swirling shades in Suzi's Iyes. They didn't seem unemotional, hypnotic, or angry. Now they were filled with deep fathoms of sadness.

Jenny relented. "Don't stand over me like that. It's intimidating. Sit down. Right here."

She patted the log next to her.

Suzi stayed still, considering her options, then slowly, and somewhat awkwardly, sat next to Jenny. Together, they watched the boys running across the oval.

"You haven't got a family either, huh?" Jenny asked.

"Only a cousin," Suzi replied. "I pushed to be seconded to this world so I could look for her. I found you instead."

"What's her name? Or don't you have names on your world?"

Suzi didn't like revealing too much about herself, but felt an affinity with Jenny, and so answered her. "We have names, but those of us who join the Agency forfeit them. It's part of the streamlining process to assimilate and purge us of our identities. My cousin liked to play games as an infant. She made a childish title for herself which we continued to call her as she got older. It is… Rags."

"Cool."

"She loved to dress up in them. I found it strange." She sounded confused. "Very strange."

"Is she like you? All robot and dark glasses?"

"No," Suzi answered. "She is not an Agent, and I am not a robot. I am a Symbiant. This body is not my true form. It is a vehicle."

"Yeah, I figured as much."

"My real self lies within. It is deep down, below my reinforced exterior battle shell."

"Yeah. Same goes with me, I guess. So, the thing with your glasses —"

"I was forced to sacrifice my eyes from my organic body and become reliant on these optics. It's part of the Agency's initiation procedure, along with being granted this battle shell. This is the case for all Agents, for it increases our efficiency. Our Iyes offer far more than just sight. If they're removed, our inner Symbiant is hormonally thrown out of balance, causing our repressed emotions to resurface with a vengeance."

"Sounds feral."

"It is not pleasant. Rags is like you. A mammalian lifeform with no battle shell. It happened when one of my kind was seconded here and they bred with one of yours."

Jenny went green. "Eeeeeeew –"

"An Agent's automated body is compatible with a human's," Suzi explained.

Jenny raised her hand. "God, I don't want to know, Suze!"

"The Agent was recalled, and Rags was taken to my world. Much later, when conflict broke out, she fled here."

"Where's the rest of your family?"

Suzi's tone lowered. "There is only my cousin and I."

Jenny nodded. "Don't want to talk about it, huh?"

"No."

"I know the feeling. It's just me and my dad at home. Mum passed away a while back and our house feels so empty during the day. It kills me."

"There is an entity in your house, Jenny Campbell?"

"Feels like it." She pulled out another apple and held it up. "Apple, Suze?"

"I know."

"Do you want it?"

"No."

"Fine." She put it away. "I can't believe I'm actually sitting here on a log talking to you."

"Neither can I," Suzi replied. "Sitting on a log and talking about ourselves while our enemies gain strength is unproductive and illogical."

Jenny agreed. "Yep, welcome to real life. None of it makes sense." She rubbed her temples. "Come on, give me some answers."

Suzi looked at her cautiously and spoke. "I am an Agent. My family are no more, due to an act of recklessness that created a conflict. An act I ignited." She gazed into the sky.

"Well," Jenny said, "at least you're opening up. Where's that coming from?"

"We are alone, Jenny Campbell," Suzi stated. "I can't reach my people. You can't rely on yours. We need… support."

Jenny gave a mock laugh. "Oooh, big come down! Asking a mere mortal for help!"

"The stakes are high."

"What are we up against?"

"I have already told you too much."

"But you're here to protect me?"

"Not just you. A consequence of my world's conflict has spilled over to yours. The aim of all Agents is to enforce security. Casualties must be minimised. If you are captured, the less you know, the better."

"Feels like a conspiracy."

Suzi peered at the school building.

"New school cleaner," she noted.

"What happened to the old one?" Jenny wondered.

"That has yet to be determined."

"What about those plant things?"

"No more have been found in the area," Suzi answered. "They seem to have…" She paused. "Vanished."

Jenny shook her head. "Meaning we're up against aliens with superpowers, huh? What's next? People who can teleport?"

"My kind tried working on that," Suzi said. "There were too many problems with Zymac particles."

"With what? No, don't answer that. Like I'd understand anyway."

"Exactly."

Jenny ignored this. "What are we facing next?"

"I don't know," Suzi replied, "but whatever it is, it's linked to the Hurriflame."

"With us at the centre?"

"Correct."

"So you're, like, my bodyguard?"

"Also correct."

Jenny shrugged. "You got any weapons to protect me?"

"I do not need weapons."

"Yeah, right. You must have some little surprises hidden away."

"They're classified, Jenny Campbell."

"Oh yeah, you're great at keeping 'em a secret. Look, I can even see a piece of metal up your sleeve there. What is it? A dart gun with a truth serum or something?"

Suzi pulled her sleeve down, concealing the metal. "It is nothing."

"Oh, pull the other one!"

"Do you really want me to –?"

"Don't you dare! What is that thing you're so bad at hiding?"

Suzi relented. There'd be no harm in telling her. The girl's knowledge of it would do little to threaten the mission, especially since this device was standard issue technology to all Agents.

"Very well, Jenny Campbell," she said. "It is a projectile injector. It fires capsules holding an immobilising tranquiliser."

"I-T darts? Nice."

"No. Effective. They give the appearance of death. Their effect is temporary."

"What's the point of that?"

"I've used it on myself in the past."

"Like when the bad guys came snooping and you wanted to play dead?"

"Correct."

Jenny gave a little nod. "See? It's not that hard to open up."

Suzi cursed herself inwardly.

"With gadgets like that," Jenny said, "which I bet are only the *tip* of the iceberg –"

"What iceberg?" Suzi wondered.

Jenny continued, "It'd be cool to have you as my bodyguard. What the hell? I've got nothing to lose."

Suzi looked at her.

"What?" Jenny asked.

Suzi spoke softly. "You've always got something to lose, no matter how low you feel. Even when you don't see it, someone will always believe in you. You have so much potential."

Jenny wrapped her arms around Suzi, putting her head on her shoulder.

Suzi nearly blew outwards with rage. Somehow, she kept her temper in check.

"You're a good person," Jenny said, "and you know what? I could help you too."

"Yes," Suzi retorted. "You can stop hugging me and back three feet away."

Jenny sat up. "I was thinking about lightening you up. Your clothes are too dark. They spell trouble. You get what I'm saying?"

"To me, you babble."

"Nah, you're just scared."

"I am not scared!"

"Liar. Takes one to know one."

Suzi fumed. "You cannot manipulate me."

"Just did," Jenny replied, "which means others can too. I can teach you a lot."

Suzi looked away, muttering, "Brainless infant."

The school bell rang.

Jenny stood up. "Come on, Suze, I've got to get my school photo done. There's only one more hell-boring class after that and then we can hang out at the mall."

"No, let's not," Suzi said, also rising.

They walked across the field.

"You know," Jenny mused, "it's good to have someone in the same boat as me."

"What boat?" Suzi asked, confused.

"You know, a friend."

"We're not friends. I'm on a mission."

"No, *we're* on a mission. It's Jenny and Suzi off to save the world."

"I was saving worlds long before you were born."

"It's called teamwork."

"I never do teamwork."

"See, like this. We're communicating."

"No, we're not. You're not listening."

"Blah, blah, blah. That's what my third-grade teacher used to say to me. She thought I was a diva and used to call me a right little miss."

Inwardly, Suzi froze.

Sarah's words returned. *"Your future is linked with Little Miss."*

She'd consider the possibilities of this later.

"Fine," Suzi agreed, "but it's Suzi and Jenny off to save the world. To start with, I must know of your conversation with the Germinator."

Jenny dismissed this. "Come on, Suze." She wrapped an arm around her shoulder. "It's great to have a real conversation for once, and not a stupid online chat, which reminds me, I've got to get my phone back from Miss Ugly. You can help with that, right?"

"Easily, Jenny Campbell," Suzi replied.

Jenny beamed. "Oh, you are so my BFF!"

Suzi observed Jenny as they walked. She didn't know what BFF meant but she did know that the girl had lightened up considerably. Her migraines had ceased too. A big change from when Suzi had approached her earlier. Whatever effect she was having on Jenny was working well, and as a team, they'd face everything head-on.

Together, they entered the building, with their spirits glowing just a little bit brighter.

Countdown Minus Four:
Speed Demons

Chapter Six

"12a, you're up!"

The photographer adjusted his camera lens as one class departed the photo stands and another moved in, grumbling about having to put on happy faces.

"Collar straight please!" Miss Ford called, pointing at the boy next to Jenny. "Tuck your shirt in on that side too. Hurry it up!" She turned and nearly bumped into Suzi who stood by the curtain. Startled, she said, "Oh, I'm sorry. You're with the agency, aren't you?"

Suzi clenched her fist, ready to take the woman out.

"The photography agency?" Miss Ford pressed.

Suzi's mood changed rapidly, from fury to annoyance.

"No," she said. "Go away."

"Right."

Miss Ford turned back to the class.

Suzi watched the students move into position. She didn't have time for this. Her mind was still on her conversation with Jenny and what the girl had said about the Germinator. The one element that concerned her most was this so-called abomination and what it had put in Jenny's head. The Trans-plants had tried to extract it. Echo couldn't even detect it. That was worrying.

"We ready?" Miss Ford called.

"Yep," the photographer said, adjusting his camera, "you know what to say."

A boy smirked. "Oh, I know what to say."

Snickers rose.

A flash followed.

Two more came after that.

"Thank you," the photographer said. "Next please."

Jenny blinked from the flash. "That was quick."

She stepped off the podium, wincing a little from the Hurripain that the flash had stirred up. Flashes and other bright lights would irritate it from time to time, but the pain never lasted long. Now it subsided and she walked over to Suzi who was looking over the shoulder of the photographer's assistant. The young woman with glasses was seated at a computer, flicking through the shots uploaded from the photographer's camera.

"Cool," Jenny said, moving in.

Suzi's tone was curious. "Please explain the relevance of the ambient temperature to the photo, Jenny Campbell."

Jenny indicated Suzi to the woman and said, "She's from Iceland." She peered at the screen. "God, I look a mess." She leaned in closer. "Hey, who's that?"

"Who?" the woman asked.

"Right on the end there. He's not in my class."

"He wasn't present when the photo was taken either," Suzi added. "I'll need a printout of this image."

The woman looked up at her. "No way!"

Suzi stared at her hypnotically.

"Right away," the woman said. She pressed a button, the image printed out and she handed it to Suzi. "There you go."

Suzi took it. "Good. Now forget me."

"Okay."

They turned away from each other.

Suzi walked over to the curtain, examining the photo.

"Hey!" a boy said, coming over. "Can I see?"

Suzi glanced at him. "No."

"Right," he said, and walked off.

Jenny was impressed. "You so have to show me how to do that, Suze."

Suzi stared at Jenny, speaking hypnotically. "No. I don't."

Jenny stared back at her. "Yes. You do."

Suzi's face flared with anger, then they both examined the photo.

"This boy isn't familiar to you?" Suzi asked.

Jenny shook her head. "God no. He's creepy, especially with that short black hair and white face. He's like something out of an Asian horror film."

"Real life is scary enough, Jenny Campbell."

"You're telling me."

Suzi was confused. "I know I am."

"So who's this kid then?"

Suzi's reply was as logical as ever. "An anomaly that's worked its way into the picture."

Jenny threw her hand up. "Of course! This is everyday stuff to you, isn't it?"

"Jenny!" Miss Ford called. "Back to class please!"

Jenny huffed and called to her teacher, "Any chance of getting my phone back today?"

"After class, Campbell," came the reply. "Move it."

Jenny made a face and walked away from Suzi. "I'll catch up with you later, Suze."

Suzi was perplexed. "Why? Will I be running?"

"It means I'll see you soon," Jenny explained, heading off.

"Yes, you will," Suzi replied, quite logically.

Suzi continued examining the photo as the room emptied around her. When she was finally alone, she clicked her head to one side, activating her Earwig. "Echo, I need you to scan this room."

"Of course." A whirring sound followed. *"Clear."*

Her focus didn't waver from the picture. "There's a newcomer in this image who wasn't present when the photograph was taken. Second row, far left. Is there any information on him?"

Echo examined the image through Suzi's Iyes. *"Negative. He doesn't match any medical records from the area. I can run a global network check if you wish?"*

"Not yet, Echo. Something's sewn into his lapel."

"I see it," Echo said. *"It's the name, Gastoff. Beneath it is a sewn image of a rose amidst some trees."*

Suzi paused, recalling Sarah's words. *'Then there's Gastoff. The invisible fury.'*

"Does that name connect with any students, past or present?" she asked.

"It does not," Echo replied, *"and by the tone of your voice it seems that this anomaly unnerves you."*

"Yes, Echo. Very much so."

"Found anything on creepy ghost kid?" Jenny asked a short time later, walking out of class.

Suzi stood in the hallway, oblivious to the mass of students heading out the door behind her.

"Nothing," Suzi answered. "It is curious. Did your teacher return your phone?"

"Yeah."

"I must see it."

"Why?"

"It is important."

Jenny pulled her phone out, slapping it into Suzi's hand. Suzi examined it, back and front, flicked through a few screens, and observed the readouts inside her lenses. For a moment she stopped, stared at the phone, then flicked through a few more screens and settings.

"Satisfied?" Jenny asked.

"No," Suzi replied. Her fingers curled up, crushing the phone with superhuman strength.

Jenny was aghast. "Suze, you feral, what are you doing?"

Suzi dropped the crushed phone. "It is a threat."

"Only if you look at the wrong sites!"

"That was not your phone."

"W-what?"

"Someone replaced it with a duplicate, even down to the scratch marks. A tracking chip was within it. You were being monitored."

Jenny was taken aback. "Seriously?"

"I am always serious."

"So, who's my stalker?"

Suzi paused. "I attempted to trace the signal, but the chip deactivated once I started. The phone would have self-destructed if I'd kept going." She picked up the remains and pocketed them. "I will examine this later."

"Where's my real phone then?" Jenny pressed.

"We have bigger concerns."

"Like hell, I want my phone!" Jenny stormed down the hallway with Suzi following. "Where's that stupid teacher?"

"It's improbable that she would have done this, or had the knowhow," Suzi told her.

"Unless she's in on it. Did you ever think of that?"

"Yes." She looked out the window into the car park where Miss Ford's car was driving off. "I have examined her background thoroughly and it seems unlikely. Nevertheless, I will recheck those details."

"Later," Jenny said. "I need a new phone. Come on, let's hit the shopping mall."

"You wish to attack your own people?" Suzi asked, puzzled.

"No, it means I'll teach you to shop."

"Why?"

"To have fun for a start."

"Fun?" The word sounded alien to her.

"Yeah. It'll seriously loosen that cork up your butt."

Suzi's hand rose to her ear, ready to get Echo to do a scan.

Jenny adjusted the half-open schoolbag on her shoulder. Her diary fell to the floor, revealing a page of scribbles. "Crap! Hang on, Suze." She knelt, picked up the diary and brought it to her bag.

"Wait," Suzi ordered. "I need to see that."

Baffled, Jenny handed the diary over.

Suzi flipped through it. "Many people have written in your diary, Jenny Campbell."

"We make notes to each other in class, so what?"

Suzi reached the page of scribbles. "Who's Gastoff?"

Jenny frowned.

Suzi held out the diary, showing her some tiny words.

"Oh yeah," Jenny said. "He's new."

Suzi was unmoved. "No one called Gastoff exists in the school's database."

"What are you talking about?"

Suzi held up the school photo, indicating the intruder at the end. "That."

"Creepy ghost kid?" Jenny asked.

"Gastoff," Suzi replied.

"That's not Gastoff, Suze. I've seen Gastoff."

"Where and when?"

"It was in, um…" She paused. "Okay, this is weird. I've gone blank."

"I'm not surprised."

Jenny blinked. "What's happening here?"

Laughter came from around the corner.

"The dude's seriously cool," a voice said.

"The one about the parrot and the dead guy was the best," another added.

"Love the one about the homely melons," said a third. "Gastoff's wicked, hey?"

Suzi watched as three boys entered the hallway.

"Gastoff?" she called.

The boys stopped.

"Yeah, what about him?" one boy asked.

"Is he here?" Suzi asked back.

"Yeah," the boy replied. "On the oval."

"Thank you," Suzi said, and turned to go.

"Do you remember what he looked like?" Jenny asked.

The boys snickered.

"Duh," another scoffed. "How much have you drunk today?"

Suzi turned back. Her gaze bore into him. "Talk."

The boy frowned. "He uh, uh…"

He put a hand to his head.

The others were equally confused.

"No," the boy told her. "Not really."

"Me either," added the third.

"Oh, thank god, it's not just me," Jenny said, relieved.

"Can you remember anything else about him?" Suzi asked. "Aside from the fact that he's funny?"

The three boys went silent.

Suzi strode down the hallway. "I'm going to the oval."

Jenny ran after her. "I'll come with you."

Suzi stopped her. "Not this time, Jenny Campbell. Stay here. I will… see you soon."

She'd struggled to use the vernacular.

Jenny grinned. "You're getting better, Suze."

"Thank you, Jenny Campbell. You are too. In all areas of your life." She headed off.

Jenny sighed at Suzi's comment and went back to the boys.

"So, what else do you remember?" she asked them.

Suzi walked across the oval, into the woods. Her Iyes penetrated the surroundings, observing them for signs of this new anomaly. She hadn't been surprised to find the oval empty and had immediately ordered Echo to do an aerial scan. As expected, Echo didn't find anything, meaning that Gastoff was well hidden. Having tried the logical approach, she now decided to try an illogical one.

She walked among the trees, raised her head and called, "Gastoff?"

Silence.

The wind picked up, growing into a soft howl as the leaves rustled. A sudden crunch of woodland debris brought her attention to a nearby clump of trees. Someone had leapt out from hiding and was running down the slope, making for the main road at the bottom of the hill.

Suzi went from total stillness to rapid speed in a mere few seconds, giving pursuit and cursing herself for having detected this person too late. Her keen hearing sensed that they were a male human. Athletic too. She knew by their breaths. It was impossible to determine anything else about them from this far off. She swept down the hill and reached the main road. Alone.

The road was empty. Save for one car with its bonnet raised.

"Hey, you okay?"

The voice came from under the bonnet. A boy from Jenny's class who she recognised but couldn't put a name to. He was nearly six feet tall with a muscular build.

"Always," Suzi replied. She looked over the car. "Your vehicle needs repairing?"

"Yeah," he replied. "Engine's dead." He held up his phone. "Can't get a signal. The reception's bad out here."

Suzi agreed. "The satellite's not in position yet. It will be soon."

"You know this, how?"

She paused, refusing to tell him that she'd been tracking all satellite movements through Echo.

"Have you seen anyone else here?" she asked, changing tack.

"Sure did," he answered. "Some kid just shot across the road and went down the trail, into the trees."

"Did you recognise this individual?"

"Yeah. Gastoff."

Suzi was riled. "Do you remember anything about him? What he looked like? Or wore?"

"Yeah, I…" He stopped. "Not really, no."

Suzi scanned him. He was sweating, that much was clear. He was also covered in grease and had clearly been working on the car for a while. It was a warm day too, which made her suspicions about him even less conclusive. He may have been the person running from her, and he equally may not have been. It was hard to tell.

"Got a name?" he asked, interrupting her thoughts.

"Everyone on this world does," Suzi answered, a little too logically.

"Care to share?"

"Suzi," she said. "Suzi Chambers."

"Greg Cox," he announced, grinning. "You free on the weekend?"

"You wish to imprison me?"

"That depends," he replied cheekily.

Suzi stared at him curiously, then discreetly clicked her head, sending a signal to Echo requesting a more detailed scan of the youth. A whirr within her Earwig followed as Echo carried out her instructions via her Iyes. A click finalised the analysis and Echo spoke so softly that only she could hear her. *No abnormalities.*

"I'll be in touch," Suzi said, to both Echo and Greg, before turning and walking away.

"I'll look forward to it, Suzi Chambers," Greg called after her.

She made her way up the slope.

"So Gastoff," she murmured, scanning the area. "Where are you?"

Greg watched Suzi walk away. Once she was out of sight, his demeanour suddenly changed. His confidence faded as he tensed. His breaths turned shallow, a far cry from the cocky sports hero he'd been a few moments ago.

Like he'd become a different person.

Almost a frightened child.

He moved from the car, clutching his phone tightly, then strode up the hill, making his way back to the school oval. He soon reached the main building and entered its empty hallway, his footsteps echoing loudly.

More footsteps came from ahead.

Maria Longsworth rounded the corner, making him freeze. He shuddered, averting his eyes as she approached.

She spoke casually. "Hey Gastoff."

He gave a small nod and spoke, his voice shy and withdrawn. "Hi Maria."

"Thanks for the help in Chemistry," she said. "Appreciate it."

"Oh-oh… okay."

"Can I return the favour?"

"N-no," he stammered. "That's fine. Just do well. Pass, for me."

"Cool. Catch ya."

"Bye."

She headed down the hallway.

"Maria?" he called.

"Yeah?" she asked, turning to face him.

"I've got something for you."

She was curious. "Really?"

"Yes," he replied. "A present. From Brad Jones. He asked me to give it to you."

Maria sighed and approached him. "Why can't Brad give it to me himself?"

"He's shy, I-I guess. Scared. Happens to all of us."

"What is it?"

He held out his hand, uncurling his fingers.

She almost laughed. "A bracelet? A little tacky, but at least it's pretty. Thanks, Gastoff."

"Do you want to try it on?" he prompted.

She shrugged. "What the hell? Could be my lucky charm."

"I'm sure it will be."

She raised her wrist. "You'll have to help me."

"O-of course."

His fingers fumbled as he looped it around her wrist.

"Take it easy," Maria said. "Don't be so nervous. I'm only a girl."

The bracelet clicked into place.

"There," he whispered, gazing at it in awe. "Beautiful. Just beautiful."

"Yeah, I am," she quipped.

He looked at her aghast.

"It's a joke Gastoff!" She slapped his shoulder, making him jump. She ignored his reaction, more interested in the bracelet. "Looks pretty. Thanks." She walked away.

"Goodbye, Maria," he murmured. Once she was gone, he turned and went the opposite way in short, rapid steps. He'd barely rounded a corner when a teacher emerged from a classroom.

"Still training hard for the swim tryouts, Greg?"

The shy persona vanished, and the strong, confident Greg resurfaced. "Yeah, Coach, sure am."

"That's the way."

The teacher slapped him with a calico folder and headed off.

Grinning, Greg strode on.

Suzi entered the same hallway not long after. There was no sign of Jenny, or anyone else. The place was empty.

Almost dead.

She stopped and activated her Earwig. "No further anomalies, Echo?"

"None."

Suzi reviewed the facts. "So there's a presence that appears in a school photo, socialises with the general population and then erases itself from their memories."

"There is the possibility of it being the Toymaster or the ECG," Echo noted.

"Possibly," she considered. "What information can you give me on Greg Cox? Was he present during the Hurriflame?"

Silence followed as Echo searched her databanks, then, *"Yes. He was in the vicinity."*

"Which means he could have been affected by Homeworld technology as a result," Suzi concluded. "What do we know of his background?"

"Official records show that his parents were John and Ashleigh Cox. However, John Cox is not Greg's biological father. Greg was already born to Ashleigh and originally went by the name of Greg Rosewood."

"Rosewood," Suzi suddenly realised. She headed down the corridor.

"Agent Chambers?" Echo asked.

"The figure in the photo, Echo. An image of a rose beside some trees was sewn into his shirt. A forest, or wood. Rose and wood. Rosewood, placed right next to the name, Gastoff." She quickened her pace. "Gastoff Rosewood. Greg Rosewood. There's our connection. Advertising himself like this indicates low self-esteem, and instability. I must find Greg Cox, and fast. Thank you."

She clicked her head to the side, deactivating the Earwig, and strode on.

Maria Longsworth walked down another hallway, making for a stairwell. Her expression was no longer *'high and mighty'*, as Jenny would have called it, while her movements were as tense as hell.

Up ahead, a blonde girl in dark glasses rounded the corner, approaching her. Maria picked up her pace. This person was a threat. The girl had already interfered too much.

Sensing a change, Suzi stopped and said, "Maria?"

Maria hurried past her.

Suzi turned around. "Is something wrong?"

Maria walked on.

Suzi tried another angle. "Gastoff?"

Maria stopped, like she'd been caught, then slowly turned to face her. Her long brown hair dangled in front of her face, half-covering her shaking features and making her look like a cornered animal.

Suzi knew that her presence was no longer Maria's. It belonged to another. She stepped in. "We need to talk."

Maria shivered and recoiled. Her voice slurred as she spoke. "Leave me!"

"Does Maria still exist?" Suzi asked.

The girl paused. "Not for long." She turned away, her long hair swishing as she made for the stairwell.

Suzi lunged, turning her around and pinning her against the wall. Maria's presence snarled, struggling wildly as her wrists were held. Suzi stayed detached, bringing her gaze to Maria's and attempting to subdue her hypnotically, without success.

"You were heading for the stairs," Suzi stated. "They lead to the school roof. I know what you're planning."

Maria's presence seethed angrily. "She must learn! The same goes for you! You've botched things already!"

"You're going to kill someone. This is no game!"

Maria broke free with astonishing strength and smashed her wrist against the wall. The bracelet fell to the floor in pieces before her high heel crushed it.

Suzi stepped back as Maria doubled over with a cry, dropping to her knees. Suzi knelt, scanning the girl. No damage. At least none she could detect.

"Maria?" she asked.

Maria trembled. Her hand rose to her head, confused. "What the hell's going on?"

Suzi picked up the remains of the crushed bracelet. It wasn't technology from the Homeworld at least. She held it out before Maria. "Where did you get this?"

Maria looked at the bracelet, then stared into Suzi's dark glasses, growing entranced by their swirling shadows. "Gastoff. He gave it to me."

"Was it really him?" Suzi pressed. "Or Greg Cox?"

His name triggered a surge of anger, snapping Maria back into reality. "What's it to you? Why would I talk to Greg? We broke up a week ago!" She rose, staggering away and rubbing her temples.

"Maria…!" Suzi called.

"Get bent!" Maria snapped, storming off.

Suzi stopped, contemplating this. "Bent? Why? I do not see the purpose in looking at the floor." She dismissed the notion.

There was no point in following Maria. No further information would be gained from her. Besides, the girl was still resistant to Suzi's Iyes, thanks to Gastoff's residual strength. Humans couldn't usually break away so easily.

She examined the crushed bracelet. At least she had a way of studying Gastoff's tactics now. If she could repair it, she might even be able to contact him too, but that would take time she didn't have, and there'd be risks involved. No, Greg Cox was still her main lead, and if Maria Longsworth was too distraught to give her the information she required, then she knew the next best person.

Jenny walked across the oval, her bag over her shoulder, glad that the school day was done, but still miffed that she didn't have a phone. She'd barely made it to the car park when she saw Suzi. Wearily, she dropped her bag and called, "Tell me it's not bad news!"

Suzi approached her. "Jenny Campbell. I must know why Maria Longsworth broke up with Greg Cox. It is important."

Jenny blinked. "Y-you wh-what –?"

"It is imperative that you tell me why they parted from their pre-mating rituals."

Jenny held up her hand. "Firstly, I don't know how far they got. Secondly, I don't *want* to know how far they got, and thirdly, what are you trying to do? Naturalise yourself among us?"

"I am natural."

"That's debatable."

"By who?"

Jenny picked up her bag and moved on. "Come on, Suze, Let's talk."

Suzi walked with her.

"I didn't get anything from those three doofuses by the way," Jenny continued. "They don't remember anything about Gastoff."

"That's expected," Suzi replied, "but you must tell me, Jenny Campbell. The breakup. Why did it happen?"

"You'll be a gossip reporter in no time," Jenny said. "Okay, so Maria ditched Greg because she thought he was too weird. He only wanted to see her at school and never let her come to his house. It was, like, a big secret or something. He missed a lot of classes too. Said he was helping his father out. Greg's just creepy, you know?"

"No."

"You and he are so two of a kind."

"Two of a kind of what? Jenny Campbell, I must know about Greg Cox's father. Are you aware of anything else?"

Jenny shrugged. "Not really. His dad got sick from what I heard. Greg started helping him heaps after the Hurriflame hit."

Suzi held up the crushed bracelet. "Jenny Campbell, did you ever see Greg Cox wear a garment similar to this?"

Jenny stopped and examined it. "Please, even *I* wouldn't be seen dead wearing that."

"Why should you care what you were wearing if you were dead?"

"Oh, believe me, I would."

"That does not make sense. Did you ever see him wear a unique object that is customary to your people?"

Jenny walked on again, with Suzi following. "They're not *my* people, Suze, and yeah, I did. He wears a chain on his neck with two dragons devouring each other."

"That is logical," Suzi confirmed. "I did not see it when I spoke to him though. Perhaps it was concealed."

"Where'd you get the bracelet?"

"From Maria Longsworth. Someone under Gastoff's influence gave it to her. I studied the pieces on the way here. It's crude and primitive by my people's standards, but impressive for yours."

"Gee, thanks. So what's the deal? Does it channel ghosts or something?"

"The chain links to a hypnotic relay circuit. It's not ghosts that we're dealing with, Jenny Campbell. Someone is manipulating these students by taking over their minds through electronic circuitry."

"Hang on," Jenny cut in, "you're saying that someone's screwing with our heads through hypnosis?"

"Yes."

"How?"

Suzi held up the bracelet. "If this were fully functional and you put it on, Gastoff would have complete control of your mind and could manipulate your body. You'd be under his hypnotic suggestions and believe yourself to be him. A limited signal projecting from this device would make others around you see him too. Once the bracelet's removed, you'd have no memory of recent events. Anyone you'd spoken to under his control would only have limited recall of the encounter."

"How does that fit in with the creepy kid in the school pic?"

"It seems that someone in the photo was wearing a similar piece of circuitry," Suzi explained. "When the photo was taken, everyone around the individual would have seen Gastoff, including yourself. I only saw the people who were supposed to be in the photo, while the camera picked up the circuitry's signal and saw what you all did. Since my Iyes are far superior to that circuitry, I perceived nothing out of the ordinary. Later, when I saw Maria Longsworth, I *saw* Maria Longsworth, and not Gastoff, even though Maria was wearing his circuit. I'm also surmising that the note written in your diary from Gastoff will correlate with Greg Cox's handwriting."

"Meaning Greg Cox is the key to all this?"

"He was born with the last name of Rosewood. That matches the apparition's shirt symbol in your school photo. It's clear that Greg Cox has a connection to him."

Jenny was baffled. "So did I end up getting a bogus phone from this psycho too?"

"Possibly," Suzi replied. "We need more answers."

"Hell, yeah. So what's our next step? Hitting Greg's house?"

"No. To investigate it."

She strode away.

"That's what I meant," Jenny said, running after her.

"I do not need your assistance, Jenny Campbell," Suzi stated.

"Yeah, but I need protecting, remember?" Jenny pressed. "Come on, I want to know who's behind this just as much as you do."

"It could be a trap."

"Leaving me on my own could be one too."

Suzi stopped and thought. "Logical. Follow me."

She walked on.

Jenny eagerly picked up the pace. "Score!"

Suzi frowned as they went. "I don't think I'll ever understand humans."

"Me neither, Suze," Jenny said, slapping her shoulder. "Me neither."

Chapter Seven

Greg Cox's house was creepy.

It was older and larger than the neighbouring houses, and its gothic design seemed out of place in suburbia. The two-story building, tattered and falling apart, had textures darker than anything else in the area, along with several protrusions pointing to the sky.

Jenny felt like the building had been dragged kicking and screaming into the present, stubbornly refusing to change, yet unable to avoid the ravages of time, resulting in this suburban anomaly. Compared to the pristine houses nearby, this place should have been condemned, she thought.

"Likes to advertise itself, doesn't it?" she said as they approached.

Suzi agreed. "It does not surprise me that this structure has been allowed to exist for so long in this state, especially since its occupants can alter people's perceptions."

"So why am I not seeing my dream mansion?" Jenny wondered.

Suzi scanned the street. "It's likely that only certain individuals who've objected to this place have been affected."

The few parked cars on the road were all empty, Suzi noted. No one else was around either, which meant that she and Jenny weren't under surveillance, at least not directly.

"Suze!"

Suzi turned.

Jenny indicated an upstairs window. "Up there! Someone peered through the curtains. They backed off when I saw them."

Suzi strode for the front door.

Jenny ran ahead, reaching it first. "Whoa, hang on! Better let me deal with the formalities, here." She raised her hand to knock.

"No time," Suzi said, and booted the door in. It slammed onto the wooden floor inside, sending a mighty dust cloud billowing high and its musty stench wafting around them.

Jenny grimaced. "Or we could just get straight into it."

Suzi stepped in, unaffected by the stench.

Jenny followed her over the threshold, covering her mouth with her shirt. "Suze, this is really rude."

"Lives are at stake."

The wind blew through the doorway, sending another wave of dust rising high.

"Man, could this place use a makeover," Jenny noted. "If this Gastoff freak can do creepy stuff around school, then surely he can afford a good cleaner. This dump is so last century. *Early* last century."

Suzi observed the surroundings. The room was rife with cobwebs where long-legged spiders were poised, waiting for prey. The furniture looked disgusting. Large strips of material hung half-ripped off the couches and there were mouldy chunks on the cushions. Even worse, several bugs were crawling from a nest in one.

"You were right about the mind-altering thing," Jenny said. "Any good social worker would have spoken up about this crap by now."

Suzi made for the stairs, with Jenny trailing. A landing was at the top where several closed doors followed the wall along. Suzi determined the door they needed, placed her hand on its tarnished handle, and turned it.

The door squeaked open.

The room was empty. A bed lay in the room's centre, a dresser next to it. The bed was unmade, with half its sheets hanging off, touching the floor.

"Looks like someone left pretty quick," Jenny noted.

Suzi entered, looking over the dressing table that was littered with scribbled notes. She picked one up.

A prescription.

She paused in thought.

"Find anything?" Jenny asked from the doorway.

"No," Suzi answered.

"I'll see what else is here."

Jenny returned to the corridor and approached another door. She placed her hand on its old-fashioned lever, pushing it down and opening the door with a drawn-out squeak. She stepped in cautiously.

The door squeaked again as it slowly closed behind her, pushed gently by a figure standing in the shadows.

Smash!

An old, grey hatchback careened through the faded garage door in front of the house, shooting down the driveway and screeching out onto the street at a sickening angle before veering away.

Suzi leaped, flying through the window, shattering the glass and dropping two stories onto the concrete below.

Jenny ran back into the room, saw the broken window, and then barrelled down the stairs without a thought. She was soon outside, running after Suzi who was striding to a parked sports car on the street.

"Suze! You can't —"

Rip!

The lock broke as Suzi pulled the door open and sat in the driver's seat, ignoring the wailing car alarm. Her fist smashed part of the dashboard, silencing it, before she threw the circuitry outside and slammed the door shut.

Jenny ran to the passenger side, opened the door, and leapt in beside Suzi.

"Secure yourself," Suzi ordered, hot-wiring the car.

Jenny buckled up. "Didn't know you could drive, Suze."

"First time for everything."

"Seriously?"

Jenny lurched wildly as the car raced away with a screech of tyres.

Several car horns wailed as the old hatchback jumped a set of traffic lights, veered left and fish-tailed onto the highway, swooping in and out of the gaps between cars. Its engine grew louder as it picked up speed, heading for the city in the distance. More car horns blared as it sped past them before swerving under a bridge stretching across the highway. It was barely out the other side when Suzi's sports car soared over the railing of the bridge above, sailed through the air, landed on top of a semi-trailer, drove off it, landed in a smaller truck's trailer, reversed off that, and skidded onto the highway in a thunderous shower of sparks. Suzi controlled the skid, then revved the car after the hatchback.

Jenny glared at her, white-faced. "Don't know how to drive, huh?"

"Teething problems," Suzi replied unemotionally. "I'll get it right soon."

"That showstopper wasn't good enough for you?"

"This vehicle is too primitive for my liking."

She sped on, zipping through the traffic and coming into sight of the hatchback as it careened into the far right lane, leaving her car in the far left. She'd have moved over to join it, had the semi-trailer not caught up and come in between them. The driver glared at Suzi and raised his phone, ready to snap a shot of her.

Suzi opened her car door, ordering to Jenny, "Here, take the wheel."

"What, no!" Jenny cried, diving over and grabbing it. "I flunked my driving test!"

"Go with your instincts. I always do."

Suzi leapt out of the car, onto the semi-trailer.

Jenny unbuckled herself, scrambled behind the wheel and hit the accelerator. The car revved hard, almost slamming into the truck's rear in front of her. She braked just as hard, the car swung violently, and she nearly fell out. Somehow, she managed to grab the flailing open door that Suzi hadn't bothered to shut, pulled it closed and fell back into the car, breathing rapidly. She composed herself quickly and let her foot touch the accelerator, gently this time, moving the car to a reasonable speed that flowed along with the traffic.

Despite this, her heart was pounding.

"Just livin' the ol' dream here…" she muttered.

The driver of the semi-trailer saw his door open, then Suzi reached in, grabbing his phone.

"Hey...!"

His jaw dropped as she threw the phone onto the highway where a car's tyre crushed it.

She stared into his eyes.

"Drive on," she ordered. "Fast."

"Right," he said, looking back at the road.

The truck picked up speed.

"Shadow me," she instructed.

"Yes," he replied dully.

She moved back, slammed the door shut and climbed over the truck's exterior, heading into the gap between the truck and the semi-trailer. Halfway in, she clicked her head to the side, activating her Earwig.

"Echo, I need you to disable all security cameras in the area. Do the same for everyone's phone's too."

"At once."

She emerged from the gap onto the truck's other side. By now, the hatchback had sped ahead. A blue car was behind it.

"Completed," Echo reported.

Suzi leapt, sailing through the air with an effortless jump and landing on the blue car's roof. Its driver hit the brakes, sending its tyres screeching. She sprung off, propelled by the lurching force. Her calculated aim was correct, and she landed on top of the hatchback, holding its sides with both hands.

The car picked up speed. She leaned down a little, catching a glimpse of the side window, then the windscreen. They were covered by a dark filament that she couldn't see through. It wasn't affecting the driver, she noted, meaning it must be like a two-way mirror.

The car veered to the right, heading for a pylon.

Suicide.

Her face flared with anger. "Coward!"

Something was wrong, she concluded. Someone as manipulative as this wouldn't give in so easily.

She looked back. The semi-trailer in the next lane was closing in, with its driver obeying her orders to shadow her. She jumped onto its side, the trailer slowed, and she'd barely landed when she heard the hatchback slam into the pylon and explode.

Several vehicles came to a screeching halt, along with the semi-trailer. Bangs and crashes followed as a few cars and trucks all rammed into each other.

Suzi sprang from the truck and ran across the car rooftops to the hatchback's burning husk, then jumped onto the road and scanned the vehicle as she approached, all while relaying the scene to Echo. She reached the door, ripped it off and threw it away.

Inside was a burnt body.

"Corpse identification?" she asked Echo.

Echo analysed the relayed information. *"Solomon Gonzalez, 47 Adonis Street, Carrington."*

"Greg Cox's neighbour," Suzi confirmed. "A decoy."

"His watch has a fading electrical signal, similar to the bracelet worn by Maria Longsworth."

"Meaning our real target's fled from the house by now."

"A gas explosion occurred there ten seconds ago," Echo informed her. *"The building's destroyed."*

Suzi was annoyed. "Don't wait so long to tell me, Echo. Emergency services?"

"They're on their way."

She observed the car. "Gastoff's covering his tracks well. This also confirms what I've suspected for a while. This behaviour's too reactive for the ECG or the Toymaster. We're dealing with another entity entirely, with its own agenda."

"And one that still leaves us without a lead."

"No, we have one." She reached into her pocket, pulling out a slip of paper she'd taken from the house. "It's a morphine prescription from the local hospital, made out to Gastoff Rosewood. Someone under that name has been receiving treatment there. The signature matches the handwriting in Jenny Campbell's diary. Greg no doubt."

Echo considered the possibilities. *"The background check I completed on Greg's school records state that he has no major medical issues."*

"Exactly," Suzi confirmed. "I'll need you to scan all of Carrington Hospital's records relating to Greg Cox and Gastoff Rosewood."

"At once."

"I'm heading there for further investigation. Perhaps there'll be printed information to assist us too."

"Understood."

"You can also reactivate all cameras and digital devices in this area."

"Will do."

She moved from the car, heading along the highway's emergency lane as sirens grew among the rising tide of traffic.

"Suze!"

Jenny ran through the maze of cars towards her.

"Any luck?" Jenny asked, approaching.

"The driver was Greg Cox's neighbour," Suzi replied. "He was a decoy whose luck ran right off the highway and into that pylon where he was incinerated."

"I get it, Suze," Jenny cut in. "No luck for me either. I crashed the car."

Suzi looked at her curiously.

"Some jerk cut me off," Jenny explained. "I accelerated instead of braking. Not my car, care factor – none. What's our next step?"

"I can see why you failed your driving test," Suzi concluded. She held up the prescription. "I took this from Greg Cox's house. It's Gastoff's request for morphine from Carrington Hospital. That's where I'm going."

She walked away.

"Cool," Jenny said, following her, "but what about his house? If Greg and this Gastoff freak are hiding something else –"

"The house exploded a short time ago," Suzi cut in, "due to a gas leak."

Jenny's hand rose to her chest. "We could have been in there!"

Suzi continued. "I very much doubt that we're likely to find anything of use in its remains. The hospital is the next logical option. You can come if you wish."

Jenny nodded. "Sure. I'll come."

Suzi nodded back. "Good." She noticed Jenny's arm. "Nice bracelet, Jenny Campbell."

"Thanks, Suze."

Suzi nodded again, then walked away.

Jenny gave a little smile and ran after her. "Way to go on the small talk, Suze. You're getting there…"

Suzi strode along the hospital corridor for the supply room, with Jenny practically running to keep up. Through Echo's guidance, they'd infiltrated an office and found some papers, telling them that several supplies of morphine had been ordered over the past few months in the name of Gastoff Rosewood. There were several variations of his signature, clearly by different people under his control who'd all gone unnoticed. Gastoff had covered his tracks well, Suzi noted. Not as efficiently as she would have done, though. She'd have destroyed the paperwork. Evidently, he was still an amateur.

The supply room lay at the end of a corridor, half-hidden, which suited Gastoff's personality nicely, she observed. She headed to the door, reached for the handle, then stopped.

"What's up?" Jenny asked.

"Someone's coming."

"How do you know?"

"Hide. Now."

They snuck around the corner, peered back, and saw someone enter the corridor.

Greg Cox.

They ducked out of sight. Silence followed, before they heard the supply room door creak open. They peered again, watching Greg enter. The door closed behind him.

Suzi turned, striding in the opposite direction.

"Suze!" Jenny hissed. "Where are you going?"

"I've seen all I need to see," Suzi replied.

Jenny was aghast. "You're not going in there after him?"

"No," came the answer. "You were right. Greg Cox's house requires more investigation. You must stay and watch the door."

"Really?" Jenny asked, confused. "Okay. Cool."

Suzi turned to face her and, out of character, gave a hint of a smile. "We are a good team, Jenny Amber Campbell. We'll solve this situation."

Jenny returned the smile. "I know we will, Suze."

Suzi nodded and headed off.

Once she was gone, Jenny looked back at the door.

"Is there another way into the supply room, Echo?" Suzi asked, once out of Jenny's sight.

"*There is,*" came the reply. "*Proceed to level two. A stairwell leads to an emergency exit on the room's other side.*"

"Acknowledged."

Suzi retreated into the stairwell's shadows, moving out of sight from the door at the top of the stairs which served as an emergency exit to the supply room. She waited patiently, knowing it wouldn't take long for events to unfold.

The door above squeaked open. Someone emerged, carrying several morphine bags, before quietly and cautiously descending the stairs. They reached the bottom, touching the long handle of the opposite door.

Locked.

Suzi had ensured that. She emerged from the shadows, saying coolly, "Gastoff."

The figure whirled around.

Suzi wasn't surprised by the revelation. She'd suspected as much all along.

For before her, stood Jenny.

Only it wasn't Jenny. Her presence was gone, replaced by a child-like personality. The girl's breaths were also shallow as she clutched the morphine bags and recoiled.

Suzi spoke firmly. "You're inefficient, Gastoff. Jenny Campbell never told me her second name, nor was she wearing that bracelet when we entered your house today. I only noticed it after you killed your neighbour in that car crash."

Jenny's hands shook.

"You're in pain," Suzi said, "hence the morphine. What's going on, Gastoff?"

The opposite door squeaked open, and another figure emerged.

Jenny turned to greet them.

Suzi's head rose, satisfied that she'd drawn them out.

Greg Cox.

The door slammed shut behind him, locking them all in.

Suzi observed him curiously. His gaze was different from Jenny's. It was confident, solid, and far more focused.

Suzi's voice lowered. "Echo?"

"He holds no electronic signals," came the reply. *"It's him. Completely."*

"Understood." She addressed the newcomer. "Greg Cox. I knew you'd give yourself away. It's reckless of you to manipulate Jenny Campbell when you know I'm around."

Greg spoke, deadly serious. "As always, there's a bigger picture."

"Of course," Suzi agreed. "It's called Gastoff Rosewood. You're helping him willingly."

Greg's tone lowered. "Sometimes he lives through me. Other times I help him voluntarily. He doesn't quite understand our ways yet. He's lived apart from us for so long."

"Where is he?"

He pulled a ring out from his pocket, throwing it before her. "Put that on and find out."

"No," she replied simply.

"Do it, or Jenny's brain gets fried."

Suzi was unmoved. She tried a different tactic, gazing up at him with her hypnotic stare.

"Don't try that on me!" he warned. "Believe me, I'm very familiar with mind control. Ring!"

"I don't have to *try* anything on you," Suzi stated. "I can free Jenny and slam you to the floor easily."

"You won't do that. You need answers."

Suzi observed the ring. He was right. She required information more than anything, along with results. With no other choice, she bent down and picked up the ring. It was scratched and faded. Strangely though, it felt cold, like it had just been pulled from a freezer, and it tingled in her touch.

"Understood," she said. "Let's see what you've got."

She put it on her finger.

There was a blinding flash and then...

She hears a babble of voices. Dozens of them. They're calling from everywhere within a void. Some are close, some are distant, some are familiar, some are not. Jenny's is among them, crying out faintly.

"Suze! Suze, where are you?"

Her voice grows softer, then louder, then softer again, before diminishing as another presence sweeps in, dwarfing it.

A fierce wind billows over her.

The world changes. The void disappears. She sees a woman in a hospital bed, weary and weak. A man's by her side. A nurse approaches, a baby in her arms.

"There's been some complications with the birth..."

The woman shudders. "I don't care. I just want to see my son."

"You have to realise —"

"Show me!"

The child is handed over.

The mother sees him. A torrent of emotion bubbles up and she screams.

A disfigured child gurgles back.

A headstone. A storm. A deformed child stands by it, alongside an old lady. The headstone has the name of the child's mother on it.

His one good eye burns with rage.

The boy is much older now, and still grotesquely disfigured. He's being tormented by a group of boys in school uniform. They throw him against a classroom desk as several teachers and other adults rush in.

"I'm getting him out of here," comes the voice of his grandmother.

Now he's even older. Hunched over a desk in the study of a house that would one day belong to Greg Cox. Glumly, he watches the children outside play in the street, then his focus returns to his studies.

His ugly features curl up, consumed by hatred.

Clouds rush by as time speeds up. The image changes to night.

The boy sits at his desk, writing. His grandmother brings a tray of food in and places it down.

Always studying, she thinks sadly. It's easy to see why. Intelligence is his only hope to survive.

She walks out, closing the door behind her.

His twisted lips curl with hate as the mathematical calculations in his book expand like wildfire, flowing into a mental symphony of burning passion.

More time flies by. Chunks of jewellery lay strewn across his desk. Wires link them to bits of machinery. Switches are flicked. His disfigured face scowls in frustration. No matter how hard he tries, nothing works.

Furiously, he sweeps everything away.

The image changes to morning.

"Gastoff, this is Ashleigh. Our new maid."

A young lady steps into the study behind his grandmother. He turns to see her. The woman takes one look at him and recoils in fright, her hand over her mouth.

Despite her initial shock, the maid decides to keep her job. She cleans around Gastoff while he works with his circuitry. One day, she asks what he's doing. He tells her. She listens, interested, and they converse. Over time they talk more and more, and she sits with him, intrigued. Soon she falls under his spell, entranced as he speaks long into the night.

She clasps his hand, making him see that there is light inside of him. Compassion too.

Together, they work through his pain. They talk for many weeks until one day she can't see his features anymore. Tears roll down her smooth cheeks as she strokes his twisted moulds of flesh, before slowly leaning in and kissing them.

The maid's hands press her stomach. She stands in his dimly lit study, speaking shakily, with her words seemingly echoing around him.

"I'm pregnant…"

"Pregnant…"

"Pregnant…"

He watches from the window as his grandmother walks down the street to their house. A youth calls to her. She ignores him. The youth runs in, grabs her bag, and starts beating her.

Her grandson can only look on in rage.

"What are you doing?" the maid asks.
"We're playing a game, Ashleigh. A little game between you and me."
She gazes, transfixed, as the watch swings back and forth before her.
He's unsatisfied with the circuitry on the table behind him. It doesn't work too well just yet, meaning more traditional methods are needed.
Hypnosis it is.

"Oooh, look at this!"
The young man grins as Ashleigh approaches him in the street.
Her gaze is focused. A little too focused. Like she's in a trance.
"What do you want?" he asks cheekily, as she approaches.
She pulls out a knife and lunges, thrusting it into his stomach.
His friends cry out.
Ashleigh runs.
Further than she ever thought possible.

The disfigured youth grabs an object, hurling it across the room.
A newspaper lies on the desk nearby.
'Fugitive flees.'

Another headstone. Another tragedy. He stands in the graveyard before his grandmother's resting place, his face hidden by a hood. Several crumpled notes are in his hand. His grotesque features harden.
A man steps beside him. A private investigator.
"I've found her," the man says. "She's had the kid. Calls him Greg. They're living with a guy named John Cox. She's marrying him in September."
Gastoff scowls.

He walks out of the cemetery, seething with unrelenting hate. The storm surges in, forcing him to struggle against the howling wind. Plagued by his demons, he's oblivious to everything, even more so when the rain hits his enormous eye as he crosses the road.
A truck's headlights loom out from nowhere.
Another car swoops around the bend.
He's caught in the middle.

He *lies in a hospital bed as his bandages are removed.*

He's *burnt beyond belief.*

His *already deformed face is now a mesh of boils and scars. His limbs are stumpy mounds of flesh. Half of one lung works slightly, meaning a breathing respirator is vital. He's half blind and mostly deaf, with no sense of touch or taste, yet his mind is more alert than ever.*

As *always, intelligence is the key to his survival. It's the driving force that keeps him going, especially when he's transferred to a 'home' in the hills.*

Many years pass.

A blinding flash rips through the darkness.

The Hurriflame.

His wounded eye sees what he can of it from his bedroom window. He feels its explosive effects, despite his distance from it. The ion particles grant him the mental powers he's always yearned for. He knows how to fix his trinkets. He knows how to control the minds of others and bend them to his will. He knows he can live again.

With newfound passion, he uses standard hypnosis to manipulate a nurse into working on a bracelet. The task is soon complete. She puts it on.

The result is a success. He sees into her thoughts, knowing them intimately. She has no free will. Only one distorted mind exists between them.

His.

This home will not do. He needs somewhere private to continue his mission.

He needs help. He needs an heir, so he reaches out to the only one who has the potential to share his dream.

His son, Greg Cox.

He uses the nurse to find the boy. She does so easily, and places a chain around Greg's neck, granting him the revelation of his father's vision, and filling him with an overwhelming passion for his new life's purpose.

The boy finds his father and they develop a connection. First with the chain, then without it. Having seen and shared his father's dreams, the boy submits to him willingly.

After a time, he takes his father away to live in the only place that Gastoff desires. Home.

More circuitry's developed. Watches, chains, pendants – all created by Greg. Devices that can control people's minds. Through them, Gastoff can have the life he's always desired. The freedom to physically move, without fear or prejudice from others. He can be respectfully appreciated by everyone.

Only his constant physical pain is a reminder of the past.

"You're a freak! Deaf, dumb and stupid!"

Maria Longsworth turns away from Greg, having humiliated him in front of her friends.

A fire burns inside him. His father's presence, who knows humiliation only too well.

Father and son know what to do.

Go in for the kill.

They attempt so, but there's a setback.

Another face appears. This one's immovable, like a rock. A face no longer in the past, but the present.

Suzi's. She stares defiantly into the howling winds of Gastoff's mind amidst Greg's echoing laughter.

"I think I'll call you, Mother!" he mocks. "Let's see what's inside you. What are you hiding…?"

The winds sweep over her.

The tide's strong. A hurricane of hate streams into Suzi's head, pouring in like a thick ugly mass of slime. Her temples burn fiercely under the searing strain.

Images flash through her mind. The kind that she'd normally suppress and keep buried as deeply as possible.

She sees her Homeworld. Her life as an infant. She feels her anger from then and relives the constant fights with her family. She was born a fighter. A rebel wanting to do things her way, never listening to anyone.

Her family's voices return. She hears their screams as they cry out in despair, pleading for her not to join the Agency. Their shrieks grow louder as she sees herself walking away from them, doing things on her terms, as always. This time, it's to become an Agent for the Authority.

She's adamant that it's the best course of action. The only way to end her inner conflict. She needs to channel her energies into solving problems through facts and reason, whilst venting her anger on those who deserve it.

The Agency does little to resolve her turmoil. She works the way she wants, leading to clashes with her superiors. She never lets herself get personal and remains as tough as her diamond-shaped heart, not letting anyone in no matter how hard they try. She reasons it will make her a better fighter. Instead, it's a hindrance. One that her enemies are cunning enough to exploit. They see things about her that she's blind to, while using her arrogance as a weakness. Finally, she's betrayed by the one she trusted the most.

Flames crackle. She smells smoke. Her past horrors return with a vengeance, only this time she knows the outcome.

Deep laughter grows. It's not from Greg Coz, but from his father. Gastoff Rose-wood.

Towering flames rise above her. She watches, powerless, as her family, the ones she'd always loved but had never admitted her feelings for, burn in the debris of their home. Charred, smouldering corpses flake away in the hellfire, and all because of her reckless errors of judgement. Their burning embers sear their way into her very being, embedding themselves tightly and wounding her forever more.

Strains of guilt and shards of shame remain from that night. No matter how hard she tries to focus on her following missions, the searing residue from her faults flicker relentlessly inside her.

She speaks softly, finally saying what she'd always believed.

"Tears won't extinguish the flames."

Gastoff's presence bellows through her pain.

She feels herself drawn in as her identity starts to fade. She pulls back fiercely with her will, focussing on her inner strength that she's spent so many years building. Emotions are important too, but they're more like irrational flashes deep inside of her, resembling fires that need to be contained. Intelligence and reason are calm, controlled and objective. They can always be relied upon.

It doesn't work this time. The bellows thunder louder. The flames grow higher and, as much as she resists, Gastoff's will is simply too strong. His void of hate looms over her and she feels herself being sucked in once more.

A cry comes from behind her. Not from Gastoff, but someone else. The cry grows louder.

A higher power?

No.

A girl.

"Suze!"

Suzi responds softly. "Jenny Campbell."

She reaches for her. Their energies touch and then —
Flash!

She sees Jenny as a child. The little auburn-haired girl who weeps by her mother's hospital bed.

More images appear. Jenny's anguish from the horrendous bullying she endures at various schools. How she tries so hard to fit in with the mean girls to cover her insecurities while her father struggles to make ends meet. Like Suzi, she's become a fighter. Tough, and with a shield around her, yet still battling on, desperately trying to get somewhere in life.

Suzi senses another presence simmering in Jenny Campbell too. The strange anomaly ignited by the Hurriflame that's giving the girl headaches. Suzi can't tell what it is, for it's hidden away tightly. Whirring and growing.

She feels Jenny reaching out for her and, for the first time ever, Suzi finds herself reaching back. Suzi's head rises, whispering fiercely to the fires that torment them both. "You won't beat me."

"Me neither," Jenny says.

They push through the howling winds against the barriers of hate, illuminating the shadows beyond with their spirits.

United.

A shimmer of light appeared, growing steadily brighter, until the surroundings solidified, allowing Suzi and Jenny to step into a dark, dank basement. They watched as a dim, red halo appeared on the wall above, seemingly out of place.

This wasn't the real world, Suzi determined, although it could easily pass for it. She and Jenny were in a stable, neutral ground in a meeting of minds. In reality, Suzi was still in the stairwell wearing Gastoff's ring, while Jenny, no doubt, had his bracelet on too. Nevertheless, everything here was vivid. There was dampness in the air and an icy breeze in what was probably a mental replication of Gastoff's current location. What he sensed in that place was magnified tenfold here.

A grotesque shape shifted in the shadows.

Suzi stepped in.

There he sat. A broken figure in a wheelchair, breathing huskily into a respirator. His withered, deformed features were covered by enormous chunks of melted skin that bubbled over his body in various mounds.

Most of his face was gone, save for his right eye, half bursting from his flesh and burning with an insanity that kept him alive. It welled with hate, and fear, as he quivered before her. Shaky breaths of horror rose as he rolled his wheelchair back to protect himself from her.

Jenny stepped next to Suzi. "Nice work, Suze, we did it."

Suzi froze. She hated the notion of any kind of collaboration and always worked on her own to fix things. Echo was useful, yes, but Suzi had complete control over her. Other than that, she was a loner, and always had been, yet now it seemed that she had a... *friend?*

No! Whatever these hideous feelings were, she shouldn't be having them. There was a mission to complete, requiring her undivided focus.

Jenny indicated Gastoff and grimaced. "What's that? Looks like rectal spawn."

Gastoff glared at her.

"No," Suzi replied. "He's Gastoff Rosewood."

"The big ugly cockroach behind all this?"

"Yes."

"Then he really needs to get a life and stop leeching off everyone else's." She looked around. "How'd we get here?"

"We didn't," Suzi stated. "This isn't the real world. Physically, we're still in the stairwell wearing his objects."

"Creep. No one's going to control me with digital crap."

"Your whole society is glued to mobile devices."

"You want to take off your glasses and say that?"

Suzi paused, annoyed that Jenny had shot down her argument through sheer logic. She relented and said, "You speak truthfully, Jenny Campbell. This time though, *we're* in control. This is a mental replication of the hospital basement where Gastoff lies. I can tell by the container labels."

Jenny put a hand to her head. "Now I know I'm insane." She blinked. "So freakazoid was hiding here the whole time?"

"No," Suzi answered. "He and his son were in his house when we arrived there. The person you spotted in the window was Greg Cox observing us from his bedroom. When we entered, he and his father went into the next room. I went to the window where you'd initially seen Greg, while you wandered off and found him and Gastoff. Greg Cox placed circuitry on you. It was designed so well that not even Echo could detect it."

"What's Echo?"

Suzi ignored this. "Gastoff used you like a puppet and adapted your personality traits so I wouldn't get suspicious on the highway…"

"What highway?"

Suzi pressed on. "You wouldn't remember anything whilst wearing the bracelet. Once we were in the hospital stairwell, he had no need for your persona and dropped it, allowing his real self to seep through."

"What stairwell? What the hell are you talking about?"

Suzi continued. "His plan to use his neighbour as a decoy, and then destroy his house, was a contingency measure. With his supplies of morphine up in smoke, the next logical place he and his son would make for is the hospital. I first suspected Gastoff's influence over you when I saw you wearing that bracelet on the highway. When I called you Amber, which is not your second name according to my research, I knew you were possessed. You also showed no hesitation in coming here. My investigation into your history reveals that your mother died in a hospital and you've hated them ever since. Someone as traumatised as you would present a greater physical reaction when entering this building. You displayed nothing."

Jenny shook her head. "My life's just an open book to you, isn't it?" She paused. "Guess you know a lot about trauma, huh? Fantasy land back there showed me you've had some pretty weird family stuff too."

Suzi's Iyes flared with rage. She hated *anyone* knowing anything personal about her. Now this human infant not only knew of her past but had firsthand experience of it as well. A memory wipe would be needed in time.

Gastoff's eye widened and he shook violently in his wheelchair, half-suffocating himself in the process.

"Gof!" he slurred. "Leavef! Nowf!"

Jenny glared at him. "It's time to stop living the dream, ya freak. Reality's about to hit back, big time."

Gastoff slurred on. "I can… helpf you. You don't knowsh whatsh coming!"

Suzi dismissed this. "What do you know about the ECG and the Toymaster?"

"I… work alone. Like… bof of you."

"Just a regular psycho," Jenny scoffed.

"No," Suzi replied. "He's a lonely boy who only wants a normal life, like so many children."

Jenny swallowed hard and looked away.

It took Suzi a moment to compose her own thoughts too. Weakness wasn't an option. To show any sign of it would allow Gastoff to take advantage of her, even though she identified with both him *and* Jenny. They all had different backgrounds, and unique identities, but the forces that bound them were the same.

Gastoff pressed on, glaring at Suzi. "I can offer youf so much. The location of the Black Crosshroadsh. There'sh also the Heartbeat, where the human faction whosh replashed this girl's mobile, lies. I knowf where your cousin iss too."

Suzi's cool exterior dropped, showing a hint of emotion. "Rags? Where?"

Gastoff deflected her question. "I know your part in End-Time. I know aboutth the Toymaster. Shubmit, and I will tellsh you."

Suzi stayed silent.

Jenny spoke up. "Best not to deal with the devil, Suze. Not now, not ever."

Suzi nodded. "Thank you, Jenny Campbell. You've confirmed what I was thinking." Her voice rose. "It's over Gastoff."

The eye widened as the hideous wheelchair-bound lump shook violently, then let loose with a howling gust of mental energy, slamming Suzi and Jenny into the back wall. Various shadows on the wall opposite started moving, forming into clawed hands and long beaks.

Jenny gasped.

"Illusions, Jenny Campbell!" Suzi called over the roaring winds. "Don't let them overcome you!"

Jenny whimpered. "They're from the book! Someone read it to me as a kid 'round the time Mum died. I hate it!"

"You're not a book, Jenny Campbell!"

Jenny fell to the floor, trembling against the growing storm's might.

"Shubmit!" Gastoff bellowed to Suzi. "Shubmit or the girl diessh!"

Suzi's head lowered as she moved in. "You leave me no choice, Gastoff."

He stayed defiant. "Kill me and you'llsh never knowf! Your cousin. End-Time. What's really insidef your friend's head…"

"I'll find out one way or another," Suzi stated. "Without your help."

She pushed in mentally. His presence was red hot. Images of her burning family resurfaced once more. Those memories barely affected her now. Somehow, Jenny Campbell had given her the strength to fight back.

She pushed harder, her emotions bubbling. All those years of forcing her feelings down had taught her one thing. It was time to release them, just not too much.

Her fists clenched and she let loose, hitting him with a wave of psychic fury. Her aim was merely to incapacitate, but she knew by his horrified expression that she'd done more than that. His will had crumbled. He'd made his resolve.

To self-destruct.

A strong wind blew her backwards. She skidded, holding her ground as he burst into flames.

"It doesn't have to be like this!" she called over his piercing screams. "I can help you!"

The flames grew higher. His eye widened as they inched closer to him while his enormous misshapen head rocked back and forth in terror. His boiling skin melted to liquid as a final cry erupted in Suzi's mind, along with several numbers.

"7-5-1-2-1-5!"

The flames grew louder, before a final blast of psychic energy blew out the whole room, dropping it into a void. A crushing force sucked her into the darkness. Into silence. Into solace. Into…

"God, that hurts!"

Suzi came to and saw Jenny lying on the stairwell floor, wincing. They'd returned to the physical world, where Suzi's legs had mechanically locked into place, allowing her to remain standing the whole time. Jenny, however, had collapsed.

Jenny groaned and sat up, placing a hand on her head.

"Damn," she said groggily. "I thought I was having an after-party nightmare."

Suzi was confused. "Why would such a dream happen after a social experience, Jenny Campbell?"

"Yeah, I should have known you've never been wasted," Jenny grumbled. "You know, intoxicated?"

"Neither have you," Suzi said. "We linked minds, remember?"

Jenny winced again. Suzi knew that Gastoff was gone from Jenny Campbell, yet the remnants of his psychosis clearly remained, along with the Hurripain. Suzi waited for things to settle, and once they did, she reached out. Jenny took her hand and yelped as she was hoisted to her feet with such strength that she practically flew up from the floor.

"Whoa!" Jenny exclaimed. "Where do you keep your muscles, Suze?"

Suzi frowned. "Inside myself of course."

"Of course," Jenny retorted. "So you, uh, saw a lot in my head, huh?"

Suzi nodded. "Yes."

"Awkward," Jenny muttered. "Well, I saw into your life too."

"I know," Suzi replied crossly, then glared at her. "You say *nothing*."

"Chill, Suze, it's okay. Who'd believe me anyway?"

"Greg Cox. My superiors –"

"Yeah, but that's stuff they already know, and even if it isn't there's not much they can do with it. We're pretty strong, right?"

Suzi considered this and relented. There was no point in being angry at the girl. It wasn't her fault she'd seen what she had. There'd been no choice.

Suzi spoke softly. "We've experienced a lot of pain, Jenny Campbell."

Jenny shrugged. "At least we've got each other."

Suzi submitted, wondering if the mind link had affected her more than she thought. "Yes. We do."

Jenny leaned over, hugging her.

Suzi remained motionless, unsure how to react.

Jenny pulled away. "I won't tell if you don't."

"I will not tell, Jenny Campbell."

"Pinky swear?"

"Explain."

Jenny reached down, taking Suzi's hand. "You link your little fingers like this, see? That's what we call a pinky swear."

"How does this coax us into silence?"

"Just does. It's our bond."

Suzi considered this. "Is this a custom of your planet?"

"For some of us, yeah."

Suzi indicated the empty stairwell. "We must find Greg Cox."

"Was he here too?"

"Yes."

"So his father fries and he just bails?"

Suzi headed for the steps. "I think I know where he is."

They found him in the hospital basement, kneeling by his father's lifeless husk. Gastoff's abnormal head was slumped sideways, dead to the world.

Suzi addressed Greg, relaying the information that Echo had given her. "Several hospital records have been falsified. They now state that you've escaped from a psychiatric ward over east. Orderlies are on their way here to transfer you to the nearest mental health facility. I will ensure that it protects you from all threats. There is no doubt you will be a target from this point on."

Greg trembled. "This isn't over…"

She leaned down, glaring at him. "First, you'll tell me everything. From where your father's circuits are located, to the work he'd planned. We cannot allow it to fall into the wrong hands."

He shook his head. "I don't care anymore."

Her gaze bored into his. "I do. Talk!"

Greg submitted and did so.

Suzi stood in the school corridor, aloof. Hordes of kids flooded past, ignoring her. Her mind filtered out their banter. Social trivialities were never her focus. Only the mission mattered.

She pondered on Gastoff's words. End-Time. Sarah had mentioned it too, just before the battle with the Trans-plants. Then there were the humans who'd bugged Jenny's phone. They were undoubtedly observing things from a distance.

Maria Longsworth walked by, with a posse of girls.

"What's the story with Greg?" a girl asked.

"Heard he got pulled from school," replied another.

"*I* heard he's in a mental home," Maria said flippantly. "The jerk can stay there too. I'm going to the river to ditch the ring he gave me a while back. Wanna come?"

"Hell yeah," a third girl sparked up.

They walked on.

Suzi thought about what they'd said. How did they know about Greg already? She'd covered her tracks thoroughly, with Echo's help. Perhaps their banter was speculative gossip. Greg couldn't have said anything to anyone and *was* safely locked away in a psychiatric ward. Whatever the case, it seemed nothing got past high school girls.

Much to her annoyance, Greg had been resistant to her Iyes, thanks to Gastoff, and he remembered everything. The hospital staff were another story. Once Echo had falsified Greg's medical records, she'd personally seen the senior staff one by one, pressing into their minds that Greg was delusional. The staff had then found the nearest matching syndrome for him and ensured that his identity was changed, and impossible to trace. With no real family or friends, no one would search for him, especially since his mother and adopted father had recently died, again the result of Gastoff's work.

Suzi felt no sense of victory, despite her success with this mission. Greg was completely alone, and she knew only too well how that hurt.

She stood silently in the fading crowd.

Maria rounded the corner, still in flippant conversation with her posse.

A boy approached her. "Maria, can we talk?"

She stopped. "What about, Brad?"

"Alone?" he pressed.

Maria's posse moved away, giggling, with some eager "Ooohs" thrown in. Once they were gone, Maria stepped in closer, grinning slyly. "What do you want?"

He motioned her to one side, discreetly pulling out a badge. "My name's not Brad. It's Deck Turner, ECG Taskforce. I need you to tell me about Jenny Campbell and the girl she's been hanging out with."

Maria's jaw dropped, like she'd been insulted.

Jenny found Suzi standing motionless in the school hallway.

"Hey Suze," Jenny said, approaching her. "You okay?"

Suzi gave a little nod. "Yes, Jenny Campbell. I was considering the possibilities from our encounter with Gastoff."

Jenny sighed. "God, Suze, don't you ever just chill?"

"You mean freeze, Jenny Campbell?"

"No, relax. Come on, forget about him. You've got me now. We're bound by pinky swear." She put an arm over her shoulder and led her down the hallway.

Suzi glanced at Jenny's arm. "Is it customary for you to put your arm around me, Jenny Campbell?"

"Kinda," Jenny replied. "Try doing it back."

Suzi put her arm around Jenny.

"See?" Jenny said.

"I do not," Suzi answered, "but I have seen your people doing it and it does seem to improve their mood."

Two boys rounded the corner, walking past them and looking cross.

"Excuse me?" Suzi called.

They turned to her.

"What?" one asked gruffly.

"Try doing this," Suzi said, indicating her arm around Jenny. "It is supposed to make you feel better."

Jenny grinned. "Yeah. Hug it out!"

"Screw you!" the boy snapped. He stormed away, with the other boy following.

Suzi frowned. "Is there a tool big enough to screw me?"

"Yep," Jenny told her. "He's out there somewhere. One for me too."

"I do not understand."

"One day, Suze. One day." She smiled. "See, this is cool. You just need to let go of everything. Forget about Gastoff. He's fertiliser."

"Fertiliser makes plants grow, Jenny Campbell. He would kill them."

"Good point. Anyway, we've got other things to worry about. Got my award ceremony tomorrow and I *do not* want to get the Hurripain during my speech, which means as much chill time as possible. Hey, want to see how our school photo turned out?"

"No."

"Cool. I'll show you."

She parted from Suzi, took her bag off her shoulder, pulled out her copy of the class photo, and held it eagerly.

Gastoff was still on the end.

"Oh crap, they left him in," Jenny said, dismayed.

"Yes," Suzi replied. "You can see Naomi Robbins, an old girlfriend of Greg Cox, standing above him. I've since established that she wore the bracelet that transmitted Gastoff's image into this picture."

Jenny sighed. "God knows why he chose to look so ugly for the photo. Why not choose to look like Mister Universe if he can control how people see him? He looks dead here."

"Perhaps the camera saw his true self," Suzi stated. "A lost child who only wanted to belong. Now he's achieved it. Forever."

Jenny saw the numbers running up the photo's side and knew what Suzi meant. Finally, she thought, this lonely boy belonged somewhere at last.

For the numbers read 751215.

Countdown Minus Three: Acceleration

Chapter Eight

The great blades of the military helicopter whirled fiercely as they swept through the sky's grey mists, high above the desert. Far ahead, several black clouds loomed like angry giants.

A storm was brewing.

The helicopter descended, veering to the right and heading for a dark patch below. As it drew closer, numerous abandoned buildings appeared, revealing a ghost town.

The helicopter's sensors activated, scanning it. Once complete, a transmission was sent.

"Talon Strike to base, we have confirmation, repeat, we have confirmation..."

JT grinned, more than happy with the report. The news had come sooner than expected.

The bridge's mechanical hums were soothing. He'd always found machines easier to get along with than people. Several of his top scientists were working on some tech beauties a few floors down, deep in the ECG's base of operations, fittingly called the Heartbeat.

A figure stepped in, gazing at the wallscreen with him. He didn't have to turn to see who it was. They were slightly taller than him and wore dark glasses like Suzi's. Unlike her, however, this being was completely under his control.

Assimilate or destroy, that had always been JT's mantra. He preferred assimilation. The more allies the better. The figure beside him proved that even an outside race could be made subservient, after some rewiring. This being, a metal body holding a Symbiant life form, was another treasure from the Hurriflame. The ECG had found it in the burning valley, barely alive. Several mutations, like Trans-plants, but originating from insects, had been attacking it. The Symbiant, in critical condition, had deactivated its systems and played dead. The mutant attackers couldn't penetrate its metal shell, at least not easily, and were making little progress when the ECG arrived to gun down many of them, and capture even more.

Once this being, this *Agent*, was taken back to base, it was augmented. Yesterday, their latest recruit had finally come online. The Agent's security protocols meant that most of its secrets remained hidden, but JT was above and beyond satisfied. This find was worth its weight in gold. Almost as much as the recent discovery of the Shockwave, a unique energy source that kept their base off the main power grid.

The ECG scientists hadn't been able to penetrate the Agent's metal body to reach the Symbiant inside, so external improvements were made instead, ensuring the Agent's unquestioning obedience. They'd also increased his combat capabilities. One of JT's favourite augmentations was a little trick where the Agent's teeth rotated to become razor sharp. A single bite would absorb all the information out of a human's brain, sucking it dry. That knowledge could later be downloaded onto an external hard drive, which was why JT had named this individual, Terror-Byte.

Terror-Byte spoke unemotionally. "Confirmation of the Black Crossroads has come sooner than expected."

JT nodded. "Yeah, it's early. Way too early, but we're close. We're *that* close —" He paused. "Most of our projects are ready. Not all."

"Can we afford to wait?" Terror-Byte asked.

"For the moment, yes," came the reply. "First, we'll deal with our biggest problem." He glanced to a technician, calling, "Put her up!"

The wallscreen flickered, revealing Suzi's image.

"One of your friends, I believe?" JT prompted.

"That individual is not my friend," Terror-Byte answered.

"Don't matter," JT said. "She's sticking her nose in where it doesn't belong. She took care of the Trans-plants, and Gastoff too. She'll be a great ally."

"You have me."

"There's no such thing as too much power —"

"I disagree," Terror-Byte cut in. "Your physical forms are limited compared to your desires."

"Yeah, but you're the one working for me, remember?" He indicated the screen. "I said she *could* be an ally. I didn't say she'd come willingly. Like you, she'll be resistant at first. We'll have to shock her into place. Two converted Agents on my team'll send an even clearer message to your people to back off."

Terror-Byte was unmoved. "Meaning your next step is to pursue her?"

JT smiled. He was satisfied with the work Agent Deck Turner had done. Maria Longsworth's information had paid off nicely.

"No," he said. "We'll get Jenny Campbell. There's something in her head that Chambers is protecting. We need to know what. Grab Campbell, and Chambers'll give chase. Two for the price of one."

"I know my people," Terror-Byte said bluntly. "She will not make it easy for you."

"No, she won't make it easy for *you*, sunshine. That's why you work for me. Dismissed."

"Understood."

Terror-Byte turned mechanically and left.

JT glared at Suzi's giant face on the wallscreen.

"Game on, Chambers!"

The mechanical door slid open.

The roar of an engine ignited, growing into a booming crescendo, before a sleek black motorbike soared onto the hillside, shot into the air and bounced onto the road with advanced shock absorbers.

Terror-Byte revved its engine.

A fierce eruption of several more engines rose behind him. Another bike emerged, then a second, then a third, and soon a group of riders were roaring away. They were fitted with black jumpsuits and wearing heavy helmets, unlike Terror-Byte who rode helmetless, with only a basic shirt, jeans, and a leather jacket, just like Suzi's.

The human riders all leaned their bikes to the side in formation, following him around a bend in the road. These ECG soldiers were masters of their craft. They could easily track targets on their bikes the same way killer whales did to bring down much larger prey, all through intimidation, manipulation, and the finely honed craft of hunting.

Hence why they were called, Cycologists.

Jenny Campbell gulped as the school auditorium filled with people. Her hands shook a little, holding her speech notes, as she did her best to remain calm. Nothing had started yet, and she was nowhere near the stage for God's sake. Her speech wouldn't be for a little while, so it was only a matter of ensuring that she didn't pass out in the next five minutes or, even worse, when she was up there in front of everybody.

"I've never spoken in front of a crowd before," she told Suzi. "God, I hate this! Why did it happen to me?"

"You won the award for your age group," Suzi answered logically. "You brought it upon yourself."

"Along with vicious death stares from Maria Longsworth for beating her. I sure hope my heart holds out and – oh my God!" Her eyes lit up as she forgot about everything, ran across the room and straight into the arms of… "Dad! You made it!"

"Hey, shortcake!" He hugged her tightly.

Jenny beamed. "How'd you get the time off work?"

He smiled. "Wasn't easy, but I made the boss see sense. Couldn't miss this honour for my little girl."

"Congratulations, Jen," another voice said.

Jenny leaned over, hugging the woman next to him. "Thanks Aunty Gwen! You didn't have to come."

"She was the only one I could rustle up on such short notice," Mister Campbell said happily. "She didn't want to miss this either and, hey, guess what? I got some overtime hours, so I'll be able to get you a new phone in no time. Only remember not to drop this one."

"I won't, Dad. I feel so bad. If only I could pass an interview and actually *get* a job –"

"Hey, hey, hey…" he said, putting a finger to her lips, cutting her off. "We don't talk about that today. This is your special moment. Remember?"

Jenny grinned. "I know."

She hugged him tighter.

Suzi kept her distance, observing their interaction. She was curious at first, then felt a tinge of sadness for Jenny. The girl had confided to her that she couldn't pass a job interview because the stress would ignite the Hurripain, making her lose concentration. Suzi's sadness grew and it took a moment to become aware of this. She rapidly refocused on her immediate priorities. This was no time for emotion. There was work to do.

"Could everyone take their seats please?" a voice from the stage called.

Suzi walked to a chair and picked it up, ready to take it somewhere.

"No, no, no," Jenny said, hurrying over. "Just sit on it."

Suzi was dumbfounded. "That would be impractical should our enemies attack, Jenny Campbell."

"Yeah, like that's gonna happen…"

The Cycologists sped towards the centre of town in a deafening roar. Cars wailed as the mass of riders swept by. Neither Terror-Byte nor the Cycologists were concerned about the authorities being alerted. All digital signals in the area had been scrambled, thanks to the scientists back at base.

The riders raced on.

"Just stand by the door then," Jenny told Suzi. "Oh God! I'm so nervous I could cry."

"Laughter is more beneficial," Suzi stated.

Jenny nodded. "You're right, Suze. Wish me luck."

"You do not need luck, Jenny Campbell, you need success."

"Oh, you think?"

Suzi frowned. "Always."

Jenny made her way to the stage.

"That's my girl," Mister Campbell said to his sister with a grin.

They sat down.

The announcer started speaking.

The bikes picked up speed, weaving expertly in and out of traffic, following Terror-Byte to the school up ahead.

"… so it gives me great pleasure to announce the honoured lady of the hour, Miss Jenny Campbell."

Applause ignited, the loudest coming from Jenny's father, who pointed her out to a few other people as she approached the microphone.

Only Suzi remained detached from it all, scanning for threats.

The bikes came closer.

Jenny cleared her throat.

"Uh… hi," she began a little hesitantly. "Th-thank you all so much. It's a great honour to receive this award. My inspiration throughout all of this has been my family. My dad, especially. Thanks Dad."

Mister Campbell waved her away with a smile.

Jenny continued. "My desire to create this work was born as an outlet from the challenges that we all face in our world today…"

A sharp brake and slide brought the bikes to a standstill in the school car park.

The Cycologists dismounted. Terror-Byte indicated for a few to stand on guard, then entered a building through its emergency exit.

The rest followed.

"I thank you all for this honour…" Jenny concluded.

The figures in black marched down the passageway.

"Thanks everyone, I'm really glad you liked my work."

Another round of applause went up. Jenny beamed over the crowd, gave a little half-bow, walked across the stage and descended the steps.

The announcer took the stand. "Thank you very much for that, Jenny, I'm sure we've all been inspired by you here today —"

Jenny had barely reached the bottom step when an emergency door opened and a man in black riding gear stepped out.

Suzi's head shot up.

"This way please," the man ordered, putting an arm over Jenny's shoulder and guiding her into the passageway beyond.

"Wha-what…?"

Caught in the moment, she complied and went with him. Apart from Suzi, nobody sensed anything out of the ordinary. The crowd's attention was focused solely on the announcer.

Suzi moved to follow.

Another Agent emerged from the doorway, making Suzi stop in her tracks. He glared across the room, his Iyes boring into hers.

Suzi clicked her head to the side. "Echo, empty the building."

"Acknowledged."

Echo's holographic face shimmered in Suzi's ship as she hacked into the school surveillance cameras. One showed Jenny being led past a stairwell by a group of dark figures. Another showed a layout of the building's electrical systems.

"Logging onto the main grid," Echo stated.

Several pipes roared to life, making the audience cry out as they were hit by sprays of water. The howling wails of fire alarms came next.

The crowd leapt to their feet, blocking their ears and covering their heads to avoid getting soaked whilst hurrying for the door.

Jenny grimaced as she was marched along the passageway. "Okay, this isn't right, this is so not right…"

A sprinkler above activated, hitting them with a blast of cold water.

Seizing the opportunity, Jenny shouldered her handler and ran. Another man lunged for her. Desperation made her dodge his grasp and she sprinted, gaining some ground.

"Activating security door three," Echo said.

Slam!

Jenny jumped as a metal door thundered shut behind her, blocking her off from her pursuers.

"Okay that was random," she quipped. "Big time…"

She turned and ran.

A Cycologist smacked the door, then touched his earpiece. "Sir, we have a problem…"

JT drew an angry breath.

A technician spoke from behind him. "An outside force has just patched into the local area network. We can't identify its source."

JT's lips pursed. "I see." He called out over the room. "Mister Margrave?"

"Yes, sir?"

"I think it's time we put our Shockwave to the test."

Lights flickered throughout the school.

"Interference?"

Echo analysed the new information. Something was pushing back against her energy.

Her face flickered, concentrating hard.

"Echo, I'm losing your signal."

Suzi's tone stayed cool and her gaze never left the other Agent's as the crowd fled the room. She stood motionless, listening as Echo's voice faded in a wave of static.

"In… fer… ence… disrupting our sig…"

Suzi didn't budge. "Looks like I'm alone on this one."

The metal door that blocked the Cycologists off from Jenny rose with a hum, care of the ECG.

The black-clad figures ran through.

Unaffected by the sprinklers' chill, Suzi's stare locked with the rogue Agent's as they strode towards each other. They stopped in the room's centre, just as the last of the crowd ran out.

Suzi's head leaned to the side a little, examining him curiously.

He did the same to her.

She spoke first. "You've been augmented."

His response was cold. "The correct term is *upgraded*."

"The correct term is *defiled*."

"With empowering results."

"Delusional and corrupting ones too," she observed. "Part of my mission to this world was to find you. I wish I hadn't. In time, you'll wish the same."

He stepped in, looming over her. Unafraid, she too stepped in, glaring right back at him.

"My mission was also to find you," he stated. "You are to be taken into the custody of the ECG."

Suzi saw a small light flash behind his ear. A device. One that controlled him, she concluded.

Her response was resolute. "I will not go with you."

"You speak illogically," he said. "As an Agent, you would wish to find the source of your opposition and investigate it."

"Not as a prisoner," she replied firmly. "That would also be illogical. Since you're clearly in the power of another, I can therefore conclude that this conversation is being monitored."

She stared even deeper into his Iyes.

JT saw Suzi's face boring at him from the wallscreen.

"Tell your boss I'm coming for him," she warned. *"Personally."*

JT smacked the panel beside him. Growling to Terror-Byte, he ordered, "Okay boy, show her what you're made of. Grab the information we need. Stat!"

Terror-Byte's mouth opened with a whirr and his teeth rotated, growing sharp.

He lunged.

Suzi punched him straight in the mouth. His head flew back, then he lurched in again. She evaded the bite, grabbing his biceps. He grabbed hers too. Their arms locked in place and they swung each other around, first crashing into the stage and smashing part of it in with their colossal strength, then whirling sideways into the wall, denting it heavily.

Seizing the opportunity, Suzi reached up, ripping the device from his ear.

JT snarled as Terror-Byte's relay feed blipped out.

Suzi pocketed his device, kicked him away, raised her arm and fired her last I-T dart from her sleeve. Terror-Byte dodged the shot, leaving the dart to thud into a chair.

She ripped a fire extinguisher off a wall, ramming it into his face. Once, twice, three times. The alloy that made up his Iyes was barely scratched and her blows had little effect on anything else. She swung a fourth time. He weaved aside, wrenched it from her, then kicked her back, swept in and struck her with the extinguisher in a savage uppercut. The blow sent her flying into the room's centre where she landed with a thump. She started to rise. He threw the extinguisher at her in a direct hit, making her slump under its impact. He strode towards her, his teeth growing longer.

Suzi leapt for the extinguisher, reaching it just in time. She interlocked her fingers and clubbed them down hard as a single fist. Her enormous strength burst it open and it flew up like a missile, slamming into Terror-Byte's chest, sending him flying across the room, crashing through the rear wall and dropping like a stone.

Suzi rose, making for the emergency door. She had what she wanted now. The device she'd taken from Terror-Byte was her connection to the ECG base. She only needed to re-establish her link to Echo to trace its source, but first she needed to find Jenny.

The building's rear door flew open and Jenny stumbled onto the street, straight into another black-clad man standing on guard.

She recoiled.

He grabbed her before she could flee.

His team ran out behind them.

She shuddered. "Great! I knew today was too good to be true. I finally get the best day of my life and what happens? The crapocalypse!"

A hand clamped over her mouth. She gave a muffled cry as she was hoisted to a parked van. A man smashed its side window in, opened the door, and sat in the driver's seat. Another man entered the passenger's side, climbed in the back and opened the rear doors.

Jenny whimpered as she was half-carried inside.

The doors slammed shut behind her.

The van took off with a roar. The remaining Cycologists mounted their bikes and followed, save for three who stayed behind. One entered the emergency exit, looking for Suzi, while the other two made for the building's entrance, intending to cover it.

Silence followed, then the Cycologist in the emergency exit flew out onto the street, backwards. He hit a wall, slumped down and lay still.

Suzi emerged after him, moving like a well-oiled machine.

Things weren't good, she thought. The ECG were though. Too good. They'd worked efficiently. Jenny was gone, Echo was out of the loop, and she heard a heavy military chopper overhead, along with the roar of several vehicles coming her way.

She moved around the corner and stopped at the sight of the two Cycologists.

She assessed the road's layout in a microsecond. Numerous cars were parked on the street, as well as a semi-trailer behind her enemies.

She ran at them head-on.

They raised their guns, firing.

She dropped to the ground, sliding hard. Their shots flew over her head as she swept between them, slid under the truck and rolled out the other side. She rose, turned, lifted the vehicle with her enormous strength and tipped it over, trapping them underneath. She'd planned it carefully, knowing it wouldn't crush them. They were already pushing back and would soon struggle out, but it would take time and effort.

Despite everything, she was no killer.

A glance at the street told her it was empty, save for a stunned man who stood frozen to the spot. He held a phone in one hand and an ice-cream in the other.

"Excuse me," Suzi said, plucking the phone from him.

He fainted dead away.

Suzi looked at him, confused, then opened the back of the phone. She fiddled with its circuitry, pulled out the device she'd taken from the rogue Agent, and attached it. Once it was in place, she turned it over, activated its screen, and brought up its GPS. Soft beeps followed, along with the coordinates to the ECG base.

Its location didn't surprise her. The impact point of the Hurriflame.

Satisfied, she strode to a pick-up truck and pulled open its door, breaking the lock. She slid behind the wheel and had barely started the hot-wiring process when her phone's screen flickered and JT's face appeared, having locked onto her signal through Terror-Byte's earpiece.

"*So…*" he began.

"Coming for you now," Suzi stated. She crushed the phone in half, threw it out the window, and hit the rogue Agent in the head as he emerged from the building.

Her expression hardened as she started the engine and hit the accelerator.

The truck roared away.

Behind her, Terror-Byte strode to the semi-trailer that the Cycologists were under and righted it.

Jenny wailed sickly as the van veered around a corner.

A patchy voice came through a radio link. *"All units, we have a moving target. Repeat. We have a moving target!"*

Suzi swerved the truck to the left, driving it through a narrow stretch between two buildings, and following the route she'd seen from the phone. Her expression was angrier than usual. What the ECG were doing was immoral, especially after Jenny's victory at school this morning. Suzi had lost too many people by not being good enough. Not this time, she vowed. No one else would die because of her negligence. The ECG would pay.

The truck rounded a bend.

Several bursts of gunfire ignited from above, accompanied by the looming shadow of an ECG helicopter. Behind her, a semi-trailer rounded the corner, driven by the rogue Agent. Before her, loomed several motor-bike riders, moving in fast.

She was surrounded.

Her anger grew. This was more of an annoyance than anything else. It was unlikely they'd kill her. The other Agent wanted her taken into custody. It didn't mean they wouldn't change their minds about killing her, but it gave her an advantage for now.

She revved her truck for the bikes, then veered to the side, smacking into the nearest rider. A sharp turn sent another flying off their bike. A few bikes sped away, allowing her to shoot through the group. She'd only just cleared them when –

Bang!

She lurched violently as the semi-trailer slammed into her truck's rear. She accelerated, weaving her truck onto the footpath, then back onto the road again. The semi-trailer followed, smashing several cars to the side with thunderous crashes and knocking over a few streetlamps.

Up ahead, lay a hotel.

The helicopter loomed closer.

She knew what she had to do: use both to her advantage.

She gave a sharp kick, sending the door of her pick-up flying open, before leaping onto the road and running for the hotel. A couple cried out as she flew past them and entered the building through its revolving door. Behind her, the semi-trailer's shadow approached the hotel's window.

Several people screamed and scattered. They'd barely cleared the area when the truck smashed through the entrance, bursting into the foyer. The motorbikes swept past it, revving after Suzi who made for the stairwell door beside the lift.

She shouldered the door in, breaking it off its hinges, and ran up the stairs, practically flying in her ascent.

A lone motorcyclist gave pursuit, revving his bike up the stairs after her. Its monstrous roar echoed throughout the stairwell as it veered around each bend.

Terror-Byte brought his truck to a halt and kicked its door open hard, sending it flying across the foyer and knocking a security guard out cold. Mechanically, he dismounted, and strode over to the stairwell after Suzi.

He wasn't worried about the building's security systems. The Shockwave had taken care of that.

"Maintain surveillance," JT ordered the helicopter pilot through a COM link. *"We'll take care of the authorities. You just sit tight."*

The helicopter pilot nodded. "Acknowledged."

The chopper held its aerial position over the building.

Suzi reached the eighth floor, smashed the door open, and emerged into the lift lobby.

An elderly couple stared at her, aghast.

"Excuse me," she said, grabbing the elderly lady's walking frame from her.

The woman's arms flailed as she fell back against her husband who caught her with great difficulty.

An engine roar rose as the pursuing motorbike entered the lobby.

Smack!

Suzi's smooth blow from the woman's walking frame sent him flying off his bike. He barely had time to rise when her sharp kick knocked him out.

Suzi returned the dented walking frame to the elderly lady. "Here, and thank you. Your generosity has surely aided the human race."

The couple stared at her, horrified.

Smartly, she picked up the bike, sat on it, and revved it so loudly that it almost gave the old couple a heart attack.

She looked at each of them. "This situation cannot be good for your physical health, especially at such an advanced age. Forget."

They stared into her Iyes, entranced.

Her task complete, she revved the bike towards the *ding* of a lift door that opened ahead. She entered, sending another startled couple running out in horror. Swiftly, she turned the bike around whilst kicking the button for the top floor.

The lift doors started closing.

She stared at the new couple.

"Forget," she ordered again.

The doors slid shut and the lift ascended.

Once it was gone, silence followed, then the pair from the lift faced the elderly couple, their expressions changed.

"So how are you, Elspeth?" the young woman asked the elderly one, completely oblivious to the surrounding damage.

"Very well, dear," came the reply. "Thank you so much for asking."

"It's lovely to see you again."

"Yes, you too. I must ask, how are the children?"

"Little devils, would you believe?"

"Oh, I say!"

"Yes well, they've made me say a lot of things too…"

"If it's one thing I can't stand, it's bad behaviour…"

The half-hanging door nearby dropped to the floor. They barely noticed and kept talking, engrossed in their conversation.

The lift doors on the top floor opened and Suzi revved out.

"Now what are you playing at?" JT wondered.

Terror-Byte's voice came through. *"I know her tactics. Leave her to me."*

JT brushed this aside. "I don't think so. You're part of a team, soldier."

The link went dead, severed by Terror-Byte.

"TB?" JT snapped. "TB?"

No response.

"Galvey!" he called. "How the hell did he shut us out?"

The Tech Officer analysed his readings. "He made some changes to himself before leaving. Looks like he's been snooping around in our databanks for a while. Now he's resistant to our commands."

"Get that damn fool back on the line!"

"Yes, sir. Won't be easy.

JT seethed. Terror-Byte had just slapped him right in the ego. With him and Suzi out there together…

"Problem doubled," he murmured, thinking aloud.

The chopper hovered over the hotel in surveillance mode, overshadowing the growing mass of cop cars below. They didn't bother the pilot. What did was the rooftop door bursting open and Suzi racing through it on a bike. He pulled the chopper up, making it ascend rapidly with a loud whine.

Too late.

Suzi raced over the rooftop, flew off it, leapt from the bike in mid-air and shot solo for the chopper, leaving the bike to fall away.

"I tell ya," an old man said to a younger one in the hotel alleyway amidst the rising wail of police sirens, "it's all in the Bible. Any second now, the heavens are gonna open and hell's gonna rain down —"

Smash!

Suzi's bike plummeted into the dumpster nearby.

"See," he said. "What'd I tell ya?"

Suzi grabbed onto the chopper's railing, smoothly climbed up, and ripped the door open, breaking its electronic lock.

A soldier inside lunged for her. She stepped in, held her ground, and took several of his blows, which had little effect, hurting him more than her.

Finally, enough was enough for Suzi.

"Go away," she said, hurling him out of the chopper. He flew to the hotel roof's ledge and caught on, dangling high over the ground, struggling to maintain his grip.

An engine roar almost deafened him, coming from a motorbike ridden by Terror-Byte who raced across the rooftop, picking up speed for a jump, just like Suzi had done.

Within the chopper, Suzi made for the pilot. He reached for his gun but barely touched it when she hoisted him from his seat. He struggled helplessly as she took him to the exit and threw him outside, just as Terror-Byte's bike soared off the roof for her. The pilot cried out as he pummelled into Terror-Byte, then spiralled onto the rooftop.

Terror-Byte, however, dropped like a stone.

"Yes, sir," the old man said, "any minute now there's gonna be demons descending from them there skies –"

A thud followed as another bike plummeted into the dumpster.

The younger man's jaw dropped. "Okay, now I'm convinced."

"You want to pray?"

"Yep."

Suzi sat in the pilot's seat, steering the chopper away from the building and picking up speed.

JT's face appeared on a small screen. *"Give it up now or your friend's a goner, along with half the city."*

"Stop wasting my time," Suzi said, and smashed the screen in with her fist, severing the connection.

"Infant threats," she said crossly.

She turned the chopper for the hills in the distance.

The two men with their heads bowed in prayer, looked up as Terror-Byte slammed into the ground nearby, forming a small crater. To their horror, he rose, intact.

"Lord almighty," the younger man whispered.

"The dead shall be resurrected," the old man trembled.

"I believe," the younger man said softly. "Lord, do I believe!"

Terror-Byte ignored their awestruck faces and started walking by, then stopped, looking at each of them.

"Forget," he ordered.

They nodded.

Satisfied, Terror-Byte headed around the corner, out of sight. Once he was gone, something switched in the men's minds, and the older one turned to the younger one and said, "So, son, you changed your mind 'bout comin' to church yet?"

The younger man shook his head. "Told ya once, told ya a thousand times, never gonna happen."

"Ah, go to hell then!"

They waved each other away and walked off.

Jenny listened as JT's voice came through a COM link. *"Hostiles in the area, people. Get back here, stat. That's an order."*

She grinned at the report. "Boy, do you guys suck. Still think you're elite, huh?"

The van went over a bump, making her yelp and lurch sideways.

A short way ahead of the van, a large metal hatch in the woodland hillside hummed open. Three choppers emerged from a hangar within, flying in formation and picking up speed as they raced for Suzi's chopper in the distance.

They'd barely cleared the area, when the van carrying Jenny veered off the road and into the forest, heading for the metal opening. It entered smoothly, leaving the hatch to whirr shut behind it.

Suzi saw the black military choppers rising like hawks, ready to swoop in. She zeroed in on them with a high-tech camera, glancing at the readings. Her enemies were heavily armed, preparing to let loose with a barrage of fury, which was exactly what she wanted.

She knew that the ECG's headquarters – the Heartbeat as they called it – lay ahead. The chopper's hard drives had told her that, once she'd bypassed the security protocols, of course.

The choppers came for her.

She aimed hers at the centre one and accelerated.

"Target approaching on a direct collision course."

JT frowned at the pilot's tone. "What in the hell does she think she's doing?" He paused as realisation dawned. "She's playing chicken!"

The central chopper's pilot grew more unnerved by the moment.

"Collision course imminent," he reported to JT. "With all due respect, sir –"

JT's voice cut in. *"Nobody treats us like crap. Maintain your position."*

The COM link went scratchy, then Suzi's voice broke through, addressing the pilot. *"Your boss has no regard for your existence. You can't trust him, and you can't avoid a collision. Get out of the machine. Now!"*

The pilot grabbed a parachute and opened the door.

Suzi watched the man jump from the chopper, then targeted her own for the hillside below. The other choppers opened fire. Unfazed, she kicked the door open and dived into the sky, parachute-free, aiming for the tip of a tall tree.

Her chopper soared on, swooping into the forest on a pre-programmed course. Her intention had never been to hit the other choppers. They flew aside, leaving hers to tear between them, shooting for the ground.

Like a large missile.

"Incoming!" came a cry.

JT snarled. "God damn…!"

The chopper hit the forest floor, bursting into flames.

Waves of fiery debris billowed high. The two remaining choppers maintained their distance as their pilots scanned for signs of Suzi. The third empty chopper, that the pilot had sprung from, spiralled and exploded into an open area, causing several far-off observers to reach for their phones.

No casualties, and the authorities alerted.

Exactly how Suzi had planned.

Suzi leapt from one tree to another, staying out of sight of the choppers. A sharp jump from a great height brought her to the forest floor.

She soon found her chopper's wreckage lying as a mangled, twisted heap of burning debris. More importantly, it had rammed into the hillside, creating a flaming opening that descended into a metal tunnel beyond.

"Target's been sighted entering the Heartbeat, sir."

JT was impressed. "She's good, I'll give her that."

Suzi strode through the empty hangar, up to a security door. She took off her Earwig and pocketed it. It was too valuable for the ECG to get hold of, not that she expected it to happen, but she didn't know her enemy's arsenal just yet, so it was best to be cautious.

Her heavy kick sent the door flying open in a shower of sparks. Thundering footsteps rose, before several black-suited soldiers rounded the corner, aiming their weapons at her.

She leaned her head to the side, analysing them curiously. Each wore a thick balaclava and tinted goggles, no doubt to protect them from her gaze, she reasoned. She'd have to fix that.

She lunged.

A burst of gunfire ignited.

She dived under the hail of bullets, sliding across the floor and tripping the nearest assailant up. The others barely had time to re-aim their weapons before they were all smacked unconscious.

Only one was left. She hoisted him to his feet and pulled him around the corner, out of sight of a camera. There, she ripped his headgear off, revealing a young man's face underneath.

She glared into his eyes. He shut them tightly. A sharp press from her thumb into his throat's pivotal point made him open them again, while her other hand removed his earpiece and pocketed it. No doubt it would be useful later.

"Obey," she ordered, gazing deep into his pupils.

He stared at her, entranced.

"Here's what I want you to do…" she began.

"I like the girl," JT said, admiringly. "Proves my point that we need her on our team."

"We calling for reinforcements?" the Tech Officer asked.

"Hell no, she and I are just gonna have a little talk, that's all…"

Suzi headed deep into the belly of the Heartbeat. The place was empty. Not good, she reasoned. People weren't attacking her. Attacks meant panic. The leader behind all of this wasn't panicking. They were thinking. Calculating. Drawing her in. They hadn't even tried to stop her from accessing the security systems showing the Heartbeat's primary operation centre. She soon found it in a physical sense too, and coolly approached its door, ready to boot it in.

It slid open.

JT stood in the room's centre, somewhat relaxed. "Why hello there, missy."

She entered of her own accord. She didn't need, nor want, an invitation.

He wasn't intimidated as she strode towards him. "Well I expect – mmf!"

She clasped his jaw tightly with one hand, pushing him up against the wall and staring deep into his eyes.

"Jenny Campbell," she said darkly. "Where is she?"

"Now, now…" he began, then winced as the pain grew.

Hisses rose from nearby. Rustling leaves followed, telling Suzi exactly what they were.

Trans-plants.

This annoyed her. When she'd taken Jenny Campbell into her ship and attempted to scan the girl's brain, things had backfired and most of her vessel's systems had temporarily gone offline. It had been impossible to patch into the local area network, or else she'd have seen the ECG rummaging through the nursery after her fight with the Germinator. She'd returned there shortly after for her own clean-up operation, finding no trace of any Trans-plant remains. There'd been no sign of the ECG either. They'd worked rapidly, she concluded, leaving them with several obedient Trans-plants as weapons.

She glanced at them. They were stronger than those from Carrington Nursery, like they'd been augmented.

Her grip tightened on JT.

"I won't ask again," she said coldly. "I want Jenny Campbell."

JT wasn't intimidated. "Well, Missy, that little eye trick's not gonna work on me, now. I've never underestimated your kind, especially when one of you's workin' for me too. Optic implants, see?"

She peered in and saw he spoke the truth. This privilege was just for him, evidently, since he hadn't extended the courtesy to those who'd attacked her, meaning it was still a work in progress.

"Galvey!" he called to the Tech Officer. "Plan B!"

The Tech Officer flicked a switch, activating the wallscreen showing a ghost town in a desert.

Suzi's gaze shot to it. Huddled beside a building, was a familiar little girl.

"She's one of your lot, ain't she?" JT pressed. "That other Agent said so. She's related to you. A cousin or somethin'? Goes by the name of Rags?"

She looked back at him, her Iyes filling with rage as she spoke in a dangerously low voice. "I'm going to rip your eyes out."

"You do and you won't reach that kid or Miss Campbell," came the hasty reply, "and the Black Crossroads is where we all wanna go."

Smash!

He jumped as her fist slammed into the wall next to his head.

A Trans-plant came in for her.

"Hold it!" JT ordered.

It halted, with its crackling tendrils wavering over Suzi.

"Game's outta your hands," he warned her. "You want it back, you gotta follow me."

Suzi wasn't swayed. "Prove that your information is genuine first."

"The only way to find out is to come with us," JT told her. "We weren't gonna hurt Miss Campbell. We only brought her here 'cause we need your help. We've been trackin' you for a while now. The nursery, the hospital room where you spoke to Sarah Eastman, we've seen it all."

Suzi glared at him. "I know. You've threatened me with the lives of innocents."

"We've got results," JT corrected. "Another group of Trans-Plants infiltrated the Black Crossroads a while back to do some spyin'. They were sent there by that big boss of theirs, what's his name? The Germinator or somethin'?" He probed Suzi's Iyes for a reaction but got none. "When you sent that nursery up in flames, we went in and grew our own Transplant buds behind you there, who linked minds with their leafy buddies in the Crossroads. That place is the real deal. We know that somethin' big's goin' down. Whatever it is, we want it stopped."

"Stopped or assimilated?" Suzi asked. "You cannot be trusted."

"Yeah, but we've also got access to everything you want," JT pointed out. "Miss Campbell and that kid on the screen are only the start. We've got the best military tech you'll need to get into the Crossroads, which is where you wanna go anyway. Doin' it your way's only gonna take longer, and while we're standin' here arguing, the big uglies are sittin' back laughin' at us."

Suzi considered the possibilities. Being a threat to this idiot wasn't a practical option. She could do more as an ally, gain the information she needed, then play things her way. For the moment, however, there was no choice but to submit. A notion she hated.

Reluctantly, she released her grip and lowered her arm. "Very well. I will comply, for now."

JT rubbed his throat. "I knew you'd see it my way…"

"No, I see a much bigger picture. One without you in it."

"Play nice —"

"I never do. I must see Jenny Campbell before we continue."

JT motioned to his Tech Officer who hit a button on the wall. The rear door whirred open and Jenny was pushed inside.

"Oi!" she yelled to the man behind her. "Don't take your anger out on me, micro-nuts!" She caught sight of… "Suze!"

"Jenny Campbell," Suzi replied simply.

Jenny ran over and hugged her.

Suzi stayed motionless throughout the embrace.

"They got you too, huh?" Jenny asked, breaking away.

"No," Suzi answered, "I came here willingly. For you, Jenny Campbell."

Jenny was astounded. "What? You mean you fought your way into psycho central just for me?"

"Yes. You are important."

"Don't get all mushy on me."

Suzi ran an internal check of herself. "I appear to be as solid as you are."

JT spoke up. "You're important in quite a few ways, Miss Campbell. We're a military unit that's here to protect the earth from external threats."

"Are you kidding?" Jenny asked in disbelief. "Is this, like, some research scientist, military hellhole?"

"Yes," Suzi stated.

"Go figure."

JT addressed Suzi. "See? You can trust us. You're friend's okay, right?"

"Yeah, no thanks to you…" Jenny scoffed.

"She's not," Suzi cut in. "Her blood pressure's raised, along with her breath. Her heart's also showing physical signs of stress."

"Suze, it's called saving face," Jenny said quickly.

"You're not saving anything," Suzi said back, logically.

"Which leaves us as one big happy family," JT finished. "We better get to work."

"I'm not happy, nor are we a family," Suzi pressed firmly.

"Work on what?" Jenny asked, then saw the towering figures looming nearby. "Hang on, are those…?"

"It's not surprising you only noticed them now," Suzi told her. "Especially with your physical signs of stress."

"Suze, shut up already…" Jenny retorted.

"See?" Suzi pointed out.

Jenny threw an arm up.

Suzi returned her focus to JT. "I will need to assess and improve on your planned operation against the Black Crossroads. Jenny Campbell will stay with me at all times."

JT dismissed this notion. "No deal. Little Miss'll only provide a distraction."

Little Miss, thought Suzi. *There's that name again.*

"Hey!" Jenny snapped, returning Suzi's focus to the present.

"Like that," JT indicated.

"I understand," Suzi agreed.

"Bulldust!" Jenny protested.

JT motioned to a guard. "Get her out of here. Treat her real nice though."

Jenny looked at Suzi. "Don't ditch me like this…"

Suzi spoke firmly. "I fought hard to get to you, Jenny Campbell. I'm not going to abandon you now. For the moment, I must make some compromises. Have no fear. I will not be far."

Jenny relented. "You better not be. See you soon, Suze."

"Yes, Jenny Campbell."

Jenny gave her one last glance and walked out the door.

"Got any food?" Jenny asked the guard on the way out.

"Just say what you want!" JT called after her.

"I want my damn phone back!" Jenny retorted, recalling what Gastoff had told Suzi in that creepy netherworld. "You guys stole it from me, re-member? I want it now, or I'm so gonna crack open your ba–"

The door slammed shut.

JT addressed Suzi.

"Now," he said smugly. "Where were we?"

Chapter Nine

Jenny frowned as she was taken down a corridor.

"This doesn't look like the way to your psycho café," she said.

"No," the man replied. "We're heading for a lab."

"Why?"

"For your brain scan."

She stopped. "I don't need a – arrrrgh!" She raised her palm to her forehead, wincing.

"Boss's orders," the man told her. "You want those headaches stopped, right? We can help with that."

Jenny submitted. "Fine, but you better not do anything dodgy." A thought struck her. "Can we also call my dad and let him know I'm okay?"

He nodded. "I'll have to run it past the chief first. Should be fine. The less questions from your old man, the better, for all of us. We can make the call in the lab."

"Great. Lead the way."

"No, that's your job," he ordered.

She sighed wearily, swearing under her breath.

The liquid inside the giant glass cylinder bubbled as the bulging eyes of its green humanoid occupant gazed out. Through its fragmented vision, it saw a door hiss open, and watched as JT and Suzi entered the enormous chamber surrounding its cylinder. The creature could only make out a few words here and there, not that it cared what they were saying. It was in too much pain for that.

Suzi scanned the room observantly. Dozens of huge cylinders stood over a vast area, all holding hybrids of humans. Many were morphed with other life forms, such as reptiles and amphibians. Each of these abhorrent, grotesque mutations floated in their prisons of green liquid, seemingly in agony.

JT indicated them proudly. "Impressive, aint they? We call 'em War Operational Medical Buoys, or WOMBs for short. They hold my babies, here."

Suzi wasn't impressed. He could tell.

"We didn't create these mutations, we just house 'em," he continued. "Hell, we only found 'em on the Hurriflame site when everything was fresh." He motioned to a mutation, composed of three species in one. "Things got a little mixed up that night, for everybody. Now we keep 'em here to stop 'em hurtin' anyone."

Suzi was unswayed by his argument. "You augmented my fellow Agent. You're manipulating these creatures too. I can tell."

JT was unfazed. "We don't want 'em mutatin' out of control now, do we? The world's best fighters don't come out of nowhere. They evolve, meaning improvements are necessary. It takes time to create the perfect super race."

"Someone in your planet's history tried that once before. They failed."

JT ignored her. "This way."

He guided Suzi along.

"This is so illegal," Jenny said.

She did her best to stop herself from flinching from the two warm wires strapped to her temples. She lay on an operating table while two scientists, a man and a woman, worked over her.

"Relax," the woman said. "We're just doing a basic brain scan to check for abnormalities."

"I'm so glad we didn't tell my dad about this," Jenny huffed, referring to the brief conversation she'd had with him on the phone a few minutes ago. He'd been concerned about her, and relieved she was all right, but confused as to her whereabouts. She'd had to think fast and told him that she was helping a friend on the other side of town, which was as close to the truth as she could get. Thankfully, he was needed back at work and couldn't talk for long, much to her relief.

"So what are you looking for?" she asked the woman. "To see if I've got two brains or something?"

"No," came the reply, "but I can tell you're in two minds about this. There's no need to be. Our records indicate you've been getting headaches since the Hurriflame. We bugged your hospital room when you were admitted after it happened. We did some tests on you too. They were inconclusive at the time…"

"Psychos…"

"…but we did detect slight traces of radiation in your brain. Since then, we've located a red patch that's getting steadily bigger. We need to know what it is."

"Don't I get a say in this?"

"You don't have a choice. Sit tight."

The woman got to work.

Jenny shivered, feeling a tingle of energy flow into her head.

JT stopped before another WOMB. Suzi did the same. This one was larger than the rest and didn't house a creature. A blinding light shone from inside, and in its centre hovered a shape resembling an enormous genome strand, swirling on an axis and pulsating rhythmically.

High above them were bridges, platforms and walkways, littered with terminals and workstations, where ECG personnel monitored the giant WOMB. All of them, along with JT, wore goggles to shield themselves from the sheer intensity of the glow. Only Suzi remained unaffected by the WOMB's brilliant luminance. Her anger, however, at the realisation of what lay inside, was another matter. Zymac particles. This concerned her greatly.

"Beautiful, ain't it?" JT said. "My it's pretty, and it's all our doing with none of your alien help. We've named this WOMB, Mother. Her real prize is what we call the Shockwave. A single spark is enough to power this whole base for decades. It's undetectable to the rest of the world, and we've enhanced its lifespan by a thousand years or more."

Suzi thought this over. So this was the energy source that Sarah Eastman had spoken of in the hospital. The Shockwave had been in the girl's bloodstream too. Mixed with the ship's ion particles from the Hurriflame, it had granted Sarah extra-sensory abilities, and also affected Gastoff. Now, the ECG had a whole host of mutations resulting from the lethal combination of these two elements.

She glanced over another set of readings showing some dates, confirming her suspicions.

"You were experimenting with the Shockwave right before the Hurriflame hit," she observed.

"Ain't just a pretty face, are ya?" JT replied. "We were in the next town but, yeah, we were playin' around with the prototypes."

"Resulting in what Sarah Eastman became," Suzi concluded. "The ship's ion particles, combined with your Shockwave, turned her into this monstrosity."

"I prefer the term *evolved*," JT corrected. "She just learnt to think outside the box, that's all. We tried talkin' to her a couple of times after it happened. She never said much."

This didn't surprise Suzi. "Naturally. It's hard trying to manipulate someone who can see right through you."

"Well, she opened up a little more to you," JT pointed out. "Good thing we bugged her room, wasn't it? Not even you picked up on that, thanks to the new tech we'd acquired, courtesy of your people, and the Hurriflame."

Suzi flicked through a terminal screen, further examining the readings. "This power source is dangerous."

He shrugged. "Needs to be tweaked a bit, but so far it's doin' okay, if I say so myself."

"Then what?" she pressed. "You'll keep it all to yourself instead of using it to benefit billions of people?"

"Wouldn't you?" JT asked. "They'd only squabble and kill each other over it anyway. We don't want it getting into the wrong hands now, do we?"

"It is in the wrong hands. You know nothing about it. There are imitators and there are originals, and you're only imitating the best. You're about to initiate a battle with forces who have tactics far superior to yours, in every way possible."

"That's why we take precautions, Missy. The ship that set off the Hurri-flame brought a whole stack of goodies down with it. We salvaged what we could, set up camp at ground zero, and started monitorin' your con-versations with everyone, everywhere. We've taken measures against other threats too." He pressed the terminal screen, bringing up an image of a wooden box. "This went online two and a half hours ago. The ultimate prison, courtesy of your planet's tech, with a little of our Shockwave thrown in. We call it the Toybox. We're a little unsure of just how power-ful this so-called Toymaster I've heard about is. Thanks to the Shockwave, that box has enough power to contain the blast of a thermonuclear explo-sion, meaning it can hold him too."

"Don't be so sure," Suzi warned. "He's a lot smarter than you are."

"I know," JT replied. "That's why you're gonna lead the mission against him."

"Really?" she retorted.

"A good leader leads from the front," he pointed out.

"While you remain hidden in your rear?" she pointed back.

"Someone's gotta stay in charge in case worst comes to worst," he said. "Not that I'm expecting you to fail."

Suzi observed him curiously. "Billions of years of evolution on this planet and what drops out from the bottom of it all? You!" Her anger grew. "You mustn't attack the Black Crossroads. You'll wake a beast that will annihilate you on pure instinct."

"What about your cousin?"

"My point exactly. Our enemies are aware of our emotional triggers, and your giant ego. They're not as stupid as you are."

"So we're just gonna sit pretty while they mass up and strike us, is that it?"

"We must assess the situation thoroughly first."

JT brushed off the very idea. "No time for that. We have Mother, as well as Trans-plants, Cycologists, soldiers –"

"I fought my way into this base easily. Alone. Why not send your aug-mented Agent in?"

"He's not as expendable as you, and I need him on standby. Besides, he's got nothing to lose. You, on the other hand, have your cousin and Miss Campbell to look out for. If you get caught, you'll fight your way out through sheer desperation. Stakes are high."

"I'm not desperate. Your actions are."

"We're fighting a war…"

"You're starting a war."

"Maybe, but we can easily do to you what we did to your fellow Agent. You won't fight back with lives at stake now, will you? That means you've got a choice. Soon, you won't have one."

A Trans-plant rustled loudly.

Suzi spoke coldly. "You've just signed the death warrant for this operation. Your Heartbeat's not going on for much longer."

JT was unmoved. "No more threats. Well?"

"I'll do it," Suzi said.

JT was slightly taken aback. "Really?"

"I never lie. I will lead your taskforce into the Black Crossroads. No deceptions. Just facts."

"You were threatening me a second ago –"

"Lives are at stake and your argument is valid. The outcome of your action will change, and not in your favour. I will comply with your demands for my cousin, and for Jenny Campbell."

JT nodded, slightly unsure of her about-turn. "I'm glad you see it my way. Okay, let's get you ready."

"I am ready. You, clearly, are not."

"Everything has to be taken into account," he said, now irritated by her dominating attitude which infringed on his ego. "We all want it to run smoothly, don't we? Make yourself comfy. We'll move out in a little bit."

"I am comfortable. You're always shifting."

JT scowled and turned away, issuing instructions to his people.

With his attention off her, Suzi went to a terminal and rapidly typed a numerical sequence. Several systems were bypassed and she brought up an image showing Jenny strapped to a table, overlooked by two scientists. One male, one female. She hit a switch and spoke softly. "Do it."

"The malignant ratio's increased by twenty-four percent…"

The female scientist frowned at her colleague's words. They baffled her as she examined a screenshot of Jenny's brain.

Jenny was unnerved. "Translation, please?"

The woman spoke. "The red patch in your left hemisphere's expanding, meaning the radiation level's growing. That's what's giving you headaches."

"Which means what? Something's frying my brain?"

"Not frying, agitating," the woman corrected. "Rather like what you're doing to mine."

"Can you stop it?"

"We need to know what's causing it first. It's not easy to get to. We —"

A sharp buzz cut her off. Her eyes rolled back and she slumped to the ground, care of a tech device to her neck. Jenny watched as the male scientist stepped over his colleague's unconscious body and began undoing her straps. The second they were off, Jenny scrambled off the bench and backed away.

"Okay, what was that?" she demanded, indicating the body on the floor.

"Standard-issue taser," he replied. "Relax, I'm on your side."

"I don't buy it!" she snapped.

He ignored her. "My orders were to attack your friend when she entered the base, but she got to me with her glasses. They overrode the mind control used around here, and she told me what to do. Two scientists were assigned to you. I got rid of one and took his place. The other's on the floor there."

"I still don't trust you."

"Believe what you want, but we have to move, like, two minutes ago."

He pulled the door open.

Jenny stayed still.

"Still not sure?" he asked. "Wait a few minutes, blow the opportunity, then you'll know. Your friend's just given me an order through this." He indicated the earpiece he wore. "She tapped into it, keeping my buddies out of the loop and making them only hear static. It's not my usual piece either. She took that and gave me one she pinched off a guy she smacked out."

"I know how she feels. Let me speak to her."

"She's offline so there may be trouble at her end," he explained. "She asked me to tell you one word. Rags. Her cousin's name. She says she told you about her when you were sitting on a log under a tree in the schoolyard, shortly after –"

"Okay, you got a deal," Jenny cut in.

He motioned to the door. "Coming?"

"Hell yeah."

They moved into the corridor.

"What is this place?" Jenny asked, following him.

"Gold, by the way," he said.

"What is?"

"I am. That's my name. Cadet Anthony Holden. Someone liked my work and called me a golden boy, so it's just Gold now."

"How'd you end up here?"

"Not really sure to be honest," he answered. "I was a cop. A junior area driver. Pretty good too. Straight of school and into the force. I'd only been there a year when my bosses told me about a recruitment program, then things got a little blurry."

"Tell me about it." A Hurripain stab overcame her and she placed her palm on her forehead. "Arrrrgh!"

"You okay?" he asked.

She waved him away. "It's fine. It only comes when I'm jittery."

They headed down the corridor.

"What's being worked on here?" she wanted to know.

"Anything and everything," he replied. "The big find is an energy source called the Shockwave. The ECG wants to turn it into the world's primary power supply, then use it to hypnotically manipulate everyone through their digital technology. I worked with a team to implement a few systems. Now they're almost ready. The only obstacle is the Black Cross-roads. Once that's gone, they're in business."

"So what do we do? Ditch this place and call the cops?"

"God no," he said. "The ECG control the police and have contacts everywhere. They've hacked into all major surveillance networks and can track you twenty-four seven."

"Sounds like my mum when I was little, only she did it on instinct. Now there was a real champ." She paused. "What about Gastoff? Did he slip under the radar or what?"

"He was always an ECG target," Gold told her. "They just couldn't find or contain him. He was good. When your friend took him out, we were alerted. She was deemed a significant threat after that. We ransacked the remains of Greg Cox's house and took Gastoff's trinkets. God knows what the ECG intends to do with them. They're searching for Greg as we speak and are closing in on him. There's still more Hurriflame mutations out there too, and the ECG are rounding them up into a massive freakshow. We need to get out of here. Fast."

"What about fighting back?" Jenny asked.

"You can't. My people are too strong."

"They've never messed with a teenage girl scorned and I really want to run amok in this place. There must be something we can do."

Footsteps came from down the hallway.

Gold opened a door. "Yeah. Hide!"

He pushed her towards it. She smacked his arm away and entered.

Suzi walked by a giant WOMB, not quite as large as Mother, but still impressive in size. She stopped at the sight of the mutant inside. It stared back at her just as curiously. Although she and it were alien to each other, there was still a familiarity between them. She recognised its pain, knowing that the ECG who held this poor thing captive was far more monstrous than how this creature appeared. Now, more than ever, she vowed to bring the ECG to an end for good.

JT stood by the opposite WOMB, preparing for the battle with two of his commanders, yet occasionally glancing at Suzi, suspicious of what she might be doing. She knew he wouldn't let her out of his sight for long, meaning she'd have to play things carefully.

She walked around another WOMB and stopped. It was empty, save for a single ring on a small podium inside. The WOMB's terminal told her that the ring fluctuated with an energy signature.

She brought up its readout on the WOMB's side screen, not liking it one bit.

GR – Master-Ring.

GR. That could only stand for one name: Gastoff Rosewood.

So he did survive, she realised. She scrolled through the screen's information, reading rapidly. The reports stated that Greg Cox, some time ago, and under the influence of Gastoff, had given Maria Longsworth the ring. She'd kept it in her locker and never worn it, so Gastoff had reached her through a bracelet instead, an attempt which Suzi had stopped. Maria then intended to throw the ring into the river, but an Agent Deck Turner had found and questioned her about the whole Greg/Gastoff situation first, then had broken into her locker and taken it. At least Turner's move was effective, Suzi noted. It allowed Gastoff to be neutralised as a prisoner, for the time being.

She walked around the side of another WOMB, keeping herself partly in JT's line of vision. Subtly, she reached out, activating its terminal. Spending time in the Heartbeat had allowed her to identify several codes and passwords for various operating systems. Most were only minor digital commands, but every little bit helped.

A visual feed appeared, showing the room that Jenny had been in. There was no sign of her, only the female scientist splayed out on the floor. Suzi saw, by the numbers on the screen, that the woman had fallen in the last few minutes. No one else had seen this image, no doubt due to her agent's influence. If they had, alarms would be wailing by now.

She rewound the surveillance footage to see what had occurred. All was satisfactory. She then found ten minutes of previous footage and replayed it through the system on a continuous loop. Anyone who saw it would only see two scientists working around Jenny. They'd have to watch closely to notice their repeated actions.

She keyed in a few commands, tightening the security on the locked door. The room was soundproof too, making the woman a prisoner. If anyone tried to enter, it would take time to get in, and the woman wouldn't be able to contact them or leave. Now all Suzi had to do was locate Jenny's current position.

Her fingers ran across the screen, bypassing several systems, before coming to a halt. An image had appeared. A layout of the ECG's Mother WOMB, holding the Shockwave. This was practical to know, she reasoned. She could use this information.

She took several screenshots with her Iyes, then resumed her search
for Jenny. It took a few moments until… there! Jenny, and the man that
Suzi had selected, were heading through a small conduit beneath the base.
On camera.

"Clumsy," Suzi noted.

Discreetly, she pulled out the earpiece she'd taken from the man when
she'd first issued her orders to him. She raised it to her ear, clicking it into
place.

"Cobwebs!"

Jenny grimaced, ducking under the webs stretched between the pipes
in the cramped tunnel. They were on their way to the kitchen, or so Gold
had said, then they'd figure out where to go from there. Jenny wondered
if they'd make it out alive with so many cobwebs around. Worse still, the
spiders on them were massive.

Gold grinned. "Not scared of 'em, are you?"

"It's what you guys did to them that bothers me," Jenny replied, grimly.

His earpiece buzzed loudly. He flinched in surprise, tapping it. "I think
your friend wants to talk."

"Seriously?" Jenny asked.

He held his hand up, motioning her to keep quiet, and listened as Suzi's
voice came through.

*"Your surrounding cameras are offline. My signal to your earpiece is scrambled.
Take the device off and turn its volume to maximum."*

"It's her," Gold said quickly. He pulled the earpiece away, tapping it
once more.

"Suze!" Jenny cried, grabbing Gold's hands and calling into them.
"Where are you? You okay?"

"Yes, Jenny Campbell," Suzi answered, now loud enough for both of
them to hear. *"Why would you think I'm not performing at optimum efficiency? Our
new ally is not. His methods, like those of this whole base, should be improved significantly. The room where you escaped from was not sealed correctly, nor was the security
footage he initiated suitable. I can see why he's still a cadet. Clearly, he is not elite
material."*

"Nice to hear from you too," Gold retorted.

"You gonna get us out of here?" Jenny asked quickly.

"*No,*" Suzi replied.

"What, are you nuts?" Jenny protested. "You want to bring this place down, right?"

"*Yes, but first I must lead an assault on the Black Crossroads.*"

Gold frowned. "What the hell?"

"*Listen to me, both of you,*" Suzi ordered. "*This base holds an emergency override centre, fifty metres below you. Everything in this complex can be controlled from there. It's easy to reach, and even easier to break into digitally. Cadet Holden was part of the team assigned to it.*"

"Just doin' my job," Gold mumbled.

"*An inefficient worker follows inefficient commands…*"

"Enough already!"

"*You are to take Jenny Campbell there, Cadet Holden.*"

"Hang on," Gold cut in. "I only helped set things up system-wise. I've never actually seen it."

"*Once again, you are inefficient. I will assist you by helping you avoid detection. Now hurry. We don't have much time before I return to my battle.*"

"*Your* battle?" Jenny shot back. "Suze, what's the deal here?"

"*No deal has been made, Jenny Campbell. I cannot reveal too much. If you get captured, it will put my plans in jeopardy, especially if the man beside you speaks. He is much too responsive.*"

"Garbage!" Gold snapped.

"*See?*" Suzi pointed out. "*Whatever happens from now on, the ECG mustn't be allowed to continue.*"

"So you're going to fix it all by going to war?"

"*Yes, but not in the way that you think. I have a plan to eliminate the Black Crossroads, and destroy the Heartbeat, but I need you both in position first.*"

"It's to do with that girl, right?" Gold asked.

Silence.

"What girl?" Jenny pressed.

Gold spoke. "We have surveillance footage of a kid in the Crossroads. Scans show she's not human."

Jenny addressed the earpiece. "Suze? Is it Rags?"

More silence, then Suzi spoke softly. "*I must know, Jenny Campbell.*"

Jenny nodded. "Yeah, of course, Suze. We'll help you out."

"Thank you," Suzi replied. *"Thirty metres ahead of you lies a hatch. It's under the third grille to your right. I've disabled its alarm, allowing you easy access. Its ladder will take you to the emergency override centre."* Static crackled through the transmission. *"I must go. I'm drawing attention to myself and there's an important task to complete before I leave."*

"Thanks, Suze," Jenny said.

The earpiece went dead.

Jenny walked away from Gold, looking back at him. "Come on, golden boy."

"Watch out for cobwebs!" Gold warned.

Jenny walked straight into one and screamed.

JT was curious. Suzi stood half-hidden behind a WOMB. She'd been slipping in and out of his sight for the past few minutes and he didn't like it at all. Suspicious, he approached her.

"We're ready to leave," he said.

"Good," she replied automatically. "Let's go."

Suzi went with JT, passing the WOMB that held Gastoff's ring, satisfied that he'd failed to notice that ring now flickering every thirty seconds. He'd missed seeing the new bulge in her pocket too. A small lead-lined case the ECG used for handling hazardous materials. She'd pinched it from one of their stations, then infiltrated the WOMB and removed the ring without touching it directly. No one suspected anything, nor noticed the WOMB's new ring; a holographic projection of the original.

Her face gave nothing away as she walked on.

Jenny and Gold stood by a terminal in the cramped, dimly lit emergency override centre. They were thankful that no one was here, and that Suzi had allowed them to enter undetected. Several screens linked to the base's camera feeds were before them. Hacking into the Heartbeat's primary systems without detection hadn't been easy for Gold, but had paid off.

One screen showed the hangar bay where ECG troops were making for their choppers. Suzi strode with them, heading for her own.

Jenny inhaled sharply. "This is it."

Gold nodded. "Yeah." He paused. "It's just us now. In a tight spot. Waiting for the end of everything."

He looked at her.

Sensing his gaze, she looked back at him.

"Eeeeewwww, no!" she cringed, suddenly aware of his intentions. "No! No, just… no!"

She shifted uncomfortably.

Gold sighed and returned his attention to the screen.

"Fine," he said. "Work it is."

Jenny gulped, then frowned, looked at him baffled, shook her head in disbelief, and focused on the screen.

The Heartbeat's hanger doors opened and Suzi's chopper ascended into the night. She sat at its controls, alone in the speedy vessel. The ECG had attached several cameras over the chopper's exterior, allowing live feeds they could monitor. JT had also insisted on several hidden cameras inside the chopper, should Suzi try and double-cross him, and had made her wear an ECG earpiece, leaving him as close to her as possible.

Several other choppers emerged from the Heartbeat and followed her, albeit at a distance. They were larger, heavier, double-bladed, and armed to the hilt. Their duty was to maintain surveillance from afar, with their cameras trained on her. Suzi would lead the way since she was the most expendable, but this mission was also delicate. JT knew she couldn't be trusted, and the Black Crossroads remained a wildcard. All information was vital, meaning that everything would be recorded.

Suzi, however, knew that her enemies in the Black Crossroads were expecting her, and was prepared for the worst.

Chapter Ten

A light breeze swept through the desert town, lifting a mass of dust into a swirling funnel before dissipating. Another breeze followed, gliding along the deserted streets, swooping in between two empty buildings, and making their rotting foundations creak softly.

A small figure stood in the town's dead centre, gazing at the sky. Several dirtied bits of material hung from their small body, while a few animal bones were tangled in their knotted hair. That hair may have been blonde once. Now it was little more than a scruffy mess, covering a face blackened with dirt.

The face of a child.

A girl.

She shivered, clutching her broken doll whilst listening to a faint sound approaching steadily.

Choppers.

She hugged her doll tightly.

Suzi had dealt with her chopper's internal cameras, both standard and hidden. Any observers would once again see a continuous loop of old footage, just like she'd done with Gastoff's ring in the Heartbeat WOMB, as well as Jenny on the lab table too.

Idiots, Suzi thought. They kept falling for the same old tricks. That's what happens with self-centred apes. Still, she knew it wouldn't be long before one of them detected something wrong.

She removed the crude earpiece that JT had given her and worked on it. In no time at all she'd created two extra audio channels. She now had links to Jenny Campbell, Echo, and the ECG, and could determine who heard what.

Her task complete, she put the earpiece back on, clicked her head to the side and said, "Jenny Campbell, can you hear me?"

A scratchy voice spoke. *"Loud and clear, Suze."*

Suzi clicked her head again, blocking off Jenny's channel and opening another. "Come in, Echo."

A wave of static followed, then, *"I hear you."*

"We need to talk."

Her chopper picked up speed.

The Heartbeat's Tech Officer flicked a switch. "Primary chopper's approaching the Crossroads."

JT nodded. "Right, boys, let's see what we got here…"

"There she goes," Gold said softly.

He and Jenny watched the live feeds from various choppers.

"We're with you, Suze…" Jenny whispered.

Suzi's chopper landed in the dirt, sending dust waves billowing high. The whirring blades slowed to a halt as Suzi emerged, stepping into the desert and heading for the town. All three feeds behind her ear were live, allowing the ECG, Jenny, and Echo to hear everything, except each other.

The only sounds that came were from her shoes crunching on the rocky surface, along with the winds rising, and the slow squeaks of old signs, shutters and rotting doorways.

A figure appeared before her, surrounded by a swirling dust cloud.

"Sir, we have a visual!"

JT leaned in, peering into the Heartbeat's wallscreen. Several smaller feeds were active on it too, showing exterior footage from Suzi's chopper, along with scans from the choppers above.

Curiously, he examined the person facing Suzi and ordered, "Zero in."

"Tread lightly Suze," Jenny warned, gazing into the screen.

Suzi moved in. She'd only taken a few steps when there came a shrill cry, "Stop!"

Suzi did so.

The dust cleared, revealing a child covered in rags, holding a broken doll.

Suzi clicked her head to the side, blocking out the audio channels to the ECG and to Jenny, but not Echo.

"We've lost audio," the Tech Officer reported.

"Get it back!" JT snapped.

"Echo?" Suzi asked.

"Preliminary scans indicate it's her. One hundred percent."

"Is she rigged?"

"No explosive devices detected, but it doesn't mean they aren't there."

Suzi clicked her head again, bringing the three audio channels back online, even though she didn't like the ECG listening in. Echo was essential and had to hear everything. Jenny Campbell, she could let in a little, but the ECG were a hindrance. Still, if she shut them out completely, they'd only come racing in. There was no choice but to let them listen.

For now.

"Audio's up again," the Tech Officer reported.

JT inhaled sharply, satisfied.

"Rags," Suzi said.

The younger girl shuddered. "Cousin."

Suzi paused. "I came for you, like I promised. I never break promises. Ever."

"I know," came the reply.

The wind picked up.

"Are you alone?" Suzi asked.

Rags shook her head. "No. You're not either."

"You are correct," Suzi stated. "I have a military taskforce on standby."

JT was aghast. "*You* have a military taskforce on standby?"

"I'm here to help," Suzi continued. "To make amends if I can."

Tears welled in the child's eyes. "Are they all gone?"

Suzi's response was sombre. "Yes. We are the only survivors of our family line. You needn't be afraid of the Homeworld anymore. I've eradicated our enemies there." She paused. "It's time to stop running."

The girl bit her lips. "For you too, cousin."

"I never run."

The girl gave a small smile. "Liar. I know when you're covering things up. You can't hide it, no matter how hard you try."

Suzi felt a sharp twinge of sadness and did her best to conceal it. She changed tack and said, "We can start again. Just the two of us. The war's over. We can go home. It's safe now."

Rags quivered. "I don't want to go back there. I want to go somewhere beautiful where I can help people."

Suzi's voice grew quieter, almost cracking. "I missed you."

"I missed you too," Rags replied.

"Come to me."

Rags clutched her doll tighter. "I can't. No more than you can come to me. You see…" She paused. "Our fires still burn. You're here on behalf of your side, while I'm here… on behalf of mine."

Suzi's logic took over once more. "I'd anticipated that. There's no doubt that your side wants mine to surrender."

Rags gazed at her tearfully. "Just as your side wants mine to well. It's back to square one. The war zone. Seems we never left."

Suzi's expression darkened. "I won't leave you again, Rags. I will make amends."

Rags spoke grimly. "Once again, cousin, the game's out of your hands."

Suzi's face hardened. "Then we change the rules. Neither side wins but us."

"What the damn hell's she talkin' bout?" JT snapped.

"You can't win," Rags warned. "The Toymaster won't let you. He's too powerful. He would have killed you when you came to this world, but when he found out we were cousins he wanted to play instead. Just like he's played everyone, all along."

Suzi suddenly understood. "We're not in the Black Crossroads, are we?"

Rags nodded. "It's a decoy. Not even the Trans-plants could tell it from the real thing, and don't ask me where that's hidden."

"I wasn't —" Suzi began.

"You're lying again," Rags cut in. "Everyone you've brought here's bait for the Toymaster to pick off, one by one."

Suzi was unmoved. "I suspected as much. No matter. I've allowed for that."

"There's more," said Rags. "He wants someone. A girl you know. Jenny Campbell. She's the key to all this."

Jenny froze.

"How?" Suzi asked.

Rags tensed. "He just said that a little too much power had gone to her head."

Jenny put a hand to her temple, sensing the buzzing growing once more.

Rags shuddered. "You have to hand her over, or I die." She shrugged, defeated. "No win."

The desert winds rose.

Suzi stared at her. "Don't ask me to make this choice, Rags…"

"It's not me that's asking," Rags told her. "It's him." She glanced at the wooden sign above them, squeaking eerily in the breeze. Upon it, was a clown's leering face.

"He's here?" Suzi pressed.

"He's everywhere."

Suzi gave a little nod. "As expected, meaning we're caught between two equally powerful forces. The most logical choice is to side with one." She paused. "Very well. He can have Jenny Campbell."

Jenny's heart skipped a beat. "What? Wait, Suze, no! Where the hell's my say…?"

Rags spoke solemnly. "He thought you might see it his way. First, he wants access to the Heartbeat where his *'toy soldiers'* are playing."

Suzi clicked her head to the side, shutting out Echo's signal completely, then took off her earpiece. "This is a direct line. He only needs to lock onto their power source. The Shockwave."

JT tensed. "Okay, this has gone belly up! All units, move in!"

Suzi didn't flinch to the rising sound of ECG choppers. They were expected. She could read the ECG's actions as clear as a billboard.

Rags raised a hand to her ear, removing her own device from beneath a mass of grimy hair.

"Here," she said, throwing it to Suzi who snatched it out of the air. "Send him in."

Suzi clicked the two devices together.

A spark flashed between them.

Several Heartbeat screens died suddenly.

"Okay, what's happenin' here?" JT asked, slightly concerned.

The Tech Officer spoke quickly. "A big ugly's hit our system. I'll start a digital immunisation sweep."

JT bit his lip worriedly.

Suzi watched as the ECG's earpiece, linked with Rags's own, fizzled loudly. Thankfully, she still had her Earwig from the Homeworld. She took it out, placing it behind her ear. "Are you there, Echo?"

Echo's voice came through scratchily. *"I am."*

"We've created a link between the Heartbeat and this town. I need you to join in and strengthen the connection. Wait until I give the command."

"Understood."

"Patch me through to Jenny Campbell, please."

"At once."

A screen self-activated before Jenny and Gold.

Suzi's voice came through. *"Cadet Holden, you must deactivate the Heartbeat's security protocols from your relay station."*

"Suze!" Jenny cried.

"I got it," Gold said, working on the terminal.

"Wait a sec," Jenny cut in. "What the hell are you playing at, Suze?"

"My aim is to eliminate both sides in this war," Suzi answered. *"I've no doubt that the Toymaster was listening when I said he could have you. That's not the truth but part of the plan. We need him reacting. Now hurry!"*

Gold's fingers flashed across the keyboard.

Suzi's gaze didn't waver from Rags. It never had, and never would.

"You can't fight the whole world," Rags warned.

"Yes," Suzi replied firmly. "I can."

Rags was adamant. "I can't go with you. You must come with me, or he'll force you to."

Suzi's jaw hardened. "Not if I can help it."

The choppers grew louder.

She pulled off her Earwig, attaching it to the interlocked devices from Rags and the Heartbeat.

Echo, now in the loop, boosted the link between the two sides.

The Heartbeat's sirens wailed.

"All defences disabled!" the Tech Officer reported. "I —"

The terminal exploded, hurtling him across the room and silencing him forever.

Another terminal blew, then another, then another, all at distinct levels, pitches, and rhythms, like musical cues.

JT watched as the wallscreen reactivated, revealing two blood-red lips encompassed by a painted white face.

The lips shrieked with laughter.

Jenny recoiled, clawing at her temples as the Hurripain grew sharper than ever. The cackles on her terminal screen, along with *every* screen in the Heartbeat, fizzled furiously.

Gold cringed. "I hope your friend knows what she's doing."

Jenny flinched over the hideous laughter. "She does, I think!"

Suzi's voice bellowed around them. *"Get out of there now, Jenny Campbell! Evacuate the base!"*

"No need to tell me twice," Gold said, pulling Jenny away.

"I wasn't," Suzi stated.

Suzi changed her Earwig's settings on the linked devices. "Echo, can you get us into the Heartbeat's operational systems without interacting with the Shockwave?"

"I can," Echo replied, *"but not for long. I've allowed the Toymaster to cross into the Heartbeat, but it's taking all of my reserves to keep him out of our ship's systems. His power's immense."*

"I only need you to unlock a few Heartbeat doors to let Jenny Campbell out."

"Acknowledged."

Jenny and Gold climbed out of a hatch, emerging into a tunnel. It was empty, save for the mocking laughs from the speaker system.

A hiss rose from a second hatch nearby, sliding open to reveal a long ladder in a confined space.

"This way," Gold ordered.

"Why?" she asked. "What's up there?"

"Emergency exit to the surface. Seems we've got friends in high places."

Jenny entered and started climbing.

Suzi saw the choppers approaching.

Rags shivered. "It's happening again, cousin. You can't fight them all. You can't take me. It's over."

Suzi was unmoved. "Not this time. I'm coming back for you. Hold tight."

She pocketed the three linked devices and broke into a sprint, running for the abandoned hotel. The choppers fired, just for her and just as expected. She knew that Rags would be far more valuable to the ECG as a prisoner.

The bullets thundered into the ground, hot on her heels. She ignored them and mechanically propelled herself through the hotel doorway, flying up the stairs.

The chopper let loose with a missile. She reached a second-story window on the hotel's opposite side and a giant leap smashed her through the glass, sending her sailing into the night and leaving the building to explode with a deafening roar behind her. The mighty boom and the flaming heat barely affected her as she landed in a run, heading away from Rags, against all her gut instincts. Despite what she wanted; her logic had to overrule her emotions. Feelings would only get her killed. A retreat was necessary, temporarily at least, before a counterattack could be made.

She picked up speed.

Rags watched a chopper land. Its soldiers ran for her.

"Better stay back!" she called. "He won't let you near me!"

The soldiers slowed.

"What's he gonna do?" one retorted. "Kill us with candy?"

Rags nodded. "Yeah. Totally."

Several multi-coloured balloons, hovering in a window, caught their attention. Red, purple, green, all filled with bubbling liquids. The balloons floated from the building, slowly at first, then picked up speed, targeting the soldiers.

Rags tensed. "Careful. They go off with a bang."

She shut her eyes.

A green balloon approached a soldier. He stood still, unsure how to react.

Silence followed.

Bang!

The balloon exploded with a deafening roar. A wave of fire billowed from it, blasting him and two other soldiers off their feet, killing them instantly.

More balloons flowed from the surrounding buildings as sinister carnival music, filled with static, played throughout the dead town.

"Happy Deathday to you…"

The voice was childlike.

The soldiers fired. The bullets hit the balloons, erupting burning cacophonies of toxic flames soaring outwards.

It made little difference.

From every doorway, every window, every opening of every building, more and more balloons emerged in great tides, swooping in from all directions.

Rags covered her ears, falling to her knees as the firing grew.

Laughter screeched from above.

She looked up.

Swirling over the chaos were several toy clowns, resembling marionettes, with propulsion units strapped to their backs. They circled menacingly, carrying armfuls of black candy canes.

"I love games!" one called down. *"Won't you play with me? Pleeeeeeassssse?"*

They soared in.

"I love you," another chuckled, dropping a sweet onto an ECG soldier.

The sweet exploded, blowing him apart.

The marionette giggled. *"I always love to kill with kindness."*

The sheer multitude of balloons left the soldiers little room to manoeuvre, leaving them to be slaughtered by the dozen.

JT stood frozen.

The deadly smile on the Heartbeat's wallscreen had minimised into a corner, allowing him to witness the full horror of the massacre. He watched as the balloons and marionettes made for the ECG choppers trying to flee. Two left the ground, firing relentlessly, before they were blown up in mid-air.

His face fell. "Hardly seems fair now, does it?"

Rags crouched with her eyes closed, unable to move amidst the horrific blasts and screams. The hideous cries of the damned were all too familiar to her. She'd heard them not so long ago, back home.

The grotesque creations swarmed over the soldiers, silencing them forever.

Suzi ran.

She weaved from side to side. Several sweets rained past, accompanied by insane marionette laughter from above. She'd planned to outmanoeuvre the ECG, but there was no chance of that now. Not with an ocean of balloons around. She batted some falling sweets away, knowing she was being diverted from Rags.

A marionette swooped in.

She turned, grabbed the flying monstrosity and flew up with it, knocking the explosive from its wooden hand and hearing it ignite below. She swiftly ripped the clothing off its wooden frame, made of broomsticks, and watched as its laughter grew and its head rotated to face her, its blood-red lips parting to reveal a set of jagged teeth.

They bit for her savagely.

Unfazed, she ripped its head off, cast it aside, controlled the sick device's descent, then leapt off and hit the ground running, making for Rags. With a single sweep, she grabbed the girl and fled.

"No!" Rags cried.

Her cousin's cries were drowned out by a sudden rumbling as the ground shook violently. Suzi rounded a corner, the tremors grew, and the land cracked open into a long ripple in the middle of the street. She tried veering away.

Too late.

A white-gloved hand with frills shot up, grabbing Rag's leg and pulling her down.

Suzi stopped, still holding Rags. Whatever clutched her cousin was far stronger than she was.

Another deadly toy from the Toymaster.

The surrounding balloons and marionettes halted their approach, hovering in silence and observing the struggle.

Suzi analysed the opening in the ground. The rumbles grew, and she knew that more deadly hands would soon be reaching up.

"Forget me!" Rags cried pleadingly. "Let go!"

Suzi's tone was resolute. "Never!"

She reached into her pocket, pulled out the three linked devices, brought them to her face and nimbly flicked a switch. "Echo?"

"I hear you."

"The Shockwave's composed of Zymac particles, correct?"

"Correct."

Rags wailed as the hideous grip on her leg tightened.

Suzi spoke quickly. "Cheat's way out, Echo. Remember when the Authority tried to use those particles for the Homeworld's war efforts?"

"I also recall the early experiments. The prototypes were extremely dangerous."

"I'm prepared to take that risk, Echo. You know the scientific theory. Put it into practice. When it's done, send one of your own stocked viruses into the Mother WOMB."

"Acknowledged."

Echo's presence entered the Heartbeat, via Suzi's linked devices. Skilfully, she evaded her rival digital intruder, reached the Mother WOMB and deactivated several codes.

The Shockwave latched onto Echo's wavelength, making for Suzi.

Suzi felt the linked devices tingle in her hand, then saw a dim glow emanating from it.

The Shockwave. Complete with Zymac particles.

With Echo's modifications to her Earwig, after manipulating those particles, Suzi now held a prototypical tool. Long ago, her people had observed a cosmic race far superior to their own, and attempted to duplicate their abilities. The initial results were disastrous for the Homeworld's scientists, but right now she was prepared to risk everything for Rags.

She raised her arm high, hit a switch, and let loose with a stream of golden energy that burst into the sky.

To create a flickering blue sphere of a miniature Gateway.

One that would take her and Rags to safety. They wouldn't go far, perhaps even as little as a few kilometres away, but at least it would help.

A blood-red balloon swept in.

She dropped the linked device into her pocket, picked up a rock and hurled it at the balloon. The shot was direct and the balloon exploded, taking out a marionette. She kicked out, severing the monstrous arm from Rags's leg, then pulled the girl away as the ground split open further. More hands rose, stretching out for the child, while the balloons and marionettes surged in.

Suzi leapt high, taking Rags with her, and together they were sucked up by the Gateway's gravitational field.

A marionette spat a bomb in after them.

Halfway in, the bomb exploded.

Rags wailed against the howling winds of the Gateway's Slipstream. Her arm was wrenched to the limit in Suzi's grip, amidst flying fire tendrils and bomb fragments that shook the already unstable conduit. Not good, Suzi thought, struggling to hold her cousin against the sheer hell they swept through. Not good at all.

Rags winced. "Let me go or you'll be forced to! My arm'll be ripped off if you don't!"

Suzi ignored her, holding on tightly.

Echo opened a Gateway, preparing to evacuate Mother.

Her work was complete, having introduced her virus into the Mother WOMB. It would start as a small black blip, then grow into a malignant sphere to render the Shockwave ineffective, first within the Heartbeat, then throughout all ECG bases globally, thanks to a cyber cyst. A digital form of warfare from the Homeworld called the Acystance Package.

Echo withdrew. She felt the Toymaster's presence targeting her through a digital frequency. Swiftly, she retreated…

… right back into Suzi's vessel where she activated the security filters to block the Toymaster out. When done, she took further measures to protect Suzi by adding digital shields to her linked devices. Those measures wouldn't protect Suzi completely but would buy her more time.

JT ran along a dimly lit corridor. Most of his people were dead. His

Heartbeat was going up in flames, while the clown's laughter, accompanied by sinister carnival music, echoed throughout its dying embers.

He swore repeatedly, filled with fury. No way in hell was he letting his Heartbeat go to the enemy.

He ripped open a wall panel and bypassed a system to activate a self-destruct sequence, whilst ensuring that the Shockwave would stop any alien presence from disabling it.

He made the countdown minimal. Less than a minute was all he needed.

Rags sensed Suzi's long-suppressed emotions taking over. For the first time ever, Suzi shuddered, and Rags felt it ripple through them both.

"I'm finished!" Rags called. "Leave me!"

Suzi remained as stubborn as all hell. "I won't!"

Rags stared at her firmly, with a maturity far more advanced than her years. "I forgive you! You have to forgive yourself! Go!"

"I —"

A savage wind blast surged in, breaking their hold. Suzi reached desperately for Rags, failed, and watched helplessly as the final member of her family was sucked into the void. There was no time to react, for the Slipstream's howling winds sent her spiralling the opposite way in a blurring rush.

The Heartbeat exploded.

Jenny's cry was engulfed by the titanic bellow from deep in the valley behind her. A blast as large and as fierce as the Hurriflame itself blew high, again splitting the night open in a deafening roar and leaving the air red-hot. Several black and gold flaming clouds billowed over her head, along with Gold's, as they dropped to the ground. A further eruption sent a second flame wave shooting far into the sky, along with the Shockwave's golden halo.

Jenny felt the earth tremble as further explosions rippled through the Heartbeat's tunnels far below.

Terror-Byte too, saw the explosion from another part of the valley, unaffected by its blinding glare. He'd been returning to the Heartbeat when the place had blown to smithereens. It didn't surprise him that the situation had spiralled out of control. The ECG were inefficient as always, he concluded. None of this would have happened if he'd been in command.

A wave of fire soared high into the night, changed course in mid-air and dived straight for him, churning ferociously whilst forming into a great flaming mouth.

There was no time to run.

He held his ground, defiant against all odds.

High above, within the flames, the Toymaster sneered, watching Terror-Byte's cold expression. Here was an ally who'd work nicely, he determined.

The Toymaster reviewed the situation, pleased with his progress. He'd entered the Mother WOMB, evaded the cyst, and only just touched the Shockwave when the base went up. A few seconds of contact were all that he needed to evolve.

Now he had a new plan.

He swept in for Terror-Byte, engulfing him in a blinding flash.

Jenny coughed amidst the smoke, wiping her eyes. She barely saw the mass of overturned trees, and the rumbling in the ground made her as nauseous as hell, aggravating the Hurripain. Finally, the rumbling faded and the smoke cleared, if only a little.

"We made it," she said to Gold, feeling like she was half-choking.

He spoke quietly from beside her. "Yeah. We did."

The Hurripain subsided and she flicked some ash from her face. "God knows how many other bases you guys have out there. None, I hope."

"A few," Gold answered, "but that one was the heart. Rip that out, and you're empty."

"I know the feeling. Come on. We better move before we're fried."

"Not this time."

Jenny looked down and gasped in horror. A jagged strip of iron had run right through his torso to protrude bloodily from both sides. Her hand rose to her mouth and she shuddered in shock. Somehow, she kept it together. "We-We'll get help…"

Gold smiled weakly. "I don't think so, soldier. Some wounds are just too deep."

"There's always a chance…" she began.

His eyelids lowered. "If only. You know, for a brief second there, you actually made my heartbeat glow. I needed that. Thanks."

She swallowed hard. "Any time."

His smile faded as his head rolled lifelessly into the mud.

Suzi fell from the Gateway, back into reality. She landed on the ground with a thump and stood motionless, feeling hollow. She couldn't move, and barely registered Echo's voice from the linked devices in her pocket.

"Agent Chambers?"

She didn't react.

"Agent Chambers?"

Still nothing.

A sinister laugh came from one device.

The Toymaster.

The laughter grew louder. She knew he was riding its signal straight for her.

She pulled out the linked bits of tech, took her Earwig off, dropped the other parts into the dirt and stamped heavily, crushing them to pieces and halting his path. Her hand rose robotically as she attached her Earwig in place and spoke, devoid of emotion. "I hear you, Echo."

"Your plan was effective," Echo reported. *"The Heartbeat is no more. Satellite sensors state that a self-destruct sequence recently activated. It seems that the ECG would rather die than surrender."*

"Cowards," Suzi said bitterly.

"In any case," Echo continued, *"their network is crippled. I ensured that several cysts were transmitted along the Heartbeat's digital channels and into their global bases. Their occupants will have time to evacuate, but their finances and resources, along with the Shockwave, will be obliterated. It's fair to say that the ECG are no longer a threat to anyone, for the time being at least. That's another faction down."*

Suzi stayed formal. "Follow-up measures must be implemented to ensure our success. Did the Toymaster reach Mother before the base blew?"

"Yes," Echo answered. *"Thankfully, our Acystance Package worked fast. It eradicated the Shockwave's Zymac particles which means —"*

"No more teleporting for anybody," Suzi concluded. "Does the Toy-master know of our ship's location?"

"*Negative,*" replied Echo. "*I took strong precautions to shield it. We're as invisible to him as he is to us.*"

"Thank you, Echo. What's my current location?"

"*Two point four kilometres from the Heartbeat's remains. You're at the exact centre of the Hurriflame's blast.*"

Suzi observed the four-sided patch of ground she stood on. "Back to square one." Her shades seemed to darken. "All I wanted was… Rags."

"*I know,*" Echo said. "*If it's any comfort to you, your cousin didn't return to her the decoy town. I'm unable to detect any trace of her there, nor anywhere else for that matter, meaning we have no proof of her demise.*"

Suzi thought this over. "Then where is she?"

Rags opened her eyes.

The air was crisp. A gentle mist hung over the cool stream beside her. She focused on several dust granules mystically swirling in the sunlight.

A reeling sound came from nearby as a large shape was pulled out of the water.

"My, my," a voice said. "We've caught a real beauty here. This one's special."

Rags sat up to find herself in a forest with a man who was fishing. This place was beautiful, she realised. Almost perfect. At least it would have been if not for the towering skyscraper frames under construction in the distance.

The man unhooked the fish from his line.

"You'll bring us much joy," he noted.

She wasn't sure if he was talking about her or his catch. She spoke cautiously. "I've never seen a fish that big before."

"Times are changing," the man, the *Fisherman*, said, indicating the buildings ahead. "It's called progress, apparently. Our small town's being swamped by it."

"Town?" Rags asked nervously. "You mean the Black Crossroads?"

The Fisherman dropped the fish into the bucket beside him. "This place is far from black, but it's heading that way, especially with this trickledown effect that's supposed to make us all richer."

A raindrop hit Rags's nose, making her blink. Cautious of the man, she moved into a suspicious crouch. "How did I get here?"

He threw his line back into the water. "Same way as I did. Through a reel-life experience."

Rags frowned. "That doesn't make sense."

His gaze rose to the towers. "Not very much does in this day and age, I'm afraid."

"Got a name?" she asked.

"Many," he answered. "Now I'm just a simple fisherman. What about you?"

Rags paused. There was no way she was going to tell him her real name from the Homeworld. She'd made up many names for herself in her short life and could do so again. She thought about what to say.

A sniff came from nearby. She turned to see a dog by a tree. The animal seemed friendly enough, with large sorrowful eyes that brought up a memory.

When she'd first arrived on Earth, she'd lived in the city streets. The only friend she'd had was a dog with a faded nametag. The animal had been good to her, and she now decided to adopt its name, at least until she found out more about this place. So, with a deep breath, she said,

"Bluey. My name's Bluey."

The Fisherman nodded. "I'm very pleased to meet you, Bluey."

"Yeah, you too," she replied. "Can you tell me how I got here? Or how to get back?"

He gave a little smile. "You fell from the sky. I saw the whole thing. You were surrounded by a halo that carried you down to the marigolds."

She was wary of his tone. "You don't seem surprised."

"You could say that we're a very tolerant sort around here," he stated, "or we used to be until all that started rising." He motioned to the skyscrapers. "You're no threat. After all, there's always bigger fish to fry." He peered into the water, as if searching for one. "As for how to get home? Well, the only way to get anywhere is to go through something else."

"You mean the city?" asked Rags.

"I mean a good piece of fish." He patted the bucket beside him. "That means lunch. Now I know a little town not far from here. Or what's left of one anyway. It's a short walk that way." He indicated a trail behind her.

"You can eat there."

Rags turned and looked. The mist had drifted amidst the trees and, for a brief second, she thought she heard laughter in the forest. Strangely, it resonated with a deep yearning inside her, bringing back memories of her home before the downfall. Her heart glowed and she felt the urge to run towards it.

"From Rags to riches," she murmured.

"Mmmmm?" the Fisherman asked.

Rags thought of Suzi. She didn't want to leave her cousin, but this place was captivating, and she was hungry too.

"You know," she said, "I think I'll take you up on that." She stood up, then hesitated, suspicious from years of hardship. "Just don't screw me over."

"Oh, I wouldn't dream of it," the Fisherman replied. He nodded to the forest. "Just follow that path there, you'll find the village soon enough."

"You're not coming?"

He focused on the water. "I've got a few more fish left to catch. There's a big one that keeps getting away. It's so fast that I haven't even caught its name yet." He looked back at her. "Look at you. You need to eat. You're nothing but rags."

"Not anymore," she said happily. "I'm Bluey now. See you there."

Her mind firmly set on food, she turned and headed into the forest. The mist enveloped her as she walked along the path while the laughter rose around her. As she delved deeper into this newfound realm, she suddenly realised that, for the first time in a long time, she felt happy.

She failed to see a sign at the base of a tree, covered by shrubs. Its paint was scented with just a touch of vanilla, while its words indicated that she was at a crossroads of another kind, for it read simply,

Welcome to Sanders Crossing.

In a very different forest, much further away, Suzi's face was sombre as she walked amidst the burning, ravaged and battle-scarred terrain. There was no laughter here. No beauty. No joy. Just thick clouds of smoke, accompanied by fiery harsh crackles.

She made her way into the shadows, as she'd always done.

Alone.

JT pushed himself up off the ground, bloodied, wearied, and having barely made it out of the Heartbeat alive. He rose, stumbling over the smouldering remains of his ECG base, as well as the lifeless bodies of Cycologists, Trans-plants and other mutations.

Everything was gone, save for Mother. She was practically indestructible, even against the most powerful nuclear blasts. The Toybox also lay buried deep in the debris, intact. It would activate if anyone tried to access Mother, thereby imprisoning them, in an order that couldn't be countermanded. Mother was also shielding herself from the human authorities detecting her, and from Suzi's technology too. It brought JT some comfort to know that Mother wouldn't be found any time soon. Still, with the Shockwave gone, he'd lost everything.

Damn that girl.

Damn Suzi.

It seemed like such a waste.

Still, he had an opportunity to rebuild. It would take time to find his old contacts, but he'd do it. That stupid girl had put the whole damn planet in danger. She'd pay for it. Big time.

A bright light descended over him. No, he suddenly realised. Not just a light. An energy sphere, growing brighter and hotter as it swept in.

His face filled with dread. "Awwwww hell…"

The phenomenon smacked into him, searing his face to a crisp. The last thing he felt was its presence surging into his mind, along with shrieks of clown-like laughter.

Terror-Byte scanned the barren terrain before him. He'd been transported far from the forest. Very far. To a ravaged desert town by the looks of it. The last thing he recalled was standing outside the Heartbeat's remains when a fireball had hit him. He'd seen part of a burning face among its flames, leading him to conclude that whatever had invaded the Heartbeat still survived.

He vaguely remembered spinning through a blue light stream. A Gateway. He'd heard about their prototypes on the Homeworld. Clearly, the Heartbeat's invader had reached a power source, interacted with it, and created a Gateway to bring him here.

A wooden sign creaked in the wind. One holding a clown's face that read simply, *Welcome.*

Terror-Byte didn't move, knowing he was at the decoy ghost town. He recognised it after tapping into the ECG surveillance transmissions. His presence here indicated that something of significance remained, which he was expected to be a part of.

Soft carnival music rose as several balloons floated from a building. They didn't attack, and merely hovered.

The door to an empty saloon opened and a figure emerged. Their hand rose in a gesture of welcome.

Terror-Byte observed them curiously.

Suzi walked through the forest, heading to a road that would lead her to Carrington. She pushed on, out of duty, promising herself that she wouldn't give way to tears. All that mattered was the mission. Nothing else.

Her face twitched.

Her emotions were getting the better of her.

Stand firm, Agent, stand firm, she told herself.

She couldn't keep the bubble down no matter how hard she tried. She cursed herself for her weakness. Just as she felt ready to erupt, someone appeared ahead, walking towards her.

She jumped inwardly. Could it be Rags? Was there even a slight possibility? Even the slightest –

"Suze?"

The voice was older. Different.

Jenny Campbell.

Suzi stopped. At least half the battle was won. She was grateful for that. She stood motionless as Jenny ran in and hugged her.

"You okay, Suze?"

Suzi stayed formal. "Yes, Jenny Campbell."

Jenny moved back a little, sensing her mood. "You're not though, are you? I can tell. Where's your cousin?"

Silence.

"Oh Suze, I'm sorry!"

She came in to hug her again.

Suzi stopped her. "I have yet to determine her fate. I will find her."

"I know you will, Suze. I know."

Jenny rubbed Suzi's shoulder warmly.

Suzi scanned her friend. "Are you intact, Jenny Campbell?"

Jenny stepped away from her. "Mostly."

"What of Cadet Holden?"

"He, uh, didn't make it."

Suzi paused. "Did he go with dignity?"

Jenny held off her tears. "Yeah. He did."

"Then I chose well," Suzi confirmed. "I always do."

They gazed into the forest. The flames were growing, along with the sounds of fire engines and helicopters.

"Hurriflame Two," Jenny said sadly. She winced as the Hurripain flared up. "Did we get all the bad guys?" she asked through the pain.

"To a degree," Suzi answered. "The Heartbeat's no more. The ghost town, however, was part of someone's sick game. Our enemies in the real Black Crossroads have grown more powerful than ever. There's always a bigger threat. Always."

Jenny blinked as the pain in her head dissipated. "We took out the ECG at least. No more Heartbeat. Now, I guess, all we have left is, heart."

Suzi frowned. "I do not understand, Jenny Campbell."

Jenny smiled. "Look at the bigger picture, Suze. I still have my Macadamia award, and we got the creeps who disrupted my ceremony this morning. That's what happens to anyone who ruins our day."

Suzi spoke, her voice barely audible. "I lost Rags."

"Yeah, but you still have me," Jenny pointed out, "and I'm a bonus to anyone. Come on. Let's get away from this… deadbeat, and go hang out somewhere."

"I am not entangled, Jenny Campbell."

"Yeah you are, Suze. More than you think, just like me." She sighed. "God, what a day. You've been through hell, and I –" She stopped, thinking of Gold, then shook the feeling away. "I just want to do something normal. Watch a movie. Get some ice-cream. Look at boys. Can you do that with me?"

Suzi dismissed this. "I'm not interested in the male infants of your planet."

"Oh, so you're into women? That's cool too."

"No, Jenny Campbell." She paused, trying to find the right words. "I loved once. Long ago. He died because of my errors."

Jenny nodded in sympathy. "Sorry to hear that, but I want to forget today. Let's ditch this crap and get some ice-cream."

"That is illogical."

"Yeah, but it's yum. Come on." She took hold of Suzi's shoulder, leading her through the decimated forest towards the main road.

Suzi relented. "I will eat ice-cream with you, Jenny Campbell."

"Thanks," Jenny said. "I tend to go for choc-chip. I know this great little place by the shops near my house. You'll love it."

"I do not love anything, Jenny Campbell."

"You'll love this."

Jenny babbled away excitedly, lost in the moment.

Suzi observed her. Her voice had the same pitch as Rags at times. In many ways, Jenny Campbell reminded Suzi of her cousin.

Of family.

Suzi felt a glimmer inside her. Strangely, she didn't dismiss it. Maybe she was changing, she thought, or perhaps she was too tired to resist. For some reason, Jenny's words were making her feel better. She didn't know why. They just did.

Together, they walked through the darkness, making for the main road and the dim glow of headlights steadily approaching.

Countdown Minus Two:
Collision

Chapter Eleven

Suzi reactivated and was not impressed.

She never deactivated unless it was necessary, and last night, she deemed, *was* absolutely necessary.

After a few hours of sitting with Jenny Campbell at the ice cream parlour, Suzi had been persuaded to return to Jenny's house to watch some images on one of those TV screens that these humans seemed to like. Jenny's father was working the nightshift, so it was just the two of them. Jenny had called to let him know that she was okay, although she had to practically yell at him to stay and do his shift, which he reluctantly did. He was still more than a little concerned for her after the aftermath of her awards ceremony.

Suzi stayed with Jenny, still feeling empty after the loss of Rags, though refusing to admit it. She told herself that it was her duty to protect Jenny Campbell, and after everything they'd gone through, it seemed that the only people they could rely on now were each other.

Watching TV turned out to be a waste of time in Suzi's opinion. It was impractical and boring. Still, sitting with Jenny Campbell in front of something called a romantic comedy seemed better than being alone. Suzi didn't have a clue what these visual patterns were about, but Jenny seemed to be enjoying them and Suzi liked seeing Jenny laugh. Besides, it took Suzi's mind away from the battles ahead, but one movie was more than enough. She hadn't understood any of it, and when the second movie started, she deactivated ten minutes into it.

Now, the next morning had arrived, and she found herself lying awkwardly on the couch, having been pushed over by a gently snoring Jenny who snuggled into her while clutching a blanket filled with teddy bear images.

Suzi's Iyes darkened.

"Infants!" she seethed, pushing Jenny off her.

Jenny rolled back, then forwards, then fell off the couch and hit the floor where she continued to snore down there.

Suzi stood up and started walking away, then stopped and looked back.

"Compassion," she mused thoughtfully. "Regulation 78 of my training protocols. I must practice it."

Robotically, she picked up the blanket from the couch and dumped it on Jenny, covering the top half of her body. Satisfied, Suzi nodded, walked into the kitchen, clicked her head to the side, lowered her voice and ordered, "Report, Echo."

A beep followed. *"Human emergency service personnel are clearing the Heartbeat's remains. Three humans in the area last night were wounded. There are no civilian casualties."*

"What of the global ECG bases?" Suzi asked.

"Destroyed by our cysts," Echo answered. *"Once again, no casualties. Civilian or ECG."*

"Good," said Suzi. "Now we must stop the human authorities accessing any Trans-plant remains or other such experiments."

"Much of the Heartbeat's research was eliminated by the explosion," Echo stated. *"However, I detected several Trans-plants and other individuals fleeing the area. They appear to have vanished."*

"Locate them immediately."

"I'm afraid there's a much more pressing matter to attend to," Echo cut in.

"Go ahead," Suzi ordered.

"There's been a significant change in Miss Campbell's physiology."

"Which is?"

"She's dying."

Echo's words thudded into Suzi like bullets. They hurt. Greatly. She wondered if she'd heard the truth. Echo would never deceive her. It was impossible. Echo was surely being manipulated. That had to be it.

"Explain!" she demanded.

"There's been a significant increase of radioactivity in her brain…"

"Are you certain, Echo?"

"I am. We injected neuro-monitors into her system when we brought her into our vessel. Whatever's hiding in her head has expanded to become lethal. She only has days to live. If that."

Suzi looked back at Jenny. The girl lay on the ground with a blanket over her head.

Like a corpse.

Suzi averted her gaze, feeling like a dark cloud was descending over the whole world. She'd seen too many deaths in her time and recalled their final cries far too vividly. Now they returned with a roaring vengeance.

"Options!" she snapped.

Echo spoke coolly. *"There's little I can do to halt the radiation's progress. However, I'm almost able to contact the Homeworld. I only need to break through the final portions of our enemy's atmospheric shield that prevents us from doing so. Once I'm done, we can call for assistance, then take the girl home and examine her there, with our more advanced technology."*

"Agreed. How long will it take to penetrate the shield?"

"Another hour or so."

"Do it. It's our only hope."

"What is?" Jenny asked, groggily walking into the kitchen. "And keep your voice down. It's enough to wake the dead."

Suzi cursed herself. No one ever sneaked up on her like that. She'd been so concerned for this one human that she'd let herself be distracted to the point where everything else had fallen away. That was unacceptable.

Jenny yawned. "Everything okay?"

"Yes," Suzi replied, turning to face her.

"Liar," Jenny scoffed. She opened the fridge, pulled out an apple, and walked back into the lounge.

Suzi stepped out of sight from Jenny.

"Break through the shield, Echo," she ordered. "Fast!"

"Will do."

The signal went dead.

Suzi stared out of the window, her mind racing with options.

"Is everything cool?" Jenny called out.

Suzi stayed silent, filled with dread. With no other choice but to suppress it, she went into the lounge.

"No," she said, formal as ever. "We are in the correct temperature for this environment, Jenny Campbell."

"No, I meant is everything okay?" Jenny asked, flopping onto the couch.

"There is no threat from the ECG," Suzi stated, "or from the Black Crossroads, yet."

"That's good." Jenny picked up a remote and switched on the TV. The entertainment news appeared. She turned the sound down and said, "Thanks for staying over, Suze."

"It is my duty," Suzi answered logically.

Jenny became absorbed in the words on the screen.

Suzi stood confused, wondering what to do next. She observed Jenny on the couch, then slowly walked over and sat mechanically next to her, rigid and straight.

"It's great having someone here," Jenny said. "Things get a bit rough with my dad working so much. Nightshifts and empty houses are hard on both of us. God, it's so good to actually have people in the house for once."

Suzi struggled to find her words. "Yes. It is… nice."

"Did you like the movie last night?"

"I did not understand it," Suzi replied truthfully.

"You liked the ice-cream. I could see that."

"I liked the ice-cream," Suzi agreed.

"We should do this more often."

Suzi didn't respond. Echo's news burnt deep into her mind. Despite that, the thought of sitting through another movie like last night's was torture. Nevertheless, she spoke, letting her emotions slip. "It is good to spend time with you too, Jenny Campbell."

She regretted her words immediately. They weren't logical, and against protocol. Things were getting too personal.

Jenny nodded. "Yeah. Same goes, Suze." She stretched out and sat up. "I'd better get ready."

"For what?" Suzi asked. "Is there a war on?"

"Yeah," Jenny answered. "It's called school." She stood up and went into her bedroom.

Suzi rose too. "It is better that you rest today, Jenny Campbell. Especially after recent events."

"Normally I'd say yes," Jenny called from her room, "but I want to go in and grab my report. Stupid Miss Ford refuses to a send digital copy, which is sooooo last century. I also want to get out of the house and do something normal, you know?"

"I do not," Suzi replied. "This report card, it is important to you?"

"Hell yeah," said Jenny. "They're my final grades which'll show if I graduate or not. Dad loves it when I'm doing well. You saw him when I got my Macadamia yesterday. I like making him proud. We've gotta have some things in life to look forward to, right?"

Suzi agreed. "Yes, we do, Jenny Campbell." Her protocols lapsed once more and she slipped out with, "I admire your energy."

"Thanks, Suze."

Music rose from the bedroom radio as Jenny changed.

"Just not that kind of energy," Suzi said, turning away.

Her Iyes welled with anger. She hated the music, she hated the movies and she hated so many things about this culture, but one thing was certain, she'd defend it to the death.

Her face hardened as she once again gazed out the window into the darkening sky beyond.

Jenny walked down the school hallway, stunned. It was the end of the school day, almost the school year, and she should have been over the moon, but no. She was exhausted from yesterday, it was raining outside, and her headaches were getting worse. Aside from that, she'd turned up late for class that morning and been yelled at by Miss Ford for it. That didn't bug her so much. What did was that yesterday morning she'd been on top of the world when she'd received her Macadamia.

Not anymore.

She stopped in the middle of the hallway, looking glumly at her report card. The icing on the cake to this crappy day.

"Oh, man…"

Suzi was equally sombre in her ship. Echo had finally established a link to the Homeworld, but it hadn't lasted for long. It wasn't an enemy who'd cut the link, nor a freak occurrence. It was her superiors. They'd ended the conversation abruptly and Suzi hadn't liked it one bit.

"Brainless idiots!" she seethed.

"They're merely taking precautions," Echo explained. *"Despite your fondness for Jenny Campbell, they see her as a threat to Homeworld security. Nobody knows what's in her head. Taking her before the Authority may well be part of our enemy's plan to wipe them out."*

"It's not confirmed that she is a threat, Echo," Suzi stated firmly. "It would be better, strategically, to remove her from this planet."

Echo remained calm. *"We were told that the girl could be transported there only —"*

"As a dissected corpse!" Suzi finished. "That's insulting!"

Echo's glow dimmed at what she said next. *"Nevertheless, you were given a direct order. The Authority has dispatched another vessel to this world. Its priority is to take us both home."*

Bang!

Suzi had punched into a structural beam, creating a large metal dent.

"They're afraid," Echo pointed out.

"Afraid that I'll misjudge the situation and mess things up again!" Suzi snapped. "A girl is dying, and they expect me to retreat and let our enemies win! No, Echo, no! If I leave, everybody loses!"

"If you stay, you'll bring the Authority's wrath upon us."

"I can fix this!"

"The odds are too great."

Suzi glared at Echo furiously. "I've lost everything on the Homeworld, including my reputation. That's why we're here. It's not because they wanted the best. It's because I'm expendable!"

"Agent Chambers —"

"I've lost everyone I care about, I've lost the confidence of my superiors and now I've lost Rags. There's no way, Echo, *no way*, that I'm losing Jenny Campbell!"

"We don't have a choice. The Authority believes that your personal attachment to this girl has clouded your judgement on this operation…"

"I have no personal attachment!"

"… and a replacement Agent has been assigned. He will remain while his vessel transports you and Jenny Campbell to the Homeworld on an automated course."

"That's insulting and stupid," Suzi retorted. "This will be the third secondment of an Agent to this world in a short space of time. That's not efficiency, that's an embarrassment." She glanced at a screen, calculating the stakes. "There'll be a few hours before the replacement Agent arrives. We must do what we can for Jenny Campbell, right to the end. I need you to help me uncover what's in her head, and look for the Black Crossroads too. I'm also out of I-T darts, as Jenny Campbell calls them."

"I do not understand the terminology."

"Tranquilising projectiles for my sleeve. I need more."

"Of course I will aid you but —"

"Good! Let's get to work."

She typed rapidly on a terminal, fighting against her greatest enemy: time.

"Your move," she whispered to the odds. "I'm ready!"

Jenny leaned against her school locker in silence, clutching her report card. The world seemed to fade as she stared at it in shock.

A shadow came over her and a sly voice asked, "Not so great, huh?"

Jenny didn't have to look up to know that it was Maria Longsworth who'd thrown the bitch grenade in. The cow had caught a glimpse of her report back in class and smiled smugly, much to Jenny's disgust.

Jenny crumpled the results up quickly, snapping, "It's none of your damn business!"

She headed down the hall.

Maria followed, calling. "Pretty poor showing for someone who got a Macadamia yesterday!"

Jenny whirled around, glaring at her. "What's up your butt, Longsworth? Besides the school hockey team?"

Maria stepped in. "The Macadamia was mine! I don't know how *you* could get it and then end up with a report like that. It reeks of a dodgy deal, Campbell!"

"You're the only one that reeks around here!" Jenny shot back.

Maria held up her own report card. "One B! The rest A's!"

"Yeah, and I know what the B stands for!" Jenny retorted. She turned and stormed down the hallway.

"You've peaked, Campbell!" Maria called after her. "Peaked!"

Jenny punched a locker door shut and rounded the corner.

"Damn stupid –"

Crash!

A bin dropped heavily, care of Jenny's savage kick.

A cold drizzle of rain tingled over her skin as she stood outside the school's science building. Furiously, she picked up a rock and hurled it over the empty basketball courts, then slammed her bag into a fence, once, twice, three times, before falling back against the wall and sliding down it with her face in her hands, sobbing.

A shadow came over her. Wearily, she looked up to see Suzi, silhouetted against the black clouds.

Jenny sniffed.

Suzi broke the silence. "Your day was not beneficial, Jenny Campbell?"

Jenny reached into her bag, pulled out her crumpled report and held it up. "Cs and Ds. You read 'em. I'll weep."

"That is not good?"

"With these grades I won't make uni." She tossed the card into a nearby puddle.

Suzi paused. "It is discouraging. You received an award yesterday. I expected you to obtain a greater result."

Jenny shook her head. "I've had these stupid headaches ever since the Hurriflame. They're damn distracting and I can't always recall what I want to. The Macadamia Award was for something submitted six months ago, *before* the Hurriflame. These grades were from more recent work, and I'm not like feral Longsworth. I don't have a posse to help me study. Do you know what that feels like?"

"Yes," Suzi answered.

Jenny shuddered, then scrambled to her feet and hugged Suzi tightly. "Oh God, Suze! I'm sorry. I was just letting off a little steam."

Suzi broke away and looked down at Jenny's rear.

Jenny half snickered through the sobs. "No, not like that. It's just Longsworth's gloating. It gets to me. That's all." She wiped her teary eyes with the base of her palm. "I'll make her pay, don't worry."

"I'm not worried," Suzi said.

"Things can't get any worse, right?"

"Yes," Suzi replied. "They can."

Jenny swallowed hard. "Why? What do you know?"

"Jenny Campbell…"

"Go on, Suze, hit me!"

Suzi raised her fist, confused.

"No, just tell me, Suze," Jenny pushed.

Suzi's fist lowered. "You are right, Jenny Campbell. Hitting you would not help."

"Then talk!"

Suzi saw no other choice but to speak the truth. "I've been recalled. Home."

Jenny stared at her in disbelief. "Oh, you are joking, right?"

"I never joke."

"Yeah, I should know. So, you mean…"

"I am to return to the Homeworld. My superiors have deemed me as inefficient. Another vessel is soon to arrive. I will depart with it."

"But you can't!" Jenny blurted out.

"I have no say in the matter," Suzi explained. "If I do not go, others will come for me."

"So, when's that gonna happen? An hour from now?"

"Two point four."

Jenny gasped, raising her hand to her mouth and doing her best to keep it together. "W-well, that really makes things perfect, doesn't it?" She sniffed again. "I mean, there's nothing else that can go wrong, is there?"

Suzi stayed silent.

Dead silent.

Jenny shuddered. "Those bastards. Two and a bit hours, and after everything you've done for 'em they're just replacing you?"

Suzi's tone was resolute. "Whatever happens, you must remember how important you are, Jenny Campbell. Do not let Maria Longsworth discourage you. Your value is much higher than hers."

"Yeah, I know." She hugged Suzi again as the rain fell harder, growing colder by the moment. "I know."

Suzi's hands rose slowly to her own neck and she reached behind it, pressing gently. A click followed and she removed an object. Jenny stepped back, looking at it. It seemed like a piece of jewellery. A chain with a strange design, holding a small white orb in the middle.

Suzi spoke. "I want you to have this, Jenny Campbell."

Jenny bit her lip. "So underneath your hardcore commando crap you're a closet human, huh?"

Suzi ignored this. "This object is called a Dragon Slayer. Religion was outlawed on my Homeworld long ago, in favour of reason and logic."

"I can't see you as the religious type, Suze."

"I am not. My family were. This belonged to my maternal sire."

"It was your mum's? Oh God, no Suze, I can't…"

Suzi struggled to speak, finding it hard to get the words out. "You are the closest thing I have felt to family in a long time, Jenny Campbell. The Slayer is said to grant protective powers to those who believe in it. You need protection."

"Yeah, but who'll protect you, hot shot?"

"I can look after myself. Take it."

"Suze…"

"Take it."

Jenny submitted. The Slayer tingled in her fingers. "It's beautiful. I like the colour."

"The texture comes from an alloy I coated it with," Suzi explained. "It prevented my superiors from detecting it on me. The switch on its back renders it invisible."

Jenny grinned. "That's hell rebel." She put it around her neck, touching the chains together. They linked automatically.

"Thanks," she said softly. "This means a lot, Suze."

Suzi's reply was equally soft. "It means a lot to me too, Jenny Campbell."

"I'll take good care of it."

"It will take good care of you as well," Suzi told her. "Seraphim Dragon Slayers have been highly effective in the past."

"What Dragon Slayers?"

"Seraphim. It is…" She paused, then spoke hesitantly. "The name of my Homeworld."

Jenny nodded.

A thunderclap came from overhead.

"What do you say we get out of here?" Jenny asked. "Go somewhere and celebrate your last couple of hours on earth?"

Suzi peered over Jenny's shoulder and her gaze darkened. "I think someone's already decided that for us."

Jenny turned and gasped.

A red balloon hovered over the oval's edge, by the woods, with a cartoon image of sunglasses on its side. Another balloon ascended, also with sunglasses. A blue one followed, then an orange, then a pink. All rose to a certain height and stayed there, as if making an announcement.

Or an invitation.

Jenny tensed. "Looks like hell's having a party and we're the guests of honour."

Suzi spoke darkly. "For the Toymaster."

"So how come we're still here?" Jenny wondered. "With the ECG, the Germinator and Gastoff out of the way, why are we not being hit by Hurricane Psycho?"

Suzi considered the possibilities. "It's because we have something he wants." Her tone hardened. "I'm going in."

"You sure about that?" Jenny asked. "You've seen what he can do, right?"

"I have no choice, Jenny Campbell."

"Then I'm going too."

Suzi's head turned mechanically to face her.

Jenny shrugged. "What can he do to make my day worse?"

"Many things. From the evidence I have seen he can —"

"Enough, Suze," Jenny cut in, holding up the Dragon Slayer. "Protective locket, remember? We might as well spend your last few hours here doing something useful. We can't run and hide from this garbage. Let's just face it. Together."

"Yes," Suzi agreed. "Together."

Jenny held her hand out. Suzi copied this by raising her own hand and leaving it out in the air. Jenny reached in, clasped Suzi's hand around her own, and the two of them headed into the rain, making for the looming balloons in the distance.

Chapter Twelve

Suzi and Jenny entered the woods. They came to the river, followed it to where the balloons were hovering, emerged into a clearing and stopped.

Sitting against the trees were two dead bodies, propped up like toys. Their faces were covered in white make-up, with black circles encompassing their eyes. Their lips were bright red, pinned up into forced smiles, while their clothes had been replaced by colourful clown costumes. Dark gloves covered their hands. Frills surrounded their ankles, wrists, and necks, and on either side of them were two giant human-sized teddy bears, with metal spikes for teeth.

The balloons held their position, bobbing in the wind.

Jenny cringed. "This is the sickest teddy bears' picnic I've ever been on."

Suzi approached the bodies, scanned them, clicked her head to one side and spoke softly, out of earshot from Jenny. "Analysis, Echo?"

"James Sears and Matt Koresh," came the reply. *"Two students from Carrington High. They're dead and gutted. A transference has also taken place."*

Suzi picked up a stick from the ground, jabbed it into a boy's hand and broke the skin.

Jenny grimaced. "Suze!"

No blood emerged, only stuffing and sawdust flaking in the breeze.

Jenny was confused. "Is that supposed to be in there?"

Suzi dropped the stick. "No."

"Then where's what's supposed to be there?"

Suzi indicated the giant teddy bears. "In there." She kicked one lightly. It wobbled like a waterbed.

Jenny went green and backed away. "I'm gonna gag!"

"It will not be beneficial," Suzi warned.

Jenny leaned on a tree to support her queasiness. She shut her eyes tightly and asked, "Why would anyone do that to 'em?"

"It's a declaration of war," Suzi answered darkly. "Once again, the innocent have died so the guilty can gain my attention." She controlled her anger and refocused. "Did you know these boys, Jenny Campbell? They were from your school. Their names were James Sears and Matt Koresh."

Jenny's knees gave way, crunching onto a pile of leaves below, as she trembled. "They were in my English class. They were miffed that I beat them for the Macadamias." She rested her head on the tree again.

Suzi saw an envelope protruding from one boy's pocket. A pair of black sunglasses was drawn on the front, like the balloons.

Another invitation, she concluded. This one more formal.

She ripped it open.

"What's that?" Jenny asked, looking up.

Suzi read the contents. They showed a series of cartoons. The first was of a girl with headaches who resembled Jenny Cambell. That was easy enough to see. The second cartoon was of the girl approaching a grave. The third portrayed a clown. A marionette-like figure descending from the sky, reaching for the sick girl's head. The fourth showed several orbs ascending from her forehead as she smiled, now healed. The fifth revealed the clown hovering over a building with a cross on top.

One that was familiar.

"Suze?" Jenny pressed.

"X marks the spot," Suzi murmured. She crumpled up the note, putting it in her pocket. "It's our official invitation, to the Black Crossroads."

The rain on Jenny's cheek felt colder than ever. "Boy, when it rains it pours. Does it say where it is?"

Suzi nodded. "Yes."

"So where then?"

Suzi went silent, like a heavy cloud from the black sky above had descended, covering her.

"Where is it?" Jenny pushed. "Where's the damn Crossroads?"

Suzi didn't answer.

"Tell me!" Jenny demanded.

Suzi glanced ahead, indicating for her to turn around.

Jenny did so.

A lone balloon had broken away from the rest and was hovering over the only building in sight, as if to guide them there.

"Of course," Jenny realised. "The one place on the planet more terrifying than anywhere else." She swallowed hard. "Bloody high school!"

Suzi stepped forwards, gazing at it. "He's been like a spider hiding among us the whole time, manipulating events since the beginning, and using us to get rid of his rival factions who couldn't detect him. Now they're gone, and he wants what's in your head."

Jenny stepped beside Suzi, looking at the ominous building before them "Sounds like he's getting desperate."

Suzi's head rose. "The only way to discover the truth is to go in and find it."

Jenny trembled. "You sure about that? We could be giving him just what he wants and –" She placed her palm on her forehead. "Arrrrgh!"

Suzi saw the bodies behind them. The wind had picked up, along with the rain, smearing their white make-up and red clown lipstick, making it seem like they were crying long tears of blood.

Suzi's gaze returned to the school as she considered her options. Jenny Campbell could easily end up as another corpse, she thought. Then again, if they didn't go in at all, the girl would surely die. There had to be a way to save her, but they'd be walking into the beast's lair. When it came to Jenny Campbell's life, however, there was no choice. Suzi wasn't letting her out of her sight. They'd have to go in.

Suzi knew there'd be very little room for error, and she'd be walking a fine line between life and death. Jenny Campbell's that was. One wrong move and Jenny would be lost, just like Rags and the rest of Suzi's family, and so many others along the way too. Suzi vowed not to let history repeat itself.

"We're going in," she said firmly.

"Odds aren't good," Jenny said back. "I think we can beat 'em though."

"Logic suggests –"

"Stuff logic. We're fighters, aren't we?"

Suzi was impressed. "You inspire great faith in me, Jenny Campbell. You are correct. The odds are against us. Others of my kind are coming to take me home but I'm finishing this job before they do. Permanently."

"Yeah, let's kick his butt!"

Suzi thought this over. What good would that do, she wondered. A more effective measure would be to kick an enemy in the stomach or the head or somewhere useful.

Her Earwig buzzed and Echo, who'd been monitoring the conversation, spoke. *"I'd advise extreme caution, Agent Chambers. I know you can't ignore the possibility of a cure for Jenny Campbell, but the risk is immense. You're being manipulated into entering the building."*

Jenny wailed, half doubling over from a searing Hurripain burst.

Suzi lowered her voice. "This is the only chance we have, Echo. I came here to do a job and I'm finishing it. If I fail, I die, which I have no problem with since I'm in no hurry to go home, especially not as a failure. My judgement's clear."

Echo was wary. *"Once you're inside I won't be able to contact you. If I couldn't detect our enemies in there after all this time, then I won't be able to locate you either."*

"I know the risks, Echo, but our enemies have declared war. I'll make sure they get it."

"Wars always have casualties. You know that."

"Yes," Suzi replied. "Too well."

Echo relented. *"Very well. I'll do what I can to assist you."*

Jenny blinked away her tears as the Hurripain subsided. "God! That was a bad one! I feel sick." She drew a shaky breath. "Were you talking to someone?"

"I was reviewing the situation," Suzi answered truthfully.

"Whatever." She rubbed away the final remnants of the Hurripain from her temples. "All right, Suze, I'm over taking crap from freakin' everything. Let's finish this. Once and for all, huh?"

"You are right, Jenny Campbell," Suzi agreed. "Let's finish this. Once and for all."

They stood motionless, staring at the school.

"Why aren't you moving?" Suzi asked.

"Why aren't you?" Jenny asked back.

"I'm waiting for you."

Jenny gave a little smile. "Nah, you're scared, just like me. You're holding off for as long as possible and hanging onto what you've got. You don't want to lose anything else."

Suzi indicated a storm cloud, circling over the school. "Interesting. The eye of the storm is always its calmest point."

Jenny pulled Suzi forward with one hand whilst clasping the Dragon Slayer on her neck with the other. "Got that right."

Together, they headed for the building.

Suzi gazed ahead, addressing the enormously high stakes in a dangerously low tone. "You want to play games?" Her tone lowered further. "Game on!"

Chapter Thirteen

The school's great double doors stood wide open.

They were welcoming.

A little too welcoming.

Suzi and Jenny stepped inside.

Everything about this place felt different to Jenny. It didn't help that the storm outside was gaining momentum. The rain thudded loudly onto the roof, echoing throughout the hallway. The growing thunder enflamed her Hurripain, as did the freezing wind billowing in from the main doors, engulfing them in its path. To Jenny, it was laughing. Childishly.

Her hand rose to her neck, clutching the Dragon Slayer and feeling it tingle between her fingers.

Suzi clicked her head to one side and whispered, "Echo?"

The only response was static. There were traces of Echo's voice, but nothing clear.

Her Echo was fading.

She walked with Jenny to the end of the hallway. They rounded a corner, then stopped abruptly.

"Whoa!" Jenny whispered in shock.

Hanging by their necks and dangling from the ceiling, were dozens of mannequins. Most were the size of adults, some were baby-sized, and all were made from different materials. Plastic, metal, glass, even china, there

were so many kinds. Each had strings around their wrists and ankles, link-
ing their limbs to the ceiling and making them twist in perverse macabre
dances. Even worse, they were all bleeding, with great wet red patches
dripping from their distorted faces onto the blood-splattered floor.

Jenny placed a hand over her mouth. "This dude's sick."

"More than you think," Suzi said.

"What do you mean?"

Silence.

A thought hit Jenny. "Do you know 'em, Suze?"

Suzi relented. "Yes. They're all casualties of war. Replications of my
family and others on the Homeworld who perished. Rags is there too.
That raggedy one by that locker."

She glanced up at it.

Jenny followed her gaze.

"What bothers me is that one," Suzi said, with a nod. "The clown in
the middle there."

Jenny noticed the white-faced figure with spiked orange hair and
blood-red lips. His clothes were colourful, though dominated by green,
and his face seemed familiar.

"Is that…" Jenny began.

"Yes," Suzi replied. "It's the ECG commander. The one who calls himself JT."

"Why's he dribbling blood?"

"I'm more concerned about the symbol on his neck."

The speaker system clicked.

Eerie carnival music began playing throughout the hallway.

A cord on another mannequin snapped, sending it falling to the floor,
crashing heavily and bursting into a torrent of blood upon impact. Suzi
and Jenny leapt back as another mannequin fell, then another, then a
whole heap, as waves of blood burst around them. The china one went
next, shattering loudly and half-deafening Jenny. The glass one followed,
shooting spinning shards that forced them to duck. One by one the mannequins fell, until only the clown with JT's face remained.

Jenny shuddered. "I always said that school was a stupid bloody place
full of clowns!"

Suzi's tone was dark. "This one knows exactly what he's doing though."

"So why hasn't he fallen like the rest of 'em?"

The clown's eyes snapped open.

Jenny gave a cry.

The thing was alive.

Its lips curled into a mocking grin, revealing two long fangs as its head rose slowly, as if waking from a slumber.

"Yesssssss," he announced in a crackling purr. "This has always been my favourite place to –" his neck twisted awkwardly within the noose, "– hang out!"

He clicked his fingers sharply. His wrist strings detached, along with the cord on his neck, dropping to the ground and leaving him hovering in mid-air with his frilly arms outstretched. Gracefully, he descended to the slimy red floor as the breeze whistled around them.

Silence followed.

He sneered, before his arm flew up in an operatic sweep.

Several lockers burst open, releasing waves of blood into the hallway. Long streams of fire came next, bringing sickening cocktails of flames and thick ooze.

Jenny averted her gaze.

Suzi stood robotically, staring detached at the demonic clown.

He spoke over the roaring chaos. "Finally, my dears, your inner child has been –" He grinned. "Unleashed!"

He cackled and swung an arm in their direction. The savage blow of his will slammed them back against the open lockers where the hot metal and bubbling blood burnt their backs.

Jenny tried to move but couldn't. Suzi was unable to either. His telekinetic powers held them in place.

Jenny winced, from the heat on her back and the Hurripain in her head. She fought against the pain and asked Suzi, "JT?"

"That's not him," Suzi replied. "That thing took his form."

"Okay, so he's stuffed," Jenny quipped, indicating several feathers sticking out from the clown's costume. "Who is he?"

"The Toymaster," Suzi answered.

The hideous clown moved his face in close to Jenny's, like a wolf sniffing its prey. "Yes. All that potential. Just waiting to be released!"

Jenny knew he wasn't referring to her character and did her best to keep her emotions in check.

His long fingers rose, holding her chin with an icy grip. She tried to cry out but couldn't, for her lips were pushed outwards.

"You're going as white as I am," he purred, taking glee at the blood draining from her face. "You're coming along nicely."

Suzi struggled to break free from the locker, without success. "Let the girl go! I'm the one you want!"

"No, you're on a whole different level in this game," the Toymaster retorted. "It's called snakes and ladders. You fight the snakes while I climb the ladders." He glanced at each of them in turn, then leaned in, peering into Jenny's eyes. "Do you remember me? Hmmm?"

Jenny trembled.

"We've met before," the Toymaster whispered.

Jenny flinched as the memories returned...

She's back in the Hurriflame, lying in the burning woods holding a soft, squishy object. She looks down, seeing a sinister clown's face staring up at her. Her eyes widen as its malignant force flows into her head...

"You took something of mine," he pressed. "You didn't mean to, of course. I had to hide it somewhere. You were the perfect living doll." He moved in closer. "What you hold in that precious little head of yours, my girl, has a place close to my heart. You could say it's my birthday presence."

Jenny cringed. "What the hell did you put there?"

His icy breath streamed across her face. "Exactly what's killing you, my dear. Didn't your best friend tell you? You're dying."

Jenny glanced at Suzi. "Is he serious?"

"Don't listen to him, Jenny Campbell," Suzi warned.

"This is my damn life we're talking about!"

"Not for looonnnggggg," the Toymaster sang playfully. He released his grip and stepped back.

"He's creeping me out, Suze! Is he telling the truth or what?"

Suzi relented. "Yes, but —"

"WHAT…?" Jenny shrieked, cutting her off.

"Music to my ears," the Toymaster swooned. "Bliss!"

"I'm dying?" Jenny cried to Suzi.

"We don't have time for this…" Suzi cut in.

"I have less!" Jenny protested. "I'm dying, Suze? How could you not tell me?"

"He's the enemy, Jenny Campbell, not me."

"Yeah, sometimes I wonder! How long have I got?"

"Hours."

"If that," the Toymaster pointed out.

The shock hit Jenny hard and she would have collapsed if the Toymaster's will hadn't held her up like a ragdoll. The Hurripain flared again, along with the realisation that this big black pain cloud was killing her. It was an effort to fight against it and cry, "Haven't I been through enough? Hasn't Suze?"

A door squeaked loudly behind them and a figure emerged from a classroom. Jenny could only move her head slightly to see them.

"Miss Ford?" she asked, confused.

"Jenny Campbell," her teacher said. "Come with me, please."

The sharp jab of a syringe pierced Jenny's leg and she felt a warm rush of fluid flow into her veins. The Toymaster's will fell away as dizziness overcame her and she slumped into Miss Ford's arms, groaned, and looked up at her teacher groggily. "You? That's no surprise. You always acted possessed."

Miss Ford threw the syringe away. "Not this time. This is all me."

"What…?" Her vision blurred as she was turned around and half-carried down the hallway. "Where are you taking me?"

The Toymaster spoke up. "To my *lav-oratory*. We need to flush out those nasty little demons in that head of yours."

Jenny felt weaker by the moment. "Suze…"

"You needn't worry," Suzi said. "I'll be coming for you."

"So she says…" the Toymaster mused.

Jenny struggled to stay awake.

"I bet my grades were forged too," she told Miss Ford bitterly.

"Naturally," her teacher replied, taking her away. "You needed to be in a depressive state. You'll find out why soon enough. Your real grades were quite impressive."

"You're a bi—"

Her head dropped.

"Wake up, Jenny," Miss Ford said, shaking her. "We're not there yet."

Jenny stirred, opening her eyes a little.

Suzi watched as they rounded a corner and were gone.

The Toymaster loomed over her. "We need to talk, mother dear, but not rationally. At least not on your part."

He stretched out with his will.

Suzi felt her Iyes vibrate. Sparks ignited as they flew off her face and into his outstretched hand. Waves of searing, unfiltered light made her let loose with an anguished cry as he released her from his grasp. She dropped to her knees, covering her empty eye sockets and doing her best to block out the world.

His fingers encompassed her glasses as he mocked, "I'd always intended for you'd bow to me one day…"

He made a twisting motion in the air, raising her head to face him. She growled, fighting against the pain, as trickles of dark liquid streamed from her face. He grinned, pocketed her glasses smartly, and said, "I'm so privileged for being the one to finally make you see the light. If it's one thing I love, it's having my own wind-up toy. Now let's play!" He leaned in and whispered, "… In my Playpen!"

Jenny awoke feeling sick. The Hurripain was burning through her forehead. Her vision was blinding. Sounds were magnified to the extreme. Metal coverings had been placed on her temples, which irritated her too, making her want to rip them off. That, however, was impossible, for she found herself upright, strapped to the wall. She struggled a little, to no avail, and did her best to recall how she'd got here. There were vague memories of blacking out intermittently whilst being carried by Miss Ford, but it was the shock of seeing this room that had given her the big fade-out. Waking up to see it all again made her want to hurl.

She was in a psycho child's toyroom. There were enormous black teddy bears, hideous mannequins, a stuffed jester strapped into an electric chair, and a giant jack-in-the-box with a dagger on its side. Luckily, the box was closed. She hoped it would stay that way.

She shut her eyes, blocking out the horror.

Another Hurripain flareup made her cringe and open them again.

"Hold still," Miss Ford ordered from behind a terminal.

She flicked a switch.

Jenny winced. "It hurts."

"It's about to get a whole lot worse," Miss Ford warned. "Count yourself lucky. You'll have no more headaches when we're done."

"Doesn't matter," Jenny said wearily. "I'm dying, apparently."

"Only if we allow what's in there to stay put," Miss Ford told her. "My job's to remove it. I've put a couple of chips in your ears. They'll allow this tech to interface directly with your brain. Thing is, you may not survive the process, but you've got a chance at least. I give it a sixty-forty shot, not in your favour. Either way, no more headaches for you."

"Gee, thanks, teach." She blinked the tears out of her eyes. "How'd you get mixed up in all this?"

"Child at heart," Miss Ford answered.

"Or just a sad old lady, huh?"

Miss Ford stopped. "I didn't choose this. The Toymaster found me during the Hurriflame."

Jenny cringed from the pain. "What were you doing there?"

"I was at the party, same as you," came the reply. "You didn't see me. I made sure of that. I was having a little too much fun out the back."

Jenny grimaced. "God, you're sick!"

Miss Ford shrugged. "As I said, child at heart. If it's one thing I hate, it's getting older. I like to feel young. I love revisiting my youth and… doing things." She grinned at a cheeky memory. "It was great too, until I looked out the window and saw the Hurriflame sweeping in, so I split. Sure, I wanted to save my butt, but I also knew that we were about to get a heap of attention that'd bring the cops. They wouldn't understand what I was doing there. To them it would look dodgy."

"It's more than dodgy, ya sad old perv!"

"The point is, I got out of there and found you, stretched out before a toy clown. I liked its look and picked it up. It showed me things. Pretty things. I like pretty things. That's why I became a teacher."

"Ugh!"

Miss Ford continued. "He wasn't the Toymaster then. Just a toy on the run from its creator, with some very big secrets. He hid the biggest in your head." She keyed in a sequence. "My first job was to kill his creator, a Fugitive from their Homeworld. That was easy. The idiot was so absorbed by the Hurriflame that I only had to run up and push him into a flame pit. I also dealt with another snooping Agent by guiding some big ugly weeds in his direction. When everything settled down, my little doll gave me a crash course in his tech. He modified my eyes too, making me resistant to your friend's glasses, just like you, only now he sees everything I see. I pretended to obey your friend a few times, just to keep up the act, but everything I did for the Toymaster was my choice. He needed a human agent. If he'd used any alien tech, your friend would have picked it up."

Jenny shut her eyes again, more tightly this time. "So what is he?"

"A computer program."

Suzi flinched after saying these words, resisting the pain. The white glow around her intensified as she stood in a giant cylinder, aptly termed the Playpen.

The Toymaster loomed before it, leering at her. Behind him, working at a terminal like the one Miss Ford was using, was Terror-Byte. Nearby, were several grotesque Trans-plants, taken from the Heartbeat's remains and further adapted by the Toymaster.

Not that Suzi saw much of it. She wasn't totally blind without her Iyes, and could make out a few shadowy shapes in a swirling black mass, but her head throbbed in agony, making it painful to speak. Nevertheless, she rose above it.

"You're a digital lifeform," she reinforced. "Nothing more. A more accurate term would be 'a psycho-pathogen'."

The Toymaster loved this description. "We all start off as blips in someone's imagination. Reality happens when curious energies want to play."

Suzi continued, recalling what she'd seen with her Iyes. "The symbol on your neck shows that you're a Sigma Virus. A sick form of cyber warfare that the Homeworld factions used to attack the Authority with."

"Oh, he's much more than a Sigma Virus," Miss Ford said. "He's long since evolved from that. Now he's a weapon that can literally transform planets. You could call him —"

"A Terror-Former," the Toymaster sneered.

"The Shockwave helped him evolve," Miss Ford explained, "plus the body of that ECG Captain. The Toymaster needed someone with a childish mentality. JT was perfect." She twisted a dial. "The other Agent, the one the ECG called Terror-Byte, would have made a better vessel for the Toymaster. Trouble is, Agent bodies lack the creativity the Toymaster craves. Besides, the lifeforms tucked away deep inside Agent bodies are so paranoid that their metal casings hold dozens of counter-security measures, including a self-destruct mechanism. No one can get near them. The Toymaster would've struggled to get inside. That's the problem with Agents. They bury everything deep down and are so repressed. Still, Terror-Byte had his uses and, like me, was *persuaded* to work for us."

She initiated another command and continued.

"The Toymaster was different when he was brought to this world. Very different. He wasn't even a toy clown then. Just a mutation of a Sigma Virus created by the Fugitive. When the Fugitive landed, he took samples of the ECG's Shockwave and played around with 'em to use as a weapon against the Homeworld. The Sigma Virus got curious, merged with the Shockwave, and a sentient life form was created. The Fugitive didn't know the results of his experiments, the new lifeform stayed hidden, and its first and only instinct was to strive for power. For that it needed a body, but its capacity was limited, so it entered a toy clown instead. One from a kid called Rags."

Jenny gasped in realisation.

Miss Ford spoke on. "Once the virus entered the toy, it could move slightly. When the Hurriflame hit, the clown stole the Fugitive's big secret, hitched a ride in his rucksack, and dropped itself off in the forest. I found the clown right after you did and became his plaything. If he said dance, I danced. If he said play, I played, and if he said kill then I did it without hesitation. Thing is, you got to the clown first and took exactly what it had stolen."

"What did Jenny Campbell take from you?" Suzi asked the scowling clown face that had once belonged to JT. "You said she took it unintentionally. Logic indicates that you let her keep it as part of your twisted game. What is it? What's in her head that you so desperately want back?"

"Go on," Jenny encouraged. "What's the big vomit bag want?"
Miss Ford relented. "Fine. It's called the Black Circuit. It's for his PET. What you have is the key to opening its cage."

"My darling, darling PET," the Toymaster whispered.
Suzi suddenly understood. "A Planetary Eruption Trigger. An outlawed weapon that the Fugitive stole from the Homeworld. You're going to use it as a deterrent to force the Authority to back off or you'll rip this planet in half." Her anger rose. "And the operating circuit, the *Black* Circuit, lies in Jenny Campbell's head!"

"You're saying there's a bomb switch in my brain?" Jenny asked in disbelief.
Miss Ford activated a sequence. "It's not in solid form. It was broken into particles and disguised so minutely that it's pretty much invisible. Its instinct is to reform, but every time it does it grows a little and you get headaches. A sneeze'll soon be enough to blow your head off."
Jenny shuddered. "You're going to take it out though, right?"
"Yes, but it won't be painless," came the reply. "Getting it in there was easy. Getting it out is also a breeze, normally. Thing is, it uploaded itself into your head during the Hurriflame. Mix in the ion particles with the Shockwave, and abnormalities are born. The circuit's growing, and evolving too. We need it at a certain density for extraction. The only way to get it to that level, without any tech, is to make you depressed."
"Which is why you forged my grades, huh?"
"As well as organising a few triggers over the last couple of months."

"You mean like stuffing those boys down by the river to get me here," Jenny said sourly.

"Oh yeah," her teacher confirmed. "Lowered your mood, didn't it? Getting the circuit out's a delicate procedure and if you die, it dissipates. Same thing happens if it's extracted wrongly. You felt the effects when the Germinator tried forcing it from your brain. If it was that easy to rip out, then the Toymaster would've swooped into the greenhouse and saved you from the Trans-plants himself. Your problem, Jenny Campbell, is that you're not as dense as we thought. You're too much of a fighter. We'll have to change that."

"So why go to all this trouble, teach? Why not just kidnap me when all this started? Rags was held in the ghost town. Why wasn't I?"

"We needed to get rid of the other factions first, kid. You and your friend were pretty good at doing that. Anyway, that wasn't part of the plan."

"Part?" Jenny retorted. "What's the rest? The Toymaster can teleport now, right? He hit the Shockwave so that should make a difference."

"Not quite, Campbell. Your friend was smart. She introduced a mutation into the Shockwave, erasing its Zymac particles, which means teleporting's no longer an option for anyone. The Toymaster's working on fixing that, but he has other priorities first."

"I'm still alive," Suzi said to the Toymaster. "You need me. What for?" Terror-Byte hit a switch.

"We have to move fast," Miss Ford stated.

"Hang on," Jenny retorted. "I need to know –"

Her temples flared and she flinched. It wasn't from the Hurripain this time, but Miss Ford's commands. Jenny winced as the chips in her ears heated up, making her scream.

Suzi tensed as the Playpen's blinding white light became excruciating. Despite her resolve, its forces were overwhelming, and she quivered as their immense pressures enveloped her.

Jenny wailed as the Hurriflame ignited, care of the terminal. It felt like a giant object was being sucked out of her nose, splitting her head in half.

Miss Ford observed the readouts. The Black Circuit was being extracted nicely, but the possibility of Jenny's survival had dropped from forty to thirty percent. She ignored the girl's cries and focused on ensuring a smooth extraction.

Jenny's head rose defiantly. "Suze…!"

"Jenny Campbell," Suzi whispered, fighting against the pain. "Jenny…"

The Toymaster leered over Suzi's weakening form. She shook violently, on the verge of breaking apart.

He stepped in, his eyes widening with manic glee. "Yesssssssss…"

His frilly white hand rose for her.

Suzi prepared for the worst.

Chapter Fourteen

Bang!

The lab door flew in, shooting across the room and slamming a Trans-plant into a wall, leaving it dazed.

Several figures entered.

Agents.

Ones who'd arrived with the help of Suzi's Echo.

The Toymaster turned to them, delighted. The one thing this psycho-pathogen loved was a battle.

He started to speak. "Well, this is —"

A fierce laser blast hurled him into the wall. He slumped to the floor as several objects fell from his pockets.

More shots fired, felling the Trans-plants and sending the rogue Agent Terror-Byte diving for cover. He fled through the rear door, unable to fight against such odds.

Two Agents moved to pursue him.

Tendrils from below clasped their necks. Unfazed, the Agents fired into the Trans-plant on the floor. The tendrils loosened and they stepped away.

The Toymaster, unaffected by the gun blast to his chest, popped back up to his feet. "A battle? For me? Oh, you shouldn't have!" His arm rose. "I always loved being the *torcher-er!*"

His arm swiped down. The sheer force of his will sent every Agent recoiling as fierce electrical bursts hit the surroundings.

An Agent leapt up, lunging for him. Another blow from the Toymaster's will hurled the Agent through a terminal. A second Agent reached the Toymaster, struck out and sent the clown reeling, head over heels, into a wall.

The Agent moved in, stating unemotionally, "You cannot win this conflict."

The Toymaster twirled the fingers of one hand. "Liar, liar, pants on fire!"

The Agent erupted into flames and was flippantly discarded.

The remaining agents fired. The Toymaster brushed the shots away, diverting them all over the place.

One hit the Playpen, weakening it.

Suzi couldn't see the impact, but sure felt it. Seizing the opportunity, she lunged, crashing through the barrier and dropping to the floor. Her hand landed on an object, wrapping around it.

Her Iyes.

They'd fallen from the Toymaster's pocket.

Suzi refused to believe in miracles but right now she made an exception, for she hadn't expected to find them so easily. She brought them to her face and locked them in with a click. A hum followed, her pain subsided and her vision returned, along with an immense wave of relief.

Several hazy shapes came into focus. They morphed, sharpening and solidifying in her perception, to show the four remaining Agents trying to outmanoeuvre the Toymaster.

One ran at him from the side while another fired.

The Toymaster laughed playfully and spun on the spot, as if in a dance. Fluidly, he dodged the shots, grabbed the running Agent by the neck and hurled him into his comrade, sending them crashing to the floor. Before either could rise, the Toymaster ran in and let loose with a savage kick, booting their heads off in a fiery blaze.

The third Agent dived at him.

The Toymaster raised his hand, forming it into a long metal pole.

"I always loved clubbing," he said, and smacked that Agent's head off too.

Only one Agent remained.

The Toymaster leaned his head to one side, observing him curiously. The angle was so awkward that the Toymaster's head seemed painfully out of position. He sneered mockingly. "Crack open the pain jug, I'm about to go on a binge!"

His mouth opened, revealing his fangs, and he ran for the Agent.

The Agent ran back at him.

The two leapt in the air, swept in, then the Toymaster vanished.

The Agent dropped to the ground, alert. There was no sign of the Toymaster. Only Suzi was left. She stood behind a terminal, her fingers a blur as they flickered across it. High above, in the wallscreen behind her head, the Toymaster's hideous face gazed down from inside it.

"The other side of the looking glass?" he jeered, now speaking through the digital mainframe.

Suzi smacked the mute button and continued working.

The Agent approached her.

"Is the situation contained?" he asked.

Her response was cool. "Hardly. It's a very big situation. The Sigma Virus is overriding my commands. My control over it will only be temporary."

Several sparks sizzled from the wallscreen.

She hit another button, stabilising it.

The Agent stepped behind the terminal, alongside her. Her head rose and she met his gaze. Shadows flickered in their Iyes, like waves of emotion, before they returned their attention to the terminal.

"Agent," Suzi said formally.

"Agent," he replied, equally formally.

She worked fast on the touchscreen. "There can be little doubt that you volunteered for this mission."

"That is correct," he answered, assisting her with her work. "You left the Homeworld hurriedly, without even a farewell as I recall."

"I was reassigned."

"Records state that you not only requested a reassignment, but manipulated several digital systems to ensure it would happen. Your deception was discovered after you left. You should have known better. No one can sneak into the Catacombs undetected."

Suzi cursed inwardly.

He continued. "Your psychological profile reveals much fear in you. It's a genetic trait of your family, hence why you're so reckless, even for an Agent."

The shadows in Suzi's Iyes swirled again and she spoke with great restraint. "Your subordinates lie dead around us while you still stand, thanks to me."

The Agent wasn't fazed. "Your physical reactions indicate that you are indeed grateful. My technology does not lie. It states that you desire me just as much as I desire you. Our next logical step, once this mission is over, is to develop an intense, intimate relationship."

"We have no relationship."

"My technology's readings say otherwise."

Crunch!

She'd kneed him hard in the thigh, knowing exactly where to aim.

His face displayed no emotion. "You've broken my technology."

"It was only a minor piece," she stated.

They glared at each other so fiercely that their faces nearly changed colour.

The monitor behind them sparked.

Their attention returned to the terminal and their fingers rapidly worked the screens, trying to keep the Toymaster contained.

Suzi spoke, using the Agent's designated serial number. "I have the situation under control, 421."

Agent 421 spoke coolly. "Arrogance is also specified in your reports. The Authority is concerned about it."

Suzi ignored this. "How informed are you on current events?"

"Fully," he answered. "Your Echo told me everything."

"I have learnt more," she stated. "A Black Circuit lies in Jenny Campbell's head. It's an operating mechanism for a Planetary Eruption Trigger, that the Toymaster calls his PET, which can split this planet in two. He wishes to play games with such a device."

"Where is this PET now?" 421 pressed.

"I'm about to determine that." She changed the digital screen, then stopped.

"You've discovered something?" he asked.

Suzi went silent.

He examined the readouts, which did indeed show the location of the PET. "This location is significant to you?"

"Yes," Suzi answered. "It's emanating from a human command post, once known as the Heartbeat. An area, which Jenny Campbell has since termed, the Deadbeat." She paused. "Records state that the ECG discovered the PET shortly after the Hurriflame hit and stored it there. Evidence indicates that they didn't know what the PET was, or how to use it." She paused again. "If the Black Circuit from Jenny Campbell's head activates the PET, it will bring about another Hurriflame. This one will be global."

421 showed no emotion. "Is the PET secure in the Deadbeat?"

Suzi analysed the readings. "For now. It's currently in the 'Before Cataclysm,' or the BC stage. Soon it will enter the 'After Detonation,' or AD phase. We need to attend to it, fast!"

The wallscreen flickered and its sound returned, bringing soft carnival music amidst the Toymaster's cackling. *'Mummy, Daddy, and the baby. Oh, how sickeningly lovely!'*

Suzi tried switching the monitor off. Her efforts were countermanded.

"Why did I get sick, Mummy?" the Toymaster taunted. *"I'm hungry. I need food. I need to –"* He bared his fangs. *"Breastfeed!"*

Suzi picked up a nearby monitor and hurled it hard, shattering it against his menacing scowl and fracturing the wallscreen down the middle.

His sick grin widened amidst the rising circus music. *'I'll be coming home soon! Mummy, your little boy will be coming home!'*

Suzi resumed working on the terminal.

"I can't do any more to limit his power," she told 421.

"Your records state that digital security is your specialty," he recalled.

"Yes, but something's preventing me from initiating the procedure. My mind turns hazy when I attempt it."

"How is this possible?"

Suzi gazed up at the Toymaster's broken, grinning face.

"It's his work," she concluded bitterly, "from when I was imprisoned in his Playpen."

421 nodded. "Can I assist in strengthening his containment field?"

"No," she answered. "You do not have the practical skills. I've contained him as effectively as I can for now. It will not be long before he breaks free and the more time we waste, the stronger he'll grow. I've also discovered Jenny Campbell's location. We must reach her while there's still time."

"Agreed."

They made for the door.

The Toymaster's laughter grew behind them, accompanied by the rising carnival music.

"Come on, damn you…!"

Miss Ford worked rapidly over the terminal.

Jenny lay across a school desk, her face deathly pale.

Miss Ford was worried. It wasn't the girl's death that concerned her. The Black Circuit was only sixty percent extracted, leaving the rest wedged in Jenny's mind, refusing to budge. If the girl died, it would be lost, leaving the Toymaster's ultimate weapon without a primary circuit.

An act that he would find unforgivable.

A flatline rose from the terminal.

Jenny's head slumped forward.

"No!" Miss Ford cried, typing rapidly. "No, no, no! Not good, not good…!"

Suzi and 421 strode down the hallway.

Suzi spoke fast. "Have you assigned your taskforce to the recovery of Jenny Campbell?"

"I have," he answered. "Your Echo informed me that her retrieval is paramount. My team will not fail."

They rounded a corner and stopped.

Several Agents were spewed out on the floor in a mass of severed limbs and body parts. A crackling group of Trans-plants stood over them, with Terror-Byte in the middle.

Suzi glared at 421. "No matter what the situation, I refuse to train under you. Ever!"

421 ignored her and observed Terror-Byte curiously.

Terror-Byte returned his gaze.

"An augmentation?" 421 speculated to Suzi.

Terror-Byte's lips curled up, revealing his razor-sharp teeth.

"Confrontation will not be beneficial," Suzi warned, indicating the fallen Agents.

"We do not have a choice," 421 told her. "Jenny Campbell must be retrieved. Only one of us can do that."

Suzi's mood darkened. So many had died. More were set to follow. The casualties were high and the last thing she wanted was to lose Agent 421 too. Her feelings for him were still bubbling, now more than ever. He was ready to sacrifice himself for her and the mission, like so many others had done in the past.

She glared at the Trans-plants. They returned her gaze from their eye fragments beneath their botanical growths.

All were hungry.

All except one who seemed familiar. Extremely so. They held a presence she'd seen before.

Realisation dawned.

Reason and logic wouldn't help here, she concluded. She needed the faith that her maternal sire had tried so hard to teach her. She'd absorbed some of it in her youth, and resisted the rest, resulting in chaos. Still, part of her had never given up on what she'd learnt, which was why she'd kept a Dragon Slayer around her neck for so many years. Now, she no longer needed the Slayer to remind her of her family's faith. It was time to finally use what she'd learned.

"Enough's enough," she whispered.

She moved in.

"Agent!" 421 called.

She defied him and kept going.

"Explain your actions!" he ordered.

She ignored him.

"There's no victory in sacrifice!" he pressed.

Terror-Byte tensed, poised for battle, as the Trans-plants rustled louder than ever.

Suzi focused on the lone Trans-plant she'd singled out, then stopped and called, "Sarah Eastman!"

The creature stared at her, somewhat curiously.

Suzi knew the Trans-plant wasn't Sarah. At least not completely. The girl had exploded into an oozing green mess after being absorbed by a lone Trans-plant which had then self-destructed. Suzi concluded that some of Sarah's characteristics must have been integrated into the greater Trans-plant collective. Sarah had also been exposed to the Hurriflame's ion particles, and the Shockwave too, possibly allowing her to resist the Trans-plants group mind and retain enough willpower to assist Suzi.

Suzi's emotions were fluctuating. The Playpen experience, plus the memories of her maternal sire, *and* her feelings for 421, were all churning furiously. Now it was time to relent and do the one thing she'd vowed she never would and hated more than anything else.

It was time to sacrifice her ego and surrender.

Her gaze bore into the Trans-plant's eye, connecting with Sarah's presence, and it took a great deal of effort to stop her voice from quivering.

"Help us."

The lone Trans-plant crackled. Its grotesque eye widened beneath a long, green leaf, recognising an affinity with Suzi. The girl was familiar. A tiny voice in its mind, small and distant, told it to believe in a much higher mindset than its fellow Trans-plants had. The creature knew that it was like Suzi in so many ways. Inwardly, they were both frightened little girls disguised as monsters.

Things weren't supposed to be like this, it thought. They were meant to kill each other. Suzi shouldn't be able to see the roots of its pain, yet somehow could. This curious girl with the jet-black glasses had insight. The Trans-plant respected her for that. It bristled, then its eye blinked.

Suzi nodded.

Terror-Byte sensed treachery. Mechanically, he strode through the jungle of Trans-plants towards Suzi.

The Trans-plant with Sarah's presence rustled again. This time, its fellow Trans-plants all lowered their leafy heads, subdued, like they were communicating.

Terror-Byte picked up speed and…

Snap!

A tendril clasped his neck, pulling him back. A second wrenched his arm sideways. A third smacked his legs out from under him, slamming him to the floor. He struggled fiercely under a ravenous mass of leaves.

His razor-like teeth severed a few tendrils, making little difference. Sparks flew as he was guzzled upon, unable to fight against so many.

Terror-Byte's violently writhing reflection shimmered in Suzi's Iyes, along with the Trans-plants gorging indulgence. She found it difficult to watch. As much as she wanted him dealt with, she hated seeing anything in pain, and so turned and rounded a corner, with 421 following. What made her feel worse was that Sarah had aided her twice now, and the favour couldn't be returned. Suzi was annoyed that she couldn't make Sarah human again. If only –

"That tactic was incompatible with Agent protocol," 421 said, interrupting her thoughts.

"I'm not just any Agent," Suzi replied. "I didn't sacrifice everything when I joined the Agency, especially not who I am. I merely became distracted by other things and forgot what was important."

421 analysed this information.

"Interesting," he noted. "I sense that your time on this world has affected you more than you realise. You are almost… human."

Suzi stopped, clearly annoyed by this notion.

He too stopped, returning her glare.

Not wanting a conflict, but now extremely agitated, she headed along the hallway to the door ahead, with him following.

Beads of sweat trickled down Miss Ford's face as she desperately tried to resuscitate Jenny, fearing the worst if she failed.

She'd barely started when the room door was booted off its hinges, flew in, slammed her into the far wall and sent her collapsing into an unconscious heap.

Suzi didn't bother with Miss Ford as she entered the room, leaving 421 in the doorway. Her expression darkened as she approached Jenny. She'd seen bodies strewn out on benches like this before. Far too many times.

She scanned Jenny. The readings from her Iyes reported that the girl's life signs were almost gone. She dismissed this. Her experience in defying the Trans-plants and breaking through to Sarah's presence in the hallway had encouraged her greatly. Logic and reason were important, but they were nothing without believing that the impossible could be accomplished. The Dragon Slayer on Jenny's neck only strengthened Suzi's resolve to use faith once more.

Full of determination, she moved behind the terminal and got to work.

Unseen by her, 421 picked up a long metal device by the wall, retreated into the hallway and strode away.

Terror-Byte's head was a mess of black liquid and machinery.

Sparking wires protruded from his neck. Half his face was gone, revealing a skeletal metal mask, while his grotesque mouth snapped violently at the Trans-plants who delved hungrily into him.

Footsteps came from ahead.

Through the fractured lens of his Iyes, he saw another figure. The Agent who'd been with Suzi earlier, now carrying a long metal device that Terror-Byte had stored in the toyroom where Jenny Campbell was taken.

A flamethrower.

Terror-Byte observed this Agent. He wasn't like Suzi. She was plagued with inner demons and played by her own rules. This Agent followed protocol completely, unhindered by emotions. He was simply cleaning up an interplanetary mess in a swift, effective operation, which meant killing everything in sight and leaving no evidence.

The flamethrower activated.

A rush of fire engulfed the Trans-plants who erupted with piercing shrieks. Their grip on Terror-Byte loosened as they fell away, leaving him to dodge a second burst of flames, then leap up and run.

His speed grew as he rounded the corner.

421 was angry. He hadn't been efficient at all. He'd misjudged Terror-Byte's strength and the target had escaped. No matter. There was still work to do.

He widened the flamethrower's nozzle to maximum.

Whoosh!

The Trans-plants flailed in squealing agony. Their leaves blackened. A few stumbled towards him on pure instinct but their attempt was futile, and they collapsed with the rest of their kin, leaving a dark mass of burning compost twitching before him. Moments later, they were motionless.

He observed their corpses coldly. His mission wasn't complete. It wouldn't be until Terror-Byte joined the Trans-plants in death and the school was burnt to the ground. Secrecy had to be maintained at all costs. No part of this botched affair could be allowed to survive, especially not as evidence for the humans to study.

His Iyes reflected the flames as he walked over the Trans-plant remains and headed down the smouldering hallway, clutching the flamethrower tightly.

The terminal screen blipped.

Suzi's heart almost leapt with it.

More blips followed. She analysed the readings.

Jenny Campbell's life signs were returning. Her heartbeat was rising too, along with her breathing and brain activity. Her other bodily functions were stabilising as well.

Suzi only wanted to feel satisfaction. She needed to be objective and detached, nothing more. Instead, she felt an overwhelming sense of relief and other strange emotions. It took some effort to contain them all.

She glanced at Miss Ford. The unconscious woman on the floor was evidently a novice to this technology. Suzi knew that much from the readouts. The Toymaster had been ineffective in training the woman properly. Suzi had found it easy to operate this machinery and had easily stabilised Jenny Campbell.

A full recovery was another matter.

Further readouts told her that Jenny's consciousness was returning. This was good. What wasn't so good was that part of the Black Circuit remained wedged in the girl's head. Unless it was removed completely, or restored there, Jenny Campbell would wake up with a fragmented perception that would eventually lead to insanity. Conditions were still favourable for a full and smooth retrieval without a fatality. Hiding the circuit somewhere safe was another issue.

Suzi's head lowered as she reviewed the possibilities available, then assessed the outcome of each one. The circuit was the prime component of a powerful weapon that had to be destroyed. This planet and her Homeworld were in jeopardy, leaving only one real option. She hated it, but there was no other way. This had to end.

She made up her mind in a second and was absolute about it. There'd be no looking back.

She entered a sequence of numbers. She'd barely begun her work when a static-like crackle diverted her attention.

She stopped, listening curiously.

The basement door crashed to the floor.

421 stepped inside, his Iyes changing to night vision as he descended the stairs and scanned the dimly lit area. The Toymaster had severed the school's power from the main grid and used an alternative energy source in its place. That source wasn't active down here. The only light either came from the doorway or the flickering flamethrower.

He reached the bottom of the stairs. There was no sign of Terror-Byte, who he'd tracked here.

A shape shuffled in the shadows.

He whirled around.

Nothing.

He sensed a presence behind him, before two hands grabbed his weapon's long burning nozzle, pulling it back into his neck.

Terror-Byte.

421 held onto the nozzle, pushing against it.

Terror-Byte hissed, his mouth opened wide and his teeth grew longer, ready to bite down hard.

421 raised his leg, kicking himself off the wall. They flew back into the opposite wall, sandwiching Terror-Byte.

Terror-Byte tried to bite again. 421 whirled them both around, slamming Terror-Byte into the side wall. Terror-Byte refused to let go and bit down savagely into 421's neck, igniting a shower of sparks.

421 faltered in his grasp.

Chapter Fifteen

A light beam pierced the shadows and widened, bringing with it a massive headache.

Jenny's eyes opened and she groaned. In the light's centre, she saw a black patch. That patch split into two, solidifying, to become a pair of dark glasses staring down at her.

Suzi.

Jenny spoke, her voice hoarse. "Must have been some party, huh?"

Suzi's face twitched.

Jenny couldn't tell if it was with sorrow or joy. Anyway, it hurt to think, and her head throbbed like hell. She closed her eyes, the pain dissipated, and when she opened them again Suzi's emotions were gone, leaving the familiar objectivity that Jenny knew so well.

Suzi spoke formally, taking things as literally as ever. "There were no festivities, Jenny Campbell, nor is there any reason to celebrate. There was a battle. It was bloody and with many casualties. Heads were severed. Limbs were torn off, many were ripped in half –"

Jenny grimaced. "Enough, Suze! God, I feel sick enough as it is."

"You should do," Suzi said. "You nearly died."

Jenny tried to rise. "What…?"

Dizziness hit her and she fell back down.

"Be mindful of your movements," Suzi warned. "You're still vulnerable."

"Speak for yourself," Jenny retorted, fighting against her horrendous nausea and sitting up again.

Suzi was confused. "I always do, Jenny Campbell. I never let anyone else speak for me."

"You know what I mean," Jenny said groggily. "So what's the deal? Am I still at death's door?"

"Jenny Campbell, I have never heard of this place called death's door."

"Am I still about to cark it?"

Suzi opened her mouth to speak.

Jenny cut in quickly, "No, don't answer that. You'll only ask another question that'll split my head open even wider. I just want to know if I'm okay. Have you fixed everything up? What's the story?"

Suzi paused, trying to find the right words.

"Just tell me," Jenny ordered. "What's happening with the junk in my head? Is it out?"

Suzi's answer was blunt. "No."

Jenny gave a little nod. "Okay, I accept that. What I don't accept is you not telling me about the crap in my brain to begin with. Mission or not, there's no way you can justify that bull."

"There's a bull?" Suzi asked.

"Rubbish, Suze, rubbish!"

"It's not rubbish, you said there was a bull…"

"Bull means rubbish! There's no way you can justify hiding stuff from me! Screw the mission, screw protocols, screw orders and screw everything else, you had no right not to say anything! None! Nada! Zilch! Zero! You should have told me!"

Suzi paused, then spoke softly. "I know."

Jenny composed herself. "Best not to argue though, since I've only got a short time left and I don't want to spend it screaming at my best friend."

Suzi stared at her.

Jenny averted her eyes, feeling awkward.

"Sorry," she mumbled with a little shrug.

"Do not worry, Jenny Campbell," Suzi said. "I do not want to spend time arguing with someone who's the closest thing I have to a family either."

Jenny's heart leapt. Fighting against the pain, she acted on impulse, rising and hugging Suzi tightly with tears welling in her eyes.

Suzi didn't return the embrace. She remained still, not knowing why she'd said what she had. Her emotions had taken over again, to the detriment of her logic.

Jenny sniffed. "Thanks, Suze. You really are like a big sister, y'know?"

"No," Suzi replied, "but you, Jenny Campbell, are similar to the one I lost."

"Really?"

"Yes," Suzi answered. "She too was defiant, insubordinate, and had a lot to say with that loud mouth of hers."

"Hey!"

"Just like that. Same pitch too. I miss her."

Jenny bit her lip. "I'd have loved to have met her. Oh God, Suze, the things that could have been! What we could have done! It's so unfair!" She moved back. "So what? I've only got a couple of hours left?"

"No," Suzi stated.

The response shook Jenny. "Really?"

"I speak the truth, Jenny Campbell."

Jenny braced herself. "So how long have I got?"

Suzi spoke sombrely. "Three months."

"Three months?" It took Jenny a few moments to process this before she smacked Suzi's arm. "Three months! Three *whole* months! That's more than I had before! God, Suze, you made it sound like I only had three minutes left!"

"It got down to one point four. I know three months is not much —"

"Not much?" Jenny cut in. "Suze, I never thought I'd be so happy to be alive for another three months! Thank you!"

She hugged her again.

Suzi returned the hug.

Tightly.

A little too tight.

Jenny cringed. "Ow, Suze! Ow, ow, ow! You're hurting me!"

"My apologies, Jenny Campbell," Suzi said, retracting her hold and stepping back. "I've never done that before."

"Getting emotional, are we?" Jenny asked, smirking.

"No!" Suzi snapped.

Jenny half jumped. "Whoa! Okay, we'll just leave it at that. So what's up with the toy freak? You said it wasn't over?"

"It is not," Suzi stated. "There's a Black Circuit in your head. It's primed for a Planetary Eruption Trigger that must be disabled."

"Do you know where it is?"

"Yes," Suzi answered. "It was stored in the Heartbeat by the ECG."

Jenny spoke resolutely. "I'll come with you. Although taking the trigger in my head straight to the weapon it's primed for is hell risky…"

"… Leaving you alone is equally risky," Suzi cut in. "I am not letting you out of my sight, Jenny Campbell."

"Me neither, sis," Jenny said, moving off the desk and pulling her to the door.

Suzi was uncomfortable with this notion. "Do not call me that, and do not lead the way. It is childish."

"Oh, come on, ya wimp! What have you got against kid's stuff?"

A whimsical hum rose from behind them, like a chilling nursery rhyme. They turned back.

Miss Ford was on her feet, grinning macabrely with a presence that wasn't hers, but the Toymaster's.

Suzi concluded that he'd bypassed the security blocks that she'd keyed into the terminal mainframe and wormed his way into Miss Ford's head. It also seemed likely that he'd placed a loyalty mechanism on her too, monitoring her actions and keeping her in line. Miss Ford had acted as his eyes and ears. Now she was his puppet completely.

The woman spoke playfully. "Naughty, naughty children. You tried to abort my *labour* of love."

She rubbed her stomach gingerly, indicating a pregnancy.

This went right over Jenny. "Always knew you were a psycho." She glanced at a large volume on the desk. "For once I'd like to take her advice and hit the books, only really hard on her head."

"That's not your teacher," Suzi warned. "It's our enemy. He's inside of her."

Jenny made a face. "Eeeewwww! The way you said that made it sound really gross…"

"There was nothing wrong with the way I said it, only the way you understood it."

"No, it was definitely the way you said it. You didn't mean it but still –"

"Clearly there's a communication barrier between our cultures…"

Miss Ford's hand rose. "So let's break down those barriers, shall we?" She rubbed her stomach again. "Children?"

Her belly expanded.

Rapidly.

"Move!" Suzi ordered, pushing Jenny out the door.

"Don't push me, Suze!" Jenny snapped. "I hate being pushed! Why don't you smack her out?"

"It won't stop him from materialising fully. We only have a few moments."

"Before what? She pops something out?"

"Yes."

"Oh sweet Jesus!"

They ran outside.

Miss Ford didn't follow. She smiled insanely as her stomach grew, becoming disproportionate to the rest of her, then her face contorted into a mask of agony and she screamed.

A squeal erupted inside her. A hideous squelch followed as her belly ripped open, revealing the Toymaster's wailing head which burst out, covered in red and white bodily fluids. She crumpled to the floor, lying splayed out like a broken doll.

Bit by bit, he emerged. His shoulders came first, and he used his floppy arms to push himself free, growing larger by the moment. When he'd reverted to his normal size he stood over her bloodied corpse, snarling, "Pop goes the weasel!" The wet blood from his red lips splashed onto hers. "I love you, Mummy. Thank you for my birth!"

He turned away. He had no tolerance for failures.

His hand rose and he clicked his fingers.

"Lights!"

The lights dimmed and the surroundings hummed.

Jenny cringed, running down the hallway after Suzi. "Oh crap…"

The Toymaster raised his arms like a maestro. "Music!"

Carnival music played eerily throughout the school, chilling Jenny to the bone.

"Action!"
His arms rose high.
Swirling lights materialised around him as he ascended off the floor, spinning like a mannequin on a string and grinning maniacally to the dark music that filled his very being. His arms opened wide as he announced, "Let the carni-voral of animals… begin!"
His hands burst into orbs of fire, then he swung them out, letting loose with his fury. The walls ignited into flames, illuminating his horrific face.
His laughter grew as he hovered through the burning doorway, in hot pursuit of his prey.

Smoke filled the hallway, growing thicker by the moment.
Jenny covered her mouth to block it out. She rounded a corner with Suzi, then came to a sudden halt.
Smouldering Trans-plant remains littered the floor between the two flaming walls.
"Your work, Suze?" Jenny quipped.
"No," came the reply. "There's a rogue Agent missing from these corpses. Another Agent called 421, who came to this world to rectify this matter, is also missing. That's concerning."
Jenny coughed heavily and fell against the wall, struggling to hold herself up in the billowing smoke.
Suzi moved over to her. "My apologies, Jenny Campbell. I was distracted from your limitations."
"It's okay, Suze, really…" Jenny said through her coughs. "I can take care of my – whoa!"
She almost doubled over.
Suzi pulled her in close and half-carried her down the hallway. Jenny helped by pushing herself along as best she could.

Suzi spoke quickly. "Fourteen seconds until we're out of the worst part. Stay conscious, Jenny Campbell."

Jenny blinked hard. "Yeah, who else is gonna see you through this crap?"

The Toymaster's mocking laugh echoed from the school speaker system, along with circus music. *"Where are my red-blooded riding hoods? Will they come out and play with nice Mister Wolf?"*

Suzi rounded a corner and propped Jenny up against a locker. Jenny clasped the handle for support while Suzi ripped another locker off the wall, hurled it at the roof, struck the ceiling, and sent a mass of debris plummeting into the hallway. Jenny covered her mouth with one hand, an ear with the other, and watched as Suzi hurled a second locker, then a third, then a fourth.

Jenny struggled to speak. "That won't stop him, Suze!"

"No," Suzi called over the noise, "but it will block some of the smoke off."

Jenny frowned. "Why not just keep running?"

Suzi pulled open a junction box cover on the wall. "I established a link to my ship while you were unconscious." She clicked her head to the side. "Echo, can you hear me?"

Jenny coughed heavily again.

Suzi tapped her Earwig. "Echo!"

Still nothing.

"I need you to restore the school's power," Suzi pressed,

Silence.

Jenny coughed harder.

A hum rose and several lights activated, care of Echo. Suzi pulled some wires out from the junction box, fiddling with them.

Jenny got her breath back and asked, "Whatcha doing?"

"I'm tired of running," Suzi answered. "I'm sending a message."

"Which is?" Jenny pushed.

"Blowing up the school," came the reply.

Jenny's eyes lit up. "Oh God, Suze! Can I do it? Oh please! I'd love nothing more! Come on! I'll be your best friend!"

"You are my best friend," Suzi replied.

Jenny was startled. "Really?"

"Of course," Suzi said logically. "I do not have any other friends."

"Hey! Although come to think of it, I don't either…"

Echo whirred into action on Suzi's ship, plugging herself into the school's digital mainframe and redirecting the flow of its gas pipes.

The Toymaster floated along another hallway, his arms outstretched and his hands ablaze, igniting the walls on either side of him. His eye colour changed from red to black as he sang blissfully, with the words almost dripping from his blood-red lips.

"To the sound of bells from the realms of hell and dead maids basked in its glow…"

Suzi stepped to the side, indicating the junction box. "Red button, Jenny Campbell."

"It's ready?" Jenny asked eagerly.

"Yes. The gas pipes are filled to maximum capacity."

"Cool." Her hand rose. "Hang on, is the school empty? I don't want to kill anyone and…"

She coughed again.

Suzi turned away. "Echo?"

A scratchy voice came through. *The building is empty of all life signs.*

Suzi was grateful but didn't show it.

"What of the other Agents?" she asked, referring to 421 and Terror-Byte.

None detected, came the reply. *There's only Miss Campbell, the Toymaster and yourself.*

Suzi's face hardened. "I don't like this."

Nevertheless, Echo said, *time's running out.*

The Toymaster's laughter grew louder from the school speaker system.

Suzi turned back. Jenny was coughing violently and almost doubling over.

"I'm pressing the button," Suzi stated.

Sheer willpower restored Jenny's breath and she rose, gasping. "L-Like hell you will! No one's robbing me of the greatest day of my life."

Suzi indicated the button with a small nod.

Jenny's hand rose, forming a fist. "Welcome to graduation!"
Smack!
The button slid in.
The building rumbled.

The Toymaster spoke, his cruel voice resonating throughout the school. "Now children, your rollercoaster ride is about to begin –"
A build-up of pressure rumbled in the walls, growing louder.
He halted in his burning tracks, looking curious.

"Hang on," Jenny said. "If we're still in the school and it's about to blow…"
"Run!" Suzi ordered.
Jenny yelped and felt her arm nearly wrenched from its socket as she was pulled away.

"The jack thinks outside the box," the Toymaster mused, amidst the building's growing rumblings. "No matter." He raised his hand, twirling his fingers playfully. "System shutdown, please."
No response.
The rumbling grew louder.
He clicked his fingers with a loud snap. "Obey!"
Still no response.
A voice rose in his mind.
His own.
"System shutdown, please."
The Toymaster grinned. "Oh! I sense an Echo…"

Echo knew that confronting the Toymaster was risky, but there was no other option. She had to buy Suzi time to get Jenny and the Black Circuit to safety.
Gathering her power, she leapt onto the Toymaster's wavelength, surging into his sick mind.

The Toymaster stood motionless.

Suzi's Echo, small as it was, had entered his head, latched on, and was refusing to let go. His face twisted in pain as he raised his blood-stained hands to his temples and dropped to his knees.

"Why am I being punished? I've been a good boy, Mummy, don't hurt me! Have I really been that bad? Moi? No, no, no! It's time to *perish* the thought!"

His soft face bunched up, distorted to the extreme, and he concentrated hard.

The sheer force of the Toymaster's will blew Echo back into Suzi's ship. The vessel's dim lights faded momentarily, leaving only darkness, before reactivating. Several small explosions burst throughout the bridge, accompanied by the Toymaster's gleeful howls as he tried to penetrate the ship's digital mainframe.

This time, Echo was prepared.

"Secondary systems online," she stated.

She moved fast, containing the flames with long jets of billowing gas, diminishing them.

"System power increasing by thirty percent."

The bridge's hum grew louder as Echo struggled against the Toymaster's might.

Suzi and Jenny ran out of the school's front entrance and down the steps as the building rumbled behind them. Jenny wondered how long they'd been in there. Night had fallen, and the stars were out, not that she'd time to notice.

They ran for the road.

A sleek police car veered around the corner, coming to a skidding halt before them. The door opened automatically, and to Jenny's amazement, there was no driver inside.

A voice spoke from the car's speakers. *"Agent Chambers."*

Jenny was aghast. "What the —?"

She was cut off as Suzi threw her into the car and leapt in after her. They landed with a crunch on several objects in the back seat. Jenny winced, pulled a police baton out from under her and tossed it away.

"How does this work?" she asked, referring to the car.

"It's powered by a friend of mine," Suzi replied. "She's interfaced with the vehicle's systems."

The door started closing.

Jenny saw someone running in for the car. "Suze…!"

The figure swept inside, landing on top of them.

Suzi's Iyes flared with annoyance at the sudden appearance of 421. *Now he shows up,* she thought, frustrated by his recent lack of communication. She'd demand an explanation from him in due course. Part of her was angry, part of her was relieved, and part of her was confused because the other two parts were so emotional. She'd have to fix that.

The door slammed shut. Echo revved the car and it screeched away, weaving from side to side and picking up speed.

Jenny's head rose, dishevelled, from under the two Agents,

"Okay," she began, "I get that some people spend their graduation day like this in a whole different way. Whatever. Me, I get to spend it by dying in a driverless car on the run from a psycho clown while my school's about to blow. The showers of prosperity are just raining down on my future, hey?"

The car veered around a corner.

The Toymaster clawed at his temples as he stumbled along the hallway, annoyed that Echo's presence was more irritating than he expected. Finally, he ran up to the wall, banging his head on it repeatedly.

"Must. Get. The. Echo. Out!"

He turned and lunged into the opposite wall, smashing his head right through it and creating a gaping hole. Glumly, he pulled his bloodied, flaming head out, and the expression on his face was miserable as he said, "This is so not funny…"

The school erupted.

A fiery blast blew out the principal's office, churning in a mixture of golden flames and thick black smoke. Another surge exploded from the science lab. The maths department went up next, then room after room ignited as the underground pressure was released and the building detonated in a searing roar.

The police car came to a skidding halt, swinging to the side.

The doors opened.

421 emerged onto the street, with Suzi following. Jenny hopped out after them, more dishevelled than ever.

The two Agents gazed at the school in the distance as part of it shot up in a deafening blast. Jenny covered her ears, looking away, while Suzi and 421 simply watched the searing spectacle, unaffected. Several more eruptions followed, each one larger than the last, until a final burst finished Carrington High off for good.

The blasts subsided and Jenny's head rose.

"Yep," she said satisfied. "That's my graduation speech done." She grinned. "I blew up my school. How cool is that? I actually blew up my school!"

Suzi ignored this and activated her Earwig. "Casualties, Echo?"

"None," came the reply.

"The Toymaster?"

"No trace of him detected. That doesn't mean he's perished."

"Agreed," Suzi stated. "He's evolved to the point where we need much more firepower to destroy him."

"Who are you talking to?" Jenny asked.

"Echo," Suzi replied. "My Echo to be exact."

"Is this Echo, like, your friend back home?"

"Not quite," Suzi answered. "Echo's my Holler-Gram. She's in my ship."

"A hologram?" Jenny wondered. "Like, a super-computer assistant?"

"A personalised digital interface," Suzi corrected. "She's a reflection of my dominant traits personified into a superior intellect."

Jenny was impressed. "Good thing no one on this planet's thought of that yet. Imagine the reality shows."

Suzi didn't answer and walked around the car, entering the driver's side. 421 got into the passenger seat while Jenny moved into the back, catching a glimpse of his reflection in the rearview mirror. Her heart leapt through her head at the sight of him.

"Jenny Campbell," she announced, leaning on the front seat, holding her hand out.

"I know," he said coolly.

"Echo, give me manual control," Suzi ordered.

The dashboard blipped and Suzi revved the car, making Jenny fall backwards with a yelp.

The car swerved down the road, racing away.

Jenny leaned on 421's seat once more. "Gotta name?"

"No," he answered.

"Your face is hard, like a rock," she noted. "It's stony. How 'bout I call you, Mister Stone? Maybe, Steven Stone? Sounds sexy. I like that."

"I do not."

"Suits you, though. What are you doing after the mission, Agent Stone?"

"Another mission."

"Come on, give me a break here. I think you're cute."

"That is no basis for a relationship," he replied. "Unless one wishes to make it purely sexual."

Jenny shrugged. "I'm dying. Could be fun."

"Not for me. You wouldn't have the stamina for my kind."

Jenny waved this away. "Doesn't matter. I've been screwed to death by so many people in my life that I might as well go out with a bang."

No laughter.

Jenny sighed. "You guys suck." She sat back and asked Suzi, "He a friend of yours?"

"He's Agent 421," Suzi said, "and he needs to explain his actions." She addressed him. "The burning of the Trans-plants in the school corridor, was that your work?"

421's response was formal. "I was merely following the protocols of a standard clean-up operation, which you have clearly ignored."

Suzi fumed. "We could have used the Trans-plants as allies. I'd persuaded them to assist us."

"They were unstable, unreliable, and untrustworthy."

Suzi was furious. How could someone she'd once had feelings for be so heartless and cruel? Maybe she was changing, she thought. Or maybe, he had.

"What you did was murder, Agent 421," she said coldly.

"Nevertheless," 421 responded, "there are consequences for not following protocol."

Suzi glared at him.

He glared right back.

Jenny sighed. "Get a room already. Anyway, if you two lovebirds can ditch the hormones for a second, there's a job to do, remember?"

Silence.

"We'll need more than a second," 421 said, as both he and Suzi focused on the road ahead, "and we are Symbiants, not lovebirds."

"Symbolic expression, douche bag," Jenny retorted.

He addressed Suzi. "I do not understand her."

"I don't either," Suzi agreed, "but she is correct. There's a mission to complete. What of the rogue Agent? I did not see his body."

"Who?" Jenny asked.

421 ignored her and said to Suzi, "That is another of your failings. You did not stay to see him destroyed. He escaped the Trans-plants and entered the building's basement. I found him, we clashed, I won. Now we must find and disable the Planetary Eruption Trigger. It must not fall into the wrong hands."

"Yes," Suzi agreed. "Echo?"

"Yes?"

Suzi paused.

"Your question?" Echo prompted.

"Talk already, Suze," Jenny pressed, having heard traces of Echo from Suzi's Earwig.

Suzi spoke to Echo. "Priority one check, Echo. State my birth name from the Homeworld."

Echo responded formally. *"Security clearance code 101. Your birth name is Athena."*

Suzi ripped her Earwig off, crushing it.

"Echo's gone," she said flatly, throwing the remains away.

421 was curious. "From what I understand, Agent, your birth name is Athena."

"Wrong," she stated. "I manipulated several Authority records just before joining the Agency. Our superiors are so complacent that they never verified the false name I entered. I couldn't hide my true identity from

Echo, since my mind was linked with hers, so I placed a failsafe mechanism in my ship. If someone were ever to interface with her, my false name would be given, leaving my real one a secret. My Echo's been with me every step of the way since the beginning, anticipating my operational needs. She even brought us this vehicle. This time, I sensed a change in her voice. The pitch was incorrect."

"Meaning what?" Jenny asked.

Suzi paused, trying to control her emotions. "I suspect she confronted the Toymaster to gain us some time." Her tone lowered, almost cracking with sorrow. "My Echo is gone. First I lost Rags, now Echo. I am alone."

Jenny placed a hand on Suzi's shoulder. "You're not alone, Suze. You have us. Well, me, anyway. I'll see you through this."

She gave a little smile.

Suzi stayed motionless.

The car sped on.

The Toymaster's giant holographic face snickered, having replaced Echo onboard Suzi's ship.

"Let's toy with this sweet shop," he mused, speaking through the ship's systems. Gleefully, he began probing them, searching for Echo's classified files. Finally, he found what he was looking for, digitally sealed away.

"Huff and puff…" he whispered.

His macabre eyes closed, concentrating on blowing the digital lock. He didn't get far. A siren wailed, activating a recording of Echo's voice.

"System breach! Intruder detected! Security protocols activated!"

The terminals whined.

The Toymaster tried subduing the automated emergency system, without success.

He wasn't scared. Just annoyed.

"Paranoid idiots!" he scowled.

Fiery bursts ignited from the terminals as the Toymaster's wrath collided with the ship's security systems.

Neither side won.

The ship whined ever louder, then the bridge exploded.

A deafening boom shook the suburban streets as an enormous fireball blew out the windows of Suzi's house. Thick black smoke clouds followed, swirling high, twisting and morphing into the Toymaster's cruel features. His mouth opened in a silent scream, not of pain but defeat, then his face dissipated as larger explosions ignited, incinerating the building and the vessel below.

"My ship is no more," Suzi reported coldly.

Jenny spoke softly. "So you've got no way of getting home?"

"There are ways," 421 said, objectively.

"Yes, but they won't be on my terms," Suzi corrected. "I've no desire to go anyway. There's nothing left for me there."

The dashboard's GPS beeped, changing images.

To reveal a grinning clown face.

Jenny fell to the side as the car skidded violently, coming to a screeching halt by the roadside while the doors and windows locked automatically.

"Suze, what the hell are you doing?" Jenny cried.

"It's not me, Jenny Campbell," Suzi replied. "The Toymaster's latched onto this vehicle. He controls it now."

Jenny hit 421's shoulder. "Haven't you got an Echo that can help us?"

"No," he answered. "I've no need of assistance, and do not hit me."

"I'm so glad you ordered a supersize on your ego!"

The Toymaster's white hands shot out of the GPS, clasping Suzi's and 421's throats. Waves of steam sizzled from his grasp as he steadily emerged from the screen. His head, shoulders and arms all slithered out while Suzi and 421 smacked him repeatedly, to no avail.

He scowled cruelly and said, "Why did you hurt me, Mummy? Your precious baby who only wants to play in the Garden of Eden, to be a happy little boy." His face contorted angrily. "You punished me. You made me a bad boy…"

Suzi and 421 kept hitting him.

Jenny also lunged for a strike.

He snapped at her savagely.

She yelped and fell back.

The car filled with steam as Suzi and 421 convulsed from his burning wrath.

"Jenny Campbell!" Suzi called through the pain. "My left pocket!"

Jenny plunged her hand into the side of Suzi's leather jacket, finding a small box. She blinked away some steam and her fingers fumbled as she opened it. A small ring lay inside.

"Do not handle it directly," Suzi struggled to say. "It's for him."

Jenny grabbed a heavy book from the back seat and smacked the Toymaster's face. His arm rose, pulling Suzi up with it, then he raised a sizzling finger that made a rude sign at first, before he turned it on its side, ready to blast her.

Jenny threw the box at him. The ring flew out, touching his soft, white digit, a spark fizzled, and it latched on, clamping tightly.

"A gift?" he sneered. "For me? Oh, how pretty. How beautifully exquisite! Thank you so very, very —"

He stopped, sensing a presence enter his mind. His jaw dropped in horror and he released his grip from Suzi and 421, wailing, "No! Not fair! Cheats! You're all cheats and bullies!" He clawed at his temples. "Get out! Get out now!"

His face twisted horrifically.

Suzi and 421 slid their seats back fiercely, breaking them off their grooves and almost crushing Jenny in the process. The Agents raised their legs, gave an almighty kick, and sent the Toymaster flying through the windscreen and far into the night. His body flailed, dancing like a leaf in the wind, before disappearing.

"Move!" Suzi ordered, kicking the door open.

421 did the same on his side and they leapt out.

Jenny had no hesitation in following. Once they'd all emerged, she asked, "What's the deal with that ring?"

421 addressed Suzi. "It would be beneficial for me to know as well."

Suzi headed for a tavern in the distance.

"It was something I took from the ECG…" she began.

"Help me!"

The faint whimpers from up ahead stopped the young couple in their tracks. They hesitated, hearing the rising sobs from around the corner. Since they both worked in hospitals, neither of them wanted to deal with another crisis. All Jason and Tina Argus yearned for was a quiet after-dinner walk. That's what they got, until the explosion from Carrington High several streets away shattered everything. Wailing sirens had risen, indicating something big had gone down.

"Stop! Please…!" the voice pleaded.

Jason moved forward.

Tina grabbed his hand, stopping him. "No…"

"I can't leave it," he cut in. "It's my job, remember?"

"You're off duty, *remember*?" she pointed out.

He dismissed this. "I have to. It'll be okay. Trust me."

Tina released her grip reluctantly, and watched as he rounded the corner, then heard his footsteps stop.

Along with the whimpering.

"Jason?" she called. "You okay?"

No response.

"Jason?"

The wind blew noisily.

Summoning up her courage, she rounded the corner too, and halted in her tracks.

Jason stood before a twisted bundle of rags on the ground. Those rags shifted, forming into what seemed like a discarded ragdoll with a repulsive clown face, contorting in pain. Long wisps of steam rose from a ring on his finger that he was desperately trying to wrench off, but couldn't. He stared up at them with bloodied tears streaming down his white face as he bawled, "There's a pain in my head that won't go away!"

Tina fainted.

Jason froze, unsure of what to do.

The clown arched up, howling, as a dark mist materialised over its grotesque head. Gradually, the mist morphed into an even uglier face, superimposing itself over the clown's hideous features. One with a mesh of scars, boils, burns, and one twisted blazing eye.

"No!" the clown roared, and bit angrily into the air.

The face vanished.

Jason went for Tina. Enough was enough. This was too weird. He had to get her out of here. Now.

"Don't go!" the clown cried. "Stay and play!"

He threw an arm out, slamming Jason hard into a wall and sending him slumping to the ground, passing out next to Tina.

The Toymaster swung his arm sideways, making several bins burst into flames, then rose with a hiss.

He closed his eyes, delving deep into his warped psyche.

"How I wonder what you are…" he whispered.

"We'll need these," Suzi said.

Jenny's eyes lit up. "Hell yeah!"

Suzi mounted a motorbike. Jenny leapt behind her. 421 sat on another.

Suzi leaned down, ripped some metal away, and fiddled with the wires below. Seconds later, the bike roared to life so suddenly that Jenny nearly fell off. Ruffled, she fought against its sickening vibrations, holding onto Suzi tightly.

Soon all three were racing away.

Two bikers in leather jackets ran out from the tavern behind them, stopping at the sight of their bikes vanishing into the night. The largest and broadest pursed his lips, then put two fingers into his mouth and whistled loudly.

Several more bikers emerged from the building.

Not long after, engines revved, a roar erupted, and a mass of bikes went streaming down the street, heading for the highway.

"Down the rabbit hole and straight into Wonderland!"

The Toymaster curiously observed this new mental realm. He was engulfed by a thick, black mist of suffocating thoughts that, much to his dismay, weren't his. His own were constantly exploding like operatic fireworks. These gloomy clouds were filled with a murky, dripping heaviness, with no sense of fun whatsoever.

He wore no ring now. That was back in the real world, along with his body. The ring had brought him here, and kept him in this realm too, controlled by whatever presence lay ahead.

Dramatically, he held his arms out, like he was being crucified, and bellowed, "Let there be light!"

His hands erupted into burning orbs of fire. Their brightness grew as he summoned his strength, ready to let loose.

A fierce, freezing wind blew in, extinguishing his flames. He looked up, annoyed. "How rude!"

He hurled two long fire streams into the darkness so ferociously that they blew the mists apart, revealing an enormous frightened eye peering out from the shadows.

"I see," he observed slyly. "The eye of the storm!"

The icy wind picked up again. He dismissed it and headed for the anomaly, much more easily this time, parting the mists as he went.

The eye was afraid. He sensed it. The closer he came, the more the eye shrank, growing smaller and smaller until morphing into two human eyes belonging to a scowling dark-haired boy.

The Toymaster sneered. "My, my treacle pie, what an interesting little phenomenon you are."

He took note of the two letters sown into the boy's lapel.

GR.

"Ah yes," he growled, almost spitting the words off his slimy, black tongue. "Gastoff Rosewood!"

The Toymaster knew all about him, thanks to Suzi's work, JT's memories and one or two other insights. The Toymaster had admired Gastoff from afar, even if this mutated overgrown kid's tactics were too crude for his liking. Now Gastoff had reverted to what he truly was, and had been all along. A frightened child in a black mind, hidden in a ring in the real world.

"You're no fun," the Toymaster said bitterly. "I do so like to *play* with children. They have so much imagination. We could have a splendid time, you and I. Oh yes! I'd love to be your toy."

Gastoff's head lowered, summoning his strength. A roaring blast of psychic energy sent the Toymaster flying backwards, with his legs rising so high that they almost went over his head. He landed upside down, his limbs flopping apart in both directions.

Gastoff smirked.

The Toymaster rose crossly.

"How undignified," he muttered, stomping in. "I see that you're a difficult child. How very sad. You should lighten up." He twirled his fingers, creating small flames flickering from their tips. He savoured the moment, before unleashing another torrent of fire.

The boy's icy will extinguished it.

The Toymaster stepped in. "Do you like party tricks? I've got a few up my sleeve." He waved his hand and several cards appeared. "Pick a card, any card."

No response.

"Take this one," he hissed, pulling one out and showing him. A glistening spike flipped out from its top. "The death card!"

He hurled it at the child.

The boy lowered his head, welcoming it.

Jenny hung onto Suzi tightly as they roared along the empty highway. The monster bike's vibrations were making her as sick as hell. She tried to keep the contents of her stomach down and focus on the job at hand, although thinking of what lay ahead did little to ease her pain.

Suzi kept looking back. Jenny wanted to know why, and when she yelled into her friend's ear to find out, she barely heard her own voice, let alone Suzi's answer. All she saw was Suzi give a small nod to 421, who nodded in return, then Jenny nearly gagged as both bikes came to a skidding, screeching half-turn halt in the middle of the road. Somehow, she kept her hold on Suzi as they came to a dead stop.

"Dismount the bike, Jenny Campbell," Suzi ordered, getting off.

Jenny blinked and stumbled off it. The world still spun, and she cringed at the discomfort from the ride. "Ow, ow, ow, sore, sore, sore! I should have stretched before getting on. God, that hurts!"

Suzi spoke, sounding clinical. "Physical activity for your kind is required for optimum efficiency. You are in less than peak physical condition."

Jenny made a face, mimicking in a high voice, "You're in less than peak physical condition!"

421 turned to face the way they'd come from, unfazed that they were smack bang in the middle of the highway.

"What are we waiting for?" Jenny asked. "Don't tell me we're going to make a last stand against the toy freak right here?"

"No, Jenny Campbell," Suzi replied. "There's another hindrance."

"What kind?"

It was 421 who answered. "The most irritating. Humans."

"Yeah, and who brought all this crap here to begin with?" Jenny retorted bitterly.

421 didn't respond.

The steady roar of bikes grew from up ahead.

The Toymaster lashed out, releasing another fiery burst from his fingertips. Within those flames were faces. Ghostly images from Gastoff's past, screaming, howling and sweeping for the boy.

They never reached him. Gastoff's defensive clouds were cold and heavy. Nothing could penetrate his mighty barriers.

The flames faltered, dissipating.

The Toymaster frowned, knowing he needed to divert this young idiot's attention.

He clicked his fingers.

Two clouds morphed, forming a face that hovered over Gastoff, solidifying into an old lady's features.

The boy's grandmother.

Gastoff shuddered. His defensive clouds faded momentarily, then strengthened with a vengeance as he belted her image into oblivion.

"Hmmm," the Toymaster mused. "There must be another way into your black heart."

He merged the shadows again, forming a second face.

The maid, Ashleigh.

Gastoff's lips pursed and he retaliated with a freezing wind, sending the Toymaster recoiling, then he too brought up an image.

The Toymaster barely regained his balance when he saw an apparition of two giant Iyes hovering over him. They stared coldly and he realised, with horror, that they belonged to the engineer who'd created him.

"Mother?" he whispered.

His lips scrunched with hate and his hands rose, turning those Iyes into two screaming balls of fire and smacking them at Gastoff. The flames hit the boy's icy black clouds and vanished.

The Toymaster shook away his mother's face from his mind. He'd always hated her. She'd been too strict with him. That's why he'd killed her.

He pressed in with his will.

Gastoff retaliated.

A white sphere of light grew between them, flickering wildly with demons from each of their pasts.

Death Grudge, the appointed Commander of the Blood Warriors, spotted his bikes up ahead. His followers rose behind him, certain that the bikes had been stolen by a rival gang.

They were surprised, however, to find three people standing in the middle of the highway, waiting for them. Two of them, unfazed by the possibility of oncoming traffic, wore leather jackets and sunglasses.

Grudge raised a gloved hand, bringing his bike, and posse, to a halt. Menacingly, he dismounted and approached Suzi, glaring fiercely. She didn't react as his gang moved off their bikes and stood tall, arms folded.

Grudge brought his face close to hers.

"We have a problem," he said, his voice dangerously low.

"Yes," Suzi agreed, "we do. You're violating my body space. Back off."

He pushed her shoulder. "Gonna make me?"

Suzi pushed his shoulder right back, with far more strength, sending him flying into two Blood Warriors who caught him. They struggled to hold him up.

"Yes," she replied.

His gang whipped out their guns, taking aim.

Jenny cringed. "Mother of crap!"

Suzi gave a satisfied nod.

"I suspected as much," she confirmed. "You're the useless kind who follow orders without question, then blame others for the failures in their lives. The correct term for you is, idiots."

Jenny tensed. "Yeah, not helping Suze."

Suzi and 421 stepped in, glaring at each of the bikers in turn, and spoke in unison.

"Lower the weapons."

The bikers, entranced by the hypnotic, swirling shades of their Iyes, did so.

Suzi focused on Grudge. "You. Approach me. Now."

Grudge rose and stepped in obediently.

"I wish I could get dates that way," Jenny muttered, under her breath.

"Listen carefully…" Suzi began.

She spoke.

Grudge hung onto every word.

Soon after, Grudge and his gang were roaring back down the highway, with no intention of returning to the tavern.

The chances of the Toymaster overcoming Gastoff were high, Suzi had concluded. Her orders to the bikers were to delay him from afar, whilst taking all measures to ensure no casualties. She didn't like putting them in harm's way, but with the planet at risk she needed to buy time.

421's face hardened. Unknown to Suzi, he'd discreetly countermanded her orders with his own subliminal commands, instructing them to engage in direct combat with the enemy, no matter what the cost.

The bikers picked up speed, racing away.

Suzi, Jenny and 421 mounted their own bikes, making for the site of the Hurriflame.

Countdown Minus One:
Crash and Burn

Chapter Sixteen

The Toymaster's face clenched in rage.

So did Gastoff's.

The psychic energy sphere between them tremored to bursting point. Countless faces inside it were rapidly forming, howling, and vanishing. Sparks flew as the two demonic beings poured their wills into the great ball of light, each trying to smash the other's barriers.

The sphere moved in for Gastoff. He pushed it back, with immense effort, towards the Toymaster who retaliated. The sphere wavered between them, with several long black streaks rippling through it, ready to crack open.

Gastoff struggled to hold his ground.

The Toymaster snickered.

"What comes first?" he mused, first glaring into Gastoff's frightened face, then at the glimmering white oval between them. "The chicken or the egg?"

The sphere shook violently before blowing outwards, blasting the Toymaster back to reality.

The Toymaster awoke by a dumpster. He groaned and rose shakily to his feet, stumbling along.

"There was a crooked man —" he began.

He stopped, horrified. A line of black liquid was dripping from his sleeve.

Blood.

He raised his hands to his cheeks. They bled too. There were cuts all over him.

He dropped to his knees, staring into a puddle of water. Rivers of dark blood were flowing down his pale face. His blackened mouth gasped in horror.

"Now you've done it," he seethed. "You've broken my favourite toy!"

A creeping sensation drifted over him.

Gastoff.

That overgrown baby was trying to sneak into his mind.

The Toymaster scowled. "Time for you later!"

He ripped the bloodied ring off his finger and tossed it away. Mumbling curses, he staggered along the street.

The ring rolled to a dumpster and fell to one side, lying amidst a discarded newspaper, a rotten banana peel, and an old tin, fitting among them like standard junk.

At least until it glowed.

The glow was dim at first, then brightened a little, before the ring suddenly stood up by itself. Fuelled with a dark presence, it spun over the pavement to an outstretched finger.

Tina's.

The ring latched on, its presence swept in, and a dark halo encompassed her. That halo flared and expanded, then retracted, dimmed and faded.

Tina remained motionless.

Until her eyes snapped open, now with a very different persona.

"Back into hell!"

Jenny trudged through the forest after Suzi and 421, trying as best she could to follow their shapes in the darkness. They, on the other hand, were having no trouble navigating the terrain.

"Reptile, Jenny Campbell," Suzi pointed out.

Jenny looked down. A snake had slithered past Suzi's foot and was heading for her own. She screamed, leapt out of its way, and ran ahead, nearly crashing into Suzi who'd stopped to stare at the sky.

Jenny trembled. "I hate this place. Always did. It's so… natural." She followed Suzi's gaze. "What are you looking at?"

421 answered bluntly. "Seraphim."

Jenny did her best to try and see something, anything, through the small gap in the clouds. "Is that your home?"

"No," Suzi responded, redirecting Jenny's gaze to a different star. "That is."

Jenny nodded. "I bet you miss it, huh?"

"I do not," Suzi said. "I am merely contemplating what's at stake. I've lost too much to lose the Homeworld as well."

"Yeah, you miss it," Jenny confirmed. "Believe me, it takes a liar to know one."

"Just like you miss school?"

"Yeah, like a killer wedgie."

"Now who's lying?"

"Shut up."

She placed her arm around Suzi and they moved on, making for the Hurriflame's impact point.

The Toymaster smacked his head. He'd always believed it was the best way to clear cobwebs out. Those of others, that was. He relished his own.

Gastoff was gone, yet psychic remnants of his sickening presence remained. The Toymaster was merely grateful to hear the many voices between his cotton ears again. No more hindrances, he determined. Now that his cuts had sealed and he'd returned to being fully functional, nothing would stop him from reaching the Black Circuit and his beloved PET.

A roar of engines bellowed behind him.

He whirled around.

He'd barely time to register anything when the rattle of gunfire made his body jolt awkwardly and a spray of bullets blew the stuffing out of him. He writhed wildly, jolting under the impact, as big, bloodied holes burst out of his chest, making him recoil and ready to fall.

The shooting ceased and the bikers dismounted. Long wisps of smoke ascended from the guns as they stared at the bullet-riddled freak before them.

The Toymaster's lips parted and he spoke hoarsely. "If it's one thing I refuse to do, it's bite the bullet!"

He spat one out, shooting it at a large woman and sending it thudding into her brain. She fell to the ground, dead, with smoke rising from her head.

The Toymaster shook himself. Masses of bullets dropped out of his light body as his wounds sealed up. When the last bullet fell, he stared into a biker's eyes, sensing what Suzi and 421 had done to them.

"Yes," he confirmed. "The mindless sheep have had the wool pulled over their eyes. So, you're all working for the Agent-see now, hmm? Well then, consider yourselves free from your employment. You've all been fired!"

He raised his hand, letting loose. A fierce rush of flames engulfed the bikers in a searing ferocity. They flailed wildly, either crashing to the ground or falling on their bikes, which tipped over in burning heaps.

Grudge hit a dumpster's side, groaning painfully. He couldn't see the gun he'd dropped in the fall, only the enraged Toymaster looming in through the flickering embers. His gang were either dead, dazed, or too wounded to attack.

Grudge searched desperately for his gun. There was no sign of it.

The Toymaster reached in for him, sneering cruelly. "Everyone has to *face* themselves sometime…"

His fingers rose.

With each digit turning into a razor blade.

421 heard the bikers' screams in his mind. His mental abilities were more advanced than Suzi's, leaving him able to monitor the situation via Grudge's head. He knew those primitive apes would fail. If Suzi's Echo had fallen, there wasn't much hope for these pack animals.

Still, he'd had his reasons for instigating the attack. His plans were going as anticipated.

Soon, they'd pay off.

The Toymaster peered into Grudge's hollow eyes.

The biker's face stared back at him.

It was just Grudge's face. A thin mask dangling limply off the Toymaster's white finger. Grudge's dead body, stripped of its facial features, lay crumpled on the road nearby.

A cry rose as a surviving biker surged in, holding his knife high.

"Kissy, kissy," the Toymaster said, throwing the face forward.

The biker skidded to a halt as it hit him in the head.

The Toymaster lunged, ready for a kiss himself.

Grudge's face dropped to the road, watching through its sightless eye sockets as droplets of blood fell onto its dead cheeks, growing with the biker's screams as he was devoured hungrily.

The forest ended.

Jenny reached the clearing's edge and stood with Suzi and 421. They gazed at the crater ahead where everything had begun, and would now end.

The site of the Hurriflame.

Suzi scanned the area with 421. Their Iyes whirred with soft hums, searching for energy signatures.

421 spoke. "Our target is twenty-five point eight metres below the surface."

"Makes sense," Jenny said. "No one would want to leave it smack bang in the middle of a forest where any old drunken hobo could find it. How do we get there and bust the crap out of it?"

Suzi turned, looking behind them. "There are other hindrances to be concerned with first, Jenny Campbell. The ECG were working on numerous experiments. Many were released before the Heartbeat's destruction."

"So there's big uglies lurking down there?"

"No, Jenny Campbell. Up here."

A screech rose from the forest.

Jenny whirled around. "This day just keeps getting better and better!"

The Toymaster leapt in the air, his hunger satisfied.

His arms spread wide as he ascended, soaring high and illuminating the night sky as a colourful dot.

"Send in the clowns…" he whispered.

Jenny stood rooted to the spot. Several creatures were emerging from the forest. The long strands of their leafy green hair indicated they were Trans-Plants, yet their bodies, much to Jenny's dismay, were of scuttling giant ants.

Jenny shuddered.

"Trans-plant rejects?" she asked.

"Deviants," Suzi corrected. "Insects that have mutated and now exist as a cross between human beings and Trans-plants."

"You mean Devi-Ants, huh, Suze?"

"I do not understand."

"God, aren't there any humans 'round here anymore? Can't you do your glasses stuff on 'em like you did with the bikers?"

"No," Suzi said. "The Agent who was present when the Hurriflame hit was subdued by these creatures. He tried to communicate with them and failed."

"How do you know that?"

"His Iyes transmitted the attack to the Homeworld. Nevertheless, he survived, with his Iyes damaged and unable to contact the Authority. The ECG found him soon after, augmenting him into one of their own. One Agent has fallen. No more will follow."

A Devi-Ant sprang at her. She grabbed its two front limbs, dodging a stream of saliva spraying from its ugly mouth and sizzling into a tree. Fiercely, she swung the beast around, hurling it into the forest.

Jenny ran for the crater, then stopped.

Several Devi-Ants were emerging.

One lunged for her.

She ducked as it flew in, sweeping over her and landing on 421's back. He arched up, slamming himself backwards into a tree. The Devi-Ant gurgled under the sickening thud, before 421 turned, kneeing it in half.

Suzi's uppercut sent a Devi-Ant's head flying off, then she kicked the beast's body into its own kind, all while masses of its kin swarmed from the forest, rapidly growing in numbers. She knew she could hold them off, but not for long. For one thing, she didn't know the size of their army. For another, a colourful object was streaming through the night sky towards them.

Her Iyes zeroed in on it and her anger grew.

The Toymaster beamed at the sight of Devi-Ant heads and severed limbs flying high into the air, with many screeching in blood-curdling agony. The more horrific the cries, the more delighted he grew. He gazed at the spectacle in wide-eyed awe, as if witnessing paradise.

"What a wonderful world…" he sang.

"We don't have time for this," Suzi fumed, kicking another Devi-Ant away.

"Agreed," 421 said. "Find the PET. I will ensure you have the time you need."

"There's too many for you to fight," Suzi indicated.

"Debating is illogical," 421 stated. "Go!"

Suzi grabbed Jenny's arm, hoisting her through the nightmare mass of Devi-Ants. Thankfully, no more were emerging from the crater, only the forest.

Jenny followed Suzi onto the crater's slippery slope, half-skidding and struggling to keep her balance. Suzi practically slid down it and reached the bottom smoothly, then turned and caught Jenny who tumbled into her. She steadied the girl, before kneeling over a sealed hatch in the ground and punching it. Hard.

The impact half-deafened Jenny who recoiled, clutching her ears.

Suzi pounded on it several more times until the lock finally broke. She pulled the hatch open, grabbed Jenny and threw her inside. Jenny tumbled in with a cry while Suzi whirled around, booted a Devi-Ant aside, then leapt in after her.

The fall was only a few metres. Suzi landed smoothly on her feet, right next to Jenny who lay sprawled on the floor.

A Devi-Ant made for the entrance. Suzi jumped up, smacked it away, then gripped the hatch's handle, slamming it shut. That also half-deafened Jenny, for every sound in this metal tunnel was magnified tenfold.

Suzi ripped a metal beam off the wall, sliding it through a gap in the hatch's handholds. Jenny watched, impressed, as Suzi wound the beam up like a knot. It wouldn't buy them much time, Jenny figured, but every little bit helped. That other dream-faced Agent above could take care of himself and find a way in later, she thought, yet something about him irritated her too. He didn't seem quite right, and his vocal tones bugged her, like they'd changed somehow. Whatever the case, she felt uneasy with him around.

The hatch rattled loudly as the Devi-Ants tried to break in.

Suzi moved into the darkened tunnel.

Jenny ran after her along the descending path. They hadn't gone far when Jenny's foot hit some debris. She yelped and brought her leg up, wincing.

Suzi stopped and turned back. "My apologies, Jenny Campbell. I was so focused on the mission that I omitted your limitations. Here, I will help you."

She clicked her head and her Iyes glowed, illuminating the darkness. It wasn't much. Just enough to see a short way ahead.

"Thanks," Jenny said. "Great shades. They'd go off like a bomb at a party."

Suzi seemed confused. "How are you aware of their self-destruct mode?"

"Never mind. Are they battery powered?"

"No. Solar phosphorescent."

"Silly me."

"Understandable. You are only human."

Suzi walked on.

"Hey," Jenny called, running after her. "What do you think you are? A higher species or something?"

"Yes," Suzi replied simply, "and I don't think, I know."

A whimper came from ahead. Footsteps went with it.

"Friendly?" Jenny asked.

"Ask it yourself," Suzi indicated. "It's one of yours."

A familiar face appeared in the light.

Jenny was astounded. "Longsworth?"

She hardly believed her eyes. Maria Longsworth appearing from the shadows? The queen bee of Carrington High looked dishevelled as hell and totally freaked out.

Suzi spoke. "You did say you wanted more humans around, Jenny Campbell."

Jenny drew a sharp breath. "Yeah, but she's not exactly human."

"Deal with it," Suzi ordered, and moved past them, though not too far. The glow of her Iyes allowed Jenny and Maria to see each other.

Maria shuddered. "Take it you've seen what's outside?"

"Duh," Jenny scoffed. "How'd you get in? The hatch was locked when we found it."

"I was speculating on that too," Suzi said darkly.

"Double duh," Maria retorted. "*I* locked it. It was open when I got here."

"So what?" Jenny pressed. "You thought you'd take a trip to hellsville in the middle of the night?"

"Kind of," came the reply. "I came with Mike Adams. We wanted this place to be special for, you know, our first time."

"Explain!" Suzi demanded.

"Later," Jenny shot back, then asked Maria, "So where's your big man now?"

"Freakin' out down there somewhere," Maria answered. "He couldn't deal with what's outside."

"Is this area secure?" Suzi asked.

Maria was confused. "Huh?"

"She means are there any unfriendlies around?" Jenny clarified.

Maria shook her head. "No. Have you got a phone? Mine's dead."

Jenny stepped in. "Okay, first, Longsworth, I'm a little busy. Second, I've peaked. Remember?"

Maria shivered. "Can't you just forget about that now, Campbell?"

"Nuh uh!" Jenny snapped. "Everything bad that's happened to me all goes back to *you*! I left the party and hit the Hurriflame because of *you*! I ended up with all this crap in my head thanks to *you*!"

"I didn't ignite the damn Hurriflame!"

"No, but you pushed me into it!"

"I know, Campbell, I know —"

"You know squat! You've been a pain right up my friggin' butt from day one!"

Suzi raised her eyebrows inquisitively.

"Please –" Maria pleaded.

"No!" Jenny cut in. "I've had it! No more crap from you, Longsworth! That's it!"

She lashed out, striking Maria hard and sending her flying into the wall. Maria's head hit it with a sickening thud and she slumped to the ground, unconscious.

Suzi observed Maria's prostrate form. "Now we have another problem to deal with, Jenny Campbell. We cannot leave this individual here."

Jenny shrugged. "Yeah, we can. We'll grab her on the way out, *if* something doesn't get to her first." She headed down the tunnel. "Come on, we're wasting time."

Suzi ripped open a metal door in the tunnel wall, leading to a small storage area. Coolly, she picked up Maria with one hand, dumped her inside, then slammed the hatch shut, leaving it unlocked. "She'll be safe in there for the time being, though will be afraid when she wakes up."

"Good!" Jenny called back.

"She will hate you too."

Jenny stopped. "Yeah well, I mightn't have got another chance to smack her out."

"In time you may live to regret that action, Jenny Campbell."

"Speaking from experience, huh?"

"Yes," Suzi replied, walking past her.

"Okay, so I may regret it," Jenny said, following. "Then again, with everything that's going on around here, I may not even live long enough to regret it, and even if I do it's only three months, so *ha!*"

Satisfied, she overtook Suzi.

Suzi followed, baffled by the girl's logic.

The Toymaster descended before a mass of Devi-Ants, observing their corpses.

"Hmmm," he mused, "I always get so jealous when someone smashes my wreck-ord."

He sniffed the air, sensing Suzi. Jenny too. There was no trace of 421.

He looked around curiously.

Suzi approached a door at the tunnel's end. A quick scan from her Iyes told her that the wallscreen beside it was still active. She keyed in a few commands, bringing it to life. The screen's data appeared, making her angry.

"So it did survive," she said softly.

The Heartbeat's primary WOMB, known as Mother, was operational, complete with the Shockwave. The readings told her that shortly before the Heartbeat exploded, the Toymaster had reached Mother. He'd touched the Shockwave, then Mother had expelled him just as the Heartbeat blew. The blast didn't spiral into a colossal explosion, thanks to JT's commands. Most of the base had gone up, but Mother remained shielded. She'd self-repaired after the blast, implementing safety measures to avoid detection from Echo, or anyone else. True, Echo's Acystance Package had wiped out the Shockwave in all ECG bases throughout the world, and also placed a cyst in Mother's WOMB. The cyst was growing, yet its growth rate was contained, and Mother was once again functioning at full capacity. Despite this, Suzi was grateful that Mother was still around, meaning she could use her to her advantage.

She flicked through a few more screens, taking the information she needed, then entered another command.

The door slid open.

"This way," she ordered.

She stepped into a tunnel, with Jenny following. Together, they headed along it, and when they reached the end, they found themselves on another crater's edge. This crater was much broader and deeper than the one in the forest. The devastated remains of the Heartbeat's Operations Centre lay before them, sunk by a massive explosion. Fallen beams hung amidst dangling cables and wires, none of which were active. Suzi concluded that Mother only powered some things here and not others, for now anyway. She couldn't tell if Mother was making further repairs but didn't underestimate the possibility.

Interwoven among the cables, beams and twisted bits of machinery, were tree roots and forest debris from above, forming a path to the bottom of the crater. With all doors in this place obliterated, several open doorways encompassed the area. Some were high up, a few were below, and most had caved in.

"Looks like my room just before rental inspection," Jenny said. "What are we looking for, Suze?"

Suzi indicated with a nod. An old-fashioned wooden chest, with a padlock, stood by a wall at the crater's base.

"That's it?" Jenny asked, dumbstruck.

"Yes," Suzi answered, at the sight of the Toybox.

Despite the ravaged surroundings, it looked the same as when she'd last seen it with JT. There wasn't even a blemish. Nevertheless, she sensed something wrong. The Toybox was a safety protocol created by the ECG to hold the Toymaster. Worryingly, a signal from his ultimate weapon, the PET, was emanating from inside it.

Jenny interrupted her train of thought. "So, that box and my head are triggers for blowing up the whole damn world?"

Suzi climbed onto a girder and started descending. "The most powerful factors are often the smallest, Jenny Campbell."

Jenny followed, climbing after her. "Are you saying my head's small?"

"No," came the reply, "Although I have heard people at your school say that it's big at times."

"I'm so glad I blew that place up!"

They continued their descent. The girder squeaked under their weight, then part of it gave way beneath Jenny's foot, making her yelp and tip outwards.

Suzi reached out, grabbing her.

"I have your back," she said, pulling her in.

"You always did," Jenny replied shakily. She regained her hold, "and I appreciate that."

They moved on, somewhat more carefully.

"We make a good team," Jenny said. "I brighten you up, and you protect me. You're right, Suze. We're like family."

Suzi stopped abruptly.

Jenny nearly overbalanced from the sudden halt. "Whoa! You okay?"

Suzi shook the notion of family away. She hated being attacked by surprise emotions.

"Yes, Jenny Campbell," she answered, and continued descending.

They soon reached the ground.

Jenny dusted herself off. "Just two messed-up kids saving the world. So our lives are hell. Doesn't mean everyone else has to burn in flames. Let's end this."

She took Suzi's hand and they approached the Toybox. Once there, Suzi removed her hand from Jenny's, touched the padlock, and stopped.

It was already open.

"Suze?" Jenny asked.

Suzi did her best to quell her unease as she unhooked the padlock, threw it to one side and lifted the lid, raising it with an electronic hum.

A toy clown lay inside. The shell of what the Toymaster had once been. It hummed electronically, with an eerie cackle.

Jenny stepped in to see. She quivered at the sight of it. "God, it's the freaky thing I touched in the Hurriflame. Is that what we're after?"

"No," Suzi answered. Her tone grew darker. "This is only a standard-issue beacon."

"Beacon?" Jenny wondered, confused. "What? From your planet? You have toy clowns there?"

"The doll is from this world. I can hear the beacon inside it."

"So where's what we want?"

"Not here," Suzi replied. "Beacons can replicate energy signatures. They're issued for one purpose only." Her face hardened. "As decoys!"

A shape emerged from the shadows. They turned to see a blood-red balloon hovering amidst the debris.

Jenny spoke grimly. "Don't tell me we've failed, Suze."

"I never fail," Suzi stated.

"First time for everything."

"Not for me," Suzi said firmly.

Jenny felt her spine tingle, then realisation dawned. "He wanted us here. He baited us and we fell for it. Hook, line and sinker."

The roof shook, sending trickles of dust falling.

Jenny continued. "Everything up top was all part of his sick game to get us here, wasn't it?"

Suzi stayed quiet.

"Wasn't it?" Jenny pressed.

Suzi answered softly. "Yes, Jenny Campbell."

Jenny tensed. "There's gotta be something we can do, right? Maybe if we can use some of the stuff 'round here to –"

"There's nothing," Suzi cut in. "We've no time to find the Planetary Eruption Trigger."

"He can't be that close."

Suzi looked up. "He's closer."

"What?"

A crash came from above. Jenny recoiled as several chunks of debris thundered past, hitting the crater. She watched, horrified, as the Toymaster descended through the opening, his arms wide and his grin wider. Soft cradle music tinkled from his bloodied red lips, with notes so sharp they almost stung her. He landed gently, relishing the moment and speaking with a snarl.

"I do so love to *crash* a party! Or should that be *crush*?"

Suzi stood statuesque.

The tension mounted.

Jenny ran.

The Toymaster waved a finger.

She flew against the wall, held fast by his will.

"Wherever there's a will, there's a wall," he sneered.

"Suze!" she cried.

Suzi stood rooted to the spot. Her mouth barely moved as she spoke. "It's time to stop running, Jenny Campbell. We must stand and face our greatest fear. The most frightening of all."

"A big circus drag queen?" Jenny quipped.

"No," Suzi replied. "Losing."

"That's just your dumb ego talking," Jenny retorted.

"Not when it's referring to losing you."

A lump formed in Jenny's throat. "We, uh, didn't have a good run, did we, Suze? We've been swimming up this tsunami of crap from day one." She paused. "Tell me straight. We never stood a chance, did we?"

Silence.

"Suze?"

Suzi's answer was sombre. "No."

Tears welled in Jenny's eyes. "Then why did we fight for so long? What the hell was it for?"

Suzi hesitated. "Because going through it together made the pain more bearable, that's why."

The Toymaster raised a finger, stroking the red balloon gingerly. His long nail made a screeching noise across it as he brought it to the point of bursting, then he stopped, savouring the moment. "Nearly time for bed-die-byes. Oh, how I'll love to cuddle up to you both in bed. There are so many *games* we could play."

He approached Jenny. Her terror grew as he lowered his monstrous face before hers and his icy hand stroked her cheek. Delicately, he leered in and said, "You'll look so good hanging on my bedroom wall."

She trembled, averting her gaze.

"She's helpless," Suzi warned. "I'm not. Try intimidating me." She indicated the Toybox with a glance. "The ECG set that up as your prison. It's risky to bait us with the very thing that can contain you."

The Toymaster rose, facing her. "Like you, I love flirting with the dark side, and you, my dear, are so very dark. You really need to –" His fingers ignited with flaming crackles. "Lighten up!"

"You're inflating yourself through words, rather than actions," Suzi retorted.

"Good one, Suze," Jenny quipped.

Smack!

A savage, burning blow sent Suzi flying into the cave wall. She regained her balance, with a long black mark across her cheek.

The Toymaster returned his focus to Jenny.

She shut her eyes.

"Open up," he ordered, "or I'll huff and I'll puff and I'll blow your brains in…"

She didn't move.

His flaming fist punched the rock wall beside her head, bursting through it. Jenny jumped and her eyes opened reactively, just like he wanted, and she gasped as he leaned in, staring maniacally. She found it impossible to close them again, for she was frozen, controlled by his will.

"Humans," he purred, "always tend to carry the worst secrets inside themselves."

"Where's your PET now?" Suzi asked him.

Her question set off a spark in the Toymaster and he faced her delightedly.

Jenny blinked and shook her head, free from his hold.

"Where it's always been," he revealed. "The lion's den."

He blew the flames out from each hand and made a signalling motion.

Footsteps rose from the shadows behind him as a figure emerged, stepping into the light.

Jenny thought she was hallucinating.

"No way," she whispered.

Suzi wasn't surprised by the revelation. Nothing surprised her anymore. She'd lost too much to care.

Jenny, however, was in shock.

For standing there was Maria Longsworth.

"Maria?" Jenny asked in disbelief. "I always knew you were a demonic cow, but seriously?"

Suzi indicated the Toymaster. "She's here on his commands."

"Meaning what?" Jenny pressed. "There's a bomb in her head?"

"No," Suzi replied. "She is the bomb."

The Toymaster snapped his fingers.

A halo engulfed Maria and she stared ahead, her eyes shining like golden orbs.

Jenny tensed. "I always said she was full of crap. Now I know." She shook her head. "So she comes to power and it's the end of the world? Fitting, Longsworth. Real fitting."

Maria spoke, her voice half-computerised. *"You took a piece of me, Campbell. I want it back."*

"I didn't *choose* to take it," Jenny retorted, knowing that Maria was referring to the Black Circuit. "Mister Inflatable here put it in my head. He screwed us both over."

"That's not Maria Longsworth," Suzi stated. "Only a template."

"A toy actually," the Toymaster corrected. "The real girl went to pieces some time ago. She brought a boy down here for a breeding session, but they were caught in the Hurriflame. He ran, leaving me to find her. The poor child was almost death warmed up. Almost, but not quite. I needed my PET to have a larger kennel and she was the logical choice. When she finally died, I kept her template, combining logic with technology to turn her into a *techno-logical* air of brilliance."

He passed his hand through Maria.

"How'd you do that?" Jenny wondered. "I smacked her a good one earlier."

"Her density can be changed," Suzi said.

"S'pose it helps when you're pretty dense to begin with," Jenny scoffed. "Seems Mike Adams didn't know the difference either. I'm guessing he's back at the pre-grad party right now sleazing onto every chick in sight."

"Oh, he's merely off somewhere playing games as usual," the Toymaster sneered. "Smart boy."

Jenny glared at him. "So she's what? A weapon? Yeah, that'd be right! She always was a time bomb. I can't believe no one spotted that earlier."

Suzi spoke. "The Hurriflame's ion particles, along with the Shockwave, allowed certain people deep insights. That's why Sarah Eastman and Gastoff Rosewood had extra-sensory abilities. Luckily for us, neither could see the Black Crossroads real location, or that Maria Longsworth was the PET."

A thought struck Jenny.

"Hang on," she said to the Toymaster. "If you knew there was bad stuff in my head, and that you had to combine it with her…" she indicated Maria, "why wait so long to bring us together? You had that old slapper Ford using your tech at school, so why not finish everything ages ago?"

"He couldn't risk extracting the Black Circuit incorrectly and having it dissipate," Suzi answered. "The ECG and the Trans-plants were also around, and the more trials we faced, the more stressed you became, thereby accelerating the process for the Black Circuit's extraction. He also manipulated your school results and initiated other environmental factors too."

"I think the correct term is environ-*mental*," the Toymaster mused.

"Meaning my school really did run on negative energy," Jenny concluded. "I knew that already."

Suzi scanned Maria with her Iyes. "Shortly before we blew the school, the Toymaster assigned Miss Ford to extract the Black Circuit from your head. We gained the upper hand in this battle, so he used Maria to place the decoy beacon in the Toybox to bait us here. If any more Agents close in now, the Devi-Ants in the forest will provide a hindrance." She observed Maria. "I couldn't sense her true nature, nor could Echo. When we encountered her a few levels above, she tried to manipulate you into a lower emotional state to get to the Black Circuit. Instead, you became angry and struck her."

"Let's just say I learnt how to fight from the best," Jenny said.

Suzi dismissed this uneasy feeling and continued. "This holoprojection is impressive. Her true nature was no doubt hidden from Gastoff when he possessed her. The Toymaster clearly allowed this possession as a means of investigating Gastoff further. I also suspected Maria's true nature back in the tunnel when she mentioned Mike Adams. He is currently dating another girl at your school."

"You know this how?" Jenny wondered.

Suzi ignored her. "When Maria said she brought him down here to be intimate, I was suspicious. I now realise that her mode and memories have reverted to the events of the Hurriflame."

The Toymaster spoke slyly. "Let's not forget that she also kept a few seductive human traits to turn the Agent, you call Terror-Byte, inside out. They met just after the Heartbeat was destroyed, when I took him to my little desert town, the decoy Black Crossroads. They played doctors and nurses, and she *persuaded* him to see the light."

Jenny glanced at Suzi. "So how are they hoping to get the crap out of my head? I hope Slimeball Sicko here doesn't want to see her and I do a makeout session."

The Toymaster scowled. "I'm more interested in children's games, and we're going to play one final one. The last drop of bloody icing on my cake. You see, everything that's happened 'till now has been planned to the last detail." He moved towards Suzi and leaned in, gazing deeply into her jet-black Iyes.

She didn't flinch.

"It's time to *open up* the sad one," he continued. "The wounded girl who walks with permanent black eyes. The hurt child so bullied by life. There's no family for her anymore. They're all dead or missing. As for friends, well she never really had any, did she?" He twisted his head to the side with a maniacal expression, staring deeper into her Iyes. "An infant ravaged by war. A home destroyed. She fights on, her mission failing. Her personal casualties are high, as always. A little girl lost, just like her young cousin. How many others have died because of her failures? Can't remember, can you? Well, here's another one. Just look at my face."

He righted his head.

JT's face stared back at her, filled with the Toymaster's presence.

He walked around her, sliding a long white finger across her neck. "Failure after failure after failure, including this mission. You're a casualty of existence, just like your puppy dog Miss Campbell, and the oh-so-great Maria Longsworth too. The lower orders like you three must suffer so the higher ones like myself can evolve. You're only building blocks. My toy castles to build up and tear down." He moved before her. "I can see the device in your friend's mind. It's wedged tightly. Halfway in, halfway out, all in that halfway house of a brain. There's only one way to free it." He clamped a soft hand on Suzi's shoulder. "You know what to do. What you've always done." His blood-red lips curled into a grin. "You must fail. Again."

Suzi didn't budge.

"What's he saying, Suze?" Jenny asked. "Tell me he's just talking crap."

Suzi stayed silent.

"Suze!" Jenny pressed.

No response.

An awful notion struck her. "Tell me."

Still nothing.

Jenny shuddered, realising the awful truth. Her voice shook as she said, "H-he wants you to kill me, doesn't he?"

Suzi's lips parted, and she spoke in a whisper. "Yes, Jenny Campbell."

Jenny struggled to keep it together. "Won't the circuit go up in smoke if I die?"

"He'll make sure there's time to retrieve it before you're fully gone," came the reply. "Dying by my hand will allow your brain chemistry to ensure a perfect extraction."

The Toymaster cackled. "It's a killer solution. Or rather, a *kill-her* solution."

Jenny trembled.

"The final tragedy of both your pathetic lives," he purred. "You two only met because *I* made it happen." He glanced at Jenny. "Your fight in class with Maria, the first meeting between you two in detention, it was all my design. You were my puppets who obliterated every last ounce of opposition leading up to this moment. I wanted you to be friends. Best friends. Besties that turn into beasties. Makes the tragedy all the more powerful. It was simply part of a game. My game." His tone hardened. "Game over."

Suzi heard Jenny's heart racing.

"Isn't there something we can offer you?" Jenny pleaded to the clown.

The Toymaster was unmoved. "Only your lives. My darling Black Circuit will be extracted from your head and placed into your dear friend's. I'll then put my PET in there too, where it will combine with the Black Circuit to create one very big birthday bomb."

Jenny tensed.

He continued. "It won't be used straight away. I'll need access to Mother first. Her Shockwave will give me the growth spurt I've always dreamt of." He patted Suzi's shoulder. "You, dear one, will help me with that. Alas, I can't access Mother on my own, or she'll contain me in her spare womb." He indicated the Toybox. "Once I've absorbed the Shockwave, then you, Miss dark Iyes, will have one last task to complete. You'll be returned to the Homeworld to be the candle on my birthday cake, getting those big bullies off my back once and for all. When your spark ignites, your world will be broken in two in a very, very happy birthday to me. With it gone, I'll be free to turn this planet into my own little playpen, thus ending the final act of my Toy-master-plan."

He whirled Suzi around with his will, making her grip Jenny's neck tightly. The hold was vice-like and crushing, making Jenny choke helplessly into the cold stare of Suzi's glasses that felt like two black pools swamping her.

"Suze!" she blurted out, but could say no more.

The grip tightened.

Jenny choked with wide-eyed horror. Her friend wasn't even trying to fight back, leaving her terrified. Why would Suzi give up so easily? Her best friend? Her protector? How could she do this? How? Right now, Suzi seemed more alien than ever.

Suzi spoke flatly. "Goodbye, Jenny Campbell."

Jenny wanted to cry. To scream. Vivid memories swept through her mind. Her award ceremony. She and Suzi sitting on a log. The two of them at Jenny's house on the couch eating ice-cream, right after smacking their enemies straight back into hell. So many good times.

The world started to fade as past voices returned. People and places who'd been so special. Friends and family. There hadn't been many, and they were few and far between, but all were important.

Finally, there came the most special voice of all.

"Dinner's ready, shortcake! It's on the table!"

Jenny's heart leapt.

"Mum?" she called, with her voice clear in her mind.

"Come on, sweet stuff," the older woman called back, *"we're waiting for you!"*

"Mum, I…?"

"You just want me to come over and carry you inside, don't you?" A sigh. *"Okay shortcake, I guess I've got no choice…"*

A presence swept in.

"Let's go home, Jenny. Play time's over."

Jenny resisted. She didn't want to go. She wanted to stay right here and do whatever it was she'd been doing, only now she couldn't recall what. Her mother's voice was captivating, as were the two ghostly arms embracing her, ready to carry her away. She'd no idea where she was going, but it felt like home.

Everything went black, like her mental signal had suddenly switched off, leaving her disconnected from reality. There were no images, sounds, feelings, emotions, or sensations. Just emptiness, as pure darkness engulfed her.

She reconnected again just as suddenly, and the feeling of her mother's embrace returned once more.

This time it felt different.

The last thing she heard was the crack of her neck, and then nothing else mattered.

Only the light ahead.

She soared towards it.

Chapter Seventeen

Suzi watched blankly as Jenny's head slumped down. She let the girl's body drop limply to the floor and stood motionless, feeling the Toymaster release his invisible grasp from her.

"Two broken dolls," he mocked. "I always love ripping them to shreds. Inside and out. Now I have the best of both worlds. Literally."

He snapped his fingers to extract the Black Circuit from Jenny's mind. A dim glow appeared over her body.

A halo, Suzi observed, growing brighter.

High above, and unseen by either of them, a figure stepped out from a rocky passageway and moved to the crater's edge. Hidden by the shadows and bits of half-fallen debris, the newcomer coolly watched events unfold.

The Toymaster sensed treachery. The Black Circuit was meant to be black, and black meant shadows. Not a blue luminescent glow.

"Trick or treat?" he wondered.

He knelt before Jenny, running a hand over her face and letting the white frills of his wrist flicker in her light. He sniffed the air, sensing her powers, then his hideous features curled in rage. "Trick!"

A fierce blow from his will sent Suzi slamming into the wall.

"No circuit!" he snarled, coming for her. "Only an *echo* of one."

His fingers made a crushing motion.

Suzi felt her face squeezed in excruciating pain as he delved into her mind, searching through her memories.

"Agent Chambers? Can you hear me?"

Suzi hears Echo's scratchy voice in her Earwig, whilst observing the unconscious Jenny lying on a desk in Carrington High. It's just the two of them. Agent 421's off somewhere, either fighting the Trans-plants or dealing with Terror-Byte.

She clicks her head to the side. "I hear you, Echo."

"I'm up to speed on events," Echo states. "I've contained the Toymaster as best I can in his system mainframe. It won't be for long."

"Right now I need your help in another matter, Echo. Can you work on several fronts?"

"Indeed."

"The Black Circuit's wedged in Jenny Campbell's head. We need to extract it completely."

"What do you intend to do with the circuit once it's out?"

Suzi ignores this. "Can you create a decoy to put in its place?"

"I can, but I'll need to know your full intentions. What is it you hope to achieve?"

"You won't approve."

"Another gamble?"

"Yes. You'll have to work with me on this."

She stops momentarily. Her plans are clear. She knows exactly what to do once the Black Circuit's extracted. She doesn't like it one bit, but fate has chosen otherwise.

"The decoy, Echo," she says. "Work fast."

"Where have you hidden it?" the Toymaster screeched. "Where?"

He grabbed her neck.

Suzi displayed no pain as his grip tightened and he raised her high, pushing her against the cave wall.

"Kill me," she said, devoid of emotion. "You've lost. Now you're a Toymaster with no toys."

His other hand rose, making a fist. "Either you spill, or I do. With your blood!"

He opened his hand, tickling the air.

Her Iyes wobbled, ready to detach. She glanced at Maria Longsworth's hologram. The ghostly girl stared back, not blankly, but with a tiny spark. A human element. One that meant her memories and emotions were still there.

Suzi felt the circuits on her Iyes ready to break.

"Nice and easy doesn't do it…" the Toymaster scowled bitterly.

Maria started flickering.

Suzi sensed the girl's presence rising and tensed. She hated relying on others for help, but right now, for the second time in a mere few hours, she needed it. She'd been successful in getting through to Sarah Eastman as a Trans-plant. She could only hope to do the same again with Maria Longsworth. It took a titanic effort to push her ego aside and mouth, *"Assistance!"*

Her Iyes were wrenched from her face, flying into the wall as the Toymaster's grip tightened over her neck, growing hotter. Wisps of steam rose as he leaned in, sneering. "Let's take a look-see inside your head…"

His presence surged in. He barely touched her mind before his arms were grabbed from behind and he was wrenched off her. He wailed as two ghostly limbs stretched tightly around him and a glow illuminated his frilly shoulder.

Maria Longsworth.

His PET.

Suzi dropped to the floor, covering her eye sockets. Ignoring the pain, she scrambled away, forming a mental map of the area, and thankful that the remnants of Maria's humanity had responded to her call.

Maria's hold on him tightened as they ascended in a heavenly halo for the cave roof.

The Toymaster wailed hysterically. "No! I've been a good boy, Mummy! Don't hurt me! I've been a good boy…!"

His red balloon exploded with a deafening bang as they rose higher, with Maria glowing ever brighter.

Suzi scrambled blindly over the floor, reaching for her Iyes. Her eye sockets filled with liquid. Without her Iyes, her emotions were taking over and her panic levels were rising. She quickly refocused. Logic, intelligence, and the mission were all that mattered. Goals were needed. Not hindrances.

Her hand swept to the left, landing on Jenny's face.

Suzi froze. Despite her lack of vision, she could feel Jenny's features. It wasn't an image she'd have wanted to see.

She removed her hand and resumed her search in her blurred nightmare of pain, penetrated by flickering halos from the battle above. She pushed on through the hazy world of shapes and shadows, making for the spot where she'd heard her Iyes land. She knew they were close. She'd been so connected to them for so long that she practically sensed them. Much to her relief, her hands finally wrapped around their frames and then –

Click!

They attached to her face, like they were returning home.

Her pain eased. The world solidified and her insides settled. Her temples were sore and her headache searing, but at least things had stabilised.

High above, she saw the Toymaster fighting against Maria's template. The girl was strong, but his strength was also growing. It wouldn't be long before he broke free of her hold, which didn't leave Suzi much time.

Still on all fours, she scrambled over to Jenny's body. The sight of the girl's deathly white features shook Suzi to the core, and she wondered if she was getting weaker.

She paused, considering this.

No, not weaker, she concluded. She was allowing herself to feel emotions. If anything, that made her stronger.

She placed her hand on Jenny's cheek. "I am sorry."

She leaned down, hugging her friend. She didn't want to let go, even though it was the logical thing to do. Something deep inside her was overriding that logic.

She spoke, her voice a whisper. "I did not want this. Any of it." She sat up, touching Jenny's cheek again. "Goodbye, Jenny Campbell."

It was almost impossible to break away. When she rose and ran, it was like ripping her heart out.

High above, on the crater's edge, the shadowy figure watched her climb the opposite slope and enter a passageway. When she was gone, the figure turned and entered a tunnel, intending to cut her off, leaving the Toymaster and his PET to slam from one wall into another.

All while masses of rubble thundered down around Jenny's motionless body, enclosing her in a makeshift tomb.

A bloodbath lay on the road.

Police Sergeant Donna Vertigo stood in a blocked-off section of the highway where the bikers mutilated corpses lay. There weren't too many cars on the road tonight. That was lucky. Even luckier was that the media hadn't got wind of this yet.

Detective Angelo Trident stood by her side. Vertigo sensed that he was trying hard to keep his stomach contents down and remain professional. She always made a habit of keeping half an eye on him. He was a little older than her. Good-looking too. Too bad he was married, she thought. Rumours at the station hinted that he was planning on being a judge one day. She, on the other hand, was going nowhere fast.

"Right," she began grimly, "what's your expert opinion, detective?"

Trident scratched the back of his neck, not disguising that he was turning greener by the moment. "Best I can tell is that some animal did this. Or animals. It's like a pack of wolves ripped 'em to shreds."

"Yeah, but animals leave tracks."

"I know, which suggests that whatever did this was intelligent."

Vertigo shook her head. "You call this intelligent? Where do we even start?"

A ground tremor answered her question as a streaming light ascended from the forest ahead. A beam of some kind, she realised. It flickered high into the night, changing shape and expanding into a dome over a wide area, then switched back into a beam again, before rapidly morphing from one to the other.

Trident spoke grimly. "There's your answer, Sergeant."

Vertigo nodded. "Of course, it would be there."

She knew it all too well. The site of the Hurriflame.

She reached for her radio. "I'm calling for backup."

She didn't have to give the order for her officers to kick themselves into gear. They were already running for their vehicles.

Suzi ran through the tunnels.

She'd set her Iyes to night vision to guide her along. The rumblings from the Toymaster and his PET were growing louder, shaking the walls and sending chunks of rubble crashing heavily to the cave floor, not that Suzi cared. Everything important to her was gone. Still, she determined, she wasn't running from a threat, but fighting it instead, by heading for a place to disrupt the Toymaster's plans significantly.

Her keen hearing detected machinery ahead. She knew exactly what it was.

Mother.

She rounded a corner, entering another passageway.

A figure stepped out before her.

She came to a skidding halt.

Agent 421. Or at least he appeared to be. His presence had changed for the worse.

He snarled, revealing razor-sharp teeth.

The Toymaster faced Maria.

He'd turned himself around, locking arms with her. They glared at each other furiously, amidst fierce sparks of electricity flickering in their eyes, while fireballs from them both rumbled the cave walls.

The Toymaster's rage grew. There was only one way to finish this.

"I don't want your inheritance!" he snapped. "No, I need you back in my *will*."

He punched savagely into her chest, entering her ethereal presence and delving deep, whilst aware that this move left him open to attack. He didn't care. He loved a gamble.

This one paid off.

Rapid searching brought him to the gold nugget he so desperately desired. The tiny human spark left in her template.

He growled maniacally, ripping her core out.

Maria wailed, terrified. Her heart was gone, yet its residue remained, but that would soon fade, and fast, leaving her without much time.

Summoning her reserves, she slammed him headfirst into a wall, then lunged, fully aware that she was weakening by the moment.

Suzi stood her ground.

The Agent facing her looked like 421, and had his traits, but was clearly someone else, or rather, some*thing* else. She'd suspected as much in the car outside Carrington High shortly before the school exploded. Since then, she'd had inklings that he wasn't quite right. The last time she'd truly seen him as himself was when they'd found Jenny with Miss Ford. He'd sneaked away, and now she knew he was no longer 421. It was his body, but 421's Symbiant life form was dead, replaced with another lethal bug.

A Terror-Byte.

Suzi was shaken. It took immense strength to keep her emotions in check. The real 421 had felt something for her, and she for him, only she hadn't wanted to admit it. Now he, like so many others in this accursed conflict, was another casualty.

He and Terror-Byte must have fought, she surmised, leaving Terror-Byte as the victor. Terror-Byte had then transferred his razor-like teeth over to his new body and stayed close to her. He'd skilfully aided the Toymaster, who'd even attacked him in the police car simply to keep up appearances.

They stared at each other amidst the shaking surroundings.

Terror-Byte spoke. His voice no longer resembled 421's, but the scratchy hisses of the Terror-Byte of old. "The Black Circuit. Now!"

Suzi's thoughts churned furiously, trying to stay focused on the face she'd once had feelings for. Did he know where the Black Circuit was? How closely had he been monitoring her?

He continued. "No residue of the circuit was found in Carrington High's remains, nor in Jenny Campbell's psyche. There is only one place it can be."

"The decoy, Echo," Suzi says. "Work fast."

Echo does so.

A psychic decoy's essential, Suzi tells Echo. There are no other options. Putting a trap in Jenny's head to bait the Toymaster's out of the question. That would kill the girl.

"It's in your head," Terror-Byte concludes. "Is it not?"

Suzi stood her ground, annoyed that he'd discovered the truth. The Toymaster was another matter. Echo had cloaked the Black Circuit effectively in Suzi's mind, while the Toymaster had been too distracted by Jenny, and bound up in his ego, to notice it earlier. She'd yet to discover if Terror-Byte had told the Toymaster anything.

Terror-Byte continued. "You're no doubt making for the Mother WOMB which you know is still active. You're planning to use the Shockwave to extract the circuit safely from your head and dispose of it."

He saw a bulge in her sleeve. To any human, it would have gone unnoticed, but Terror-Byte knew exactly what to look for, and now understood completely.

"So," he hissed scornfully, "the girl lives!"

A wisp of air emerged from Jenny's lips. She stirred groggily. Vivid memories returned. The last thing she recalled was Suzi crushing her neck.

She focused intensely, thinking hard.

Jenny recalls that she's been resistant to Suzi's Iyes ever since she's known her. Now she has no resistance. Suzi's glasses are sucking her in, manipulating her mind. Not only that, she realises, she hasn't had any headaches since blowing up the school. She's barely had time to realise it, but her mind's clear.

A thought hits her. Is the stuff in her head gone completely?

The grip on her neck stops at a certain point, holding its position. A click comes from Suzi's sleeve.

Suzi mouths discreetly, "Play dead."

Jenny frowns.

Suzi speaks again before —

Thuk!

The tiny dart strikes Jenny's neck, burying itself in deeply and sending her into a dead slump.

Somehow, through the pain and confusion, another memory returns.

Jenny sits with Suzi on a log in the school grounds. She looks at Suzi's sleeve. Her friend speaks.

"It is a projectile injector. It fires capsules holding an immobilising tranquiliser."

"I-T darts? Nice."

"No. Effective. They give the appearance of death. Their effect is temporary."

Jenny opened her eyes.

Her neck hurt like hell and throbbed painfully. She recalled everything now. Well almost. Her mind was blank when it came to what Suzi had said just before firing the dart. At least the memories of hearing her's mother voice again were clear, and she was grateful for that. It might have come from some weird combination between her brain and the I-T dart, she figured.

It didn't matter. The world was blurry, she felt nauseous, and the rumbles above sounded like the gods duelling in the heavens. She blinked, trying hard to focus.

She was buried under a pile of rocks. None touched her, and all were leaning on each other for support. She just hoped to God she wasn't in too deep.

She pushed two of them away, parting them easily, and through a gap, saw Maria hovering high above her, grasping the Toymaster tightly. Her arm was wrapped around his neck as he dangled from her hold, as if in a hangman's noose.

He noticed Jenny.

"I wonder who's more hungover…" he began, then wailed as Maria's grip tightened.

Jenny pushed the surrounding rocks away and scrambled out. She'd barely emerged when she saw a glow emanating from the Toybox. Curiously, she crawled over and peered inside.

The toy clown lay in there glowing.

"What the crud…?" she whispered.

Suzi's concern grew.

Terror-Byte had surmised everything correctly. He also blocked her way to Mother and wouldn't budge without force. Time was short and she needed to get to work. That left one option which she hated more than anything.

Win him over.

She spoke formally. "You wish to be free of your master, do you not?"

Now it was Terror-Byte's turn to stay silent.

Suzi continued, "Accompany me to the Mother WOMB. There, we can remove the Black Circuit from my head and destroy it. We'll use its residue to create another virus to inject into the Toymaster and annihilate him, thereby freeing you of his control."

Terror-Byte considered this, then spoke, "Your offer is unacceptable. Your counter-offensive weapon will be untested. There will be little time to initiate it."

"I work fast…" Her Iyes darkened. "… Unless hindered."

Terror-Byte paused. The silence grew. Finally, he said, "No deal."

His tone was cold.

This angered Suzi, more so since those words came from 421's lips. Nevertheless, she kept her temper. "You wish to stay under his control when there are other options available?" Realisation dawned. "I see. You've already begun measures to break free of him, haven't you?"

Terror-Byte was unmoved. "The Shockwave shielded me from his control when I entered these decimated remains. I was therefore allowed to remove the surveillance devices he planted on me, along with his primed explosives too. I also countermanded your instructions to the aggressive humans on the highway. You ordered them not to engage with the Toymaster. I disagreed. The distraction gave me further time to free myself from his control." His head rose. "The Black Circuit must not be destroyed. If we extract it from your mind, we can manipulate both the Toymaster and the PET, effectively having two weapons. A fully primed Planetary Eruption Trigger *and* the Toymaster himself."

Now Suzi understood. Terror-Byte was making a power grab. She was annoyed. There was no time for this, especially with weapons such as these.

"You overestimate yourself and underestimate him," she warned. "My answer is the same as yours. No deal."

His head lowered menacingly. "Then we have a problem. Don't we?"

Suzi nodded. "Yes. We do."

The ground shook as the tension mounted.

Terror-Byte's jaws opened, baring his deadly teeth, then he lunged.

Jenny grimaced at the toy clown in the wooden chest. The freaky face, covered by a shimmering dark halo, was seemingly laughing at her. Even worse, she felt its hideous presence tingling against her psyche, just like during the Hurriflame.

She knew things were different this time. For one thing, the doll was free of the Toymaster who'd taken over JT's body, leaving this empty shell behind. The doll's pull was nowhere near as bad as before, yet she also sensed from its hungry glare that it yearned to consume her next. Something had to fill the void left by the Toymaster. She was it.

An unpleasant thought struck her. It was a big gamble, but a necessary risk.

A few rags lay nearby. She picked them up. They were oily and squelched in her grip. She ignored the discomfort and wrapped her hands in them. Once they were covered, she leaned in for the doll.

"Here goes everything," she muttered, and took hold of it.

The freaky hell-doll was heavy. Too heavy, and didn't feel like a toy at all, rather, a small corpse. Perhaps its contents were filled with – no! She didn't want to think about it.

She shivered, feeling the inklings of its nightmare presence that had changed her life during the Hurriflame. Now, thankfully, it held no Black Circuit, and no Toymaster either, meaning it couldn't hurt her. In fact, it might just be able to help.

She felt a bump on its back. Curiously, she turned it over and ripped part of its material away. A small metal cover, lodged in its middle, lay underneath. Crackles came from below, resembling eerie laughter.

She tried pulling the cover open with her insulated fingers. It wasn't easy.

She tried again.

It opened slightly, with a squeak, allowing her to glimpse at a red object lodged inside.

Praying like hell that she was doing the right thing, she clawed at the cover, trying to pull the whole thing away.

The cave wall burst inwards.

Suzi and Terror-Byte crashed into a tunnel, landing with a heavy thump and rolling over, their Iyes locked in a furious gaze as they grasped each other's mechanical biceps.

Suzi rose to her knees. Terror-Byte rose with her, refusing to release her arms, just as she refused to let go of his. To release their holds meant breaking the deadlock, but staying in it meant precious time wasted for Suzi. She was also out of I-T darts and knew that Terror-Byte was aware of that. They'd have little effect on him anyway, yet could have been useful as a distraction.

His rage grew. So did hers. She, however, wasn't fighting for herself, but for others. That meant taking a chance.

She fell backwards, pulling him with her, then kicked up, sending him flying over her head. He held onto her biceps, pulling her over too. They came full circle, returning to their knees, back in the deadlock.

Terror-Byte lunged for a headbutt. Suzi dodged it and rose. He went with her. She whirled him around, slamming him into the cave wall. He held on, despite the fierce impact, and their grips remained locked as they propelled each other across the tunnel, into the opposite wall. They hit it hard, before rebounding against the first wall. Suzi took the full force, then spotted a weak point in the roof. She belted him into the opposite wall again, just under it, sending a basketball-sized rock thudding onto his head. It did little to hurt him but served its purpose. She broke free of the deadlock, kicked herself away and retreated a few steps to gain some ground.

He leapt for her.

She grabbed the fallen rock that had struck his head and rammed him with it. Once, twice, three times, followed by a massive blow to his chest that sent him recoiling.

The cave rumbled, indicating that the battle between the Toymaster and his PET was growing. Trickles of dust fell past her as she scanned the roof. The readouts in her Iyes calculated the probabilities.

The tunnel was losing stability.

She knew what to do.

Terror-Byte ran at her.

She stayed motionless.

His mouth opened wide, revealing his razor-like teeth, then he dived.

She fell onto her back, raising both legs. He thudded into them and she kicked up, propelling him over her head on his own momentum to part of the roof behind her. He sailed for some way while she leapt up and bolted.

Her aim had been successful, for he hit the roof's weakest point, dropped like a stone, and landed heavily as a massive rush of debris plummeted, burying him completely.

Suzi turned and watched from a safe distance as the mound of rubble grew larger. Her Iyes scanned it, detecting his electrical readings. He was alive in there. The debris wouldn't hold him for long. Even worse, the rockfall had blocked off the tunnel, leaving her on the wrong side of it, meaning she'd have to find another way to Mother.

Still, she'd dealt with him for now. That was fortunate. He'd been a worthy opponent.

Satisfied, she ran.

The Toymaster knew that his PET, Maria Longsworth, was weakening. Every attack she made was worse than the last. All she needed, he figured, was one final push.

He moved his head to her lips, leering, "I always was a sucker for punishment!"

He pulled her in, kissing her savagely. Sparks flew between them as they twirled repeatedly amidst the shaking walls. A hideous sucking force ignited as he began absorbing her into himself.

Maria felt herself physically deflating in the Toymaster's grasp, knowing she had no chance of fighting back. Any thought she had of entering him and self-destructing was seen by the Toymaster and countermanded.

His consciousness entered her fragile psyche, delving hungrily into his weapon of choice.

Bit by bit, her template morphed into a white halo. Steadily she shrank, becoming so small that the only thing she saw was a giant clown's mouth looming over her. Finally, she entered with a scream, descending on a rollercoaster ride into the great abyss beyond.

The Toymaster licked his lips, satisfied. "I always did like the hot stuff."

He heard Maria's cries grow softer as he locked her away in one of the many monstrous dungeons of his sick mind. She wouldn't be silenced completely; he'd ensure that. After all, he reasoned, the more voices in his head, the better.

A glimmer below caught his attention. One he didn't like at all.

The girl, Jenny Campbell, lived. She was standing by the Toybox, holding his old doll.

His face fell. "Someone's not playing nice. It seems she's trying to bond with me through a recon-silly-action."

He floated down for her, watching with glee as she desperately struggled to remove the doll's back covering. Much to his delight, it had opened a little but refused to go any further.

He sneered as he descended. "I do love the way people react when I'm around. Let's start this react-or then, shall we?"

He chuckled cruelly.

Suzi heard Mother's hum.

It resonated from the end of the tunnel, behind the cave wall. She was close now. So very close.

She ran for the wall and leapt in the air, bashing into it hard. The impact was powerful, forming a massive recess. A few more blows made a hole big enough for her to crawl through. She did so quickly, shuffling along in the gap to the other side. Once there, she emerged onto a metal grilled platform and observed her surroundings.

Various platforms and stairways were stretched out before her. She recognised this area. She'd been here when the ECG were in control, only she'd seen things from far below, in front of the WOMB itself. Now she was high above that WOMB, among the aerial workstations. The terminal close by told her that Mother was currently functioning on auxiliary power. The second that power failed; this whole place would ignite. What's more, the terminal's readings stated that things were dangerously close to that point.

She saw part of the problem. Long cables dangled from the top of the cave, high over Mother, with several of them sparking. They hung from an enormous sphere that had half-crashed through the roof during the Heartbeat's destruction. That giant round piece of machinery was Mother's secondary relay station, she realised. She knew all about it, having closely examined JT's personal files when he hadn't been watching. Even better, was that she'd memorised his security codes too.

She moved over to the terminal and activated its emergency power cells. This antique piece of machinery would suffice for now, she was sure of it, but her frustration grew at its slow speed. Finally, it activated, and she entered the program she needed, typing furiously.

Two of the terminal's white panels glowed. When they reached a sufficient level of brightness, she raised her hands and placed one on each panel, then winced as the Shockwave surged up through the terminal and into her head, ready to remove the Black Circuit and send it into Mother's WOMB. Once it was in there, Suzi planned to use a cyst from Echo's Acystance Package to destroy it.

Getting the circuit into her head had been painless. There'd been no effects of the Hurripain, as Jenny Campbell had called it. Suzi's physiology was too strong for that. Getting the circuit out again was another matter. The pain from the extraction process for humans was powerful enough to kill them, and she was about to be hit by the worst of it.

Her face tightened in agony.

"Crapageddon!"

Jenny stepped back, hitting a rock wall. All the things she'd thought of as feral in her short life now paled in comparison to the monstrous white clown looming over her. She'd always believed that her high school nemesis, Maria Longsworth, had been scarier than anything else. Longsworth, however, was nothing compared to this psychopathic, schizophrenic, god-like, child-like, mental-asylum-like, freak of existence that had swallowed her up. She shivered, clutching the doll tightly and feeling like a frightened child in a dark bedroom.

A little, not a lot.

She wasn't the Toymaster.

She was Jenny Campbell.

Despite everything she'd been through, she was still a fighter, and Suzi had enhanced that to the extreme. Her best friend's words returned to her, making more impact than anything.

"You've always got something to lose, no matter how low you feel. Even when you don't see it, someone will always believe in you. You have so much potential."

Her inner spark ignited. She was worth a whole lot, she realised, meaning there was always a chance.

Now fuelled by an inner strength, she pulled at the doll's back covering again. This time it opened fully, revealing a red button. She didn't know what it would do, only that she had to take a gamble. A one in a million shot. Defiantly, she turned the doll around to face the Toymaster, her finger poised on the button.

The clown snickered cruelly. "It's always fun when people press my buttons. Go on. Do it. *Play* with me!"

Jenny hesitated. This nutjob was getting to her.

He continued. "I've always loved child's play. Especially instinctive gambles from frightened little girls playing with broken dolls. What will she do? Press the button and climb a ladder?" He indicated the girder behind him, serving as an escape route to the surface, then his long-forked tongue flickered out from his lips, making her jump. "Or will she lie down with a snake?"

Jenny's face hardened. Nobody told her what to do. Not now. Not ever.

"Suck it up, son," she seethed, "'cause Mummy's coming home for some smack-down karma!"

She pushed the button in.

Twin beams of light shot out from the doll's eyes, resting on his frills.

He froze.

So did the button. Halfway in.

Jenny swore and tried pushing it the rest of the way. It wouldn't budge.

The Toymaster snickered. This light, at minimum power, was dim, and would only halt him temporarily. He could still push on, just. He was slow, rigid, and half paralysed, but his strength was growing.

He inched towards her.

Jenny saw his confidence rising. He'd known the button would stick. *That's* why he'd urged her to press it, meaning he was unlikely to be hindered for long.

He scowled cruelly. "Miss Muffet's not meant to stand up to the spider. That's not how it goes." He inched on. "Look at her. No Mummy, no Daddy, just a single broken doll in her arms. Isn't that what we all are? Broken dolls, all in a row. Staring out at the world through cracked eyes." His own widened maniacally. "Let's fix you, little girl. We'll play a game…" He indicated himself. "This body's wearing a bit thin. It needs to be renewed. I think it's time I got in touch with my feminine side…"

Jenny shuddered.

He reached out for her. "Come into my light and be *trans*-fixed. Join the voices in my head. You'll be a lone holler in one incredibly big, unhappy family!"

Jenny had heard enough. She ran past him, clutching the toy and heading for a tunnel at the crater's edge.

The Toymaster cackled, floating delightedly around on the spot, watching her go. "Let's put the nasty into your *dy*-nasty…"

His cackle grew louder.

Chapter Eighteen

Suzi struggled to control her rising pain. The Shockwave was intense, delving deep into her mind and searching for the Black Circuit. She wouldn't cry out or scream. She'd always been up to the challenge of withstanding anything, no matter how painful. Regrettably. this technology, though far superior to the Toymaster's back at Carrington Hight, was still too slow for her liking.

The Shockwave touched the Black Circuit in her head.

She jolted, shaking violently under the excruciating pain. This was worse than anything she'd felt in a long time. Somehow, through the brightness in her mind's eye, she saw a Shockwave tendril encompass the small black dot of the Black Circuit.

Bit by bit, the circuit emerged.

Fighting against her anguish, she glanced at the terminal screen, showing the circuit's extraction rate.

A computerised voice spoke: *"Ten percent. Twenty percent. Thirty percent…"*

Far too slow for her liking.

Her hand shifted. It was painful to move. She brought it down and twisted a dial, increasing the power.

"Forty percent. Fifty percent…"

Better.

Just not fast enough.

She twisted the dial further.

"Sixty percent. Seventy percent. Eighty percent…"

Her hand jerked as she reached over, hitting another button and activating a second screen. Its image split into several smaller screens, care of the self-powered ECG surveillance cameras. Most showed empty tunnels.

One caught her attention. An image of a crater, where the Toymaster was hovering after Jenny Campbell. Suzi saw from the terminal's readouts that all the exits around Jenny were sealed shut. Now, the girl was running to the crater's edge amidst the shaking surroundings. She'd barely reached it when a girder detached, hitting the ground before her.

"Ninety percent. Ninety-five percent…"

A heavy, metal beam slammed into Suzi, striking her onto the platform. She landed solidly, feeling the Shockwave drain from her body as the terminal's touch faded. Her concern for Jenny grew, even more so when she saw Terror-Byte standing over her, holding the beam and leering through 421's face.

Dread filled her. Had she succeeded? Was she free of the Black Circuit? Did it remain in her mind, or was it in Mother, waiting to be annihilated? Whatever the case, the terminal screen still showed the Toymaster pursuing Jenny.

Terror-Byte stepped in front of it, blocking her view.

The terminal's computerised voice spoke. *"Transfer complete. New element absorbed into Mother."*

Suzi should have been pleased, but was far from it. Terror-Byte had disrupted things at a crucial juncture. The Black Circuit was in Mother's WOMB, just not in the cyst, and was hovering millimetres from it instead. If Terror-Byte wasn't here she could easily program a Shockwave tendril to pull the Black Circuit into that cyst, but with him around it would prove impossible.

Thankfully, she was a hindrance to him too.

Stalemate.

He dropped the beam loudly onto the grille. Still facing her, he half-turned his head to the side, seeing the terminal, then reached back, activating a sequence of numbers.

Suzi knew he was using the Shockwave to shield the Black Circuit with a protective sheath. That would be the only thing to prevent its destruction. Her gaze rose to the giant sphere of Mother's secondary relay station high above the Mother WOMB. She needed to get away from Terror-Byte and climb one of the several cables to reach the screen on its side which was, luckily, still active. Once there, she'd be able to help Jenny Campbell.

There was no time to think or talk, just act.

She leapt up, lunging into Terror-Byte with a flying thud. Her fist lashed out at the terminal as they flew past it, bashing its screen and making it inoperative. Sheer fury propelled her onwards as they broke through the metal rail barrier, plunging into open air among the dangling cables wavering over Mother far below. Terror-Byte grabbed a cable as Suzi held onto him tightly. Together, they swung violently over the cylinder of crackling energy.

She looked down at Mother and saw, amidst the blinding glare, that Terror-Byte had been successful in creating a basic sheath to surround the Black Circuit. It wasn't enough to fully protect it, but was getting there. For the moment though, she could still destroy it, and easily too. All she needed to do was to slam Terror-Byte into it. That was good enough for her.

She pulled on him heavily.

High above, the cable started dislodging from its socket.

Terror-Byte snarled, let go of the cable and kicked her away, just as the line dislodged. They flew in opposite directions before grabbing a cable each and spinning violently. Once they'd slowed, Terror-Byte began climbing his line, making for the digital screen in the sphere above.

Suzi cursed inwardly, knowing what he was up to. He'd worked in the Heartbeat with the ECG after all. It made sense that he'd determined her plans.

She dived over, landing on his back. Her impact made them drop a little and whirl around on his line. He bit savagely for her hand. She leapt off him, grabbed another cable, swung out, flew in, and rammed him so hard that he dropped into open air. She veered away, watching as he fell for a bit and caught a cable a short way below. It was weak, she saw. Excellent.

She used her body weight to gain momentum before releasing her grip and shooting freely for his cable. She grabbed it easily some way above him, yanking it down with both hands and sweeping past. The move was effective and the cable snapped, taking him with it. As both he and it dropped, she sailed on, propelled by her own speed, to another line.

Terror-Byte fell helplessly, with nothing to grab onto. He watched Suzi swing away while he plummeted for Mother's smooth glass surface, then smacked into it hard, splitting its casing open. A sizzling crackle of light engulfed him as a deafening siren rang out and a computerised voice bellowed, *"Containment field compromised!"*

A Shockwave tendril appeared, seizing him tightly, as more of its kind erupted around him.

Suzi saw the cracks in the WOMB growing rapidly, allowing enormous flaming bursts to erupt. The flames rose higher, coming dangerously close to her. She ignored them and kept climbing her weakened cable for the sphere above. Finally, she made it to the top, grabbed a metal handle, and released her line. It fell away, trailing down into the blinding light and hitting Terror-Byte's writhing form.

The handle she gripped was burning. This meant little to her as she looped an arm through it, holding herself in place, then worked the sphere's flickering digital screen with her other hand. Her fingers worked swiftly over the onscreen keyboard as she dangled over Mother's fiery tendrils far below.

She was making good progress, until the image wavered and died. With no other option, she ripped away a security hatch, sending it plummeting, then removed several wires and reconnected several more. When she was satisfied, she placed her hand on the live circuit board and jolted as she merged directly with the system. Ignoring the pain, she clicked her head to the side, changing her Iyes optics to allow her to interface with the sphere's camera feeds.

The first image she saw in her Iyes, via the sphere, was an empty room.

No good to her.

She changed images.

A storeroom this time.

Still no good.

She scanned through the various camera feeds. Numerous scenes rose until at last she found what she was looking for.

Jenny Campbell.

The girl was conscious and trying to find her way out of the crater.

Suzi was relieved, though would never admit it.

She watched as the Toymaster pursued Jenny, hindered by rigid movements. That was a good thing. What wasn't so good was that Jenny was trapped and there was no sign of the holographic Maria Longsworth.

Suzi zeroed in on Jenny and saw her holding the doll. She knew what to do. She had to help her… sister?

Jenny's words returned to her.

"You really are like a big sister, y'know?"

Yes. That was what she thought of Jenny Campbell now, too. A sister. It felt strange to think of her as that. For some reason, the urge to save Jenny was more important than anything else.

With her priorities firmly in order, she reactivated the sphere's digital screen. Thankfully, a short power recharge allowed her access to it once more.

Swiftly, she keyed in a sequence.

Jenny turned away from the door at the crater's edge. It was locked, just like the others she'd already tried.

Her neck tingled. The Toymaster's strength was growing. The touch of his will felt like deadly pinpricks on her skin as trickles of blood flowed down her neck.

She hit the doll's back, desperately trying to get the switch to go in further.

No luck.

The Toymaster landed, growing stronger with each step he took. She knew it wouldn't be long before she was even more screwed, and shivered as she wiped her neck, smearing blood across it.

"Beautiful," the Toymaster purred. "I do so love to get under people's skin. Why not try and get under mine?"

He'd almost overridden the doll's power and would soon be his horrific old self again, who wanted her as his horrific *new* self.

She held up the doll so it faced him, keeping her finger on the button and bracing for the worst.

Suzi keyed in a final sequence.

Done.

She'd directed some of Mother's energy into the doll Jenny held, boosting its power significantly.

She flicked a switch.

A roaring static burst erupted through the crater.

Jenny looked up with a start as Suzi spoke through the intercom.

"Press the button on the doll, Jenny Campbell. Do it!"

Jenny pressed it without question. This time the button went in. Smoothly.

The doll hummed to life. The light in its eyes grew, freezing the Toymaster to the spot.

"Looks like you're well and truly rooted now," Jenny quipped.

His face barely had enough strength to scowl.

"Bullies!" he hissed. "You're all bullies!"

Suzi rapidly programed several algorithms into the screen and reactivated the speaker system. "Throw the doll in the Toybox, Jenny Campbell. Quickly!"

Jenny hurled the doll inside.

"Score!" she cried, then muttered, "I hope you know what you're doing, Suze."

To her surprise, Suzi answered. *"I am always conscious of my actions, Jenny Campbell."*

"Oh God, you heard that?" Jenny asked.

"Unlike you, who states the obvious."

"Oh yeah, kick me while I'm down…"

"I would never do that. It would only damage you and serve no beneficial purpose."

"One of these days, Suze, we're gonna have a real good talk about stuff and – crap on a stick…!"

She leapt out of the Toymaster's path and scrambled away.

His head lowered. Rather shamefacedly, and like a spoilt child, he headed to the Toybox, manipulated by the doll.

Suzi spoke. *"The doll's recall device has been activated. It will absorb the Toymaster into itself, along with the Planetary Eruption Trigger."*

"You mean Maria?"

"Yes. Once the doll's contained them, use the padlock on the ground near your foot to seal the lid shut, then key in the numbers 458213..."

"Hang on, what...?" Jenny cut in.

"458213," Suzi repeated. *"The Toybox is a safety measure initiated by the ECG. It will hold the blast."*

"What blast?"

"I've modified the Shockwave to eradicate both the Toymaster and the Planetary Eruption Trigger he holds. Once they're inside the doll, it will self-destruct. We mustn't allow the slightest trace to escape, which is why the box must be locked before detonation. Now say that number again."

Jenny struggled to recall it. "4, 5, 8..." She thought hard. "... 2, 1, 3?"

"Correct," Suzi said. *"Congratulations, Jenny Campbell. It's fulfilling to know that I have —"* She stopped and corrected herself. *"We have completed this mission. In your language we did i—"*

The COM link went dead.

Suzi's head recoiled as a spanner shot past her, slamming into the screen and destroying it.

She looked down.

Terror-Byte was climbing a cable, his body on fire, his face a mesh of boiling liquid, but his Iyes, intact. Below him was a platform where an open toolbox lay. Several tools were inside, minus one spanner, which had just smashed the screen by her head.

Her gaze darkened as he ascended. This operation was only half-finished. Whilst talking to Jenny Campbell, she'd disabled his protective sheath around the Black Circuit. She'd next keyed in a command for one of the Mother WOMB's energy stems to pull the Black Circuit into the hovering cyst nearby. Only then could the circuit be destroyed. Trouble was, Terror-Byte had stopped her from entering the final sequence. Now, she couldn't remotely command the cyst-stem to destroy the circuit. Her screen had been demolished, upping the stakes considerably.

There was a much cruder way to obliterate the Black Circuit, she determined. Her thoughts whirred as she calculated the time factors, variables, and possible casualties. Finally, she concluded, there was no other option. If she didn't go through with it, then the Black Circuit would be up for grabs for everyone. True, it wouldn't have the Planetary Eruption Trigger, but would still be dangerous in the wrong hands. She couldn't afford to leave things unfinished. Her jaw tightened as she vowed to ensure the Black Circuit's destruction, as well as provide Jenny with an escape route to the surface *and* modify the Shockwave for one final victory.

The shades in her Iyes swirled furiously as she reached into the sphere's flaming wires, ignored the pain, and worked rapidly.

Long tears of blood trailed down the Toymaster's face as the doll's might pulled him to the Toybox, jolting him awkwardly like a puppet on a string. "No, Mummy! Don't send me to the dark place! I'll be a good boy...!"

He'd almost reached the Toybox when, to Jenny's horror, the doll's glow suddenly dimmed and his head rose gleefully.

"Oh no, no, no, no!" she cried. "Hell no...!"

She ran around him, fell to her knees, reached into the Toybox, and pulled the doll out. The button was rising from its back, thanks to a final push from his will. She pressed it hard, it slid in smoothly, and the doll's light flared brightly once more. This time she made sure to keep it in place.

"No," the Toymaster whimpered. "No, this isn't right! This isn't a happy ending, Mummy! Where's my family? My room and my toys? My soft bed? Where are you, Mummy?"

"No more games!" Jenny snapped. "You're just a spoilt, feral, out-of-control runt, and you know what? I'm sick of it! All of it! Everything you've done to me, the games you've played, the way you've conned everyone to make me think I'm crazy, but you know what's really funny deadnuts? I get to walk away from this, all of this, as me! Someone who you failed to pile your crap on! All the sick mind games you tried to bury me under – I don't want 'em, they're yours, and you know what else you can do?"

She threw the doll back in the box.

"Go play with yourself!"

The doll's power grew, pulling the Toymaster in after it.

"I can see everything," he whispered. "The Christmas lights. The presents. I can see Santa. He's coming. Coming for me. Waiting to open me up and surprise us all."

He crouched down slowly until only his head was left. The lid descended over him, leaving only his hideous eyes to stare out from the closing gap.

"Won't someone play with me?" he asked softly. "Then we can all live happily, ever... after."

The lid sealed shut.

Jenny knelt, clipping the padlock on.

"That's one can of worms that's never going to be reopened," she muttered.

She frowned, trying to recall the numbers that Suzi had given her.

Suzi worked in a blur to bypass the sphere's mainframe system. Her fingers burnt as she fiddled with the open circuit board until finally, her task was complete.

Power had been transferred to several doors in the base's remains, opening them to allow Jenny Campbell a path to the surface. Once the girl was free, Mother would explode, destroying the Black Circuit completely. Suzi had ensured that the explosion would be contained locally. Now she only needed to trigger the blast itself. There was only one way to do that.

She lowered her head. Her Iyes reflected the flames far below. Fire had been a constant element throughout the horrors of her tortured existence. Any beauty she'd seen always ended up as twisted debris in burning embers.

This time though, things were different. Jenny Campbell lived. The Toybox contained both the Toymaster and his Planetary Eruption Trigger. The planet was safe.

She'd succeeded, at a very high cost. There was a price to pay for the sins of her past. For all her guilt and shame, and everything else that made her sick at every moment of every day, it was at last time to let go. To stop fighting and finish this war so that others may live in a peace that she'd never known, and now never would.

Terror-Byte was making steady progress up the cable. He'd ruin everything if he got to her. She couldn't allow that to happen.

Sarah's words echoed in her mind.

"End-Time begins!"

Terror-Byte closed in.

Suzi found herself on the verge of shaking. Her whole life had been prepped for right here, right now.

Her voice quivered as she spoke. The words emerged, not in her calm, logical tone, nor in that of a child, but rather, an adult.

"Mission complete!"

Terror-Byte leapt.

Suzi dived.

They collided in mid-air, plummeting for Mother, with no cables to grab onto. The fires of hell rose to greet them, care of the fiery split in Mother's outer casing. Together, they surged into an engulfing fireball. So hot were its flames that their metal bodies merged into one.

Smash!

Mother's thick glass splintered as their combined lump dropped solidly into a rush of searing heat. Despite this, Suzi's mind remained intact as she defiantly fought against the excruciating pain.

Memories returned.

Agent 421's voice came first.

"You are almost... human."

Rags's little voice followed.

"I forgive you! You have to forgive yourself!"

Echo's words came next. The warm friendly charm of her Echo that had always soothed her darkest moments.

"Always a pleasure, Agent Chambers."

Lastly, there was Jenny Campbell.

Her friend.

Her best friend.

"You really are like a big sister..."

Each voice had struck a powerful chord deep inside her, easing her pain. She held onto the voices of her loved ones as her Iyes fell away, burning to a crisp and dissolving completely.

That same moment, Jenny felt an icy chill rip through her, like she'd lost something. She shook her head and refocused on the Toybox's electronic lock. There was still work to do.

"4, 5, 8, 2, 1," she began, then stopped. "No! Hang on! 4, 5, 8, 2, 1…"

The last number eluded her. She smacked her forehead with her palm. "How come I can never remember the important stuff but when it comes to reality shows from over five years ago, God friggin' damn!"

She blinked, thought hard, and tried again.

"4, 5, 8, 1… 2? Here's hoping!" She keyed in the final number and frowned. "Was it two? I sure as hell hope it wasn't three. Oh crap! Was it meant to be three?"

The lock started beeping.

The box was heating up.

Jenny rose. "Looks good anyway. Just hope it's right. I don't think I get a shot at double or nothing here…"

The box shook fiercely, like its ugly presence was trying to break loose.

The combined lumps of Suzi and Terror-Byte hit Mother's core.

Nearby, the Black Circuit they'd struck on the way past was in the final stage of its meltdown. The sequence that Suzi had started was working effectively, and the circuit was dissipating.

Within moments, it was no more.

A deafening whine followed as the cyst's tension grew, ready for a colossal blowout.

Mother trembled violently.

Bang!

The Toybox jolted from an inner blast. Almost comically, the whole chest jumped a short way up, then fell back down again, with wisps of smoke rising from its lid. Luckily, the lock held fast.

Jenny sighed with relief. "Yeah, being a blow-up doll's all you were ever good for. Game over, ya freakshow."

Several chunks of debris fell from the roof as the cave shook harder. She leapt to the side as a large rock dropped, just missing her and hitting the ground loudly. She rose quickly, feeling a cool breeze waft past her.

Strange, she thought. She was far below ground. There shouldn't be a breeze down here. Curious, she turned and saw an open door at the crater's edge.

Suzi's work, she determined.

She ran for it, stumbling over the trembling surface, weaving from side to side, and dodging the falling debris from the imploding cave. Finally, she made it to the door. A shaking tunnel lay beyond.

She ran in.

Mother exploded.

Her WOMB blew out in a deafening roar, incinerating all obstacles in its path with a raging ferocity.

Jenny felt the heat of the blast sweeping in.

"Fried alive!" she cringed. "Just the way I wanted to go! Desperate, dateless and screaming!"

There was no way she could make it out.

Tears pricked her eyes.

"Perfect end to a perfect day," she whimpered. Her voice rose as she ran. "I'm sorry, Dad. I'm so sor—"

The blast surged in.

High above, in the forest, the night lit up like day.

Thick clouds of black smoke erupted, sending huge chunks of debris spiralling high into the night and then plummeting as enormous flaming spheres. Trees splintered into burning fragments while the river bubbled furiously, boiling everything it held.

The site of the Hurriflame, the scarred landscape of wounded earth, burned once more. This time though, Mother's destructive energy held a flip side. Suzi had modified the Shockwave so that its impact would allow the site to regrow, becoming more fertile than ever. It'd take many years for Mother's healing residue to seep into the land, but would be worth the wait.

Hurriflame 1 had started this war.

Hurriflame 2 had inflamed it.

Hurriflame 3 had ended it.

Now there was a chance to start again.

The pain of the past was over.

A new age had begun.

Chapter Nineteen

"I think we've got something!"

Jenny groaned. The voices were faint. The dirt was suffocating. It was in her nose and mouth, smelling bad and tasting even worse. The world was blurry. Dark and confined, leaving her trapped so tightly that the only thing she could move was her mind.

Panic set in. Shallow breaths and rapid heartbeats followed.

Scuffling and scraping sounds of rubble came next. A few rocks shifted above, then night filtered through as a woman's face appeared.

"Can you hear me? Can you talk?"

Jenny blinked and coughed, spluttering out the dirt in her mouth and sucking in great lungfuls of air. A sharp stab of pain rippled down her spine, making her cry out in agony.

"It's okay, take it easy," the woman cautioned.

It hurt for Jenny to talk, and took most of her strength to croak, "S-Suze…"

"Donna, actually," the woman cut in. "Sergeant Donna Vertigo. It's okay. You're safe." She looked up and called, "Nick! How long's that ambulance gonna be?"

"ETA six minutes!" came a reply.

Vertigo looked back at her. "Relax. You'll live."

Jenny pushed on, fighting her discomfort. "Suze? Where is she?"

"You mean there's more of you?" Vertigo asked quickly. "How many?"

Jenny tried speaking, but coughed again, igniting a searing throb through her body. She winced and said, "Just her. You need to find... I need... need..."

"You don't need anything," Vertigo interjected. "There's an ambulance coming. Hold tight."

Jenny tried struggling up.

Vertigo pushed her back down.

"Suze," Jenny whimpered. "Suze..."

A dark shroud descended behind her eyes and her head rolled sideways. The last thing she heard was Vertigo calling, "Where's that damn ambulance?"

Then there was nothing but silence.

Dead silence.

***

Twin beams of light illuminated the darkness, waking Jenny. For a moment, just a moment, it seemed like the light came from Suzi's glasses.

No such luck.

She opened her eyes, then closed them again. She took a deep breath, opened them cautiously and blinked, observing her surroundings. She was lying flat on a bed in a cold, sterile room. There was a window nearby and a familiar smell.

A hospital.

She hated hospitals.

"Shortcake..." a voice began.

She turned her head slightly, giving a small groan as her neck twinged.

Her father spoke from the chair beside her. "Easy there."

Jenny choked hard. "D-Dad?"

Her father looked back at her; his face filled with tears.

"Yeah," he said, failing to hide his joy. "You're not alone, kiddo." He patted her hand, then retracted it quickly. "Oh God, it doesn't hurt when I do that, does it?"

"No," Jenny answered. She frowned, trying to recall as much as she could. It wasn't easy. She was drowsy, and her memories were hazy.

"Honeras Hellstorm, right?" she asked.

Her father nodded at the mention of their nickname for the hospital on the north side of town, called Honeras. "Afraid so."

"You know I hate this place, Dad."

"I do too."

"I don't want to be here. Not where Mum…"

"It's also the place that's fixing you up," he pressed. "Can't be all that bad, can it?"

Jenny relented. "Guess not."

"They, uh, don't know what kept you alive through that rockfall. I'm just grateful for whatever did." He choked back the tears. "Real grateful."

Jenny's head hurt. It was difficult to take in.

"You're not angry at me?" she murmured.

"For what?"

"For…" She indicated the room around her. "This. All this. Y'know, for disappearing on you, for being out there in the forest, for putting you through all this crap and —"

He cut her off with a small wave of his hand whilst using his other to grasp hers, albeit more carefully. "You're alive. I can't ask for anything more."

She bit her lip and closed her eyes. "God, I'm tired."

He clutched her hand. "Just rest. Those painkillers'll make you sleepy. You'll have to be on 'em for a bit too. Then you'll be right as rain." He kissed her wrist and said softly, "Go to sleep. I'll be right here watching you. Right here."

Jenny's head rolled to one side sleepily. She was alive. Her dad was with her. That was all that mattered.

Suck on that, grim reaper, she thought, and drifted into oblivion.

When she awoke, the room was empty.

It was almost dawn. Not quite, though. The sun hadn't risen but the darkness was fading. It didn't seem like morning or night, or anywhere in between, if that made sense. Not a lot did anymore.

Memories of recent events flickered in her mind. Suzi. The Toymaster. Her school blowing up. Being trapped in the rubble after another damn explosion. She should have been glad it was all over. Ecstatic. Overjoyed.

No more school, no more Miss Ford, no more Maria Longsworth, and best of all, no more psycho clowns. It was finished. She'd won.

Yet, she felt no sense of victory.

Where the hell was she supposed to go from here? Her life was a mess. Her grades were garbage and her past had gone up in flames. She may have saved the planet, but as far as it was concerned, she was nothing, a nobody, and the world wouldn't thank her for it one bit.

It was official. Jenny Campbell had peaked.

Now, only emptiness lay before her. Stretched out like a bleak highway on a three-month journey to imminent death. A gloomy spiral into…

"Jenny Campbell?"

She sat up quickly, trying to ignore the rippling pain in her body.

The person who stood before her was an Agent. The same leather jacket, white shirt, dark jeans and jet-black Iyes told her that, only this one was male.

She eased back with dismay.

"What'd you say my name like that for?" she grumbled. "You know who I am. You guys know everything about me, right? There's no need to play games, ya fruitcake."

His logical tone was frustratingly cool, just like Suzi's. "I am not an edible substance and —"

"Nor do I tease," she finished. "Yeah, I know how you guys speak. Makes me sick."

The Agent scanned her over, as if she were a specimen. "You are in-correct, Jenny Campbell. My words have done nothing to cause a decline in your current physical state. Your injuries have resulted from a rockfall. You will return to optimum efficiency in a short space of time."

"Then what?" she asked bitterly. "I get three months before I cark it?"

He opened his mouth to reply.

She knew it was going to be another question.

"It means die," she cut in.

His mouth closed and he paused. Finally, he said, "My bio-analysis of you indicates that your final demise will not occur for several decades, in accordance with the regular lifespan for your species."

Jenny frowned. "Isn't what's in my head only supposed to give me three months?"

"A deception," the Agent answered formally. "The Black Circuit was removed from your psyche by the Agent you referred to as Suzi Chambers. It has subsequently been destroyed. There is no immediate medical threat to your continued existence, for the time being."

Jenny drew in a shaky breath, absorbing this news. A flood of relief swept through her as she fought back the tears, knowing what Suzi had given her. The greatest gift of all. Life. Her best friend, her protector, her sister almost, had completed her mission.

Still, Jenny couldn't help thinking that things weren't right. Not with this weirdo around.

"Wait," she said, "if you're here, then where's she?"

Silence.

"Where?" Jenny pressed.

More silence.

She pushed herself up again, fearing the worst. "You'd better start talking, numb nuts…"

"That is not my name."

"Fine, I'll call you Blade, since you're so sharp. What have you done with her?"

"I have done nothing," he stated. "I am merely here as part of a clean-up operation."

"Which includes me, right?"

He glared at her.

She held her hand up defiantly. "Don't even think of doing that freaky glasses stuff on me! Where's Suze? Is she dead or alive?"

To her surprise, the Agent's glare lessened and he answered, "No."

Jenny threw an arm up. "No, what? What does that mean? You've gotta explain it to me, here. One-word answers don't work."

"You are correct," he agreed. "My kind use artificial bodies, or human combat vehicles, to blend in with your people. Our true forms are of much smaller, organic lifeforms, who dwell inside these casings. Agent Chambers human combat body is no more, but the organic creature of her true form survives. For now."

Jenny's heart missed a beat. "You're serious, right?"

Blade continued, "She removed the Black Circuit from your mind, transplanting it into her own. Her plan was to transfer it into the WOMB, known as Mother, and destroy it. She succeeded in the first part but was hindered with the second. Therefore, she used herself as a trigger."

Jenny shuddered. "Why the hell did she do that? Couldn't she have found another way?"

"No," Blade answered. "There wasn't time. We have since discovered that another Agent, known as 421, was eliminated by an augmented Agent called Terror-Byte. Terror-Byte's Symbiant entered 421's artificial body to deceive Agent Chambers. His aim was to possess the Black Circuit for his own gains. He failed. Agent Chambers destroyed the circuit by physically crashing into the Mother WOMB and pushing it into the Acystance Package generated by her Echo. That package terminated the circuit and saved her. Terror-Byte could not reach the sheath's protective covering in time. He is no more."

"Yeah, he deserved to fry," Jenny scoffed. "So Suzi's alive? Or her alien self is?"

"Barely," he answered. "She was found in the sheath's remains by Homeworld Agents who extracted her. Her organic form is in critical condition and has been returned to the Homeworld. Her continued existence is unclear. We are unable to confirm if she lives or dies."

Jenny swallowed hard. "If she does make it, will she come back?"

Blade spoke, with the kind of superiority that Jenny hated. "That outcome is unlikely. If she survives, she'll be held accountable to the Authority who will not be pleased with her actions. She broke several of their highest protocols on this mission, and events did not go the way the Authority planned. This is not the first time she has done this."

"She just saved two worlds! Ours and yours, douche bag!"

"Our rules are very strict," Blade countered firmly. "She failed to abide by them."

"That's 'cause she's got too much humanity for all your crap."

"We are not human."

"You got that right – arrrgh!" She winced and pinched the bridge of her nose. "I thought you said it was goodbye Hurripain?"

"I said no such thing."

"The Black Circuit's out of my head, right?"

"Yes, but there are after-effects. The circuit left many scars in your brain, both physical and mental. Do not be so emotional. It will only trigger more discomfort. Your wounds will take time to heal, along with the burns on your back."

"Burns I got doing your job." She gathered her thoughts. "What about the psycho clown we were up against? Is he gone?"

Blade's reply was as logical as ever. "The Toybox has also been returned to the Homeworld for safekeeping."

"Spoken like a true politician," Jenny retorted. "I asked if he's still alive. If he is, you guys better not be planning to bring him back as a weapon 'cause if you are you'll deserve what you get."

"I am confused by all your tenses."

"I'm confused by your lack of *tension*! How can you be so cool about having a weapon as sick as that?"

"Whatever happens is none of your concern."

"The scars on my back say otherwise. I'll ask again. Is he alive?"

"He was never alive to begin with."

"Damn it!"

Blade relented, unwillingly. "He is inactive. He can be resurrected, if needs be."

Jenny's heart sank. "Mission incomplete."

"He is contained," Blade said. "That is sufficient."

Jenny nodded. "Leaving me as the last of the loose ends, huh?"

"Correct."

"Which means that you're not just here to answer my questions."

"Also correct."

She shifted uncomfortably. This was turning ugly. Cautiously, she asked, "Okay, so what's next?"

Blade spoke. "The clean-up operation has been effective so far. The beings you've termed, the Devi-Ants, have been located and slain. The desert dwelling that served as a decoy town for the Toymaster, has also been destroyed. The entity called Gastoff is the last of this mission's elements. He must be found. You are the second last."

"Second last?" Jenny wondered. She thought this over, then the full impact of what he meant hit home. "You're here to wipe my memories, aren't you?"

Blade didn't have to answer. Jenny knew she was right. She'd seen Suzi mind-wipe people a couple of times. Suzi had even tried it on her too, but the Black Circuit had prevented it. Now the circuit was gone, and the rules had changed.

Jenny's heart thumped.

He continued. "Your knowledge is a liability to both your people and ours. As a result, your memories of recent experiences, will be erased."

Jenny should have been afraid. Instead, she was defiant. Her anger rose as she asked bitterly, "Including everything about Suzi?"

"Everything," he confirmed.

"One of the few people who actually meant something to me?"

"The Authority's influence on this world should not have been detected. All variables must be streamlined."

He stepped in.

Jenny tensed, struggling to control her emotions whilst fighting against the throbbing pain in her head. The thought of losing the only thing she had left of Suzi, her memories, was simply too much to bear. It was wrong, it was *beyond* wrong, yet there was no way to fight back.

"Please," she begged. "Take everything else, but not her. Just leave me this one thing. Just one. Can you do that? I –"

She winced as he grabbed her cheeks in a firm mechanical grip. Her lips were pushed out harshly, stretching to the point where she was gazing directly into this creep's cold, hypnotic stare. His presence was chilling as he raised her face to his own, as if examining her. The shades in his Iyes swirled like long black snakes stretching out for her brain.

"No…!"

She shut her eyes. He squeezed her face tightly, forcing her to open them again. Her defiance rose once more, angered at being told what to do by this suckhole.

She did her best to focus on Suzi's memory. Her friend. Her best friend. The two of them smacking out the Germinator, blowing up the school, speeding in a car down the highway. The more she recalled, the greater Suzi's presence grew inside her. Not only that, it seemed like Suzi was standing nearby, watching her but powerless to do anything.

The snakes entered her brain, touching her mind.

Jenny's eyes grew wider, and she froze.

An object tingled against her chest, warm against her bare skin, though hidden by her hospital nightgown. There was a little pain from it, just not as much from the solid grip pulling her face outwards.

"Forget," Blade ordered coldly. "Everything."

Her mental snakes chomped down savagely.

She winced.

"Forget," he pressed.

The snakes bit harder.

Darkness engulfed her, and she faded into oblivion.

Chapter Twenty

Jenny awoke.

A glow had enveloped her, rather like a halo.

Not a halo, she realised.

Sunlight.

It streamed in from the windows, touching her skin with its golden caress. She blinked and sat up, doing her best to recall where she was.

A sharp twinge rippled along her back, which was raw, like there were burns across it. She lay alone in a room, on a bed, in what appeared to be a hospital. Her belongings sat on the nearby dresser. Spare clothes, sunglasses, and a few of her favourite gossip magazines that only her dad could have brought her.

She rubbed her eyes and ran her hand through her hair, trying to figure out how she'd got here. It hurt to think. Finally, the memories came.

Oh yeah, she recalled. Agent Suckhole had tried to make her forget everything with his freaky glasses crap and –

She stopped dead.

She shouldn't have been able to remember that, yet she did.

"What the hell...?" she whispered.

She recalled every detail of her sick encounter with him. If that was the case, then she should also be able to remember...

She concentrated, focussing on...

There!

Somehow, miraculously, there.

Suzi's face. Smack bang in the middle of her mind. Her best friend and protector, with a solid unwavering confidence, as strong as ever.

Jenny gave a small cry and fell back on the bed, her hands on her face as tears of joy trickled through her fingers. She squealed and wept as her memories of Suzi returned. Everything was there. Absolutely everything.

Forgetting about her ailments, she sat up, pounding and kicking the bed repeatedly. "Yes, yes, yes, yes! We did it, Suze! We rock!"

She gave another squeal and flopped down in disbelief, wincing a little from her back pain which had returned with a vengeance, not that she cared.

"Suze," she whispered. "I knew you'd never leave me!"

She stared up at the ceiling. Not only were her memories there, they were as clear as day. Only thing was, how?

Had Agent Suckhole allowed her to keep them? Probably not, she reasoned. There was no way he'd let plain ol' Jenny Campbell hold onto anything that'd be a threat to his crappy Homeworld security. This had to be part of another plan.

Her chest tingled. An object was against her skin, she realised, and it sure didn't feel like medical equipment. Curiously, she rose again, albeit more slowly this time, and pulled at the top of her hospital gown to look down.

Hanging over her chest was a chain, close to her heart.

Suzi's words returned to her.

'This belonged to my maternal sire.'

Jenny pulled it out. The orb in the chain's centre prickled against her fingers as she absorbed its warmth.

The Dragon Slayer.

More of Suzi's words returned.

"The texture comes from an alloy I coated it with. It prevented my superiors from detecting it on me. The switch on its back renders it invisible."

Jenny grinned. The switch must have been activated since the beginning. The Toymaster hadn't detected it on her. Seems Agent Suckhole hadn't either, nor the hospital staff.

Hazy voices rose in her mind. Through the clouds, shapes, and shadows, she heard what could only be a doctor.

Jenny gave a little laugh. So this was what her dad was talking about when she'd first woken up. Together, she and Suzi *had* defied the odds. Jenny Campbell had made it out of hell, and Suzi's organic form still lived, if barely. Jenny still had her memories too, thanks to Suzi, who'd further defied her superiors by giving her the Dragon Slayer, thus allowing her to rebel against Agent Suckhole who'd tried to ram his stupid will into her head. Suzi had gained some humanity, not like those other losers from that feral world above. In other words, Suzi had told her bosses to shove it.

Jenny looked to the window. The sun was rising. School was over. Not only that, it was obliterated. Yes, there was still the possibility that she might graduate, but she wasn't holding her breath, and right now she didn't care. No more Miss Ford. No more Maria Longsworth. They were dead. Only she was left, and feeling far from alone.

She clasped the Dragon Slayer, thinking of Suzi. They'd overcome every obstacle imaginable, no matter how great, which meant they could do it again.

Her resolve was firm. She wouldn't let everything that Suzi had fought for go down the sewer. Something told her that she hadn't seen the last of her friend. It wasn't wishful thinking, she determined, but a damn fact. One day they'd meet again, and she'd be ready for it.

In the meantime, she now had an idea of what else was going on out there in the big bad world, besides freaky Agents with dark glasses. She'd gone through more horrors than anybody since the Hurriflame. The Trans-plants, Gastoff, secret military bases – these weren't things to simply ignore. They'd all been training for her. That couldn't go to waste. Suzi had helped her, meaning that she'd have to return the favour by helping others, though quietly, without alerting any loser Homeworld Agents lurking around.

She pulled the covers away and rose from her bed. Filled with hope, she moved to the window. Gently, she placed her hands on its warm glass, gazing out into the dawn of a new day, and a city that still stood, along with so many others all over the world, thanks to her and Suzi.

The Dragon Slayer's orb pulsed against her skin as she watched the sun rise higher.

She knew what to do.

Beneath the surface of life's everyday garbage, there was a war. Beings had come to this planet, making a mess of things, and they weren't the kind to back off easily. She welcomed the challenge of facing them head-on and was ready for anything.

She spoke, with Suzi's face in her mind as clear as the day before her. "Thanks, Suze. You made me see that I was trying to be something I wasn't." She clutched the Dragon Slayer tighter. "Time to change that."

The sun rose higher.

Her head rose with it.

Without looking back, she reached over to the dresser, picked up her sunglasses and put them on.

"This party's about to get started."

Meanwhile, at the site of the Hurriflame, in a final gift from Suzi, the land slowly healed as life began anew.

About the Author

Sam Silver is an up-and-coming and yet-to-be bestselling award-winning author. He has three university degrees, all in the interests of literature, education and information management, but puts his writing first in the interests of his true legacy.

He has been part of various literary festivals, writing groups, and stalls, and has written every day over the last twenty years, leaving several more novels ready to go after this one.

Burning Embers is the first of the burner.

He lives in Perth, Western Australia.

9 780648 607724